# THE DREAMTIME

# THE DREAMTIME

by Robert Louis Nathan

THE OVERLOOK PRESS

First published in 1975 by The Overlook Press
Lewis Hollow Road  Woodstock, New York 12498
Copyright © 1975 by Robert Louis Nathan
Library of Congress Catalog Card Number: 74-21584
SBN: 0-87951-028-5

For information address The Overlook Press.
Printed in the United States of America.

For Hope Anne

# BOOK I
# AVERY MORRÍSON

## one

Wilkulda's myth ended here in the sea. He alone chose and desired such a conclusion. There, on the continental elongation of the tidal flats, in the shallows of the ocean which had created Australia's harsh west coast, Wilkulda endured perpetual libations for a numbering of days. He, except for Kalod, would be alone in the waters until the throngs came to avail themselves of his abilities.

Late night, night dying hesitantly before fragile dawn. The sea is quiet without the fearful tides habitual to this shore. Beyond the coastal reef the ocean is as normal, shuddered with blooming swells. The shallows are a secluded passage of magically calmed waters. However, this ocean, or any other ocean, has no interest to this tale except as a watchman in no man's land.

As day's shock of hotness swarms victorious over the desolate, colorless littoral, it reveals, behind the beach of alternating black and white sand dunes, the kneeling sandstone cliffs. They are meager promontories and snuggle this bleached fringe of earth rather than overwhelming it with awesome towers. Cliffs are dilapidated. Weather of cruel extremes has conquered this world with seasons of gorging rain and seas cast up by storming winds, and then months of profound dryness. The too pliable rock has been tortured into the form of a decaying jawbone relic from the Dreamtime Age.

In the sea's revolving embrace, Wilkulda watched the dawn alone. The beach was enormous and naked. Naked too was Wilkulda. The coast was singularly empty. A desolation so vast that it had assumed a regal authority over man. Cliff, beach, sea, and sky merge in a nebulous shimmering, as if the whole immense scape were the pale beige underside of a giant oyster-shell, glazed with reflected heat.

1

Greenness, as a sign of fertility, exists not in this place except for ocean vegetation forgotton on the beach by the nurturing tides. Behind the cliffs lie extensive mulga thickets but they are dun-tinted and ugly. This bush, with attendant animals and gumtrees, parallels the seacoast for several hundred leagues. However, the mulga zone is nowhere more than five miles wide and averages less than two. Beyond the mulga strip are deserts, plateaus, and the wreckage of several mountain ranges.

Wilkulda's nakedness was unusual as he wore not even the initiate's fur badge over his pubic. Around his waist was the sole object of decoration, the human hair belt woven for his protection by the girl Mayawara. The belt carried not the wallaby bladder pouch that magicians use to hold magic objects, yet Wilkulda was a magician.

Sand is most often found to be of a tawny hue, but in this place, during the Dreamtime Age, an Ancestor had slain a maiden, and in dying, she had gifted the beach with her black skin and white teeth in common metamorphosis. The sand grains, of both shades, were uncommonly coarse. However, this is Australia, and such irregularities should not provoke undue surprise, as this world is the matrix of weirdness.

Morning's recessional tide had stranded ponds of saltwater on the beach which were clamorous with insignificant, fading traces of life. Sea's song was now as the whisper of a shellfish falling from a gull's beak. The tidal flats revealed at the last ebbing were the granaries and gardens to those mankinds that inhabited the coast. Without the rhythmic flowerings of the flats, human experience would be excluded from this shore world. The bush lands did offer a variety of food, but it was the plenitude of sea life harvested from the glistening flats that made established society possible.

The flats, and the shallows where Wilkulda stands, are protected by two major fortifications. The first line of the sea's containment is a coral reef inferior to many other such skeletons, but then this coast is inferior to all others on earth except the glaciered shores of the polar barrens. Parallel to the reef, but closer to land, is the second embrasure: a sandbar of mighty dignity that confounds the ocean with its nature of organic self-repair. It is the double barrier of reef and bar that negates the monstrous tides native to this world. It is the odd combination of coral and sand that encourages the wealth of edible life in this particular bay. Thus, the bay knows a far greater density of mankinds than is to be found at any other place on the west littoral, except for the southernmost tip.

As egocentric sun greedily sucked dry night's mist, Wilkulda spoke wistfully out over the sea, "Truly I no longer possess a name, or perhaps I have forgotten it. In my homeland of the pool every man is gifted a secret name which is his spirit's name in the Dreamtime world, but such a name was never mine. It is because Tjundaga died that I received not my secret name. My grandfather, Tjundaga, gave me my name as a child, Pilala, and after circumcision he gave me my name, Wilkulda. But that was all, for he died too soon to present me with my spirit's calling. My mankind hated me when Tjundaga was dead. Only the Sky is aware of my hidden name. I have done everything for the Sky and yet have no name beyond Wilkulda. It is quite sad. No person hears my message as I hear it. Even in the dawning I seem to men as a spectre from the darkness. After I healed my own mankind, they sent me away. I should not let failure make me despair, for it is true that it was only after I was sent away that I learned that every man must be healed."

## two

He had come unobserved into the sea three days past on a ceremonial night of the local tribe. On the fourth dawn, as light brazed the burnt-out littoral, the stranger still could be sighted secure to his upright spear that was embedded in the mud of the shallows. He clung to the weary weapon as if it were a lithe sapling rooted deep into the rock dimness that upheld the cliff behind him. Except for the aged, bleached and cracking spear, and the thin waist band, Wilkulda possessed nothing.

Each dawn since his arrival, when the limp fog was seared away, Wilkulda could be seen standing in the exact place where he had first been spied. This shore was a poor rind of the great ocean, an ephemeral sheen forefronting the deep trough outside the reef. Yet it was the sea, and Wilkulda stood in it.

Why had he not chosen to remain on the stone crest that

dominated the bleak void of the coast? High up, some thirty
feet over the dunes, it was dry and warmer. No
typhoon-beaten comber lanced to that height, or rarely.
Perhaps Wilkulda feared that the grandeur of the cliff top
would distract him from exploring what he sought. As if
standing in the sea, accepting the dread and discomfort this
entailed, would aid, not hinder, his searching.

Not even the elders of the tribe inhabiting this segment of
the coast understood what the stranger was preoccupied
with. Turtlemen were the mankind owning this coastal world.
Their womb-lands stretched twenty-five leagues along the bay
front and some six leagues inland. The Turtles, of course,
measured not by leagues but by myth creation, which is a
truer bridge. The Turtle Hero, The Ancestor-Spirit, had
created their world in the Age of Dreaming, an age whence all
truth, magical and tool sacredness had come. Extant is the
Dreamtime Age even now, for the Dreaming of wise myths is
eternal.

Whoever he was, one thing about the stranger seemed
certain. That he would enter the domain of the Turtles,
ignorant of the sorcered facts of the landscape, ignorant of its
indigenous ghouls and its myriad spirit occupiers, announced
boldly that Wilkulda was of magic surpassing reality.

By analyzing his plucked-clean jaw, the cicatrices on
thighs and buttocks in addition to the universal lateral ridge
scars raised on his chest, the lack of spear decor, the
simplicity of his circumcision, the Turtle elders surmised that
Wilkulda belonged to the deserts of the south. They could
not have comprehended how far to the south lay the
Wedgetail Eagle world of his birth. The Turtle elders thought
him obviously a barbarian and uncivilized company for them.
The Turtles were learned and proud, exalted in the creation
of magic and in their reverence for the Dreamtime Age.

A keen painter of magic in the cliffside caves and on ledge
sides publicly predicted that the fellow was a water sprite
ghost, a discard of the transcending Rainbow Snake. To
Kalod, the mankind's bone-driller, youngest but acknowledged
as the paramount elder, the fellow was a wizard with a diseased
soul. Kalod had drilled skulls for the last eight of his
thirty-nine seasons. Wilkulda at this time summed thirty-two
seasons.

Three pre-dawns past, when the Turtle mankind alertly
squatted about their smouldering mulga fires on the cliff
waiting for the sun, Kalod's oldest son, a lad of eleven who

had been defecating in the bush, on returning to camp had
noticed the stranger afloat in the moving mist down in the
sea. The Turtle elders took up their throwers and spears and
raced to the place where the boy had watched the apparition.
The women and children clung together in moaning trauma
under the three-sided windbreaks of stick and weed.

It was Kalod who had to come alone down the looping
cliffside path onto the still liquefied beach. After an instant's
hesitation, Kalod crossed the wide beach, which was fogged
in the hollows between dunes and freckled with dozens of
tidal pools, and forced himself into the sea to investigate his
son's discovery.

## three

Kalod did not return to the cliffhead until midday. The
bone-driller had already begun metamorphosis but was
unaware of his changing self. Now, on the fourth day of
Wilkulda's involvement with the sea, Kalod considered his
own daily visits into the shallows a ritual. It was the
bone-driller who, in reply to the incessant nervous
questioning of the powerful cave painter, issued his
mankind's initial judgment of the meaning of Wilkulda.

"Yes, of course I respect your opinion, Kokalaja, and
probably you are right. I should have sent him away at once.
Most likely, it was a bad mistake to give him permission to
stay in our ocean. Legally he has no rights, we can do with
him as we wish. Yes, I believe he is a man and not a ghost,
but he is quite the queerest chap I have ever encountered."

And as the elders scratched the burns and fly bites legion
to their flesh, and as they watched coils of wood smoke
finger erotically the sky's underbody, Kalod, standing as
speaker, continued, "At first glance he seemed a fool, or
worse, a madman. But I was curious and waited a bit to judge
him before spearing the fellow dead. In boredom, I suppose,
or perhaps I was just inquisitive, I soon found myself in
accidental conversation with him. I think it is good that I did
not kill him. I remember my first insight into his nature. I
judged that he was a queerness that could not be simply
exorcised by spear or bone. That first dawn when my son
came to me and I entered the waters, I looked at him and
thought, 'This awkward fellow is too tall for my tastes.' But

now I am getting used to his size."

Turtles sat with russet baked kangaroo skins over their heads and shoulders, these pelts symbolized the final stage in initiation. Turtles were buttocked to earth under a dead redgum. The tree was a giantess of a skeleton whose errant limbs slandered balance itself with confused growth. This redgum was the Crane's fire from the Dreamtime metamorphosed into a dead tree, that men might know which Hero had created the place they sat on.

"He dared to introduce himself to me by name and in our own personal tongue. I marveled at his audacity. I believe the queer fool may have used the name of his dead grandfather also aloud. Well he is certainly a lesser species as compared to us Turtles. But even though I am the bone-driller I am not yet truly confident of any of my opinions that first dawn. It was still heavy with seahair and it was altogether too mysterious for a settled observation. I confirmed to myself that he had actually spoken aloud, and not into my brain, by spitting into his weird eye while chanting the appropriate counter-magic. But he became as cocky as a little boy and nudged his spear shaft into my armpit while repeating, 'Wilkulda, Wilkulda,' several times. He seemed to be amused, yet he did not laugh or chortle as a jolly magician would have. I, as would any man exposed to such dangerous novelty, shrank from him in abhorrence, but unhappily I slipped and sank heavily into the water. I was not at this time charmed by Wilkulda's personality. I will use his name aloud. It is of no consequence to any Turtle as we have no such name. I leapt up and dashed boldly back to the beach. As I came up the path I stopped to urinate at the rib of the whale and as I watched the stream curve out of my being I believed that the urine was green and of a circumference greater than my entire member. By this I knew that everything in the world had shifted somewhat and that Wilkulda was not meant to be killed by the Turtle-men.."

The score and a half of elders, stimulated by Kalod's description of his urine metamorphosed into a sea's current, rose en masse, went to the exposed arch of the redgum and urinated. But as their lines of liquid were not original in any manner they returned to their ranked places around the redgum. Kalod took up his myth expounding once again, "And on the second day's morning when he was still there, not dissipated along with the heavier than normal fog of the previous day, I sensed that a myth of exquisite proportions might be created on our shore. Remember how we had

shouted down to him from the cliff, how he ignored our
magic oaths, how he still stood in the exact spot that he had
chosen the first night. His gaze seemed immersed in some
creeping wave. I ran along the cliff to the rock pillar that is
our relic of the Rainbow Snake, and jumped the few feet
over to it. From its position further out from the cliff I could
see into the corner of his eye. It was as if my soul was
captivated by the weird light that circles Wilkulda's head. The
light that first attracted my son to peer down. It was most
remarkable . . . In these few days since Wilkulda came and
wandered in my soul I have changed somehow, in a way I
don't grasp . . . When as a lad they bent me backwards over
the twelve elders entwined into one, and circumcised me,
then too I was changed, but this is stranger."

From the seasons of respect toward Kalod no man
laughed, or farted, or jested, or insulted him, although his
words had been childish. The bone-driller's obvious confusion
over the madman Wilkulda and his usurpation of their
shallows was scandalous. The insane stranger must be speared
dead soon, there was no other logical course. Yet Kalod was
potent, and fair, and they loved him. Thus, they listened with
pretended patience.

"This dawn, alone again I ventured to see my friend, to
see Wilkulda. To join him for a short moment in his lonely
vigil. Again none of the food I had ordered to be placed on
the beach for him had been touched. Everything had been
covered by leaves but by then all the platters were swarmed
with flies. The oysters, the mussels, the chunk of kangaroo
rump, the gull eggs, they were devoured by the flies even as I
entered the shallows.

"Yes, I see the sadness, my uncle, don't despair. You, who
confirmed that my spirit was very big with ancient seasons of
magic, I know you think me sorcered by Wilkulda, hunted in
my kidney fat by Wilkulda's evil, but I think not. And as I
am the skilled driller of skull holes, because of this work, I
judge first. For with my sacred crystal awl I vent the skull
and suck away the sorcered murder. And I am proficient in
the magic of forestalling murders by my defense of my
brother's kidney fat. And that I possess marvelous talents is
due in great measure to you, uncle, from your decision to
permit me to eat my father's heart at his funeral. It was you,
uncle, who took me on my journey after circumcision and lit
the fires of initiation, trust me uncle.

"All of you Turtles have given me fine, big favors of wives
and food. Forever that I breathe I am grateful. Yet in spite of

your concern for my brilliant mind, and your sympathy for what you think is my plight, and though I do feel perplexed and as a child in my soul, this fellow Wilkulda is a sensitive magician and not a thief of my kidney fat.

"How assuredly he waited for me this dawn. He waited patiently for me in the empty tide. Above the noise of the flocks fishing I could hear the hags shrieking for my safety from the fires . . . How poised he stood, wet and shining from the night tide's stroking. In the redness of the freed sun I could still distinguish the light about his head. Wilkulda seemed to have known of my coming although he had not turned away from the ocean to watch my progress over the beach. As I splashed out to join him, he called out his joy at seeing me, and repeated his own name again as before. As he finished his self-naming, he paused for a moment as if considering something, and then told me, 'And you should know, Kalod, I am the child of the Sky.'"

## four

Australia, the tenth planet, is age trundled imprint of a flattened grape skin, drained of juice and pleasureless. Yet it is a world electric with spiritual vitality. The men who chose to come to this planet in their nakedness lived freely among the sacred boulders, gorges, and pans. These men grew to surpass all other species in the attainment of magic. Mankinds of Australia were in perpetual involvement with the creation of their worlds in the recurring and regenerative Dreamtime.

Fellows who were bold in penis and spear, who lived their slightest act in concert with the Spirits of the sacred lands. Saucy, rollicking girls of this tenth planet were entranced with story games dramatizing the Dreamtime in the raveling and unraveling of hair string mazes of voluminous design. The boys were circumcised and initiated to inherit the Dreamtime and thenceforth their part in its protection would be daily and real. Each person on this planet-island, even if hated or feared, could never be lonely as each being was also a kangaroo, or an emu, a walrus or a wombat. A man was never only a man for he was also a replica of his Spirit Ancestor.

God was the Rainbow Snake, or the Witchetty Grub, or the Flying Fox, or indeed, the Sky Father. The mankinds were aware of their soul's existence, and thus were aware that all things have souls. Reality was one essence of spirit and death another. Conception needed a father somewhere in the vicinity, but what was of true urgency was the presence of the infant's own spirit. This baby essence might reside in a mud bog or fill a deserted pebble lying in a gully, unnoticed except by a young wife.

Before the end of their existence in our own century, five hundred mankinds were demographed in Australia, but perhaps there were more. The savants could only count bones in many instances. It doesn't matter, they are all dead men soon. Perhaps the greater 'portion of the mankinds traced their descent from an Ancestor Hero, Ant or Osprey, in the male line. A few Heroes were identified by the individual's conception spirit, and a few based their spritual tradition on maternal lineage. Relationships were rigid due to kinship laws that prescribed each social involvement. Sexual avoidance was but one of many regulations affecting each individual. When a man, or woman, disturbed that which was forbidden, even without cause, spear killings were swiftly invoked.

Wilkulda belonged to a land of the south central part of West Australia. Today it is a land almost empty of aboriginal humanity as a consequence of the Nightmare Time. This half of the outcast planet is without redeeming fertility except in a few sparse corners. In point of fact, perhaps the only solid fact to be found in this fount of fancy, water is rare in West Australia; seldom was there a river or lake that survived the dry season. Water is malproportioned to the southeast hindleg of the freakish planet. Here goodly rivers intercourse opulently. Here is where the mankinds congregated in unusual density and here in the southeast is where they were so quickly killed off in the shadows cast by the approaching Nightmare.

Also to the extreme southern tit of the western coast there exist lusher lands and ponds. There is a northern pimple where water drenches poor land futilely in the typhoon seasons. Yet today in this high peninsula mankinds still procreate even as they did thirty-five centuries past when Wilkulda healed men.

I pen and ink this story in the yearly charade of 1931. I do acknowledge that we have finished off the aborigine chaps even as the Yanks shotgunned the passenger pigeon. Better no doubt to see the abos go than the little tweet tweets, 'twas spoken in velvet-cushioned lavatories. A few other good things are also reported dead or missing. That is why in the darkness of my eye, which is perpetually lidded, I entertain this rather gaudy book, to save the last feathery passenger.

Exhibitionistic eucalyptus trees, gumtrees they was called by those blokes educated least in Greek, tenaciously teethed into the unredemptive lands with roots toughened by the eons. Tortured colors and self-voyeuristic, turnscrew limbs and trunks; individualistic and lonely the trees fulfill the empty lands of the planet with undisciplined mysticism. Weeping trees treacle resin that the brighter tribes heat-treat into a cement for spear heads and magic decoration. Fantastic woods, hard enough to repulse voracious iron axes whipped by too crude convicts, bounded blades back shockingly.

Queer planet-continent-island, poor thing forever pigeoned. Queer animals; birds, reptiles, marsupials, fish, men, what have you, all will be queer, all damned queerness. Yet all thrives till Nightmare Time. Intricate constructions impossible thrive. Flowers, beautiful to attract, but hermaphrodite weeds, scentless. And queer beyond queerness, that until moneyed Englishmen and Malays traffic o'er by watered freight, there are no herds of any cowish, deerish, antelopish, elephantish, class indigenous to this southland.

Bovines, cloven-hoofed buffaloes; not one exists in the Dreamtime Age to be re-created until cattle are thumped down Nightmarishly an age hence. Herds that to the German savage and Chinese barbarian gave meat, fuel, clothing, tools, weapons, and even milk, did not exist in Australia until this cruel modernity. No herds to force men into animal husbandry, into gardening by the cistern wall, and away from magic.

The dogs came untroubled in the dugouts and on the teak log rafts down along the keys from the sub-continent and into the kingdom of queerness. Over a montage of isles, and the extant land bridge, came the dingos and man to casually semen the newness. As drifting dust, sporelike man traverses the great island-planet. One hundred centuries to attain the granite outcrop which thrusts out for Van Dieman's land, Tasmania. Man faltered here before the incredible currents. Then, in reed stretched canoes, no room for dingos, man attacked the strait's hugeness in flimsy construction and ended the trek of treks.

Scholarly chaps believe the abo a Stone Age oddity forced out of Hindu hills by their betters. 'Tis a devil's tongue that creases over such an asp's lie. Australoids were modern men, thus evil and aware of God. This very day, here in England, circa 1931, it is obscure knowledge that a few mankinds survive yet. I do not deny this, for not even brutalized criminals and bewitched settlers, transported firstly by the courts and secondly by need of self-advancement, could eat every spore. Even then, those that wasn't dead or blinded by smuggled rum could see the abo scum were a cowardly lot of child-apes. Christian priests saw the child part more than the ape, but in self-analysis thought themselves too sympathetic toward the niggers.

And then again the mankinds, the Australoids, were, even as I, great practitioners of cruelty. Savages as true as we, but they was too dullardly to fabricate even one submersible, as did jolly cousin Henry, to drown a floating babe at dead mother's tit. Wilkulda was not cruel.

A first cruelty begat Australia. Wind was the ocean's tormenter and the sea moved by the wind tore Australia from Asia's socket and then hacked islands small and great from the sliding mass of stone.

While the colored race of New South Wales, Victoria, and the worthless outback were brown-hued, it is correct to say nigger-boy, or nigger-whore, but the latter appellation not aloud in the prescence of Christian women. The incandescent flare of the queer island carbonized their finely carved angular limbs into a false blackness. They were born brown. Mothers understood such earthy language as 'niggers,' and 'lascars,' and 'lesser races,' but the mothers of the outback knew a Spirit when they saw, heard, and felt it. Thus, the mucoused babes still fall from womb into the nest scooped out in the warm sand. Squeezed into liberation's agony the infants are creamy hued. Then, with infinite wisdom, the mothers carefully rub ash into fragile skin to hasten refreshing blackness.

In the year 1815, Kelly sailed about the whole of Tasmania in a whaleboat, with the help of four bloods as crew. Kelly viewed a six foot seven inch Stone Age creature who danced and made funny faces.

I wish the diarists had penned more information about Tasmania. It is recorded that they-them killed off the local mankinds to the last person. Tasmanian mankinds must have been persons even though they smelled badly to the convict's sensitivity. It is historically provable (trial and error methodology) that those killed off in Tasmania were disgusting in every appurtenance and activity. Disgusting in all matters as confirmed by French, Dutch, and stout English explorers. 'Twas a French chap who slew the first Australoid by European means, and that was in Tasmania. I, of course, realize that the Tsar's brave army was butchered and eventually gassed, even their corpses, to save the French Republic, but then think of Kelly and the giant clown dancing on the pristine beach.

From India, this is not fact but rather truthful myth, the mankinds trudged southward. Venturing over mountain ridges that perforated the oceans marched man. They succeeded in redeeming the spirit world that had been metamorphosed into the tenth planet during the Dreamtime. The newly created world was eager to receive inhabitants capable of spiritual brotherhood. The planet ached in its loneliness before the comrades arrived. The metamorphosed hills and plains and dried river beds accepted the tall men into their sanctuary without hesitation. The planet requested from men only the simplest commemorative ceremonies to insure the continuation of the spirit transformation as water and earth.

Tiny trickles of man defeated the vacancy and brought their heated flesh into the desolation. Only a paltry thousand succeeded in reaching the new planet of the droves that had left the north after the flood. The vast majority of these peoples had been enticed by the verdant peninsulas and archepelagos to root among wealthier races. Here they stayed to become indistinguishable from their hosts except for the odd throwback.

The thousand entered the waiting refuge as mystics with a vision of a world where they would not be persecuted because they were a peculiar race overly involved with magic. The spirit-planet thought itself wise and thus kept rain and buffaloes from the mankinds that they would ceaselessly adore the Dreamtime myths. The tenth world's Spirits did not become aware of the Nightmare until almost too late.

From this first thousand the five hundred mankinds were bred. Distinct dialects and physiques evolved as the families of the dominant males multiplied into tribes. Finally, they put away incest and seized exogamy as the surety of their self-discipline. The mankinds projected their penises into spears and feuded much but warred not. And they projected their shafts with levering throwers. These wood levers were notched at the ending catch lip to grip a slice of flint or quartz. With this cutting edge the thrower became an axe and adze. The spear thrower could also be wielded as a smashing club if a chap misplaced his knotted whopper. Boomerangs were not common to every mankind and those that possessed the wooden planes used them as simple throwing sticks for the pursuit of birds roosting.

Shields of wood, or kangaroo skins stretched on hair-tied

mulga frames, were made by several mankinds. It is factually accurate to report the savant's observation that the filthy abo knew not bow and arrow. However, the mankinds did manufacture extraordinary burial poles and massive cylinders. A few tribes created Emu masks of feathers and frames that leaned a meter into the sky over the wearer's crown.

Then, above all other artifacts of the dead mankinds, were the wood and stone boards. These objects measured from a few inches in length to six and seven feet. Always painted, and sometimes carved, these boards were the sacred holies of the Australoid race. What marvels these boards were, for indeed, they were the metamorphosed souls of dead males. Fathers, uncles, brothers, sons; these cracked and age-thinned objects were the replicas of men's spirits. A man could never truly die as long as his board existed. The mankinds trusted in afterlife, that the spirit returned to the Eternal Dreaming. And some tribes believed that the soul was perpetually reissued from the Age of Creation. A man who loved his father loved his father's board and kept it fresh in ocher and emu fat. At religious observations the relics were brought out from their secret caches and adored with fondling and singing and tears. As the men tenderly played with, and caressed the sacred holies, many would weep. The board must be intently rubbed that its soul knew it was still loved.

Women rarely possessed boards for their souls, though only a few mankinds pronounced that females had no souls. Women were slits and that was the slit of it. They were mainly ignored and degraded, yet in a few tribes older hags commanded authority proportionate to their personalities. And female religious ceremonies were not unknown. The slits, like their male counterparts, were fearless and audacious, but only with other females. A jealous hag would be widowed many times until as an old woman she was given as first wife to a young bachelor. As this fellow progressed in elderhood he would receive younger and younger wives while the hag was relegated to food-gathering. Thus, it was the old men who possessed the choice young girls, while the young fellows were lucky to be given even a hag by the jealous elders.

With breasts limp in distention to her navel, oval face withered beyond the creases of an elephant's anus, the hag would vent her frustrations by smacking a younger wife on the head with her digging stick. And with ferocity the girl would respond and the two would soon be taking alternate swings. Blows that would stun the helmeted Kaiser continued

for hours without apparent damage until a wearied male
would wander over and end the fight with a spear jab or two.

Giantress of an isle had been frictioned into being by stern
masters. Yet volcano and glacier had never scourged this
exotic world, and thus the varied queernesses were allowed to
thrive while other, deprived planets hosted only normality
and perversion.

Mything was the universe's way of idealizing its queerness.
When the thousand few came into the land the world-island
was already burnt acrid red by the orgiastic, demoniacal sun.
The men rejected the planet's queerness as a lie and thus, in
their love, they metamorphosed into the ultimate queerness.

Strange planetress of hairy egg bearers and of gruesome
unicorn cept it was a sea mammal. Marsupial, the summation
of esoteric creation with its pocket of a second womb. Thus,
the planet was fragrant with abnormal grandeur. Now,
Wilkulda, after some several ages of dying, came unto the
mankinds of our wonderland. And though he was fully aware
of their affection for cruelty, he loved them too well.

Are you properly focused with the aid of my fact? And if
not, how can I relate the loathing the Britisher felt for the
wretched abo? How with commercial distaste the Britisher
did suffer to slay the smelly abo with generous poxes,
mumpies, and venereals. This, then is the structure for my
tale and I'd be grateful if you shell-shocked chaps would
kindly delve betwixt and between that which is my fact and
your own phantasy.


# five


May I humbly introduce my powerless but souled self, my
crippled self. Name be Avery Morrison. 'Mousey chap but
fine man, good stuff,' ad'eu, ad'eu, all true once but now
ad'eu.' I once was an officer in The Indian Army. At Flanders,
in '14, I was a lieutenant in horse. At St. Loos, in '15, I was a
false captain in the infantry. Twas absurd to be at Flanders
in any organization whatsoever, and yet we did die
desperately courageously so as not to be thought ill of.

My parents are dead and it is toward jolly Uncle William,
'Billy,' Morrison that I flow with gratitude. Without Uncle
Billy I should have no roof, no hearth, no tea and Spanish
marmalade, and no Nurse Alice to fondle my silly erection.

Undoubtedly you have guessed my secret dread, that I was gassed in the Great War and am blind and laid up with several other nonsensical infirmities. This cottage of brick, with its indoor bath and lavatory, is Uncle Billy's. It overlooks Brighton harbour, the seat of my fisherman, sailor, and foundrymen antecedents.

Why is Uncle Billy involved, much to his embarrassment, in this biography of escape? Why indeed, because Billy Morrison was my father's eldest brother. My father was an Anglican priester. Hubert was his given name. And these two brothers, by my grandmother Precious Atkins Morrison, were the nephews of the infamous mystic, Captain Joseph Atkins. Thus, I am grandnephew to this crucial man, Joseph Atkins. He, Joesph Atkins, was the diarist of the Wilkuldian papers. Uncle Billy, as is documented by the Crown, is presently, and eternally, performing as muggiwug of Brighton Iron Works here on the south coast of England. The Morrison and Atkins fortunes yeasted here from the coke and lime ovens.

Joseph Atkins, free trader captain of the late Hartlepool Harvester in the beginning decade of the late, grand century, now so woefully mislaid, supplied the £ 275 needed by his younger sibling George, and brother-in-law George Morrison, yes, Georged twice, to coke up an unpretentious cupola for casting iron cannon balls to accomodate the Blackwell fleets of the Honorable East India Company. Hollow balls were the Brighton Iron Works' specialty, the ones that exploded in the interior of a wooden ship due to clever wicking.

Brighton balls served cruelly well the yellow-banded (white-banded after Trafalgar in honor of Nelson's Victory), blackened gun ports of the full-rigged frigate-merchantmen. Indiamen were damn fine artillerists and consumed tons of iron balls from my Uncles George. A novice might think the casting of a twelve pound ball a snappish order, but balance and finish were quite critical, and the explosive-charged balls were always difficult, as is all core moulding work. The Royal Navy could be cheated blatantly but the elegant Indiamen were quite particular, and it was they who had advised the Georges to set up their own shop, as the two men were regarded as superior craftsmen in another's establishment.

That there were faulty armor-piercing shells of our manufacture at Jutland, against Hipper's battle-cruisers, was most regrettable. As David Beaty duns, these shells might have been a contributing cause to the terrible losses inflicted on his far ranging command; however, his superior, Admiral Viscount Jellicoe of Scapa, passed the projectile's design and specifications. This can make no difference to the poor

British sailors exploded by the German shells; however, I am desirous of my fellow lunatics to be fully cognizant of Nurse Alice's subtle fingers.

Do you see my torch now, do you see it raised high above the other millions of dead and quenched brands? I am blind and not able to view my own lantern. I was gassed blind by the horrid chlorine fumings, outlawed, but too late. I see not my own lamp but I envision Wilkulda's quite clearly. I lurk about his curious light even as the overly excited, spotted insect is captivated and made senseless by the glow of a flickering candle.

My father, Hubert, and mother, Esther, died in Athens in 1899. They were on tour and were to leave for the pyramids the next Thursday, but died of diphtheria Monday before. I was a boy-baby of three years and eleven months when nobly solid Uncle Billy, despite his recurring sinuses, took me into his home to be raised with all my vulgarly handsome cousins; Ann, Robert, and baby Agnes. It was Uncle Billy who, seeing me become transfigured on the back of a horse, entered me into Sandhurst. It was Uncle Billy who purchased the best mounts for my use. The estates left to me by Hubert and Esther (I think of them familiarly as they were too young to remember as parents from their portraits) even when combined, were but a slender income. A few bonds in the iron works from Hubert and several unprofitable farms in Dorset from Esther. Uncle Billy stinted not and would have seen me to the expense of a Red Hat except for the chlorine business. I am gassed up and blinded and spit up flecks of Avery's dear lungs each winter dryness, but I have Nurse Alice and Wilkulda as my invalid's permanent quests.

I was gassed September 22, 1915, during the second day of the Battle for Loos. Chlorine, I must be one of the very few to survive even the least casual encounter with that chemical mist. Germany had used gas first on the French at Ypres in April of the same year. Later, chlorine was said to be too nasty for use by civilized white men and it was discarded for sweeter phosgene and mustard.

Quite comical 'twas, as it was we British who initially knobbed open the chlorine cylinders at Loos. After all, it was our attack. But our stuff had been released in a bad wind and this batch killed as many tommies as the Jerry. But 'twasn't any English gas that I whiffed. ˙

After our own gassing had failed, we attacked, although the Hun machine gun nests had not been discomforted in the least. The enemy had been sufficiently alert to regulate their oxygen devices, which gave them protection for an hour. As I motioned my men forward a battery peppered us, and among the normal explosive shells were canisters containing the poison gas. These bombs must have been experimental, for gas, at this period in the war, was normally emitted by cumbersome propulsion engines with connecting pipes.

Chlorine blinded both my twinkling orbs and chewed up much of my lung tissue, which has resulted in my invalidism and obscene dependence on Nurse Alice. Without Nurse Alice, who in actuality is Eric Smith of Belfast, a nurseyman's son who served as my horse groom in the Ferozepore brigade, 129 Duke of Connaught's Own, Baluchis, Lahore Division, Indian Army, and now metamorphosed into Nurse Alice, a tall fair lass from an equally factitious Middlesex farm, this work could not have been attempted. I will tell somewhat of Avery's war impressions but not now, as I do not wish to digress with such skill that this book's plotting becomes as untraceable as a seal's wake fading beneath the ice.

## six

Joseph Atkins, master of the three-masted ship Hartlepool *Harvester,* served from 1817 to 1853 in the Australian wool clip trade. Atkins, though spare of frame, was portly minded, a most conservative man, as are many of his profession. His countenance was as confident as are the bold ship models of waste wood that sailor hands must ceaselessly carve. Joseph was a perfected replica, in spirit, of Regina's Britain.

Above all, Atkins prided himself on his knowledge of winds and currents. Forty years of composure at the mizzenmast had apprenticed him to the innermost secrets. Atkins was a great seaman and a fine commander of men. Because of his ability to read the invisible powering that was the ship's motive force, he was a rich man at death. His yearly voyages to the wharfs of Sydney and back again to the Sunderland warehouse were made weeks swifter than could be accomplished by common masters. Invariably, clip from the *Harvester* would open the January wool market and receive a fine premium.

Atkins knew 19th-century Sydney, and New South Wales, intimately as compared to home England. And his baldness, even beneath a beaver's tall hat, as he carriaged the colony's roads must have drawn in the Australian sun deeper than imagined, into his testicles, passing first through the

sweetbread of his mind. Atkins, of bushed beard and
sidelocks, was Anglican and a devout truster in Crown and
tall masts, as are all poor boys who achieve station above
birth's oarlock. Thus, he was a sternness who plodded. Yet
was a far better seamaster than was needed for the laborious
inching of nineteenth century voyages. Pre-clipper days they
were and steam engines still properly distrusted. If a ship on
leaving Lizard's joint endured seven months under sail, as was
the average in attaining Sydney, then all was well. Rapid
voyaging was not coveted except by men of greed, as was
Joseph Atkins.

Acknowledging Atkins is a predominant counterpoint of
this vain book. This man of efficient success turned from
gold, ship, and wind to embrace the newer myth of Wilkulda.
For in December of 1853, after the slowest crossing of his
experience, after terrible stress in holding a rank crew
together, as the gold strikes in Victoria reached their frenzied
zenith, after an anxious wait of four weeks while the last
woolclip came down from the outback to be stowed away,
after sailing out from bricked and white columned Sydney,
Atkins did take in the lee braces and tacked north instead of
ESE where the firm planetary winds would have swept the
*Harvester* home. Joseph took his vessel into the doldrums
instead of down to the southern flanks of the earth's land
masses where the good winds lay.

Merino hair, dry baled and tight, does not corrupt itself,
but to a man like Atkins time was indeed gold. To sail north
around the coinless bulk of Australia, instead of running
downhill about the Horn in simplest eastward passage, was a
marked perversity in the man of wealth. To circle Australia
to make the west coast and then south to pick up the
Roaring Forties at Perth, would mean two months of
additional sailing cost. Expense to the owners, Bruce and
Whoor, that could not be expunged with profit's gold.

Then too, Atkins, somber in righteous self-will, did plainly
lie to his sailors in order that they might stay aboard and not
desert to the goldfields along the Murray. Atkins had never
lied to a crew before, yet he lied full and deep that he might
have men to work the *Harvester* to a profitless west shore. As
it was, even with the lie, the *Harvester* was manned with but
thirty souls instead of her usual complement of forty-five.
These thirty re-rigged the square sailed ship into a fore and
aft with sheets parallel to her hull that she might sail closer to
the wind while attempting a safe passage through the difficult
Torres Strait. The crew believed Atkins' lie when the august

captain told the poor men that a grandly sized gold nugget had been found in a mountain range on the western hip of the huge isle.

That he could detour so deviously wide, in his mature years, was beyond the ken of those few who knew the phlegmatic, prudent seamaster well. Yet in his sixth decade of accumulating station, at this time of ultimate material success, Atkins exhibited a profound predilection for mysticism. We wanderers of this late day have been informed of the placement of earth's primal messiah, in the shallows off West Australia in about the year 1500 B.C., only because of the change that came into Joseph's soul.

Frecht was Joseph's seducer. This Dutchman Frecht, a beached sea captain, a wrecker of his own vessel on a reef off Celebes, netted Atkins with the Wilkuldian legend. Frecht had been born in an obscure fishing village on a zee in the 1770's. He had been shipboard since his seventh birthday. He sailed first as baitboy on a tiny fore and aft smack in the herring fleets that fished off the Skagrag. Few seamen could relate the deeper lessons of ocean voyaging as could this man Frecht. At the age of fourteen he mastered a coastal schooner, a two-masted craft of eighty ton, in trading from Barcelona to Goteborg. Experienced in the storms of sea existence, Frecht captained his first planetary journey in a full rigged ship of three hundred and fifty tons from Amsterdam to Batavia. She was a chartered ship to an offshoot of the dying Dutch East India Company.

Batavia, although a profitable port of call, was a town of disease and summary death. It was a place of fetid brothels when Frecht sailed into harbor in 1801. Two months after tying to wharf his ship was finally finished with cargoing. His crew of sixty, ships were over-manned in those days due to the cheapness of hiring sailors, had been reduced to twelve by Batavia's persistent plagues. Frecht took the ship to sea with the twelve hands and sailed her with top gallants unfurled to Amsterdam with a cargo of one hundred and eighty short tons of the better grade of cinnamon. Eight sailors were on board when the ship reached home.

Frecht was considered a man of prospects with such a golden first voyage. Unfortunately the company's directors had been informed by their waterfront spies, clearance agents officially, that young Frecht had returned with more than spice. Not itemized on the ship's manifest were two Chinese sisters Frecht had purchased in Batavia for the knockdown price of $30 in bullion. The virginal ten-year-old sister had died off Madagascar, but the thirteen-year-old survived the voyage in jolly spirits, notwithstanding her pregnancy.

And though Frecht had soon discovered that the knockdown price he had paid was proportionate to the two girls' condition of maidenhood, he became attached to the older sister. They had been the daughters of a wealthy Batavia brothel owner, but after his violent death in a disputation of honor, the girls had been passed on to a Moor, also a brothel keeper, in settlement of a debt. The surviving sister had created an exquisite room of hand painted screens in Frecht's cabin. The squat, roughened Hollander was captivated by the girl's daintiness and dependence. He soon loved her as well as such a man as he could love.

That the young captain owned a yellow whore did not bother the directors, but that Frecht would marry such a creature in a church horrified them. Frecht married the girl because of her pregnancy, for he hoped that he would have a son to replace the younger brother he had lost years before. His younger brother, Wilhelm, had been employed as a bait boy on the smack that the older Frecht served as an ablebodied. In the winter of 1783, eight year old Wilhelm had been caught up in a dropping net and drowned. Frecht watched Wilhelm being dragged down through the surface until he was lost to sight among the feeding herring. He begged the fishing boat's captain to pull the seine and Wilhelm up to try to save the boy. The smack's master, a pragmatist even as was Frecht, said the boy was dead, as the net had twenty fathoms to steep where the boy's stupid foot had misbehaved. Hours later when the net was pulled in Wilhelm remained deep in the Baltic, but as the catch was abnormally good the fishermen thought well of Wilhelm's memory instead of jeering at his bad luck.

Thus, Frecht needed to legalize his baby, a son indeed, that Wilhelm might be metamorphosed in the half-caste's soul. And the Eurasian child was christened Wilhelm Frecht and the China girl was wedded, and Frecht had returned brother Willy to life. In this act of marriage to an unvirginal colored person we may perceive the essential quality of the fellow even though in future years he would become villainous.

After the church wedding Frecht was unemployed. However, a captain who had produced such a neat pile of gulden on his first long voyage, during unsettled times of war and blockade, must be found a ship, no matter his yellow whore wife. A concern owned by Amsterdam Jews, who had fled from Spain some centuries past, hired him as master of a well-founded bargue of six hundred tons. In August of 1805, some months before the battle of Trafalgar dismayed Napoleonic Europe, Frecht, his yellow bride, no given name researched even as for Frecht himself, and infant Wilhelm sailed out on a moonless night from Amsterdam.

## seven

When Joseph Atkins jostled into the banknote counting Frecht in the foyer of the New South Wales Colonial Bank in Sydney in the month of December, 1852, Frecht was in his eighth decade of Wilhelm productions while the Englander was fifty-five years counted and stacked. As Joseph knelt with the Hollander to re-constitute the fluttering flock of banknotes back into an original tidiness of wealth, he recognized the infamous scoundrel at once.

Frecht was a notorious personage in the colony and Atkins saw in the Hollander's pocked and scarred folds, the lecherous, besotten sins of a shipwrecker. Frecht had resided in disorganized Sydney since 1838. He had observed the colony's decline from its preeminence in crime and whoredom to an orderly breeder of wealth for such as Joseph Atkins.

In the monsoon season of 1829 Frecht had hurled his command onto a predesignated reef off Sangihe island in the sea of Celebes. The wreckers, Cochinchinese pirates, had proposed the arrangement. Frecht owned the ship in shares with a consortium of Calcutta jute exporters, Hebrews and distant relations of the original Amsterdam merchants who had hired Frecht in 1805. The vessel was new, an exceptional square rigger of eight hundred tons laid down in Maine in '26. She was ribbed with iron for endurance and her masts were of matured pine out of New Brunswick.

She stowed a fine cargo of pearl shell, but her main tonnage was made up of the costly aphrodisiac, Bech-De-Mer. These dried sea slugs had been amassed by Italian missioniaries in the Solomons over several years to raise funds for the establishment of a series of missions. The vessel was valued at £20,000 and the cargo of slugs and shell at £50,000. Frecht's price for gently easing her onto the

Sangihe reef was £10,000, no matter if the ship could be refloated or not.

The pirates came in two junks and several smaller dhows, perhaps four hundred men in all. The ship lay jammed but undamaged on the coral. Frecht had placed his crew on the exposed reef, according to plan, and after the ship had either been sailed away by the pirates, or looted and burned, he and his crew would be permitted to oar the ship's whale and longboats to the nearest land. It was agreed, there was to be no bloodletting.

Wilhelm, his handsome half-caste son, who served as the ship's first officer, did not know of his father's arrangement and rather foolishly attempted to make a fight of it from their disadvantaged position on the bare reef. The Cochinchinese gleefully pounded away with their brass swivel guns. The fragmented coral shredded the Lascars and Wilhelm to piteous condition. Frecht had already been taken on board the master junk, supposedly to discuss salvage terms, when the massacre ensued. The pirates left the high tide to finish their merciless work. Wilhelm Frecht was last seen by his father in myriad pieces among a school of small fish.

Five days after the wrecking Frecht was picked up out of his ship's dinghy off Boenjoe by a Russian whaler returning home after hunting sperm whale in the Tasmanian Sea. The Russian ship veered to Batavia and left Frecht to be drawn in a horse ambulance to the hospital. At first it was thought that he had been dropped off the afterdeck down into the dinghy by either a mutinous crew or by pirates. He was paralyzed and thought to have a ruptured pelvis. However, this diagnosis was discarded when Frecht disappeared from his cot after several weeks of what had appeared to be a coma that could only end in death.

No person of authority issued warrants in an attempt to locate Frecht. Officialdom was relieved to be rid of the madman. It was scandalous enough that the heathen Russians had openly gossiped that when they came upon Frecht on the open sea he was gnawing at the stump of what had been his right hand. He had already eaten partway past his wrist when the whaling men had forced his teeth apart from the dangling bone. The Cochinchinese had planted Frecht in the dinghy as proof of the vessel's foundering; they had not expected the Hollander to survive, as he had collapsed after watching the fish nibble at Wilhelm. When the pirates discovered that Frecht had lived, they arranged his departure from Batavia and paid him his commission.

Frecht was taken to Macao. Here he spent the largest part
of his £10,000 in debasement lasting well into two years.
However, with a remaining £2,000 he purchased a two
hundred ton schooner and sailed to Australian waters, where
he became a sealer in the Bass Straits. This was 1831, and
these waters were still being ravaged by escaped convicts who
guided ships onto rocks in order to loot them. Frecht had
had enough of scavenging and kept his vessel in the hunting
trade only. The straits were then humped fat with
mammillary species that provided men with marketable oil,
skins, and ivory.

Seals skins were alone worth £1 at Hobarton, chief village
of Tasmania. This town bested obscene Sydney in dissipation
and rowdyism, thus Frecht made his base there. As his profits
grew, Frecht in 1835 began to make regular voyages to
Sydney where he deposited his gold in the vaults of the
Colonial Bank, for even such a prolifigate as Frecht could not
squander all his profits in whoring and gambling. His lucky
streak seemed incredible. Not knowing what else to do with
the accumulating sums, Frecht began to purchase acreage
along the Paramatta road that led westward out of Sydney.

In '37 Frecht began to hunt along Australia's west coast.
For many seasons of mirth he slaughtered among the great
pods of seals and dugong that placidly smiled on the sands.
The dugong especially seemed to rather enjoy being clubbed
and skinned. Then a day came when, somewhere north of
Shark's Bay, Frecht stole a young lubra who was just entering
puberty. With this eleven year old girl he found a
companionship he had not felt since his Chinese wife had
died in 1807, weeks after weaning Wilhelm. The girl was
erotically sophisticated and yet innocent of all else, and
easily beguiled with the old Dutchman's magic pipe, watch,
and telescope. Frecht respected the young lubra, the first
aborigine woman he had owned, for no matter how rough the
sea the girl remained carefree and jovial. Frecht had boarded
dozens of women onto his schooner from the convict
prostitutes. He paid the white women by purchasing tickets
of freedom for them from the captains of the convict ships
that sailed to the colonies.

Frecht had tremendous catches of dugong, the sea
elephant. The market in Sydney for lamp oil was tight and he
reaped bowers of golden grave flowers for the inferior grease
of the dugong. The sea elephant's skin was not commercially
attractive, but the animal's thick belt of prosperous blubber
beneath its hide served Frecht well. Dugongs were killed

without effort or danger. Except for the expense of powder
and ball they were mined without large capital investment.
The dugong was a ponderous, slothful beast that could be
walked up to directly as it lay on the beach and tapped
smartly on its gruesome snout. As the very dumb animal
raised its mouth wide in protest, it was shot directly in the
pink delicate mouth roof.

Frecht established a residence in Sydney during the year of
1841. He kept the lubra from Shark Bay with him though
offered quite an attractive price of £ 50 for her by a
Kangaroo Island wrecking gang he knew.

Aging Frecht became bored with shooting dugong and as
he was rich, he decided to enter a semi-retired state. Besides
his schooner's activities, years before, he had taken shares in
several Hobarton whalers. During this era the sperm oil
earned a fine premium in Europe, and he was able to sell his
craft to his whaling associates without concern for the loss of
income. But he could not yet give up the sea, and he
purchased a small, broad-beamed, fifty ton schooner just
spanked out onto the Derwent by a local ship yard. She was a
tight and dry ship of well seasoned Huron pine.

He sailed the little ship along the lanes where whaling
stations perched on the tiny strands of islands that
proliferated between Southeast Cape at Tasmania and South
Cape at land's end on New Zealand. Sailing westward back to
Sydney, he would swing north to trade at Lord Howe and
Norfolk islands. The whaling stations needed endless reams of
cloth, seed, kegs of nails, and even umbrellas for sale to
captain's wife. Frecht was a dedicated sea-merchant and on
sighting a lugging whaler at sea he would close on her and
send his trading-flag mast high and hail up an offer to sell jugs
of molasses. Invariably the syrup was prized and Frecht's
banknotes would proliferate. The Shark Bay lubra shared his
schooner's bunk.

By '47 Frecht was worth £75,000 in banked deposits and
an additional £50,000 in real property. As he was now in his
seventies, he no longer relished engaging the gales and
typhoons in his fifty tonner. Frecht had begun to dream that
one night a bigger wave than the schooner could cast off
might raise her on the keel and twist her bows into the deep,
thus de-masting and tearing off hatch covers and sending her
straight to the bottom. Frecht had decided that he must be
buried on land and not lost to the ocean as had been brother
and son, Wilhelms.

Sydney was then a pretty town with gardens and farms

lying directly on the harbor. The government square was handsome, with bricked buildings and strutting uniformed fools, handsome though in their way too. Convict labor could still be hired, but this source of cheap workers was diminishing rapidly as the Crown had ceased transportation to New South Wales some years back. This city of fine streets, numerous parks, and stately official residences had been constructed by convict hands, but it was a righteous town with too many reverends, or so thought the harbor folk.

A few orchards and cornfields grew to sea's edge, but as the land values increased, and since the fierce drought of 1828 had forced agriculture back to the mountain streams, the local farmers sold out or were foreclosed, according to their luck. On holidays from Jackson Harbor to Botany Bay churned pleasure steamers crowded with picnickers. For amusement the better people sailed their skiffs from jetties built to their ocean-fronting homes.

Frecht enjoyed the whores of Sydney, and he settled comfortably into a handsome brick home he had built on acreage north of the Parramatta road. The black woman from the niggers of Shark Bay he still kept as his chief prostitute. Churchmen had not yet subverted Sydney to their pale wills, but as the seasons passed they began to drive evil from their view. Frecht, though officially a scoundrel and devil's spoor, was allowed to reside in the colony as long as he had gold, and this particular metal seemed eternally fertile in his un-Godly keeping.

In the first decades of the 19th Century Sydneytown had stunk of crude debauchery, and in the mid-century residue of this degradation, Frecht felt himself a true citizen. He fitted in, yet with each grind of his testicles' pump he believed that he was considered a revenant by society, and thus, little more than a rich outcast.

On the 3rd of December, in 1852, Joseph Atkins piloted his fine vessel, the 1200 ton *Harvester,* into Jackson Harbor and tied up at the Darling wharf after the slowest passage of his experience. By this marking in time Sydney was a stolid and adventureless city. Frecht was now worth a half a million and was the colony's sixth richest individual. Officials treated the one-handed property owner with extreme diffidence, as the Dutchman's estate was believed to be willed to the municipality in a trust to be governed by the Crown. And in time the greater part of the Dutchman's wealth came to reside in the town's treasury, but not by Frecht's design. For indeed, officialdom thwarted his will's self-redemptive thrust.

Kukika, the lubra from Shark Bay, now a matron in her late twenties, was still his bed's primary comfort. Because of his emotional attachment to the stunning whore of blackness he had acquired a community of aborigines that sought refuge from the Nightmare on his small estate. It was this odoriferous convocation of dying and diseased stone agers from several destroyed mankinds that had led him to keep his house distant from the more settled areas. Fifteen miles from Government House they were safe and could not be chopped up to feed the hunting hounds of the officers, for that is what the Australoids imagined to be the fate of blackmen taken into captivity. This mirage Kukika played like a rhapsody to inveigle Frecht into granting sanctuary to the 'dumbs niggers.' He too believed the dog food story.

There in the farmland suburbs the several score of aborigines could live outdoors by their fires and lay down peaceably with the women without a jostling crowd of christians inspecting their copulation. In 1861, when Frecht died, the stone agers were driven off the estate, and the patrimony planned for them as a memorial to the dead Wilhelms was stolen by voracious toothed things similiar to flesh-eating fish.

Atkins visited the estate in December of 1852 and found that the blacks, including Kukika, preferred to live in the apricot orchard behind the large house. The wild fruit trees, wild because they were untended, reminded the blacks of redgums. Frecht, on the first day of Atkins' visit, as he reined in his team to corner onto the trail leading to his manse, could not restrain his tongue, as he had not had a white man for a friend since his half-caste son.

"Da lubas are da best, da fuck da best den any utter vomans."

Unfortunately, Frecht had not limited himself to sleeping with black women, and he had recently contracted syphilis from a touring dance troupe girl. She had passed through Sydney in '49 and had charged the old man 100 sovereigns. Her price was normally but ten, but the aged foreigner was too obvious a mark to be resisted. She allowed Frecht but one encounter, and he was happy about his conquest as he believed her to be some aristocrat's bastard daughter. No matter her good looks and fine features, she was a convict's spawn and left Frecht with the scourge of the penal diseases. He was not unduly concerned by the infection as it was but one

more of many bodily failures that lacerated the body of the
near eighty year old fornicator. Alas, his collection of
aborigines became racked with his now tainted sperm. At his
death, when the stone agers were forced out of the apricot
orchard by officialdom and chased into foodless bushland,
these poor people laid down with the few remaining hordes
and sub-sections inland, and the Nightmare was fully and
grotesquely fulfilled.

On that first entrance into bewilderment, when Atkins
entered the rear garden to investigate Frecht's zoo of
relic-men, he found them still bold in health, as they sat
joyfully in their nakedness around their tiny three-stick fires.
He had arrived here only after a peculiar run of accidental
circumstances, so Atkins told himself. That morning when
Atkins had bumped into the Hollander in the bank's foyer,
he had instinctively dropped to his knees to help the older
man gather up his banknotes. Joseph was bemused, and
intrigued, at the accidental encounter with the four-foot
six-inch Frecht, a man with a leather blunted left wrist. Why,
after helping the old man count the notes to be sure ·that
none had flown away, he had allowed Frecht to lead him to
the Sailor's Roost on Iron Cove overlooking Jackson Harbor,
is beyond your narrator's insight. But whatever the true
reason, the spoken reason was a search for non-existent
sailors who were all down searching for gold in the mud of
the Murray. While eating a plate of sliced and pickled calf's
tongue, washed down with tanquards of hot ale, the
metamorphosis of both men was initiated, even as the
Hollander tendered a hesitant invitation for the Englisher to
pay a call at his "manor," as Frecht described his farm.

Atkins was aware of Frecht's background, for Joseph had
made thirty-six voyages to the colony and knew the major
men of the city or at least their reputations. Even though the
first luncheon had been among *wharf dregs* and compounded
ugliness, Atkins was attracted by the Hollander's salty charm
and soon the two seamen were on intimate terms. From the
night of December 10 to the 7th of January Atkins was guest
in Frecht's house. And in those few weeks the transformation
of both progressed, though neither recognized the change in
himself.

It was the whore Kukika who initiated the Englishman's
spirit flaring. Previously, she had ignited the glow in Frecht's
wasted soul. She related, in her Dutch-dialected English, the
myth of Wilkulda, the tale of human Ancestor-Hero. Atkins'

primal response to the legend was a spluttering, "My God, it
is impossible."

She spoke the name, 'Wilkulda,' with such awe that Atkins
was taken aback. He had never expected to hear such tones
of reverence in a stone ager's voice. Before hearing Kukika
speak in such a manner, Joseph had not known that the abos,
as the currency lads, the Australian born white men, had
named the mankinds, were human and aware of
transcendental beings. The only other Australoid negress
Atkins had ever heard speak aloud was an old hag who earned
her living by fornicating with a trained dingo as
entertainment in a Melbourne waterfront tavern. This hag,
who had been taught her trick on a sheep run by bored
shepherds, sang, 'God Save the Queen,' as the dingo mounted
her. In point of fact, except for those domestic servants who
died off quickly from respiratory diseases, the blacks living in
Frecht's orchard were the last normal Australoids in New
South Wales; all others were degraded and lower than house
puppies.

So Atkins had never observed a black in his traditional
surroundings before his stay with Frecht, although once he
had been blown off course in the Bass Straits by a gale and
had sheltered the Harvester on the windless shore of a tiny
isle north of Tasmania. Here the remaining survivors of the
Tasmanian mankinds had been shipped after a roundup by
dogs and convicts in the interior of Tasmania. The few score
natives captured by the hunt had been desposited on the
treeless island and when Atkins viewed them they were near
death in a strange apathy and passivity. These caged blacks
on a nude isle in the fearsome Bass Straits died away
noiselessly and could never have been magicians and hunters.

When Kukika spoke the name, 'Wilkulda,' Atkins was given
an insight into the character of the aborigine that few
Europeans had attained. Joseph realized that the stone age
woman possessed a soul, a thing the savants said was
impossible. The aborigine, they said, was at best a link
between Neanderthal and modern man, at worst an ugly,
stenched mistake of nature. And that this tiny-brained
vermin could be involved with reverential awe cast Joseph
Atkins into the state of a man wind shucked from an ancient
husk of contempt toward a newness of perception.

Frecht encouraged Kukika in her role as the teller of the
myth, although he would eagerly interrupt her and regale
Atkins with his own peculiar insights. Thus Frecht orated,

"Da ya knows dat dese peoples had once schools and histories so to speak. Dey use da love dere fathers an' old men likes we love gold. Dey can't write a word, so vat. So dey don't have no churches built of stone, so vat. Da missionaries, pissers, say da niggers ain't got da idea of God. Deys liars cause dey vant dem to kneel down only to dere own assholes.

"Dey a vild peoples just like ve vas before ve got civilized. Da white bastard-shits make da nigger old mens to be shit to da young vons so dere ain't no respect any more for da old vays. Da peoples vere here in dere millions before ve came vit our poisoned pricks an' our consumptions. Den dey die like herring in da seine, just like dat poor little boys Wilhelms. Da fuckin' missionaries never look in da old mens eyes cause dere afraid dey find wisdom in the niggers an' dey don't vant dat. Da constables say da niggers don't know about judges an' dat dey ain't got laws, da truth is dat dese peoples world is made of laws an da big fella whose cock is cut is a judge equal to da Queen's courts.

"Did ya know dat dese peoples got da vay of makin' men outa boys just like da Yews. Da sons-of-bitches Yews got most da money an dats whys I put the ship on the reef to get the Yews good . . . but I didn't figure on Wilhelm puttin' up a fight, my poors Wilhelm . . . Dese black fellas bravest mens I ever did seen. Dey do tings every day dat dey live dat we would say makes heroes but to dese niggers to be heroes all da fuckin' time is natural.

"Couple years back I vanted to take Kukika back to her peoples up on da vest coast nord of Sharks Bay. She tell me dat ve could live vit dem couple of months and dat dey would take me into da tribe right away cause some old woman would tink me to be her dead son back from da Dreamtime wheres all mans' souls go vhen da fella dies. But den Kukika changes her mind cause she don't vanna go back to sea and leave da damn apricots.

"Joe, it's ok vit da niggers, ya can get all da pussy ya vant vit a little pinch of 'bacca,' da pipe kinds dey likes da best. Da niggers give ya all da pussy ya can handle for bacca. But I took Kukika vit out nothin' cause I'm a mean bastard an' don't like da eye of her old cock husband.

"Kukika great fuck Joe. Ya should give her a good yerking. She squirts out juice from her cunt just like a man's prick. She's happy vit me even do I ain't got da hot cock like ven I vas younger man couple years back.

"Vilkulda is for real, I tink dat is so. It fits dat dese poor peoples would get a messiah cause dey ain't got nothin' else. Da land stinks for farmin' every place but rounds here. All dese lands good for really is da sheeps an' cows like da' fuckin officers brought dere merino sheeps. Dese niggers ain't got herd of nothin' dats vhy dey deserve to make a Christ. Dese da poorest niggers dat ever vas. Dey don't even got von reindeer like da eskimos got. I been all over vorld but never heard of place vit out even a camels. Dats vhy dey had da time to make a Christ, nothin' else to do.

"Da fuckin' missionaries should be shitted for saying dese peoples ain't got no Gods. Dey should be shooted like I did da seals, da fuckin' liars. Cause ven da churches say dese peoples ain't got no Gods an' da government shits dese peoples ain't got da sense of ownin' land, an' da soldiers say dere cowardly cause dey don't charge against rifles an' mounted men, an' da fartin' settlers sat dere pests likes mices, den every son-of-a-bitch in dis place says to kill da black fellas off to make da place goot.

"Dats vhy da hoity toity English ain't no better den me. Me, a fuckin' brother killer, a fuckin' son killer, a fuckin' ship killer, and a whore master, den all dese king's men vorse den me cause I knows da niggers are mens who loves dere Gods an' da land, an' dere vimen da best fucks I ever did see."

# eight

"Sky, why do you place Tjundaga's grandson in the sea without plan? Admit to me, your messenger Wilkulda, the reason that I stand here in the shallows," and musing to himself, or perhaps to the sea's soul, Wilkulda pronounced aloud a story of self-doubt therein the ocean of the Turtle-men.

"It was true that when my father, Lillywur, strode into the circle of hags straddling my mother's shoulders and waist to force me out of her womb into the blood warmed sand, that seeing me appear as a penised baby, Lillywur did seize me before I was fully breached, and wet with mother's being he lifted me into the Sky. It was true that Lillywur, my father, could barely be restrained as my grandmother chewed apart the umbilical cord and gave the severed part to my mother that she would eat it in a loving stomach. As father danced with my infant self, mother with sand did cover the afterbirth. Then she slept between the warmth of fires for though it was daytime it was the wet season and the world was chilled with mist.

"Lillywur, my talented father, danced with me beneath the morning sky and he was very happy for I was his first male child. Twirling, twirling, in screaming turns was I introduced into the revolving sky.

"Then, when hair came to my chin many seasons later, it seemed that the dance with Lillywur had made me aware that to be circumcised was to be re-made into a man, I knew it even as a soggy babe first seen by the Sky. Holy is circumcision. It is the ultimate sacredness and is second only to death when a man's spirit is interred back into the Eternal Dream.

"Myself and the two other lads who were to be circumcised waited at dawn with our heads covered by our arms. During the night we had lain prone on our stomachs but now rested nervously on our backs. We were still shaken from the preceeding night's drama when our uncles took us away from our fathers' fires to be prepared for the coming circumcisions. As if attacking an enemy people our uncles came for us. Like warriors in the press of battle, without stealth, they came to terrorize our boyish hearts. They pretended spear thrusts, but it was a testing. A testing, as had been so many things in the past seasons and as we must continue to bear for many additional years, even after circumcision.

"Captured, we three initiates were to be taken to a ritual site as the women of the Wedgetail Eagles lamented with foreboding wails. Quickly we three boys remembered our roles and calmed our fears, that the new spirits would enter us completely after our foreskins were burnt and the ashes eaten.

"All that day we lay face down into the red sand as the elders slapped at our heads with open fists and attempted to trick us into answering their entreating questions. But we were to be Wedgetail Eagles and had been properly educated, and thus we remained silent. For such indications of intelligence none of us three would be killed during the critical examinations. No females were allowed near the sacred grounds of circumcision, and we three boys were alone with the circumcised pure.

"On the second night more testing as the younger men came out of the bush to joke and sneer at the size and shape of our genitals. But we were educated and spoke not a word in reply, and their spears remained out of our lungs. We three would not fail. We had looked forward eagerly to our ciurcumcisions for many reasons. Wedgetails were not allowed to lay down with females until after we are cut into men. But girls begin to lay down in their tenth season, when the elders pull and stretch their girlish vaginas with their fingers. After the girls are made larger all the elders lay down with the tugged-open girl.

"After a season when our circumcised, new penises were perfectly healed, and after certain other ceremonies, we would be permitted to lay down with any woman or girl who came into our paths while we lived apart in the bush. However, as we Eagles do not lay down with our mothers, sisters, sisters-in-law, or mothers-in-law, and since almost all the Wedgetail females would fall into these relationships, we initiates would go through our ten summers and winters of training without laying down. Just after our season of circumcisional journey, however, we would participate in a ceremony where we would be encouraged to lay down as often as possible for sacred purposes, but this period lasted only a few days.

"I had been eager for my circumcision but not only for its religious significance, although as Tjundaga's favorite it was important to me for its holiness. But in truth I was impatient because it meant I could lay down with Kitunga, whom I loved as hotly as only an innocent boy can love. At the increase ceremony by the holy relic I would be permitted to lay down with her. Kitunga was so pretty, a young widow, beautiful and plump. When her husband died in an adjoining mankind's world, her father, who was an Eagle elder of the final rank, dared to bring her back to his fires among the Wedgetails. This was a tremendous insult to the dead husband's ghost and to his living brothers who were the rightful heirs to Kitunga.

"Kitunga's father was too fond of her and there was a suspicion of a peculiar happening. But as he was a powerful sorcerer, he was able to contend with the murderous raging of his daughter's brothers-in-law. Indeed, the old man had gone so far as to arrange a second marriage for Kitunga with a Goanna-man who had already traded four hags for the right to take Kitunga away. However, even while utilizing the hags to gather his own food, the old father continued to procrastinate and the sad Goanna wailed to the council of elders all day long. They did not care about his complaint, as Kitunga was a wondrous lover and they wished to keep her as long as they could without bloodshed.

"Kitunga had been a widow for four moons as my circumcision time approached. And in my lust for her I dreamed that she would not be taken to the Goanna land until after the laying down ceremony. But even when I could tell that the circumcision was nearing by my mother's hours of silence, I could not believe that Kitunga would still be with us then. The brothers of her dead husband were threatening a feud unless Kitunga was returned to the Mice world. As there were nineteen Mice brothers-in-law to contend with, even the Goanna-man began to offer them favors if she were allowed to come peaceably with him. It was a great scandal among the mankinds of our worlds.

"We Wedgetails have been men since the Age of Dreams when the Spirits swam out of the westing sun of fire water to create animals and land from the Sky . . . Kitunga's unmarried state had attracted many strangers to our pool encampment. I think she was in her fifteenth summer when my circumcision happened. It was a very desirable season as her breasts were still taunt and spearing, not like the drooping folds of the hags. Her buttocks were sensational and many of my older friends mewed to stroke them and some succeeded, but never was Kitunga to be mine . . . Sea's soul, why do I sing to you of the forgotten and dead days that have dwindled to narrow streams of dust? I know not why I still sing of hurts and hopes now quite meaningless.

". . . Yes, many men competed with the brothers-in-law and the Goanna-man for Kitunga. Her vulgar and dishonorable father became fattened into ugliness with the gifts of emu brain and white grubs. Mallee-hen eggs he would no longer accept as gifts, the foolish man. Kitunga, of course, would lay down with the competing fellows, but instead of the men becoming dissatisfied or bored with her as unrestricted laying down sometimes effects, they only became hotter. All this time the Mice-men had kept up a terrific row about their rights being usurped, they declared that the gifts of the various competitors should be theirs and not the treacherous father's. Kitunga's parent was reaping favors and gifts that would normally take ten seasons of trading to accumulate, he had accomplished this on the flimsiest legal grounds, claiming that Kitunga must be returned to him as the Mice-men had overlooked his burial gift at his son-in-law's funeral.

"I believe it was Kitunga's insatiable demand to lay down that made men so passionate for her. What a valuable wife she would make! Her desirability made Kitunga equally fine as a laying down gift or as a guest wife to a visiting great man. She also was a good forager even as a young girl and would provide her husband with platters of delicacies. She had a knack for searching out the witchetty grubs which are relished for their richness but will cause diarrhea if too many are consumed.

". . . When her father took her away from the Mice world she still remained a Mice woman until her next marriage, and thus the Wedgetail Eagles could lay down with her without violating the kinship laws. In truth, Kitunga laid down with almost everyone except me. At this time of the year our camp was by the pool of sweet water. It was a huge pond held by a jumble of rock. The Kangaroo Ancestor had created the pool by sitting down where the north salt pan is now and then by gliding his penis through the worthless sand surreptitiously that he might violate three sisters who were hunched to the earth urinating. The pool is where the sisters urinated and the huge rocks upholding the water are the metamorphosed sections of the Kangaroo's penis which the three women had chopped up with their digging sticks.

"We Eagles lived at the pool only in the dry season when all other water sources had been siphoned down into the bones of the earth by the Hidden Snakes. It was forbidden to drink from the pool except during the dry season and the elders stationed men by it at all times to protect the water from thieves, either other mankinds or thirsty emu who make their nests nearby. In some terribly dry seasons the emu birds were said to rush at the pool on their long legs, but the warriors' spears always bested the emu's great stride. And even with these precautions and strict rationing, seldom would the pool contain water to the very end of the dry season and we would have to walk about searching for wet soaks.

"Reeds with many seams sprout thick and green in our pond and the women plait nets and bags from the strong reeds, and things were good at the pond. Many ducks and herons lived on our pool and there were Wedgetail Eagles who lived on the highest spurs of limestone to the west over the water. We did not stalk the duck or heron although it is said they are very tasty.

"Black swans lived on the pond and there were many hundreds of them in our pool's flock. But they were forbidden food too except to the council of elders who killed two every new moon and divided the meat among themselves. A grove of whitegums roots in the high rocks at the lower end of the water and many thousands of galah nest in the swarming limbs. There are the pink-throated and underwinged galahs, those of the sun-white feathers. We do not eat galahs for they are the food of ourselves who live on the perches above and who possess wings instead of arms.

"In our pool big perch are speared easily and many clams grow in the mud. All in all, our pool is the marvel of the desert worlds and neighboring mankinds are jealous of it, but none would attempt to war it away. It is the Spirit of the Eagle which throbs in the pond's water and any stranger who drank from it without our permission would die at once, as would any stranger who falsely trod on our lands without our knowledge.

"Circumcisions were created only in the earliest part of the dry season when the pool was still almost flooded with the lost rains. We could comfortably accomodate the many guests who wished to share our joy at such heroic occasions. My own circumcision was of some consequence, for Tjundaga, my grandfather, was the greatest magician known to the world and I was his favorite and thought to be a promising magician in my own right. Thus we had a crowd of visitors camping with us. During the few weeks preceding the ceremony, Kitunga was the cause of a dozen and more spearing duels, with one poor fellow accidently killed by a mis-aimed cast that sliced his liver.

"Each morning the women and their younger children would go into the bush to gather in the day's need of seed and fruit. Young men would stealthily break away from the hunting squads and follow the women. When the girl of their passion sneaked off from the watching hags, her paramour would come to her and they would lay down. Too many fellows chased after Kitunga, and spear and club blows would be given to impede racing competitors. Kitunga was not happy with the spearings and told the men that she would lay down with each of them in turns, which is what happened anyway, but the fights did not stop. Soon even elders of the council, who should have known better, began drifting away

from the hunts and from ritual organizing to join those who
chased lustful Kitunga.

"Finally, a very great man from the vastness of a shallow
lake far to the east won Kitunga from the Goanna-man. He
was a Frog and it was said that his immense lake was the
metamorphosed bladder of an Ancestor Frog. Lilies and
myriad flocks of birds, including gulls and petrels who had
flown far inland from the seas, thrived on the Frog-man's
lakes. This I know to be true for later in my journeys I
followed an albatross from the coast to this very lake.

"This Frog was quite an aged chap and already possessed
eighteen wives. He won Kitunga by promising her father
three infant girls and two pre-puberty daughters for future
marriage, plus an exorbitant platter heavy with yellow ocher.
Such huge gifts from the sophisticated Frog proved the
extent of Kitunga's renown as a laying down person. Her
father returned the Goanna-man his hags and made
restitution to the Mice-people with a handsome share of the
yellow ocher.

"The Frog wanted Kitunga for political purposes. He
would take her back to his lake and favor his brothers and
fellow elders with her ability. This would add to his greatness
and his aura of wisdom, promoting the Frog's influence
among the mankind of his seabird-laden lake.

". . . Since my circumcision was close to enactment the
Frog-man, the Goanna-man, and the Mice-men would never
leave, as that would be a serious insult to us Eagles. They
would joyfully participate in this greatest of all services to
the Dreamtime World, to the Sky itself. And this would mean
that I might still have a chance to lay down with Kitunga if
the Frog decided to stay for the entire ceremony, which
would end only at the beginning of the wet season.

". . . I wanted her to stay very badly. I knew the reason
for Kitunga's valuation. For I had accidentally, or perhaps it
was not an accident, watched Kitunga in the power of her
laying down. As we were trekking toward the pool, across the
Southern salt pan that was created by the Ant who ate two
of his own children by mistake, the pan was the Ant's vomit,
I had wandered into a tiny gorge in order to please myself in
solitude. In the narrow crevice I came upon Kitunga and that
day's lover, Wonggu.

"Wonggu was my favorite uncle and I grieved for him
when some season in the future he was killed in a spear duel
as a result of his ˙foolish elopement with his father's
sister-in-law and thus forbidden to him. Wonggu was a

handsome giant of a fellow and the Wedgetails' best hunter
when I was a boy. He could toss his twelve-foot spear a
hundred running paces and on target. Lillywur, Tjundaga,
and Wonggu were all gone in the later bad seasons when my
people had come to hate me.

". . . That dusk in the salt pan's stone wrinkle I watched
Wonggu exhort his manhood for Kitunga. He would lift her
off the ground with his hands clasped beneath her buttocks
and draw her onto his stiffness. I had not known that a
female could become lost in her ecstasy from laying down
and for many days after this just thinking of Kitunga would
embarrass me before family and friends. I had watched laying
downs since birth and even as we walked about on our land
my father would frequently lay down with a wife as we
rested . . .

". . . but with Kitunga it was as if a wind storm had swept
rain spouts onto our pool and the gaggle of black swans had
lifted off the water to seek safety in the hidden night sky.
The passion of Kitunga was as if she were a bird sent
boomerang swiftly released in dawn, a motion of poised and
rapid excitement quivering even as if the boomerang raised
up to seek entrance into the Sky World. Wonggu, whom I
loved dearly for his joviality and strength, was like a child set
freely upon her arching, as if she might propel him into the
sky where he would become a black swan. . . . I have not
mentioned Kitunga to myself for many seasons. Mayawara
became my Kitunga.

"Then, when the second night of our initiation was at its
purest secretness, my uncles Bababa, Mushabin, and Wonggu
came to lead me closer to my actual circumcision. My two
fellow initiates and I were taken by our respective uncles to a
greater fire than I had ever witnessed before. It was massive
with flames roaring out of green bluegum trunks that sweated
dollops of steaming sap onto the fire, where the liquid
exploded. We three boys were roughly kicked and pummeled
into a small hut standing in the deep shadow of a redgum. We
were prodded to sit on our haunches with our arms wrapped
about our eyes so that we would become self-blinded.

"Terrifyingly, in a suddenness, the voice of the Rainbow
Snake existed in the reed hut and inside our covered eyes.
The father of winds lived in us three boys. None of us had
ever been so near to the Holy Snake and we were set into
wrenching trembles. Endlessly, the voice rushed into our
stomachs until I know not how my kidneys could soak all the
thunder into my blood.

"Rainbow Snake's roaring somehow came to an end and I could now hear the wailing women safely huddled back at the pool campfires. With our arms braced tightly over our eyes we boys could only rely on our ears for information. We prepared ourselves for another testing as the bangings of many objects could be heard thudding onto the curved structure's sides. First we believed the objects to be spears, but from an odor of smoke we understood that torches had been cast onto the hut. We dared not escape or evidence concern, but we three were sick with fright.

"... Then Tjundaga, Tjundaga the father to my people and my very own grandfather, came into the flamed womb of man. He pried our eyes apart that we might view the deepening volume of green-grey smoke fold into itself where the reeds were tied at the hut's conical roof. Tjundaga was radiant in the penis blood of the Wedgetail elders. The blood clung glistening to every angle and plane of his being. He had masked his identity with opossum fur, and his skull was thick with white clay in which ancient Eagle feathers had been arranged in the sacred zigzag design. Glued by the blood was an adornment of pure cockatoo whiteness. Tjundaga held in each hand kernels of red and yellow ocher and with these contrasting ripples of color he decorated us in the patterns of our mankind.

"As he painted us he sang the holy myth of a circumcision that soon we would be made into men and into Eagles that soar into the Sky's Dream. Smoke was exceedingly dense yet we boys were not desperate and breathed easily. The Eagle Spirit was with us, for it resided in the soul of Tjundaga.

'Blood races from Penis
and Blood is sacred,
'Woman is slain in man
and races the Blood of new Creation,
'Eagle circumcises man
to begin the world as Eagle,
'Forever we race the Penis Blood
and create men into Eagles.'

"Tjundaga's words left us weak and mournful, for never again would we hear these words in the exact same sequence unless one of us, in old age, should become father to the people and to the ceremony.

"With reverence Tjundaga beckoned us to merge our eyes' visions in his stomach. Singing magic, Tjundaga, with extraordinary slowness, pulled from his ribbed abdomen a thin stone some three feet in length and six inches in width. This holy stone had a hole drilled into one end, and its thinness was less than a cutting flint. Tjundaga told us that this stone was the votive voice of the Rainbow Snake, for when it was twirled from the end of a human hair cord a vibrating thunder was induced. Thus, we three boys learned the first secret of malehood, that the trumpeting of the Rainbow Snake was the magic of men. No female, or child, must ever discover the origin of the Snake's voice, and if by accident a woman wandered into the vicinity where such magic was enacted, she must be speared to death.

"This stone was marked with zigzag lines. The meaning of this magic design could not be known until a male entered the final stage of elderhood when he was an old man. I will never be made aware of the potency of the zigzag.

". . . It was not until several hours passed that we boys, caught up in the magic of the night, noticed that the hut had burned totally to earth and that the reed fastenings had burst apart at the top so that the walls sagged outward to fall, leaving a safe, flame untouched center. We followed Tjundaga over the smouldering crust of the ruined hut and the coals did not pain. Now all the male Wedgetails and the many visitors surrounded us and in intense sacredness sang magic into our souls.

"Tjundaga gently led us to an ancient stone ring of holiness and directed us to lie down in the sanctified inner space. The crowns of our skulls touched and our legs were stretched widely so our feet created a circle around our connecting heads. Around and over us, males coated in emu fat and human blood, with feather strands patterned in magic motifs crossing their faces, sang and danced ecstatically.

"And the nine uncles came to straddle over us who were to be made men. Each uncle took up a sliver of flint to make a small puncture in the undervein of his penis. Tiny spurting streams of blood issued forth, and by movement of the penises they drew the ultimate magic of our mankind on the backs, stomachs, legs, and heads of us initiates. To this night, in these shallows of a foreign sea, I can feel and hear the warm, thick liquid splattering first and then collecting in the depressions and orifices of my body. Finished with their holy honor, the uncles staunched the bleeding by compressing fresh leaves to the puncture wounds.

"Tjundaga knelt down to where our three heads converged, and with patient kindness warned us, 'If you forget your training and happen to scream when the flint cuts, your father and you will be slain. Be warriors!'

"The males began to dance with enormous energy, as if some awesome magic had been sung into their own beings instead of ours. Pumping their legs and arms dynamically, with Dreamtime·rapidity, and yet with much discipline, as if their knee joints were locking roots growing perpendicularly into the earth. The men were celebrating our re-creation.

". . . Too swiftly the dancing and singing stilled and the wails of the women and children hiding around the pool in the reeds suddenly quieted. The nine uncles again advanced to place of distinction and bent down to tenderly turn us upon our backs. I heard my wonderful uncle Wonggu lean into my mind and silently whisper, 'It is time my little Pilala for you to be made a man and possess a man's name, be proud.'

". . . Each man participating in the ceremony came past us and as each one passed he opened a vein in his forearm to caress us, and immerse us, in his life's essence. I was deeply moved and had a feeling of profound brotherhood. We three would not be allowed to wash or rub the dried blood off, ever. It must flake and crumble away, no matter if six moons should pass before the skin of blood was shed.

"It seemed to be dawn, I am not sure. Tjundaga spoke to me, 'Your spirit that lived before your birth and that will live after your death desires that you know its secret name on earth. Forever your spirit's land name will be Wilkulda, and from this day hence you shall be the Eagle, Wilkulda. One season when you are quite old, perhaps of forty summers, little one, the council will inform you of your spirit's Sky name.'

"To each of my companions he gave the name the elders had discovered through meditation many seasons before our actual circumcision. I cannot tell anyone the magic meaning of my name, Wilkulda. Tjundaga finished naming us and speaking very simply said, 'Stand up, Eagles, and walk with us your brothers, in your new skins of transcending blood, to the holiest of rocks where your re-creation will begin!'

"And now in unison, the men began chanting our new names as we solemnly walked to the rock of circumcision some hundred paces from the circle of stones. The wondrous blood drained from me with each step, and I was sad to lose any of it to the dry sands.

"How strange it all was, how different it had been from my boyish fantasies. I had not truly been afraid of it, for it had been drilled into us that it was our life's grandest moment. I would have been ashamed to waste my magic's energy with terror. Wonggu took me by his hand and led me to the boulder of the Wedgetail increase. The boulder was huge and there was ample room for the three of us to lie stretched out on its palm. There was only stillness in the wind.

"We three were suddenly straddled backwards on the rock. In the Dreamtime Age the Eagle had evacuated his bowels here and this monolith was his metamorphosed self. The rock was twice hued, the upper third being blueblack while the base was a green-white. Where the two colors had seeped into a single dark shade it seemed as if the boulder contained a moving band of water. A male would lie on this relic but once in his lifetime, when his foreskin was to be cut away. We three boys lay bent backwards on the rock's bulging end so that our penises were the part of our bodies projected highest into the Sky.

". . . Strange it was, for as I tipped backwards onto the knob I almost slid off the boulder, the blood's slipperiness I suppose, but Wonggu caught me and held me steady before I moved more than an inch. About the rock the congestion of awed men sang as Tjundaga prepared himself for the nobility of the moment. Scurrying sky whirled over our heads and existence seemed distant and unfocused, as if things had been vibrating a very long time but I had just now noticed. . . I could smell a twig fire at the other end of the boulder.

"As I lay there, waiting for the tiny flint . . . oh, I felt the flint blade. I forced myself to think of the game I best liked, pretending to spear sunfish with broken reeds from the banks of our pool . . . Oh, how painful the flint felt. I could hear the sawing noise of the flint gently but firmly cutting away my boyhood. I could not, I must not move or look or speak. My Uncles Bababa, Mushabin, and Wonggu leaned down to my ears and into my soul to sing urgent magic as my penis blood began to stain the blueblack top of the boulder, I could feel my blood collecting beneath my buttocks. How huge were the blood and feathered faces of my uncles as they peered down at my circumcised self.

"I tried to think of Kitunga but I could not remember what she looked like or anything about her. I was in tears from the pain and from the joy of it too. Very slowly the flint ate into my being and released my spirit. I thought of all the Wedgetails who had preceded me to the boulder, and I felt prouder than ever before in my life.

"Then I remember Lillywur and Tjundaga were swallowing the ash of my fire consumed foreskin that no enemy of the Wedgetail Eagles should ever possess such a potent particle of our magic ... Now I had been made a man and I was very happy."

## nine

"Noon of the seventh day of his appearance in our sea, I Kalod, bone-driller to the Turtles, again entered the shallows to visit with Wilkulda the messenger. He had eaten no food since he had been with us and had only sipped at a gourd of water my oldest son had brought out to him over the flats at lowest tides. A platter of turtle eggs, a food reserved only for elders, remained untouched and I munched them as I waded out to his station that they might not be wasted.

"By this day I understood that this fellow, Wilkulda, was the most interesting magician I had ever encountered. Already I sensed that he was a pursuer of many weird things, but especially of death. And why this saddened me, I know not for he was nothing to me, neither flesh nor bone.

"Later on, I began to believe that his terrible melancholia was caused by his own remarkable eyes, that their hugeness allowed too much light to burn into his brain, that is my opinion as the bone-driller. His eyes seemed wide enough to reflect the night sea far into the star-world. They were yellow, as are all mens' eyes from the fire smoke, but yet, even in the yellowness there did seem to be an extraordinary depth, as if in some way his soul was connected to the swelling orbs.

"Otherwise, except for the light circling his head, he was as any man. In truth I was somewhat curious about the hair band he wore about his waist. For he had told me he had no wives and had given up laying down completely, which was a weirdness in itself. And normally such hair belts were woven by wives. I did not ask, but later I guessed that the girl Mayawara must have plaited it for him.

Entering the sea that seventh day I boldly strode to where he stood facing the outer bay. This morning I had prepared myself with definitive and purposeful questions and I would insist on getting plausible answers. Yet when I noisily splashed up to him he took no notice, and as usual I became

shy and mute when close to him. Wilkulda's posture sheared
into the sky with straightness, balanced on his left foot with
his right foot entwined comfortably about his futile-looking
spear shaft that was struck down into the wet sand.

'Kalod, be free of cruelty,' he spoke out to me before I
had prepared myself to quiz him.

". . . What absurdity, what dreadful condescension and
besides I had not heard that particular word, 'cruelty,' before
and knew not its meaning. Yet I could not resist the look in
his eye, and I stepped nearer to him than I intended. As I
began to reproach him for his boorishness, Wilkulda entered
my soul through my eyes and I entered his. Never had I
known that such limitlessness could exist in one person. How
lonely and tragic was his soul. I, Kalod, who have performed
too many punctures into the skulls of desperate men and
women, had been acquainted with despair, but his sadness
was of such a boundless scope that I was myself dismayed for
him. With my fire baked kangaroo shin-bone drill I have
released many an angry ghoul, but of all the pain I had
observed none compared to that in Wilkulda's soul. He was
immersed in agony.

I fainted, and was a small, soft, wombat drowning in a rain
storm that had spurted into my burrow. The wrenching grief
that I had witnessed in Wilkulda had made me fall, eternally
shaken, into the sea. My throat began to swallow the sea and
I wondered if Wilkulda was ever coming to assist me in my
paralysis. My arms and legs were boneless. Yet nothing did
Wilkulda do or say and silently I began to chant in my mind
for the recovery of my spirit from his sorcery. As stunned as
I was I realized that I would be dead unless I saved myself.

"The chanting did not help. The muck had already begun
to ridge about my sunken frame. Still he did not move to pry
me up by my shoulders, and now I would be drowned. Then,
Wilkulda whispered. It was as if the rain storms of early
winter had at last come after a season of thirst, falling to
earth like leaping lines of dancers and pounding upon the
dryness as if it were a hollow, age-fallen tree trunk. A whisper
that rumbled into our cliffs even as the waterfall, swollen by
typhoon rains, gouges the beach below. Yet, all he had said
was, 'Kalod, my brother, get up out of the water, silly
fellow.'

". . . And indeed my strange weakness had disappeared
and I rose up. As his voice penetrated my mind, it wrought
potency unto my legs.

'Kalod,' he continued, 'you are a bit of a fool.'

"This is how he greeted me as I spewed out of the ocean in a tremendous, splashing, leap and vomited the sea out of my stomach. Ignoring his gratuitous remarks, I haltingly approached him, and as I began to slip down again I reached out to cling even as a weed wound about his spear. To me the splitting wood seemed now a patriarch and I an insignificant vine to its girth.

'Kalod,' he said, 'you are a child, for if you had but attempted it you might have raised up at any time.'

". . . This seemed to me the ultimate rudeness and I shouted that he was certainly an ungrateful guest. That he could leave our sea and seek out and bother some other mankind, 'at your convenience,' I shouted. Then too, I must admit that I made several rude suggestions. Yet my complaining only invoked a smile of sorts on Wilkulda's face. It was not a jovial smile by any means, rather it was a quiet humor around the edges of his eyes. Yet it inspired me to reconsider my anger and I remembered the pain I had witnessed in his soul. With some pity I said to him, 'Wilkulda, come out of these shallows for I fear this will not end well. By the notched scarring, and your holed scrotum, I see you are as I, a man of the Sky, a believer in the Dreaming Time. Then you must set an example for the younger men that they too will honor the Heroes and the Sky. Come out of the seas and I will respect you even as my own father. I will give you a, two, two pretty wives and a place by my fires. We will talk the nights through and share our learning . . .'

"He wistfully responded, 'Kalod, you and I have been chosen to exhibit to men the Sky's newest creation, to explore the Sky's vision that is called forgiveness. For, as I am naked to the sea, so I am in truth unblemished before the Sky. I have sojourned in the worlds and discovered that the mankinds pulsate to trust in the Sky and to make their covenant of forgiveness with the Sky Father.'

"At this I had to interrupt Wilkulda with a correction, 'You mean to speak of the Rainbow Snake as the paramount Sky Hero, don't you?'

'No, the Eagle is the Sky Father and the Rainbow Snake is but one of many Spirits while the Eagle flies the Sky in kingly solitude.' And Wilkulda continued forcefully, 'As I have abandoned deceit thus I shall cut away falsity from every man. Forever I am revealed as the Sky's messenger. In the worlds of man there is fear and cruelty, not the truth of forgiveness. Yet each mankind reflects the Sky even as I must be revealed by it night or day. Men must shed their skins of pretense. Men must discard cruelty and seek forgiveness in the Sky's light.' "

## ten

By the shaded base of the tenth planet's most sacred rock, a hump of stone of incalculable dimensions, a sober conference of a dozen men squatted on the shadowed red earth. Their bodies were patterned deftly with alternating squares of white clay and grey magnesium stone. These males were in mourning for a father-brother, who had died a moon's passage hence. Above these twelve, on the immense bulging side of the monolith, which was the actual omphalos to the Eternal Dream, thousands of painted men and beasts, startled by their universal view into the worlds, danced enthusiastically.

Around a twig fire the twelve elders listened to and watched the ancient Kalod, who spoke with both hands and tongue. It had been lost centuries since Kalod had been wetted in his meetings with Wilkulda in the sea, but his commitment still shone undimmed by the hundreds of seasons in his eyes. Kalod was still speaking, "Were not these words of Wilkulda astounding. Even as we sit here belching from bellies stuffed with kangaroo rump, is it not amazing to learn of the Sky's messenger, Wilkulda. I, Kalod, was first to be taught his death giving, and for dry season upon wet season I have walked among the mankinds that they might be informed of the many wonders he did perform.

". . . My own soul was reconstituted by Wilkulda's message. We stood there in the warming tide of that late afternoon, I still had not been able to remove my hands from his magic spear. What a poor weapon it was, with long splintering breaks down the shaft, ill-kept as if rarely fatted . . . How black was his skin, shining with the sea. His head seemed too large for his slenderness. Wilkulda was several fingers taller than I and then I was tall and not shriveled and dried up as now.

". . . Fleetingly the day sank into dusk, and the tide had completed its laying down with the ocean and was streaming backwards onto earth to now lay down with the shore. Too quick the water was circling my knees, and I became afraid, for no man willingly stays in the ocean at night. For it is in the darkness that the Rainbow Snake awakes to feed. I asked Wilkulda to release me from the spear and if he would join me as I must leave to seek refuge on the beach.

'No,' he answered as my hands became possessed of themselves again, 'you may go but I shall stay.' He had said this as if I was a child to fear such obvious spirits as those of the sea and night. The ocean was already chilled even as the sun surrendered its soul to die extinguished in the deep water.

'Let us go, Wilkulda, to the fires on the cliff and eat clam and turtle eggs. I will have my son-in-law, who killed an emu today, bring us the rump to eat,' and though he made no sign of interest I went on, 'we have many important matters to discuss. We shall bake a salmon my brother speared and the women will bring us honeyed water. And we shall lay down with many pretty girls. Wilkulda, come with me to sit beneath the windbreak and explain to me why I am no longer afraid of your name.'

'Leave me if you must,' answered my strange friend, 'I shall remain here in the Turtle sea. Days have passed and the night again begins and I am content and feel that I have become a small sea to myself. The ocean's spirit and I are brothers, as ancient to youngest. Do not worry that I will become lonely if you go, as the ocean shares my solace.

Dusk was drowning in the same grave as the sun's as I ran out of the waters of night to the nearest dune and climbed on it to observe Wilkulda. In the moon's torch I could see that he spoke out to where the waters receded into swells above the sandbar. Sky balanced as the sun's ghost had risen from the grave to shield the moon in jealousy. Only the campfires of the Ancestors in the night sky reflected a haze into the dimness. Tide rose to its fullest erection and Wilkulda was immersed to his shoulders. Yet his posture appeared composed and still content.

"I remained there on the beach through the dark's time. There was no one else about, which was not surprising considering my people's fear of Wilkulda. For some hours I was able to watch him but as the sea fog began to hide even my own feet from view, I fled up to the empty promontory behind the beach. As I stood high over the shore I could hear in my soul the messenger's discourse with the sea. I could feel the water about his throat and I remembered that the sea's spirit seemed almost to have a petulant regard for Wilkulda's welfare.

". . . At last the moon attained its summit above the low, dense sea fog. My first wife came from the camp, which was somewhat inland by a grove of redgums. The female barked and snapped at me without sense to her words. Because of the paltry nature of their intelligence, I try to show forbearance to my wives, but that night I had not a worm's patience, and without thought I jabbed Bamadja in her ample buttock with my spear. It was barely a bleeding cut but Bamadja ran in wails redundant back to the sleeping fires where turmoil ensued. I was informed later that several additional females were chastised with spear pricks until order was effected.

"Now centuries after Bamadja is sand and mud, I am ashamed and regret my past cruelties to her . . . By this historic navel-lith I oath to the Sky that I am no longer cruel to women. However, at that moment I did not consider my actions toward Bamadja critically, and without further interest in my screaming wife, I again became absorbed with what was happening in the sea.

"The night progressed and I did not die, so I ventured back down the cliffside to the beach. The fog still obscured my vision and the falling tide was a thousand winds in the mulga trees. Yet, simply I heard Wilkulda expounding on the sanctity of circumcision to the sea's spirit. Finally the waters became satiated and they slumbered into their invisible pit. The sea permitted the beach to re-appear.

"This was the eighth dawn since Wilkulda's arrival. Here and there, between expanses of cleansed sand and dying crabs and rotted plants torn off at the roots by the urgency of the sea's laying downs, were scooped out sea-water basins forever severed from the ocean. Scores of little fish were trapped in these temporary seaponds. In the briefness of pre-dawn flocks of pelicans feasted on the ocean's castoffs for miles along the coast. I watched in one shallow basin a single remaining minnow frantically dart away from a trailing pelican, whose webbed claws splashed the little pond and overthrew the imprisoned fish onto the sands. Before the pelican could gather up the flopping minnow an arrogant petrel strutted over and speared away the pelican's catch.

"Why I bothered to notice this episode I know not, for in all my previous seasons I was uninterested in such trivial happenings. As a boy playing endlessly on that beach, I had watched as many minnows, and far larger fish too, were entrapped by a fowl and often stolen by another one who had not earned the food. Sometimes we boys would chase down a gullet-laden pelican and force the bird to offer up its full pouch to us. These contents we at once devoured. But that morning, in some obscure intuition, I felt sympathy for that single, beak pierced minnow. And as if I were a weird ghost, after I watched the petrel thief hop away from the wing banging pelican, I ran from basin to basin rescuing as many little fish as I could and tossing them back into the sea.

"Finished as best I could with this hopeless task, I saw Wilkulda standing where I had left him the night before. He stood there as if he were a charcoal drawing on our cliff ledges. In the hazing bands of light and the fading dimness I could see strands of weed entwined about his body and spear. A crab, with but one huge claw, had snapped itself onto his leg below his knee at the rear. As I watched the crustacean dropped away and vaulted itself on its claw back into the shallows. Worms had burrowed into the wooden shaft that Wilkulda's hand still held. Across his chest ran a rawed streak, a reddish-pink bruise where something, either a piece of driftwood or a ghoul, had rubbed by in the night.

"To this day by this enormous navel-lith, I do not know what inspired me to singdance there on the dawn tainted sand. But the Sky shook my spirit and I began to be changed by the weirdness of Wilkulda's mystery without understanding what his secret might be.

"In that season, when I was a young man, I was a prideful magician and could singdance throughout a night and day without fatigue. So joyfully did I whirl that I stepped into the sea and enacted the Creation of Man in Its entirety. My spirit was weightless and I exhibited marvelous leapings. Happily I sang of my recognition of Wilkulda's strangeness. I was now at his side and he watched me with a contorted mien, as if undecided. Circling him in dance my voice grew in volume and filled the Sky with a force that had never existed in me before. My stampings increased their urgency as I reached toward ecstasy.

"Intently Wilkulda waited with his face now sealed in repose. Yet his gaze remained watchful even as the sea's milk began to dry from his being. The new sun rose completely from the Rainbow Snake's vagina. A moment passed and then I realized Wilkulda was singing with me. He knew the correct inflection of each word so that its magic truth would be clearly apparent. We sang, it seemed, to yesterday's tear and then began again and again. Wilkulda became Kalod and Kalod became Wilkulda and the Sky World was of our celebration.

I looked up to the cliff and saw that my people had come to watch from the heights. Even as I pondered at their courage, I tried to imagine why Wilkulda's own mankind, the

Eagles, had driven him off, for it was plain to see that he was a wonderment and must be honored deeply.

"I am proud of myself that I had begun to love him even before I had accepted that he was the messenger. It was that very morning, when I had saved a few minnows from death until the next high tide, that I realized, without understanding, that I too was to be healed."


## eleven

When I was a young army officer in the Great War, I was blinded by chlorine gas. It was the tiniest possible flaw in the placement of the left lens in its rubber-mask fitting that vented inwards the noxious filth. I was leading my section as reserve to the general attack on the beginning eve of Loos. Actually, I had believed that my men would not be involved in the battle.

There was not a gas-barrage of consequence, no frightful yellow-green cloud released at tube's end from the Hun's lines to drift across no-man's land buoyed by a southernly zephyr. No dreadful banks of gas flatulated over this shell pocked earth. A peppering of light artillery alerted us to the fact that a Hun battery was walking past the front ranks to stutter out its shells onto my poor section. Yet I was not concerned as it was an endemic bam-bamming. A chap or two blown up and that was that, all thoroughly normal.

Swiftly, in a hush between rounds, we noticed that some of the falling shells were miniature gas cannisters, a most recent and novel development. Immediately I and Lance Corporal Merrill (who today resides in the city of Birmingham employed as a millwright) vehemently dueted, "Gas, gas, gas!"

Truly it was a rare experience to be gassed from heaven, so to speak, but my men were soldiers and reacted efficiently. Only Private Sloan, a Welshman I believe, could not be given the alert, for a gas bomb had steamed out its fumes directly at his feet. I took a minor whiff myself, but with hindsight I do not believe that this initial contact was crucial. I most certainly do feel that the left lens not fitting properly was crucial. Private Sloan was in extremely bad condition as Merrill and I came up to him. He was vomiting large gouts of matter even as I shot him above his left ear with my revolver. Thankfully, the single cartridge was sufficient. As I

re-holstered my weapon, Merrill, rather pathetic in his
shyness, patted me on my shoulder for my decent behavior in
shooting Sloan. Many an officer would not assume this final
obligation to his men. Every soldier prayed that he would
have a good mate to finish him off if he inhaled a snootful of
chlorine.

However, as we continued forward behind the running
vanguard, I tasted an evilness in my mouth. Not smelled or
saw, but in my mouth I tasted the horrendous stuff burning
away the softest flesh. Ripping off the befouled mask I
dashed forward, away from the shells skipping rearward.

I was already blinded as I hurtled my frame into an empty
enemy trench. The last act I remember was groping for my
revolver which, unfortunately, had sprung out of its holster
as I crashed to earth after the eight-foot fall from the
parapet. When I awoke some hours later in the regimental aid
station, I begged a gentle-voiced Yorkshire orderly to shoot
me, but he could not as the M.O.'s were thick. To this very
moment I do not know if I truly have forgiven Merrill for not
placing a bullet into me as I raced ahead in panic. He and I
had agreed on such an arrangement a fortnight before Loos,
when I had lost my section's sergeant. Probably Merrill failed
me because he was not of the regular army but a conscript.
By Loos the majority of my men were clerks and farmlads,
and boys. Merrill's silly compassion froze his finger, at least
that is what he told me on the one visit he made here to
Brighton to see me. That time, we drank brandy and gossiped
about dead men and our good luck. After he left I was glad
he had not shot me at Loos.

It did not occur to me until 1919, four years after my
gassing, that the mask I had been issued was of faulty
construction. In 1919 I was entering my fourth hospital
(there would be still another until the authorities permitted
me to return to Brighton on the sea) when I happened to
remember that I had vouched myself a new mask only a week
before Loos. The mask that I replaced was perfectly
operable, and probably is to this day, but it had an awful
odor from its varied history as a skin-clinging apparatus.

Perhaps it was just a stray sliver of artillery housing that
punctured the hose connection. Perhaps I had fitted the mask
improperly to my face, and accidentally left a gap. As it was,
I did rage for several years after 1919 when I came to realize
that a brother Englishman, rather more likely a girl-worker
sweet soft to fondle under an elm, had betrayed me through
carelessness. It could not have been on purpose, no, it could
not have been a German agent. I mustn't think such quirky
things. Fate's damnation is what it was after all is said.

However, as the years have wandered by, after a litany of ward activities, smellings of me beyond humanity as I was corrupted alive with active chlorine, after years of clinics, nursing homes and pity, my bitterness has eased somewhat. For I have begun my treasure, my opulent of Wilkulda.

Hundreds of likely chaps have I met and heard die in varied ports of pain and I love each one still. And yet, most pecularily, I Avery, continue to live. Thousands and thousands of young chaps died in the wards of Britain and France and Germany too, died together earlier than was best for them, having made no sons and done no lasting things with their lives, while I live to write of Wilkulda.

Totally blinded, crippled by ceaseless erosion to my lungs, yes, the chlorine resides potently in my being, perhaps only a fraction of a molecule, but enough that one brightish August mid-day it will devour my final, debilitated spark.

Suicide should have been considered, you say old boy. Be cheery, why bore us old fellow, a neat stinging shot to the cranium and the sensible conclusion is luminous. Then Uncle Billy would not weep in his soul each time he comes to say, "Hello, I've come to read the *Times* to you, I love you."

It is to my Nurse that I owe my denial of suicide, my foolish refusal to seek out an ultimate quiet. Nurse's devotion to my wasting self, and to my needs, has graced my crippled state with the sole embrace since Loos. Without Nurse caring for my being I should not have dared even to the name, 'Wilkulda.' Without Nurse to ease my disgust for my sincere helplessness I would be rich manure for dandelions. Do you hear me, Wilkulda, I do love Nurse. What other than the Nurse would put up with such a loathsome cripple as I. Without the Nurse to caress me I would hole my skull to implosion and join my brother soldiers as microscopic maggot indulgence.

And this voyaging of a book, this Wilkulda, is my dream of service to my heritage and to my generations, never to be procreated. Lord God that Thou should soon end this laboring, soon now 'fore I die undone. This be the tenth year since I began the volume in 1921. God grant that I live to finish it.

## twelve

Yet I, Avery of the foundry Morrisons and of J. Atkins the changeling, now digress from Wilkulda to my personal

adventures in the Greatest Great War, Circus 1914-1918.
Make with me my journey on Nurse's pen to Ypres.
Remember the vivid monotony of death in the chalk-mud. I
cannot ever remember when the clay swamps of Ypres were
separate from my soul, and indeed, I was only adventured
there a shortish stay.

Thus, as I prose this lunatic's requiem, I implore your
patience, and beg forgiveness, as I surrender all vestige of
discipline as Wilkulda's biographer. I own a nightmare. I
envision the Ypres swamps as verdant apricot orchards and
strawberry bushes and rye and beer's best hops. The plants
are unnaturally huge, as the swamps have as manure the
finest English blood, other less distinguished Empire fertilizer
also. Yet I have proof that the agronomy of Ypres is based on
sugar beets and tobacco, not apricots and strawberries.
However, as it is my nightmare, I suppose one may do with
one's own as one wishes.

Remember the night our brigade disembarked at Le Havre,
October 1914. We, of the Ferozepore Brigade, Lahore
Division, steamed around Trafalgar into the Bay of Brittany.
Hugging the coast north to Le Havre; to its new port facilities
finished neatly in time for the Great War. We steamed into
harbor alone.

The dock, iron plated fastened to dense wood ribs
staunchened with more iron and cement, was frost white,
though it was early October. The religious structures, icicled
warehouses, slumped along harbor shores and westward to
the Seine's estuary. It had been raining in the coastal regions
of France and Belgium, except in Le Havre where a
precipitous decline in the price of mercury had penalized the
port with a glaze of winter. Our ship's massive landing-gates
were winched down to the dock where a line of high
electronics with square lantern shades were strung on a strand
of naked wire. As the wind swept the lampshades in terrible
arcs and swivels the area loomed with spectral shadowings of
the iced buildings and the ceaseless sea.

The first battle of the Marne had been fought and the
French along with our Expeditionary Force had knocked the
Germans back from Paris to a line through Flanders and
northern France below Lille. And to this front our brigade of
horse was to proceed. Allenby would take us in his command
of the Cavalry Force Division until the Lahore came up into
the line.

Our Hindu horse grooms, who were omniscient, said that
our Brigade was needed quickly for the knockout blow and

that is why we had been shipped to Le Havre. It is true that we officers did believe a knockout blow was in the planning stages, that the Huns were done in. It had been planned for fifty years that a massed cavalry charge onto a dispirited infantry would culminate the next continental war we English found ourselves in; and this was that next war. I was Lieutenant Avery Morrison then, commander of a troop of Lancers, thirty-five mounted men. Captain Frank Monthouse was squadron C.O. Our squadron was one of eight that comprised the 129 Duke of Connaught's own Baluchis Regiment. Four such regiments made up the Ferozepore Brigade; five thousand mounted men, no wonder we were wanted in Flanders, we were the cream of the Indian Army. We were the finest cavalry force in the world, we were the finest heavy horse brigade on earth. There was many a nation that could not field an entire army of horse equivalent to the power of the Ferozepore. Since Sedan in 1871, when the ubiquitous Uhlans had bested the French horse handily, we had been trained to contest these same Uhlans, the heavy Lancers of the German Cavalry Corps.

Twenty thousand of the hundred and twenty thousand mounts sequestered in England during the first twelve days of the War awaited us on the outskirts of Le Havre. These supplemental animals plus three thousand carts of forage were prepared at the Bolbec railway yards where we would entrain for Amiens. From that town we would march to the Ypres sector. The Ferozepore would prove to the doubters, to the palsied critics who wished us to become mounted riflemen, that horsemastership was the ultimate weapon. We were needed in Flanders, not to provide cover for the unlimbering guns, not to perform meaningless reconnaissance, made redundant by the telegraph and ballooners and later by the aeroplanes; Ferozepore was needed to join with England's Cavalry Division to crush the weary Hun. It would be a glorious end to the short war.

This is utterly absurd, isn't it? Suddenly I feel this paste of words is futile, a wasting, and I wonder why that tiny spew of greenish gas did not slay me instead of this maddening lingering.

Vividly that night of debarking at Le Havre after a six week voyage from Bombay summed to me all that the Empire had accomplished. No, it was not sham, it was not absurd. Vividly that night's harmony of our clatter and the profound stillness of the town holds my spirit captive.

We came into Le Havre with a snail tug coiling our

starboard aft onto the dock's rigidity. Out to sea, in our port bow, I glimpsed a ship of sail gliding without lights into the bay. A great Cape Horn, five-masted, steel ship of sails was lost to view almost as I sighted her, for there was no moon to delineate her. However, even in the sparse gleam of the star systems her beauty made a graceful longing in my throat.

Steeds on shipboard are normally restless and unhappy in the close confinement of below decks. They arrive at destination dyspeptic and worn. But our animals, even as they came up from the Bombay depot, were docile, as if pleased to share the men's thrill that we would participate in the war before the banging petered out.

Some men are quite intimate with their horses, especially if they also possess hunting dogs. Indeed, I had my pack down in the ship kennels and my steeds in the stalls, thus I was happy. Many of my fellow officers were hunters also and we anticipated sport with French stag. That was our primal misconception, that we believed the meadows of Gaul were trotted with pointed heads antelopish in profile.

How proud we of the Ferozepore were when we were informed that we would make battle promptly. The open flank of the Hun had been batted well at the Marne and victory had been close. English horse had been held in reserve when the enemy's line was chaotic and panicky. These were the right conditions for a quick victory but the opportunity had been muffed. Still, the Hun was reported to be groggy and not fully recovered from his right flank's rapid retreat, there would be another chance to end the war in this month.

Frank Monthouse was my commander and I served him gladly. Frank had five lieutenants under him and I was senior to these chaps but for one. Colonel Albert Reaches commanded the 129th while General Sir Horace Chattle was brigade C.O. Monthouse was posthumously awarded the D.C. while Reaches was posthumously awarded the V.C. Sir Chattle is somewhere or other, I suppose.

Frank and I had been of the same form at Sandhurst. He was top drawer. Frank's ruddy cheeks and red hair bespoke his open and forthright disposition. I was altogether amateurish and quite timid with women, thus whatever came my way was usually propelled by Monthouse. At Sandhurst it was I who had tagged Frank with the name, Reddy, and even his mother, the Baroness, had come to call him that. Reddy's spine would be burnt through by phosphorus as he lay in the wire before Ypres. When Reddy began to scream with the chemical burning, I became acquainted with the Great War first hand. Sergeant-Major Lamprey and I were helpless in that novel situation of your C.O. screaming, however, in a few weeks we would have been properly educated and shot dear Reddy at once.

Colonel Reaches died that dreadful night of dawn too, but with rather more decorum in that we never did find anything at all of Reaches afterwards. The Colonel was one of thousands who simply was swallowed by the swamp that the shellings had made of the chalk fields.

That star-dense night when we disembarked at Le Havre, the horses came out of the holds in remarkably good order. And as their iron hoofs beat on the iron planking of the wharf the animals became intoxicated by the marvelous hollow sounds and neighed sillily and anointed this fore-foot of France with plopping manure and steaming urine.

The horses, with the fond noises and odors, relaxed the men. Ribaldry could heard from the ranks as we lined up four abreast. All of the officers, including myself, were smoking cigars or cigarettes, and white coils of smoke rose up to surround the electric lamps with nimbuses.

Silent was the town as the thrashing single propeller of the P. & O. liner, Apollo, vibrated the wharf feverishly. The Apollo only nudged against the head of the enormous pier, engines still turning slowly to keep her in place, that she might speedily clear the space for other ships. She would make for Gibraltar to be victualed and coaled for another trip as a troop carrier. Such ships were in short supply, as Empire troops were hastily assembled for transfer to the French front.

We had paraded through Bombay preceding our embarkation on the Apollo and now as we came off the sturdy old ship the Ferozepore would make her final parade. After armistice the brigade would be disbanded, and in point of informative legacy I am one of the five officers of my regiment still alive.

The brigade pipers and the massed bands blared and we mounted to move ashore. Several hundred Franch officials and staff officers were present to review us as we went by in chilled stiffness. The great coats of the civilians were pulled up to shield them from the chilling wind. It was 2:40 a.m. as we rode the length of the wharf, six cargo ships to each side acted as blinders blocking out a view of the town. Our lances were fiercely upright, although the pennants were limp as the wind fell off. The mustaches of the French were trim and impertinent in frozen rigor. Stevedores, sullen at the pomposity of our bands, secretly content with Pernods and sausage in bellies, silently leaked farts as we, the vainglorious Ferozepore, on heavy steeds paraded from rising rust line of Apollo into the city of Le Havre.

I rode leisurely down the streets of the city. Sentries at each corner, gendarmes in frosted pairs, holding hands, I concluded, as befitted the degenerate continentals. Now a few despairing whores, ill and wet in the mist and miasma that drifted above the black pavements, as we went past a thread of blue bloused soldiers holding dulled bayonets at rifle's snout. Gas-wicked flames flickering in well kept street lights hissed to me as I went by, "We are France, we are the hoary lights of France. Who are you?"

Having no answer, I passed on and only my horse responded by squeezing turds onto the cobbled streets. Granite and marble eaved buildings, cathedral imitations, hung over us as the Ferozepore came into the squares of the city. The iron footed steeds of my fellows clacked as we rode on the stone roadways of Le Havre. What a morning it was when, without a horizon to remind us of the aging dawn, we trusted that men were eternal, good, and sane.

The sky became bolder in its whiteness as we left the suburbs by three extended trains. I wonder how many of the fraternal citizens of Le Havre the brigade had awakened as it paraded along the boulevards. Perhaps to this late decade a few of those healthy stoutish folk dream of that too-early morn when our regiments processioned by. How the warm arsed bourgeoisie must have stumbled, and stubbed toes too, as they left their rug heaped beds. In linen nightdress they came to the casement windows and peered down to find out why so many dogs were barking, both the brigade's packs and the city's, and why the timbered floors shuddered, then they saw the great mounted force pass by. How astounded the citizens must have been to view our red-plumed, silver-bright helmets and our red tunics as we cantered by! The burghers probably withdrew precipitously from the panes to huddle to one side of the stone escarpment, as if to hide from the weirdness below.

How inane these reminiscences must be to the present generation of post-war orphans. I wish my scalpel-scooped-out eyes still possessed ducts that I might weep my mind hollow, so that the orphans might understand that one comrade continues to mourn their fathers. My innocent brothers, good chaps all, even if ravaged by

gonorrhea, good chaps although some plentitude of
drunkards and whoremasters were included, but indeed, all
quite innocent. And dead now is Connaught's Own 'cept for
myself and four more. Ranks all gone, sergeant-majors and
color bearers too, all dead. We were fifty centuries that
paraded, four abreast, into and out of old Le Havre, today a
hundred wearied souls of Ferozepore remain.

What did you ask, my pretty eyed virgins, what was it for?
Honestly, I don't know anymore, anymore, but once I was
positive, sweet children, that one happy morning at Le Havre
I did know.

I realize that a soundly crafted book ought to be concise and
without these dreadful peregrinations. However, as it is my
own particular madness that this books holds checked, or at
least holds to the pace, I shall hurl forward my blindness and
dare hope that some shall follow. If you desire, dismiss any
particular page or chapter, or put me down as altogether too
ornate in depiction of cruelty and flee elsewhere in search of
delicate introspections.

For notwithstanding your irritation, I will tell you a little
of my horse Dennis. As we made to the front lines, past
Amiens, to where the killing was at its best, the Ferozepore
prayed that it would not be too late to rubber a hand or two
in battle.

Personally, I believe that any soldier who saw combat in
the Great War could only arrive at the same conclusion I did,
that machine guns were manufactured to slay either dragons
or goliaths and not puny men. Many experts insist that the
massed artillery was the ultimate technical tactic of the Great
War. It is obvious to me that these students of battle never
attacked a heavy machine gun squad nested in a concavity of
earth with additional walls of dense sandbags shielding away
grenade and rifle interdiction. It was the automatic hell
machines that forced the cruel stasis of the Great War.
Infantry could not take ground defended by machine guns,
cavalry even less. The titanic shellings were failures. Only
tanks could counter the machine guns, but they were too
late. Mobility and maneuver, this was the type of battle
European armies had been prepared for. Every officer,
especially the French, was indoctrinated with the ideal of
rapid infantry charges: the machine gun destroyed mobility
and it destroyed the infantry.

Cavalry since the American Civil War had been denied its
classic role as the reconnaissance force. Its continued
expensive utilization was mainly devoted to the protection of

the horse-drawn artillery, as a screen when the guns were
particularly exposed during unlimbering. However, we of the
mounted corps trusted that it would be horse troops that
would thrust the death stroke into the vaunted Prussians by
the stern application of a massed shock charge. Since Sedan
we English knew that if we ever returned to the continental
wars, our foe could only be Prussia. We were ready, we were
prepared, we were undaunted, and we assiduously
disregarded rumors of the mechanical excellence of the
machine guns.

Crimea had been fought two generations past and we did
not envision the historic necessity of a second Light Brigade's
debacle. Horsed forces had made enormous improvements in
mounts, men, and weaponry since Napoleon Bonaparte had
innovated on the principles of cavalry. After his terrific
casualties of 1806-7, Napoleon had concentrated artillery,
using caseshot, aimed at specific points in the enemy lines. In
the wake of this devastating bombardment he would send his
horse en masse at the weakened junctures to rupture the line
and roll it up. If at Waterloo Napoleon had possessed better
mounts to effect his charges, perhaps the Great War might
never have been.

By 1914 all nations had animals strengthened by breeding
and training to endure limits that would have been fantasy in
1814. At Waterloo English steeds could at best trot eight
hundred yards and finish with a gallop of two hundred. The
opposing musketry had an extreme range of one thousand
yards. In the Great War a horse could trot for eight thousand
yards and gallop full on for an additional mile. Rifles now
reached out to four thousand yards, but the mounted man's
tactical advantage had in the past century increased tenfold,
the rifleman's but three. Exhilarated with these scientific
truths, we had to restrain ourselves to exhibit a proper
sobriety towards future battles. Every officer understood
that the horsed charge could be successful only after the
enemy infantry had been severely weakened by heavy losses
and, equally important, by a retreat mentality. If the proper
conditions for a shock charge could be effected on a
battlefield the enemy's capacity to continue hostilities would
be destroyed. The Ferozepore believed that these a priori
conditions existed in the Ypres salient in October, 1914, that
we were moving up to deliver the knockout blow.

From Amiens to Ypres there was not sufficient rail
transport, as immense munitions trains were being assembled
for the culminating attack planned for October 20th. A full

infantry corps with two divisions, and the Ferozepore
Brigade would deliver the blow to the Hun. This would be
one third of the British Expeditionary Force's strength, not
inclusive of the 1st Calvary Division of 9,000 mounted men.
Rawlison's 3rd Cavalry Division and his Regular 7th Division
served with the courageous Belgians under Heroic Albert at
the coast proper, however, at Le Bassee Rawlison junctioned
with the Expeditionary Force.

Ironic are such paltry numbers as compared to the scores
of divisions later raised in the British Isles and in the Empire.
But in October, 1914, we were all that England could place
in Battle. We were the regular army. We would fight alone
until the volunteers, and then the conscripted would come in
their millions.

Amiens on the Somme, Brigade informs the regimental
officers that we had been detached from Lahore to serve
under Allenby. We were all very pleased at this for he was
considered the Wellington of the cavalry forces. Brigade did
not tell us that Ferozepore would attack without Allenby's
1st at Ypres: they would be held in reserve, fatal words.
October is the first congealing period after the dashing six
weeks of attack and retreat, yet the front appears still to be
elastic.

Frevent, town of Artois, where the rail line from Amiens
congests beyond comprehension. From here Ferozepore will
make up to Ypres by hoof. October 15, we are not wanted at
the front until the night of the 19th for the dawn attack of
the 20th. Leisurely we walk our mounts into Flanders on
granite-paved roads the width of a farm wagon. Rain
ceaseless, drizzle constant, hedges and trees shortening the
horizon as if one is enclosed in a labyrinth of mud. Swamp
when Caesar came, water table today only a few inches below
topsoil. Countless carts like beetles laden with the cracked
shells of sugarbeets. Dozens of canals to clump over on single
span bridges. Fields extraordinarily compacted, villages
centuries in patient gathering. Truncated cones of manure
have contaminated wells, boil water is the dictum from
Brigade. Peasants ignore us, don't like us, don't want anyone
coming to disturb their fields and prostitute their women.
Potatoes in fortified mounds of mouldering vegetation.
Tobacco sheaves on cruel and screeching conveyances.

Ferozepore gently walked until the 20th. We were the
heavy horse of the Indian Forces Field Army. We could not
help but break the Hun line. We would win victory for
England.

On the 20th there would be a fifteen-minute barrage, shrilling from a concentration of 100 guns to the two mile attack zone. We did not pretend that our horses could outrun the machine gun's spew, but it was believed that the gunners would shatter the enemy position.

October 17th, Brigade came into the village of Lizerne which lies off the fateful canal by less than a half mile and near to Stoonstreet where our attack would be launched. Here the salient curved into the German lines. Lizerne had been a Uhlan post in their deadly charge down to the Marne, and from this town the German horse had dashed south without opposition. However, just as we had been passive at Marne, the Hun had not used his own mounted troops effectively as they attempted the massive swing away from the sea onto Paris.

At Lizerne the rain ended not and Ferozepore crawled beneath broken eaves tumbled to earth by shelling and the aftermath fires. Rubble was Lizerne and stale water collected in the fallen, crushed roofs and walls. Drizzle was inevitable to Flanders, and once the topsoil's meager seal was flung awry by explosives the land regressed into the marshlike terrain that even the Legions had avoided. Lizerne, even in our brief stay, was bursting apart.

Discards of normal life were strewn everywhere. Especially noticeable were the peasants' kitchen tables. Tables that had stood sturdy through generations of feeding are now deformed and splintered. Tufted parlor sofa of singed feathers is from the imploded home of the beet mill owner. His elegant dining chairs stand exactly in their placements, but the room's roof and walls have fallen into the next space of the house, which was the parlor. Pink and green embroidered flowers have strained apart into frayed silk threads even as the colors begin to sweat in the sogginess created by the constant rain. Bare brass rods of bed steads where child and mother and husband slept yesterday, are warped into grotesqueness by the maniacal explosives. Child's red dress, a boy's dress from the white sailor boat sewn into the wide collar, flies in undamped colorfulness from a quite high branch in an untouched oak tree. From one sleeve of the tiny red garment dangles a swollen arm of the little dress's owner.

I myself, the Avery of your acquaintance, carried to the oak a clumsy, axe-hewn hay loft ladder. To this stately oak I went and to the red dress and to the child's arm. Avery, I, climbed to that singular limb and with my sabre, after all we were lancers and encouraged to own sabres and swords, did poke puffed stuff free so that it could twirl down to softly float in a puddle. Anglican priester, Major Hugh Smithfield, dead from influenza in 1918, came to the arm's pond, and with a dozen of my brother officers in attendance, offered up a prayer. Then we chaps kicked clots of earth into the puddle to bury the arm and complete the obsequies. In a month I, Avery, would not even have noticed such a treed garment of red childhood.

Brigade set up housekeeping in Lizerne with suitable wreckage as appointments. At the time it seemed amusing to walk down the tent rows on inspection and ignore, officially, such ornamentations as lace tablecloths and velvet swathes that served as mess-table and cot covers. On the 18th and 19th I hunted with my pack but unearthed only an elderly hare. After the 20th's attack the dogs would be packed off for England until armistice, when they were set free to roam in the gargantuan graveyards scenting out their masters.

Afternoon of the 19th I groomed Dennis myself. Dennis was my princely gelding, he was in splendid condition for the war even as I, Avery, was. Dennis was sixteen hands high, a chestnut jumper bred and trained on a Lincolnshire farm until Uncle Billy gifted him to me in 1908, when I joined the Indian Field Army. Dennis was eight years old in October, 1914, and was in his prime even as I, Avery, must have been too.

Raining continuously on the 19th. After dining sumptuously on beef and pudding, we junior men and Colonel Reaches went down to the regimental square where the ranks had gathered. The rain stopped at dusk and would not begin again until midnight. The regiment had formed, at rest, to sing, which was a weekly event in our lives. Several big bonfires had been lit using the village's breakage. The Hun bothered us not although the sky was glared by our fires and we were in range even of their lesser guns.

As I recall that dusk's sing I begin to weep tearlessly inward in my perpetual blackness. We sang until midnight when the rain issued again, the hour when we set out for our jump-off at Stoonstreet. We sang very well. Some tunes were accompanied by the band but in main, we were a cappella. This was very fine indeed as we had several first rate soloists to inspire us. I soon had forgotten the news given to us at supper, that only our single regiment, Connaught's Own, would participate in the morrow's attack. That the remaining regiments belonging to Ferozepore would be kept in hand as reserves. Allenby would not command or even be close to the battlefield. The current theory was that we were to be an experiment, as if by using the trial and error method of the natural sciences we might seek out the truth.

Colonel Reaches had a timbred bass voice that was richly refined by decades of tobacco and gin. He made himself gustily heard above the entire regiment. One of our lead singers would spontaneously start a new tune as the preceding faded away. Then squadron by squadron the rounds were taken up until we all joined in regimental harmony. How wholesome and fit we all looked; eight squadrons of regular heavy horse troops, the Empire's finest. Reddy was exceptionally jolly and he inspired our squadron of one hundred and forty souls to become melodious beyond previous recollection.

Stern and demanding winds off the channel, some thirty miles to the west, embossed our faces with a sexual glow. The fires shot yellow spumes that illuminated each man's boyish face. It was the finest night of my entire life, that night of the 19th October, 1914, when my regiment sang. For with the mechanical twitch of a clock's gear on the dawning I was to be deprived of my humanity by bestiality beyond my imagination.

Soldiers sang during every activity but battle during my time in the army. On march or at camp's home the army sang. There was no wireless to entertain us, newspapers were discouraged, and literacy among the ranks in the Indian Field Army was not altogether common. Yet, in truth, we sang because it was a fine, human thing to do. When I finish *Wilkulda*, Nurse and I plan to devote our next volume to the registering of the British Soldier's songs of the Great War. Nurse is as eager as I to be ended with *Wilkulda*, and to move ahead to the *Song Book, 1914-1918.* I will attempt in the *Song Book* to transfix on paper the transcending vigor of my regiment as it luted its voice that night of the 19th.

How wonderful, and yet a trifle sad, it was to observe hulking chaps sing of children and sweethearts and mothers and lost sailing ships and their harbors as they plodded up to the front lines. At the end, when our death directories listed the millionth dead destiny, the men alive had become mute. But there had been a time when Englishmen sang as they marched toward battle as if they were Spartan kings chanting their warrior codes, although infinitely wearied by the reports of modern combat techniques.

Boots on the frozen earth of winter were as bass strings in

accompaniment to the voices of the soldiers. In the beginning they marched with much pride, and their singing fully measured their inward serenity and confidence. It was not fair, the Great War devoured all the fine lads who sang so grandly.

At two thirty A.M. on the 20th we mounted. Forage nets, lances, cloaks, and blankets were left behind in the tents. We carried 120 rounds for the carbines and our swords and scabbards. At three thirty A.M. we were at Stoonstreet and breakfasted on hot tea and cold biscuits without butter. The horses were not fed and were given only a half bucket of water, as speed, not staying power, was to be demanded of them.

Dennis saved my life as he was such a tall animal in the withers. He caught several bullets that would have killed me. Dennis was an easy saddle in all gaits. Perhaps it is surprising that an ex-officer of horse remembers his steed quite fondly, but most of us cared for our animals, though it is well known that a saddle cost more than a replacement in mounts. An officer usually owned at least one gelding for active patrolling, and a mare for parade and routine training maneuvers: these precious mounts were well cared for.

At four forty-five A.M. the fifteen-minute shelling began. Its only effect was to alert the Hun to prepare strenuous countermeasures. As my fellow officers and I rode along the doubled line we were aware that it was with heavy reservations that the high command had permitted our participation in Haig's corps attack. A large percentage of the staff officers in the Imperial field armies were cavalry officers. These men had decided as early as October, 1914, that mounted troops were not to be committed to battle until after the infantry created the proper field conditions. Until then horse troops were to be held in reserve. We were, at best, an ill-trusted experiment.

Regiment saddled and moved to that quiet space before the trenches that marked our forward positions in Flanders. Wood ramps especially prepared for the 20th's attack were winched down onto the parapets and the men dismounted for a short period to lead their mounts over by bridle into no man's land to the white tapes that corps officers had laid out during the night.

It was raining determinedly and in the murkiness our damp khakied forms were camouflaged effectively. Astride our animals we gathered at the jump-off markers. The mud underfoot made queer grunts as the hoofs pulled air bubbles

from the swamp. Visibility became impossible as Colonel
Reaches rode to a slight rise, no more than twelve inches
above the mud. We could barely distinguish his form from
the other near-invisible shapes in the heavy dimness. After he
led us in a short prayer, Reaches unscabbarded his sword and,
holding it over his bared skull, inspired us to cheer for His
Majesty.

As the barrage lifted, we trotted forward, I desired, lusted,
to smoke a cigar. A thousand yards; we came to the first
enemy wire. Sappers had performed exceedingly well and the
regiment trotted over this position without loss. We had
expected only this first entanglement and I was discomfited
to hear the scouts report that they had come upon two
additional wire emplacements ahead. The second wire had
been partially opened by a squad of sappers who had
disregarded orders not to advance beyond the first defense of
steel barbs. A captured sapper might disclose pertinent
information to the enemy, however this squad did the right
thing to advance on the second wire and they had blown
several corridors in the coiled strands. The third wire defence
was not noted until our own regimental scouts came on it as
they explored ahead of the slowly moving line of heavy
horse.

Columning through the second wire we were pleased that
as yet the Hun seemed oblivious to our approach. But as we
congealed in front of the third wire, waiting for lanes to be
cut by the slow method of hand shears, the Germans laid
down a terrific fire of light and heavy machine guns
interspersed with rifle volleys. Mortar shells began to fall on
the regiment and flares sizzled high in the rain. It was a faulty
flare that burnt into Reddy's back and he, in cruel pain,
reflexed in a tremendous bound out of the saddle to fall into
the barbs.

Horses kicking each other in terror, confused shouting,
men turning their mounts onto one another as each followed
contradictory orders, Bowen, the one lieutenant senior to me
in the squadron, is down. I assume command. I lead the men
forward into the third wire at a section where the shearing
had made an inroad over a shell hole. Up and down the line
troop commanders were pursuing the same thought, to
somehow strain their men through the horrid stuff and attack
the enemy. The narrow passages were quickly shut off by the
crippled and dead horses and their unbelieving riders.

The third wire lies two hundred feet before the Hun
position may be reached, the Ferozepore is well within the

optimum range of their machine guns. Fortunately the rain and mist shield us somewhat or the entire regiment would have been finished off, as we are in a compressed jumble attempting to force through the third wire. I am shouting commands at the sergeant-major, who is in saddle next to me, until I see the holes in his chest and realize that the fellow is dead and being held in place by the compacted horses on either side. A strange thought enters my mind as I realize the sergeant-major will not be able to help me reform, is this the truth behind the Cid legend, that a man's body is held in saddle only by odd chance in a massed charge.

Colonel Reaches still lived. Every squadron captain was down and the job of leading the regiment against a prepared, entrenched enemy was in the hands of junior men, like myself, and the colonel. The eight downed squadron commanders were the true bridle and reins of the regiment; however, the attack must be carried off. There was no coward among us, we would attack again. Without Reaches nothing would have been done. He cantered nobly among our shocked ranks, a frown of unalterable will on his features. Ignoring the exhausted state of his regiment, the colonel pulled us back from the third wire to reform along the second wire one hundred yards back. He called us to order by waving his sword in wide gyrations above his head, such a strangely melodramatic act for a man like Reaches that we formed at once. He pulled in our flanks that we still might make a shortened double line. It appeared to me that our losses exceeded fifty percent at this moment.

Trotting back and forth, smiling cheerily, calling out, "hullos" to us younger officers who were still saddled, the colonel prepared the regiment to continue the attack. We must move up quickly now, for the infantry would soon close to take advantage of the break we must make in the Hun's defense.

Reaches spurred his lathered animal urgently, deep enough so that the mount shuddered, then he raced toward the third wire and leapt it clearly. It was a high jump of forty-two inches, twelve feet in breadth. I believe the Colonel was dead before his horse touched the earth. The enemy, who had stilled as we retired, unleashed their weapons as Reaches approached the hurdle. The colonel went over the wire with his sword still in hand. What a fine thing that was, to attempt the third wire with sword in hand. We watched him slither absurdly on the wet flanks of his wounded animal, and he fell under the dying horse. I, and my fellow officers, raised our own swords and took what was left of the regiment over the third wire.

Horses suffer incredible wounds that would kill a man straight off. Even mortal wounds agonize horses hour after hour. Rain smelled of fish that morning as the machine guns destroyed my regiment, killing my brothers as they lay trapped in the barbed wire cages, and as they galloped up to the German trenches. Screaming in the mist, yes, the rarest screaming of English horse and men was accomplished. I had not known that men could scream with such despair and power.

Automatic guns riveted their hot metallics into our softest parts and we, the horse and man, fell dead into the swamp. My fine mount Dennis was very brave, he had taken fifteen rounds or more. My own wounds were insignificant. Dennis faltered as we closed on the enemy. From my blood slick saddle existence was abrubtly, and insanely, disjointed. A few score of us reached the slope of the enemy trenches. At this elevation, as one rose up on the slope, the roar of the machine guns was beyond rational noise. Hulks of men without heads, torsos astride dying horses that raced in pain with all memory of discipline forgotten. Screaming in the rain that smelled of castaway fish. Screaming everywhere from the poor chaps badly wounded and in the loneliness of pre-death.

At last Dennis and I saw the enemy huge in his grey cloth. There, I viewed the monster guns. I was appalled at their diminutive snouts. I could not go on. I took coup like an Iroquois warrior by touching the sandbagged parapet, and fled on foot. Dennis dead at the base of the sandbags that were mushy sackings melting into the swamp of Flanders. Rearward I fled. I fell resurrected from terror into the British lines, "get 'im mate. Ooh what a pitch, 'e'll 'ave a bump won't 'e not likely."

The regiment killed not a single enemy. There was no victory communication. The action was forgotten promptly. As I had run back through the third wire my hand brushed a meaty thigh-chunk. That is when I screamed and as I screamed I rushed past Reddy, still enmeshed, still screaming.

The circumcision of Wilkulda was an act of purity compared to trench warfare. His cutting was holy before God even as our century's brutality to men is hallowed to the devil. Thirty-five centuries ago the mankinds of Australia were living in a state of grace as compared to the mass cruelty of my poor 20th Century.

Six weeks later, when my abrasions were sufficiently healed, I returned to the Ferozepore. There was no chance of the 129th being reformed, it was casualtied out of service. They asked me to go into an infantry regiment of the Lahore. Two of the division's rifle brigades were Indian troops commanded by English officers. The third brigade was soldiered and commanded by Britishers. The Lahore had been in the line since the end of October, somewhat east of the Ypres salient. Her company commanders had taken a terrific beating. On November 3rd, 1914, I was assigned a company of British soldiers and was breveted as a captain. I was holding this rank on September 16, when I was wounded and blinded in the battle for Loos.

Tragically, after October 20, 1914, Empire horsetroops served only as a drain on the resources of the kingdom. A huge expense had to be laid out for the daily upkeep of cavalry, and a further cost was added by the requisitioning of boxcars to haul fodder, a waste of valuable haulage space. Except for the Canadian mounted riflemen's holding effort at Moreuil Wood in March of 1918, horse troops contributed a negative burden, a seepage of strength. Allenby, late in the war on the Palestinian front, accomplished wonders with his horse against the Turk, but there he dared to take advantage of his opportunities, a thing that we were denied in September-October 1914.

I shall never stop thinking of what might have been on 20th October if English horses had been thrust aggresively. At that moment, still quite early in the war, cavalry numbered fifty thousand, this strength was available when our regiment launched its miserable blow. Fifty thousand Empire horse near Ypres the dawn of October 20, 1914. There was available a percentage of cavalry concentration to German infantry not equalled again. The best men, the strongest and the bravest in the Empire, served in the horse troops. We, the finest of the British Empire, were never unleashed in the Great War. I believe a concentrated attack, utilizing all horse under English command, on the 20th October, 1914, would have broken through the German lines. The war would never have become great, the war would have ended in early winter of 1915.

Fifty thousand horsed men at Ypres, a ten mile front, no barrage to alert the enemy. Three doubled lines of mounted men a thousand yards between; we would have smashed through. I see the fifty thousand as one immense, solitary knight holding battleaxe and griffoned embossed shield. He is astride Flanders on a marvelous stallion, he is looking seaward toward home, he is contented after fulfilling himself in honest battle.

In the years following 1918 I learned that the Germans had also launched an attack in the Ypres sector on ·20th October. But no matter their readiness, fifty thousand horse in full gallop could not have been stemmed. We would not have needed allied horse to assist us. British horsemastership alone would have carried it. The foot reserves would have marched through the ten-mile puncture to roll up the enemy line to the seacoast.

Of the fifty thousand mounted men perhaps ten thousand would have died in the attack, another twenty thousand wounded, leaving twenty thousand blooded cavalry to disrupt the German's rear. These difficult early casualities would have prevented the cruel stalemate of trench warfare. By 1915 the normal weekly wastage on the Ypres front would be several thousands of dead.

We horse troops could have done it, I know we could have done it. Why were we not given a chance on 20th October, 1914, to end the war gloriously?

# BOOK II
# MY GRANDFATHER
# TJUNDAGA

## one

I became Wilkulda when Tjundaga took away my foreskin and my father Lillywur staunched the hemorrhage with a glowing twig. For sixteen weeks after this we three initiates were banished from our mankind. In this period we traveled to the land of the Sweetwater Crab-men in the company of our nine uncles. They were a mankind of importance and possessed a fine brook left to them by their Ancestor Crab. The creek was the metamorphosed undervein of the Crab's penis. Though the Crab-men honored us highly we were happy to depart after a fortnight as they were an exceptionally fanatical mankind. Two Crab hags had been killed when they inadvertently wandered in the general direction of our forbidden camp as they foraged for roots. Thus we were content to trek to the Mosquito lands, although these were very poor. Here we had to drink our urine regularly, as the Mosquito waterholes had gone dry. The nine uncles found the Mosquito girls quite comely and thus found their hosts agreeable. After two moons with these people our penises had healed and we returned to the Eagle encampment which had just moved to the pool again. We initiates were not permitted entrance into the camp proper

69

but were taken directly to the Cave of Holiness where Tjundaga greeted us with a small blaze at the portal.

This cave connected the Sky to earth. This was the very hole where the Sky Father Eagle had hatched the first man, who was the Sky's child. This cavern was the primal sanctuary where the Eagle had slept a thousand ages while Dreaming the worlds. No person could come into this sacred place unless he be an Eagle-man, circumcised and freshly healed of sorcered evil.

The Cave of Holiness is located in a river bed that was drained forever dry by a wandering Bear in the Dreamtime. The Eagle had left the cave and river unguarded when he flew away to rescue a little boy who was being eaten by the Ant. On returning with the boy the Eagle slew the greedy bear who had emptied the river. The Bear's gonads became the sand mountains that hide the cavern from the eyes of ghosts. In the battle between the two Sky Heros the uncircumcised boy was accidently squashed by a paw. The magic black stone shelf that fronted the Cave of Holiness, where Tjundaga's fire smoked, was the reconstituted flesh of the brave lad.

For one moon's death we three initiates would remain alone in the cave where our new identities would be grafted onto our souls by the magic of the holy boards that were stored here, and by metaphysical association with the Sky Father. Food reserved for the ultimate degree of elderhood would be abundant for us three during our stay. Emu testicles we would now savor but never again until we were ancient elders.

Potent foods were ours, as we must be strong in laying down with the many females brought to the black stone ledge during the moon's period. Ten dry seasons would pass before we would again be permitted to lay down with many females. And at last, on the blackness of rock before the ledge, I would be able to lay down with Kitunga, as her Frog husband had decided to rest a season before making the long walk back to his lake. Many forbidden relationships of the minor type were disregarded during this moon as it was deemed that as many women as possible should have their vaginas cleansed by our purified penises.

Unknown to me Tjundaga, our mankind's father, had envisioned a potent dream that recurred each night I had

been on my sixteen week journey. Tjundaga had interpreted
this dream as a dictum from the Sky Father to re-initiate
brother-sister laying downs on the sacred ledge as had been
the custom when man first had exited into the worlds from
the Eternal Dream. As this tradition had been laid aside
twenty-seven generations past Tjundaga decided that I and
my youngest sister, Kitata, must be the pair to honor the
Sky, he had instructed me in the Sky's ways and Kitata was
the tribe's most popular young girl. Kitata, my full-fleshed
sister, was nine years of age, thus a season away from the
normal time for girls to begin laying down.

Tjundaga was a most original man, a renowned judge and
magician, yet those who knew him best considered him
something of an eccentric. Mainly his eccentricity seemed to
be a predilection for solitude. Seldom among men, let alone
ghouls, does one meet a person who prefers to be apart from
his fellows.

It is the combination of magic and wisdom that brings
forth those hunting skills and success in family matters that
we hold worthy for a life of devotion to the Sky. Yet
Tjundaga was not a proficient spearman and seemed to fulfil
his laying down responsibilities with a dutiful attitude rather
than with joy or affection. Added to such peculiarities,
Tjundaga seemed to be able to sing powerful magic better
alone than with the aid of surging elders or ancient and holy
objects. Grandfather was constantly beseeched to sing game
into the proximity of our spears or to create profuse rainfalls
during the dry seasons. And indeed, in Tjundaga's lifetime
the Eagle people never went thirsty or hungry. The council of
elders was somewhat unhappy at Tjundaga's perchant for
creating magic solo, but their love and faith in his person did
not permit them the twin deceits of envy and suspicion.

And yet, it was my laying down with my flesh sister,
Kitata, at Tjundaga's direction, that led to my personal pain,
and to this ending of reproof in the shallowed sea. For on
that dawn preceding the moon's re-creation, when Kitata was
brought onto the boy's metamorphosed being as the first
laying down female, as I waited with my two friends, the Age
of Dreaming issued a newer song. She came with a grin and
with skipping feet, for Kitata found it good to be given such

attention and honor. Tjundaga led her up onto the rock, her legs were short and he had to help her crawl up. The people watched with happiness as it was assumed such wondrous magic as this would bring many fine gifts to land and to the Eagle people.

My brother initiates looked on with awe as the girl laid on her back and I knelt to the stone to take her up to my newness. This would be my first actual laying down although the season preceeding my circumcision, when my penis would grow without cause, I had played with several girls I knew well. On this day of sacred increase it was considered quite important that the females express eager joyousness on the black ledge. And Kitata did welcome me into her petal like self. She seemed impish and yet mature with charming tenderness.

But my elation subdued at once as I made entrance into her child's organ and discovered that she was somehow blocked. Rather crudely in my heat, I forced the path open, but then realized with terror that Kitata was in severe pain.

She must not scream, she must not; it was a moment of dread as I have never again experienced. A female must never be anything but delighted at laying down with a man, it is our way. Women are forbidden to exhibit reluctance and are instructed at a young age in the laying down laws and what is considered desirable and attractive to men. It is our way. To allow herself the smallest discomfort at the ledge ceremony would be particularly dangerous to any female as the boy's metamorphosed being was considered the personal relic of circumcision.

I felt Kitata struggling not to give sound to her distress. Before I could withdraw my penis and conceal her failure with a pretense of my own, Kitata screamed. I do not remember, I will never remember, which old man it was who first cursed as I looked down at my sister's contorted face and then to where tiny runlets of hymen blood veined to Kitata's ankles.

With cruelest alacrity the curse was multiplied by the assemblage of peering elders, excluding Tjundaga and Lillywur who stood together, away from us, shocked. I observed every detail most clearly, as if entranced by the perfect focus of my fears for Kitata. My sister bit through her lower lip that she might exorcise her mouth of the scream. It was too late. The elders came toward us with spears tilted to the death thrust. Kitata now emitted peal upon peal of horrified screams. They dragged her away by the feet and although the dust billowings hid her form I could hear her moaning without intermission until too swiftly I knew that the spears had emptied her life's essence.

Everyone fled excepting me, Tjundaga, and my Uncle Mushabin. Mushabin was Tjundaga's older brother and his most loyal. He had been my instructor in the circumcision requirements. He was in his sixth decade and possessed a most active nature. Without waiting for direction from the stunned Tjundaga, he ran to where I still lay and tore me from the black shelf and hurriedly propelled me backwards into the Cave of Holiness.

After what seemed a very long time Mushabin, all atremble, came into the cavern where I huddled against one painted wall of stone. Mushabin was in a pitiful state, weeping and muttering as he assessed the situation. The elders had violently ranged about Tjundaga and Mushabin after I was out of sight pleading that my tainted life be forfeited. Preceded by his shock of white hair, Mushabin, in an enervated state, came close to me in the cave and I saw bewildered sadness in his eyes. For as he loved Tjundaga, he also loved me. Wearily he took up one of my wrists in his dry and delicate hands and we so touched for some moments. He, in a tearful voice, told me that I was still his favorite nephew and that all would be well.

Releasing my arm, Mushabin took out of his pouch made from a wallaby bladder, his prized magic stones. These white objects were the petrified testicles of a Dingo Ancestor. Softly vibrating the relic testicles in his cupped hands, Mushabin touched my eyes and mouth with the sacred objects. Returning the testicles to their quiet bladder home, Mushabin lifted his pointing stick, which was ornately carved with Dreamtime magic, and traced upon the cavern floor a representation of an ineffable song of sorcery. Then he touched the pointing stick first to his own penis and then to mine.

Mushabin went to the entrance of the cavern and beckoned his brother Tjundaga to enter. And as if a corpse, grandfather came to my side carrying a gourd of water. He sat down by me and placed his arm over my slumped head. Tjundaga appeared to be disturbed in his soul, as if drained by a profound depression. Ignoring both of us, Mushabin

began to dance in the stomach of the cave. He invoked the
chant of fidelity to the Spirit Eagle. From one corner of
dimness to the limitless rear, tucking himself in and then
leaping high, Mushabin sprang back and fro. He paused only
once to lick in mid-air, for a brief instant, at the rock ceiling,
as if to seep into his soul the energy of the cave through his
tongue.

From a wallet of sewn kangaroo tail Mushabin flew out
grain featherings of magic. He blew the white sands off his
extended finger tips into my face that the efficacy of the
magic dust's strength might be pure in my eyes. As he twirled
the now emptied wallet inside out, a last haze of white
granules floated in the cavern's space as if in a trance of
their own. Dots of glowing magic sparkled on our faces as
Tjundaga came closer and said softly into my ear that I must
remain alone the remainder of this day and the night in the
cavern. If the Spirit Eagle wished me dead the opportunity to
effect the killing could take place without the prying visions
of other Ancestors. If I survived, Tjundaga and I would make
a marvelous run into the Eternal Dreamtime Lands which
were located in a harsh desert world to the north. As the two
brothers left me, Mushabin suddenly pried apart my jaws and
into my mouth he dropped his sacred quartz. This was an
actual chip of the Rainbow Snake's incisor tooth. He allowed
the cold relic to absorb my being for a long moment, then he
took it back and he and Tjundaga ran.

When they were gone I leaned into the cavern wall with
my cold and wet buttocks and back. And I wept for Kitata in
that she was dead and would never know the worlds and their
happiness and the sad things too. But I was glad that the
elders had decided not to spear me as they had slain her, and
that Mushabin had taken me into the Holy Cave's sanctuary.

The shadowed beaming in the cavern was slanted beneath
earth, and I knew that outside nighting had begun and that I
had slept. Far in the sanctuary's reaches I heard the flock of
bats awake. And soon the giant swarm of downy mice were
winging out. They brushed against me gently and I was happy
at their squeals and the thrupping of their wing flapping. It
was a touch of life, a scent of food, a hope of the night's safe
passage.

Where I huddled was the central flow of the bats and I rose
to go into a deeper crevice where our sacred boards were
stored in rugs of kanagroo pelt. Carefully I probed the dark

space as not to touch even the aged wrappings. Then a bat came to me in the darkness and whispered that he was life and I caught this bat and ate it and I became life. With its warm blood I felt better and caught other stray bats and ate them. Too soon the bats glided empty the cavern to gain the beyond and I became a mourner again. I sat as near to the boards as I dared, as if they were a warming fire.

I wept for Kitata and myself. I remembered when I was a little boy of four seasons, just finished at Namana's nipples. Kitata was but a few hours old and I remembered how Namana had bit off Kitata's little finger from her right hand. How the baby had howled. Kitata was beautiful in the emu fat and ash and breast milk that Namana had rubbed into her being. I was sitting in Namana's lap, trying to get to her nipples when she had bit off Kitata's little finger. And I watched our mother as she carefully chewed and swallowed every bit and bone of the finger that her baby might be spared disfigurement by an abnormal growth. How Kitata wailed. Finished swallowing, Namana made her milk squirt on the stump and after this she covered the place with spider cloud and with tree gum. Kitata soon forgot about losing her finger as she had mama's nipple in her mouth. I tried to get to the other nipple but Namana pushed me away and gave me a lizard's tail to chew on. Never again was I allowed to drink at my mother's breast.

Thinking of all this made me tired and I went to sleep. And in this slumber I dreamt of Kitata beneath my penis and screaming up at me that she wanted her little finger back, and I had her breast in my mouth as she said this. And I knew from watching this dream as I slept, that unless I did something good the cave's Spirit must kill me. In the dream another dream at its edge instructed me that I must give up something quite valuable that I might live and that my mankind might not die out as the elders wailed and chaffed at us incessantly.

An enchantment wept from the boards that I slept close to and this spell entered my stomach and told my soul what to give to the Sky Father. Bats returning awakened me. They flew quite near to the cavern floor as they were heavier from feeding. As their faces were happy I knew that the bats had feasted and had enjoyed a night of merriment. And as I lay on my back I could distinguish the flying mice as they passed over me, outlined against the ceiling picture of the Rainbow

Snake that filled the space with its bright yellowness.

It was then that I remembered my promise given in the night's dream. It was true, I had survived, but I was much upset when I realized what I had given the cave's Spirit in return for life. I had promised never to lay down with females. I had renounced all my laying down prerogatives and my future wives; I had given up my penis rights, my very state of pridehood. It was terrible. I was appalled at what this sacrifice would mean to me.

Yet this dream's promise to desist from pleasure has returned to me enormous pleasure. But it was a very serious matter in my world to never use a penis as it was sanctified to be used. I have obeyed the promise twenty summers now, except once. This renunciation of my member has caused me and my family mortification and has engendered hate and disgust for me among my own people. From that night of promise never to release my milkfat into a woman's womb I began to differ from all others. Yet this heresy has bestowed to me a destiny that matches the Dreamtime myths. For my name is Wilkulda and although I had inadvertently damaged reality by mating with my sister Kitata, from that act's consequence I became the Sky's messenger. My great regret is that my sister died because of some strange working of the Sky's master Dream. I was never able to find where Kitata was buried and I believe her body was left in the wilderness for the dingos to eat.

I am the messenger of forgiveness. I trust in forgiveness as does the aged magician whose last son finally displays those signs of mind and heart, as verified by a personal dream of excellence, that prove him to be a potent sorcerer. And one day I believe that forgiveness will change the mankinds and that the Kitatas of the worlds will not be speared if they scream during holy ceremonies.

I was hungry in the cave and now on hands and knees stealthily made to the rearward spaces where the bats slept. Here I ate several dozen of the delicious birds and felt refreshed especially as the power of their blood is renowned as a stimulant to thought.

Tjundaga did not come as he had said though the night had

passed and I wondered what was the cause of his hesitation. I
went to the threshold of the cavern where I could be seen so
that the elders would know that I had not been killed by the
cave's guardian. I could see no movement anywhere in the
river bed or on the bare bank beyond but I was quite sure
that many eyes were on me. I understood that I must not
dare to leave the security of the cave, that as long as I stayed
in the proximity of the holy boards no harm would be mine.
This day and night walked by very slowly and I drank what
water was left and then was thirsty.

Tjundaga came into the Holy Cave the next dawn, never
did he disclose the reason for the delay. Tjundaga patted me
on the shoulder and asked kindly how was my health.
Without waiting for a reply he said that we must go at once. I
was afraid to leave the cave for I had obliged myself to the
Spirit. To me the cave was a nipple and I had sucked its
liquid and that is why I still lived. Tjundaga now exhibited
his personality's richness for any other elder hearing my
desire to stay would have fled thinking me a captive of
sorcery.

Precious boy that I was, as Tjundaga made to lead me out,
I receded further back into the stone curls and the shale roof
shunted down into a narrowness. Here were the bats and I
awoke them with my stumbling indiscretions. Screeching, the
frantic mice-birds zipped crazily in their enforced
confinement. Tjundaga sought me there at the rear where the
rock was heavy with encrusted bat excrement.

Seeking escape, the panicky bats darted about in the
recesses, and as I was about to become a bat and fly away
with my brothers, Tjundaga arrived to place his hand on my
heaving chest. Sweetly he whispered into my ear as the bats
shrilled in their blind trauma, "come from this place, Pil . . . ,
Wilkulda, come man Wilkulda. We together must run to the
immortal lands. The elders will enter soon for they worry
about the boards. You must be gone when they come.
Lillywur and Namana say that you must go. You and I shall
have a happy walkabout."

The winged creatures battered against our brows and lips.
We could hear their flying bones snap at the impact with our
skulls. "Wilkulda," grandfather continued, "come out. Do

not fear, you have committed no wrong. Thou art Wilkulda
and shall be great among the magicians.''

This high praise in the moment of my cowardice caused
me to emit a sob or two, and at this Tjundaga searched out
my boy's face and covered my wet eyes with his hands and
nuzzled me under his chin, even as if I were not a circumcised
man but still a little boy.

Both of us were mantled with settling bat dung as
Tjundaga took me from the cave and introduced me again
into day's heat. The wet of night had been inhaled fully off
the rocks by the thirsty dawn. I was somewhat hurt that we
did not see Lillywur outside. I thought he would be there
with the spear gift he had promised me after the completion
of the laying down ceremony. Before circumcision I was
permitted only a child's toy spear.

To the left of the cavern, as one makes to the north along
the dried river bed, is a deep load of red sand that extended
for several miles. Here in the redness we bathed ourselves
clean of the powdery bat excrement. After cleansing myself
I asked if we might return to the camp just to say goodby to
Namana. I had already forgotten the prohibition of speaking
to females as an initiate. Perhaps, I continued on that long
ago day, Namana might have a seed cake cooling and perhaps
Lillywur might have my spear. Sternly Tjundaga said we must
not meet any person, and he also patiently reminded me of
the laws that an initiate must observe with females.

We must trek to the Eternal lands and be recreated.
Grandfather told me it would be a curious place that I would
like. And after being renewed we could return to the pool
where no man would dare be my enemy as the magic
bestowed on me in the Dream world would be most
powerful. Tjundaga had made a walk into the Eternal lands
when he had been a younger man, during one of his solitary
sojourns. No other man in existence has been known to have
visited these awesome places except Tjundaga, I would be the
second.

Without further discourse my grandfather moved up the
crumbling sterility of the dead embankment. He ran into the
hills of stone that lift up before the escarpment. In one hand
Tjundaga carried several spears and his spear thrower, in the
other hand he carried his magic pointing stick. Attached to

his human hair belt were his wallets and pouches containing magic implements and a few handfuls of seed for food. I carried nothing.

Grandfather gained the ridge beyond the hills while I still pounded after him in a stony vale below. Up at the summit he waited without vexation for me to catch up. This height was the accepted limit of our world, then lay the flats which we shared with the Mallee Hen-Men. This mankind was sparse in numbers and were permitted to live in the flats only because they possessed an urgent segment of our Eagle dancesong that dealt with abundant rainfall.

Tjundaga, my grandfather, was a man surpassing all others in greatness. I was reminded of this as I gained the height. He stood in reverent contemplation, staring out over the colorless flats. Then, flinging wide his arms with hands tightly holding his spears and pointing stick, my grandfather jutted his heavy head skyward. He opened his eyes and mouth to admit light into his soul, and then Tjundaga spoke firmly, "Sky Father it is I, Tjundaga of your brood. I am Eagle as thou art man and I bring my grandson, Wilkulda, before thee, Spirit Eagle. This is my truest child even before his father, my son. He is my best hope and my people's best hope for increase. I trust you Sky Father and I offer up his name to you. He is Wilkulda and is Eagle as you are man. Death and dishonour have crushed me because I did as your dreaming bidded. I gave Wilkulda to his sister to lay down with as your dream instructed. I do not understand what happened. I myself applied emu fat to her female part that the lad's penis would slide without obstruction. I myself stretched her vagina with my fingers several days before her placement on the holy stone of blackness. Yet she betrayed man by her pain. I can not understand why such sadness has followed a thing you desired to take place. Sky Eagle, I beg thee not to have chosen Wilkulda as a ghoul. My people lust to destroy Wilkulda even as they slew his sister. Wilkulda will be a magician of greatness as you promised me, this I trust. You would not tell me one thing in the last season and be false in another, more difficult, day. He will be paramount among equals as you promised. He is your choice, you would not corrupt the Dream with a lie. Do not abandon Wilkulda to the skeletons of past furies. He is your choice for something

important. If a deadness is required, then take my spirit as
your purging."

Tjundaga abruptly halted his words and ignoring my tears
he ran down off the ridge even as his voice lingered out over
the pale grey flats. In the white air his smalling figure leapt
away to disappear in the shadow of a green stained monolith.
From this hidden place he called up to me, "Wilkulda, run
with me and we will be reborn in the Dreamtime's essence."

I jumped long leaps to join beloved Tjundaga, but he had
already raced ahead into a crevice lower than the flats. Here a
dying Sparrow Ancestor had dragged his tail deep as he
chased a young girl he was infatuated with. The girl escaped
and the Sparrow died of thirst. The greater portion of the
flats are his metamorphosed, outstretched, wings.

Tjundaga aimed for the giant desert to the far north where
the Dream had slept until awakened by the Spirit Eagle in
our Holy Cave. My legs became spirit to my soul as I
skimmed past the green fogged rock and entered eagerly into
the ravine behind Tjundaga's naked shadow. My young feet
leapt from hold to hold without fear's pause and I could
sense that the running was healing my soul.

Legs and arms were as one song of movement. Land
drifted by in a hazy soft light without vibrant shape or hue to
wake me from my reverie. I beheld the world's passage
beneath my running self. There were no wisps of high cloud
above to birth clots of shadow to run through. There was a
sameness of spirit on the flats that made me think and grieve
at the long ago pain and loneliness of the Sparrow.

Grandfather and I were together, matching strides on the
hot wasteland. Never had I been in the flats before as it was a
place of extreme magic. I was curious about all things and
asked questions even as we leapt. Tjundaga ran the baked dirt
in powerful strides as if he was a yearling kangaroo bounding
after a female. We were unafraid of tedium's ghost and swept
contentedly over the dead place as if we were wind demons
chased from earth to sky by mischievous spirits.

I am the very Wilkulda, who with great Tjundaga, searched
out the womb of the world, but until it was found I had
never truly believed in it. Our running feet elevated dust
trackings into the lower sky but even as this happened a
thirsty breeze came to gorge itself on the scattering sand
plumes.

We came unto the entrance of the Eternal desert, its forefoot. Here, the heroes had been created by the Sky Father, who freed them from their nests of clay with his sanctified urine. The Heros went from here each to his particular station and created the lands and the animals even unto man. Some Heros glided high above the sky and became stars, which pleased the Sky Eagle. He created night in order to view the stars better in the contrasting blackness.

A rugged system of basalt formations alerted Tjundaga to the fact that we had come upon the outer desert. Strewn among the, rare to Australia, basalt, were many score of huge boulders, red mainly in colorfulness but muted with bleached yellow crowns. In the Dreamtime these boulders had been the living testicles of a Kangaroo Hero. The Kangaroo, in highest passion, had lusted to lie down with the Black Swan Ancestor but she had no use for the Kangaroo and flew away into the sky to be rid of him. Alas, the intensity of the Kangaroo's desire was greater than his reason and he attempted to bound up into the sky to be with the Black Swan. Jump after jump and the Kangaroo went higher and higher. Yet he could not quite manage to catch the ever rising Black Swan, who eventually became a night fire star. In despair, to reduce his weight, he forsook his testicles that the last leap might succeed. The gonads fell off onto the basalt and shattered into the redyellow rocks.

We came to a place littered with petrified tree trunks rooted into stone. Thousands of trunks studded the white sand dunes that waved sluggishly through the desolation. Faster did Tjundaga lift his old legs, as if feverish to leave the reliced trees behind. He would not discuss with me their Dreamtime history as the magic involved was too profound for my young soul to comprehend.

In love he had trained me to be a keeper of the Sky's kidney fat and somehow I must measure up to his trust in me.

Wilkulda, the initiate of circumcision, ran contentedly in his grandfather's shade. Tjundaga had not slackened the pace since the two had left the cave of the boy's humiliation. Resting only at night the two had been running for the duration of a moon's confinement. They took no time to hunt, although wallabies of the smallest variety were plentiful in the sheltered places between plateaus. A few camp dingos,

who had caught up with them as they entered the desert,
were quickly eaten. Past the zone of mallee bush, which
marked the outer boundary of man's domain, they ran.
Mulga growth was the only vegetation, this ubiquitous,
multi-limbed scrub tree was a source of food to the
mankinds. In the roots of the mulga grubs, rodents, reptiles,
and insects of many types made their homes, and on the
ground beneath the short tree grew berries and seed grasses.

In these lands of perpetual dryness Tjundaga and Wilkulda
found lizards of the middle and small orders without
difficulty. Water was produced by digging soak holes where
Tjundaga scented wetness, he was never in error. Sand would
be dug to a depth of several feet or more and water would
drain into the hole. Or, a boulder's top crease might hold a
handful or two of thickened liquid. When nothing else was
available the two would lick the traces of morning dew from
age smooth stones.

And their pacing's gait did gain in strength instead of
diminishing. At night Tjundaga would friction the fire sticks
in his palms and soon a tiny blaze of twigs and dried spinifex
would comfort their chill. Wilkulda would huddle back to
back with his grandfather and this combining of body heat
would deflect the cold.

Speaking seldom, the old one and his cub's cub proceeded,
as if in union, deeper into the desert wherein existed the
Eternal Dreamtime lands. Loud were the thuds of their
flailing feet on the hot baked scab of the earth. Fluid were
their straining forms in the vacant air. As the days
compressed one into the other's void, a moment was created
that seemed of endless duration. For the running had become
essential to the existence of the universe, instinctive and
rhythmic to the cosmos even as the sea's respiration is to the
galaxy. Toward the ending of their heroic run, Tjundaga and
Wilkulda no longer thought of themselves as men but rather
as if they were the running itself. When they stopped at
endeavor of night, their bodies would spasm for a moment
until legs and arms comprehended the rested state to be.

The shame of the cave was sweated out of Wilkulda's soul
by the improbable trek. Fear and self-abhorrence became
sealed from his sight by the marvelous leaping. But Tjundaga
could not forget his own debasement and each darkness when

the boy would sleep against his buttocks, the old man would turn away from the smouldering fire and mutter chant after chant into the universal night of death.

And they came into the middle-desert, a space of bright and vivid blackness. Not even Tjundaga on his former voyage had penetrated this deep, and in the bright softness he believed they had entered the Dreaming place of creation, but this was not yet fact.

Wastes receded into a thin yellow loam and the spinifex, tufted thorn grass, became sparse in clumsy spikings. Gradually the earth relinquished even this sparse foliage and changed itself into a harridan of scorched redness. Red rock channeled with orange shadings passed beneath their feathering feet and the disturbed patina of gravel was scattered into obscure patterns.

The lad never had viewed a sky of such irrevocable blue as if clouds would not dare to thumb the rolling earth with pauses of freckled droplets. Air was dry and thus demanding of any surface liquid and provided little wetness to restore the runners. Each dawn water could only be renewed by tonguing the sheen of dew from the orange pebbles.

Sun's heat slammed incessantly through the unfiltered blue to melt the scant vapors of the purest of all atmospheres. Wilkulda became afraid in the perpetual firing and was grateful that Tjundaga was his guardian, the lad did not sense that the elder was also afraid.

Tiny runners patiently gait the volume of a gorge's mighty crease. Tjundaga has surrendered to his forebodings. He, a man of prudence and circumspection, a master-magician, ran bewildered in a novel feeling of terror, for death had revealed itself in Tjundaga's soul and the old one had interpreted the unhidden demand as a need for Wilkulda to be slain.

To kill Wilkulda became Tjundaga's dreading mission, for he now believed that only the boy's death would fulfil the Sky's expectation. As they leapt the middle isolation Tjundaga knew perfectly in his intuition that to kill Wilkulda would expunge his people's from the ignominy of the despoiled copulation cavern. That the council of elders had been right from the beginning of the tragedy, both girl and boy must be sacrificed.

The runners came between a closeting cleft of the gorge

that had been their shadowed pathway since noon. Stone
walls of ferrous oxide curved in distended cavities leaving
pillars of rouge rock projecting into the sky. Abruptly
Tjundaga halted his pace and he and the boy came to rest
after some moments of reflexed joltings. Wearied, Wilkulda
dropped down to one side and lay on the protruding crest of
a sand submerged monolith. At once the lad closed his eyes
in rest, never questioning why grandfather had called stop
while the sun lived. Quietly, he curled his limbs into the
position of repose there on the slice of exposed rock. He
barely heard Tjundaga crooning the simple song that instilled
sleep into quarrelsome children who otherwise might attract
ghouls with their whimpering.

When the boy was refuged in sincere sleep, Tjundaga began
the dance of spear-slaughter. Grandfather, even as he
prepared to instigate death, heard a solemn depression
collapse into his being. And the old one issued wails of
lamenting dignity as he took hold of the spear that would
empty Wilkulda's life.


Killing's moment arrived, obscene with its grotesque
squeal, the magic chant took control of the weapon's shank.
Drawing spear's beak back to his spine's arching, Tjundaga
prepared to. thrust it into the meek target. Spear began its
route of mortality's wound, but before it pierced screaming
flesh, Tjundaga was aware that his premonition of death had
not been scented in his grandson's soul but rather it was a
self-smelling of death to be. And spear's rush became
climaxed not in the youth's chest, but as if warped by a
shovement of force, it bounded and quivered from false
impact with rock.

"I am infirm. I cannot slay this sleeping child that is of my
flesh. What am I to do? Where is my Sky Father? Come to
me now Great Eagle. You must seek me out. Reveal yourself
for I am Tjundaga, father to your own people. My grandson
sleeps yet he must be slain. This cannot be the Dream as it
was meant to be sung. Somehow a pussing sore has damaged
the Dreaming.

"It is peculiar, this walking far without purpose, for I was
to slay Wilkulda on that first night away from the Holy Cave.

I promised the council that the boy would be killed outside
the Eagle World that there would not be a profanation. Eagle
I am not a stranger to the Sky. I am thirsty and need your
blood. I am hungry and need to suck at the marrow of your
bone. Far off my mankind wail. I am their father but know
not where I have come to. They sing to me that I must soon
return to the pool's reflection and dance for their swimming
souls.

"Events have become too complex. My kidney has
betrayed me. I should have obeyed my brother elders. I have
been clumsy. The boy must be killed and then only silent
weeping will be the people's punishment. Sky Father will you
not teach me a way to save my grandson from death. A
moment past my weapon failed but on the coming thrusting
there will be a kill for me.

"There is no Sky Father. I have always known this
secretly. He does not exist. The Dreaming is a lifeless skin of
hope. Man is alone . . . Sky Father forgive me. Come to
Tjundaga and kill him. Dreaming Eagle I deserve to be a dead
feather without soft down or flying web.

"I must deliver a chant that will kill Wilkulda with sorcery.
With a kill by magic there will be no rent in his child's
stomach where his soul could drift out of his kidney into the
space of nowhere. Wilkulda's soul would be perpetually
alone. It would become ugly and fearsome and evil.

"Slay me, for am I not aged and foolish? The boy was to
have been a river in the Dreaming. He was to have been a
magician of bigness. I have failed the Sky and the boy. How
will his killing serve the Dreamtime? I thought I was wiser
than other men. It is my fate to be made into a ghoul for the
murder of my grandson.

"I will not kill him. Let the Sky World destroy Wilkulda.
Look at him sleep. How brave he was when I took him from
the Cave and neither father nor mother came to smile into his
eyes. There is nothing as restful as to merge into a child's soul
by peering into his eyes.

"I will die here now. When I am dead Wilkulda will die for
he knows not the hidden wet creases. He will search for water
and he will fail to find it. He shall die under a mulga bush
seeking coolness among the sand covered roots.

"He soon shall awake. The enchantment was not

structured for a circumcised boy. He moves. How am I to be dead. I will have to accomplish death with my spear. To murder Tjundaga by Tjundaga's hand, this must be the Dream's will. Tjundaga must slay Tjundaga that the Dream shall not be heavy with guilt."

## two

Tjundaga sat by slumbering Wilkulda for a moment with his spear crossed over squatted thighs. The old man wept, yet as his being contained little water his weeping was tearless. Unhinging his narrow limbs the old man extended his legs along the ground. With spear in delicate balance Tjundaga did place the shaft between great toe and its minor brother. The magician bent over the toe suspended spear and was beginning to drag death into his kidney when he stayed the weapon's spurt to glance up into the Sky. And now the aged elder was wetted with tears as he became absorbed in the Sky.

"I will kill me with my spear, it doesn't matter . . . You need not bother for I am content with this vision. Yes, if that is what you desire I thank you for this magic death. I love you Sky."

And Tjundaga was dead. The untainted spear dropped from its toed platform into the sand. The single droplet of blood that had bubbled onto the spear's point from the ephemeral prick into Tjundaga's skin did leap free from the weapon's impact. The cell of blood was cast onto Wilkulda's sleeping lips. The atom of heavy moisture did startle Wilkulda from his trance. Awakened the boy did not look down to his side where grandfather was dead but up into the glared sky. Shielding his eyes from the burning vapor he felt the droplet on his lips and without pause he did tongue the spot of blood into his mouth where it fell to the waiting kidney. And thus unknowingly did Wilkulda swallow the soul of Tjundaga and make it safe.

Wilkulda located the drying corpse of his grandfather, Tjundaga. Numbly the boy swayed above the artifact that once had been personality. He noticed not the extreme calmness of earth. Wilkulda's single concern was to honorably bury his grandfather. There was not one tree in which to uplift Tjundaga's form.˙ Magicians of Tjundaga's rank were always buried in the tendrils of a bluegum, but here in the desert there was not even a skeleton of an eucalyptus. Common Eagle-men were put in the ground and that was that. Women and children were not usually accorded a grave but left in the bush for the wild things to gnaw at.

Wilkulda wondered which enemy of the Eagles had sung a murder chant into Tjundaga. The lad understood that the killer may also have sung death at himself with the aid of a pointing bone. Wilkulda worried only about his duties to his dead grandfather. He began a dancesong to defeat any plot that had to do with the humiliation of Tjundaga's ghost. As Wilkulda performed the ritual he pondered the best possible place to bury the deathing.

Wilkulda wished that he might have been alert, awake, before Tjundaga had died that he might have siphoned off the old man's extinguishing breath. By that inhalation the courage and wisdom of Tjundaga might have not been wasted. Too bad Lillywur had not been present, as it was the first son's privilege to have drunk in Tjundaga's greatness.

Wilkulda had participated in death's demands at several funeral processions and burials as a howling child. Grandfather must be tenderly graved, if not his ghost might revert to ghoulishness. The lad decided that in the absence of a tree, it would be best to carry the body to the crest of the gorge. However, as it was now night, and thus unusual to risk burying a corpse while foraging spectres were about, Wilkulda sat serenely with the deadness's head on his lap. And being a boy he forgot to wail and scrape his chest raw as was the custom, instead he slept.

At the new day's advent Wilkulda took up the stiffened husk of Tjundaga and began to porter it to the height. This draying of death was onerous and three times he slipped to the stone abrading earth and ponderously the corpse would crash upon the grieving boy. And now Wilkulda did weep and wail and carved cuttings into his flesh that the audience of spirits would observe a mourner's remorse and suffering.

Struggling with the burden, Wilkulda did reach his

destination some two hundred and seventeen feet above the cleft's floor. Upon this higher flatness there was neither wood nor a green thorn, but stones were profuse and with these Wilkulda set himself to make a raised platform. In his laboring the boy did not notice those lands that fronted the entrance to the profound ravine. He saw not, far from his apprentice tomb, the rock plateau that the gorge had sliced into. He did not see the great pan of crimson tinted clay that began beyond the plateau, or the grey and cream dunes that rose at the pan's extremity. Not halting from his efforts Wilkulda noticed neither clay, nor dunes, not the engulfing plains of sulphurous sands that lay beyond the wind-created ridges.

Now the burial mound was several feet into the sky and Wilkulda trusted that grandfather's ghost would be pleased. From Tjundaga's magic wallet the lad secured a palmful of white powder that had been trapped in the bladder creases. With these solitary grains the young man began ritual's obligation. It was a simple rite, he but danced around the catafalque while dropping the granules one by one onto the corpse. If Wilkulda had been a fully degreed Eagle the ceremony would have been quite extensive and undoubtedly Tjundaga's brain would have been drawn out through the nostrils, and the kidney fat taken from the abdomen to read the material for sorcery's crime. However, as he was but a child and not magician he performed none of these obsequies. Conscientiously Wilkulda did try to acquit those rituals that were permissible to one of his untried years. Sadly then, he sang of ancient traditions that the ghost would be aware that the board of Tjundaga would be forever fondled and reflected on. The boy danced vigorously with high knee stampings, and he made many leaps about the bier of rock that the ghost might kindly ignore the inadequacies of the funeral.

Dawn was blossomed with day, light became hotness, yet the adolescent did not slacken in his mourner's duty. In the glared shimmer of day, he a boy alone, on the forelock of the universal desert, generously sang his love for the remains of Tjundaga.

Eventually the sun lost its station in the firmament and fell into its personal grave. Night could not be denied and only now did Wilkulda stop his exertion. The final commitment was to slash long grooves with the flint blade into his facial plumpness, that the scars might appear as the metamorphosed rays of the forsaken sun. Taking grey dust from the earth he rubbed it deeply into the revealed flesh so that the wounds would heal into ridges that would commemorate Tjundaga forever. Finished with the incisions, the lad went close to the corpse there atop the large stones. He went and placed grandfather's spears, spearthrower, pointing stick, and magic utensils next to the cold arms. Wilkulda then wet his fingers in the curling blood flows on his face, and with this eternal pigment he drew the zigzag on the chest of the deadness though he knew not its symbolic meaning.

It was completed except to leave. Wilkulda hoped that he might soon return to this place when Tjundaga's flesh had dropped away, that the bones could be collected and returned to the Eagle people for distribution. Though it was but a virgin moon, thus darkness was bold, Wilkulda departed from the platform of death. He slipped down raw earth to the ravine's base and he slept at once in a sand lode for warmth as he was too weary to strike a fire.

The boy was awake at dawn. An unique decision must be confronted. Should he return home, it would not be difficult to retrace the faint tracks to family and kind, or should he walk on to complete the run into the Eternal Dreamtime lands?

And Wilkulda left behind the place of Tjundaga's putridness and advanced into the scarlet clay, in the opposite direction. All that he took with his nakedness was his destiny and a flint to cut and spark. Wilkulda had not eaten for two days and the only water, besides his own urine, was the slight morning wetness. Yet he dreaded not, for he was an Eagle and such men as these do not die easily in deserts.

He raced across the finite clays, but on entering the weird mounds of alternating hues of sand he could not leap but walked in the plunging softness. By postnoon he had come through this nothingness and entered into the flat swelling of the desert itself. Here ridges of sand exploded intermittently and along lee sides mulga shrubs grew where the slopes protected them from the wind. Among the moisture holding

roots Wilkulda worked to search out a herd of mice, or a
single bandicoot, or even a snake's egg. He dug along foliage
beneath one ridge for several hundred feet without reward
except for bark itself. However, at last he came apon a soft
substance entwined in the unyielding roots. Clawing away
dead stalks and decomposing bark, he found a writhing nest
of white grubs, the finger size witchetty.

Wilkulda swallowed the thick sweet worms convulsively
until he had eaten the entire deposit. And as he squashed the
grubs onto the roof of his mouth Wilkulda felt energy
restored with the rich juices. Refreshed he again leapt upon
the ridge crests. From one arched ball of foot to the other
the boy ran without starvation's dullness. This running
liberated him from anxiety and a surge of persistence spirited
his hopes.

As the sand was shallow on the ridge tops he made rapid
pace this first day without Tjundaga as guide. On this
vaulting firmness he gained thirty-seven miles without
fatigue. The brief dusk became cold on the sand. He had left
the mulga patch behind and with no wood to twirl fire he
again would seal warmth in a sand pit. However, the chill was
too extreme and the boy could not sleep. Now he ran the
desert in the timid light of moon and stars.

Wilkulda was young, but twelve summers and a winter,
thus, quite prideful in his strength. And in the muted dark he
became a swiftness of motion. As the night demons snarled at
the tentative approach of day, the lad searched the land for
some portrait of game but tracks and spoor there were none.
And he ran into the light of the unraveling earth, and he ran
again into the creeping shadow of sun's end. And still
Wilkulda ran.

Being an honest person he put away illusions and accepted
that death was his only companion. Now he was in his fourth
night since finding the witchetty grubs, he had not eaten
since. Water he found twice by digging soaks deeper than was
safe. He struggled to keep the pace but the lack of
nourishment was killing Wilkulda. His frame began to lose its
discipline and his legs began to falter. Then in this fourth
night, when he desired very badly to lie down into the sand's
throat and die, from out of the distance, unseen and far in
the wastes, he heard the fluttering of wings.

At first Wilkulda was afraid to think that food was truly
near. He was unsure of his own existence by now.

But the thrashing vibration of wings came rapidly nearer.
By the sound he thought the food might be a fox-bat, which
was quite large and would provide luscious mouthfuls of flesh.
"Or perhaps it is a *boobook* owl instead," he mused as into
his mind came a picture of a tawny colored bird with white
checked underwings and lustrous eyes unfiltered by
blinkings. "What good will it do me if it is an owl," thought
the lad, "it is a bird of the hunt and will easily evade me, as I
am too weak to rush at it with a stone as I should."

Whistling wings came closer and in Wilkulda's excitement
his steps quickened, no longer languid and hesitant, as if he
had been able to will them to ignore death. Wilkulda sensed
that this would be his last chance, that if he did not have
food now, the Kadaitcha, the ghoul murderer, would come
and sup on his essence.

A sudden magnificence appeared several yards ahead,
flying exactly to Wilkulda. The fowl was but a foot or two
off the flatness that was earth. It was not a mighty owl but
rather a galah, the most beautiful bird in the worlds.
Somewhat like a cockatoo with feathers luxurious in patterns
of white and pink. Normally galahs flew in swirling flocks, it
was not a creature of night. And as the galah is a tree nester,
the lad was surprised to see one in an area where even
petrified trunks were rare. The bird was startling in its
whiteness except where pinked about the head and the lucent
belly and underwings. The wings themselves ended in
single-spaced, extended, feathers of exquisite curvature.

At the first sighting Wilkulda automatically assumed the
pose of a stalking hunter, a figure in absolute stillness. As his
tongue sprayed saliva in thick white beadings onto his gums,
a tremulous shame spread in Wilkulda's soul. For the galah
was brother to the wedgetail eagle, thus cousin to Wilkulda.
The bird was forbidden food to the people of the pool. To
just dream of injuring a galah was dangerous for a boy of the
Eagle mankind.

Yet Wilkulda could not repress the instinct to hunt and to
live. As the bird softly swam in the heavy night atmosphere it
recognized the boy, yet the galah ignored its survival reflex
and glided stilly at the youth. "The bird must be confused,"

thought Wilkulda, "it sees me and is fooled by my quietness and thinks me a sapling tree."

Galah hovered a breath's limit from Wilkulda, then even as it made claws ready to land the bird glanced into the boy's eyes and slipped unhurriedly off to one side. Gentle bird, comely fowl floating, became nervously alert. Slender and delicate in the star's glower, the galah fell away to a space's safety. Incredibly at that instant, there not a stride's length from Wilkulda, a doughty bandicoot stood up into the night.

Could this be? Here in wastelands where food had been non-existent four days and nights, now rodent-marsupial and fair bird came together with Wilkulda as a sequence ending and a cycle renewed. Tiny giant bandicoot, indomitable fighter of hugest eyes, with feet of half-pig, had come nonchalantly up from its burrow to hop into the night and fight the enemy. Enraged was the bandicoot and revengeful.

In day's prosaic brightness Wilkulda would have sighted the burrow at once and enjoyed the bandicoot flesh leisurely. Now in his need, seeing the marsupial, Wilkulda forgot the galah. Thus, he did not see the bird swerve from escape to turn down upon the tiny aggressiveness of soft fur and lovely eyes, for the galah too was dying of starvation, it had been cast into the desert by a cruel wind. Before Wilkulda could react the galah lurched down on the bandicoot.

With daggers the bird burst into the bandicoot's fearlessness. Yet the bandicoot is never eager to die and even as galah struck its beak into the arrogant marsupial's heart the tiny beast reared into the fowl's throat feathers and scissored asunder important blood ducts.

Crying, denied the ecstasy of devouring, the dying galah struggled and flapped to break free. Wilkulda could restrain himself no more. Flinging his right fist he fractured the galah's breast in one blow. Galah thrashed as if to wing somewhere that it might die unmolested, but Wilkulda circled the bird's throat with his fingers and in exaltation tore the fringed head off the neck's socket. Blood of the cockatoo bubbled over Wilkulda. Without dignity the body floundered away from the boy, but Wilkulda did not notice, for he had snatched the bandicoot out of the decapitated head's beak and was swallowing the torn animal unmasticated.

In his frenzy to appease starvation he had not realized that

the brainless galah's body still harbored the will to live. Half
walking, half flying, it's talons scratching grotesquely in the
sands, the remnant bird finally managed to launch itself into
the air.

Abandoning the stripped carcass of the bandicoot,
Wilkulda gave desperate chase after the headless bird. Even as
he ran he chewed feverishly at the galah's head and drew the
brain from its bone casing with crunching teeth. This
glutinous matter was rich and gave heat to his legs. But then
the added strength became unnecessary, for a light breeze
caught under the galah's corpse and flopping wings to turn it
back on its path of senseless escape.

Food in whiteness, harshly scarlet with diminishing life,
came to Wilkulda. A step from the lad the headless corpse
collapsed in lurching confusion. Wilkulda reached down to
the bird, eating even as he first touched it. Blood and meat
were instantly consumed and the boy sat down in the sand to
crack apart each bone for the inner marrow. Soon only the
galah's feathers had not been ingested. As Wilkulda slid the
final intestine down his tongue he rolled into a sand hollow
and slept at once.

Darkened deserts are places of immense magic. Winds die
or spurt with or without cause, and ghouls are resurrected by
the radiant heat of the cooling sands. This night the only
movement is the eaten galah's feathered, splintered, skeleton
ruffled by a current of air, as if disturbed by a gaggle of
ghosts passing in the night.

Dawn steals his sleep and the boy again became the newest
of men. Away he went over the pale orange, muffled, dun
earth. His direction continued on as Tjundaga had forcast. He
ran unaccompanied except by the inchoate sun. In loping
strides he startled tiny, ephemeral, insects of the dying night
into false arousement, but quickly the infinitesimal animals
subsided. Wilkulda could not discriminate the grains of
forfeited life from the desert's costuming.

By midmorning Wilkulda tired and he had to slacken his
pace. Now the land was metallic white and the sands had
coagulated into a surface hardness. He came upon a
depression in the metallic rind where a few square yards of
spinifex had grown in the hollow's protection. The spinifex
was in blue bud and among the new foliage he came upon a
next of alligator eggs five centuries aged from the time a

swamp had lived here in the desert. Wilkulda munched the
material of decay's dust and felt himself nourished. He lay
down in the grass to rest and without realization began to
work his penis into contented erection.

Seeing his hand's creation the lad resisted, yet this delay
would not quiet the pronging penis that still hung stiff over
his navel. He dreamt of the forever lost Kitunga and
surrendered to his manipulating fingers that spurted joy. And
milk fat was jammed high into the sky and then fell heavily
into the desert's deprivation. A wind was rising some leagues
distant to the east as Wilkulda lay in the spinifex and the
minuscule wetness of his milk fat. As he rested with eyes
lidded his mind was stimulated by his milk fat reduction.

Wild thoughts reared in his relaxed mind, "I shall tear from
the Sky bloody gobs as I did to the galah. I am Wilkulda who
killed his grandfather by wickedness. How can Tjundaga be
dead? Lillywur will not understand, everything is my fault.
Everyone said I was to be a great man. Several wives were
already bound to me, promised favors. Sky, I want my penis
back, oh why did I promise? I was supposed to be a great
man and Tjundaga was going to teach me all his
secrets . . . Sky, I ate a sacred galah and only a fully initiated
man may kill one for its feathers but its flesh can never be
eaten by anyone. How grandfather would wail if he knew I
ate a galah. I was so hungry. Sky, I am so ashamed. My sister
is dead, Tjundaga is dead, I ruined the circumcisional ritual,
and I ate a galah."

As he drew his knees up into his chest, Wilkulda did not
hear the blackening clouds in the eastern sky, as all his senses
were preoccupied with guilt. A sombre silence announced the
earth's dread of the monstrous storm that was rising. The
storm's first chilling wheeze swept across the huddled youth
to awake his awareness. At once the wind ripped open the
spinifex buds and snatched off the immature blue petals.
Wilkulda believed the flailing winds to be the Sky's reply to
his lament. And he saddened for he had hoped that the Sky
would have helped him atone the shame. Swiftly rain and ice
darts began to strike the desert in sadistic cresendos, and
aroused the boy's determination. The circumcised male stood
up and turned to view the eruption of the sky. He was
astounded at the storm's dimensions.

Sometimes a decade or even three decades might pass without this particular desert fondling a single droplet of rain. And this storm was as ten centuries pent up deluge, and easily it surpassed the mists indigenous to the rainforests of Ypres. Wilkulda began to run away from the electrified billowings.

Hog winds spewed the empty wastes with gouging destruction. Spurting columns of rain snaked violently in the sky and the planet was barraged with ice bombs. For a hundred English leagues to the south and a hundred to the north, the serrating winds harrassed the Eternal Dreamtime lands. And the storm caught up to the running Wilkulda and abraded his skin with peppering wounds.

Darkness was on the wastes as the storm battled the sky for mastery. The youth continued to run but he was only a tiny stick in all the world's turbulence, a thistle's spore gusted to incomprehensible heights and unexplored regions. Unseen sky wept cascading rain even as the storm ate the light of earth. Falls of chilled water geysered downward mud volcanoes. Fragmented was the universe as the rain became a nascent flood washing away the ground beneath the boy's hurtling feet. Burned out soil, dead for too long, became an ocean without hope. The boy's charging knees were swallowed by the funneling waters. The flood was a cloying semen tugging him to death below the torrents. The rapids bullied Wilkulda and he forsaw his coming death by drowning.

Waters lifted him off the land and the liquid stung his abraded skin. Cool waters acted as a cathartic and he urinated a slight cloud of denseness. As he urinated, in this release of being, he forgot survival and allowed the flood to rush greedily into his mouth. Yet he vomited the flood out of his body and he swam. Wilkulda's lungs filled with water in spite of his spitting and his limbs were outraged by the battering of the flood. Still he did not drown. He swam the flood into the dusk of the sluiced day. And night joined with the storm and the boy was nearly finished, when with a terrific fright he crashed against a solidness huge crested in the rushing water. Terrified, Wilkulda moaned as he believed a ghoul had reached up from the depths to murder him. But touching the object again, he discovered that it was a gigantic root of some ancient redgum, shoveled up from its tomb by the flood.

Elated by his find, Wilkulda lifted himself up into the exposed maze and entwined his thin form in the root's parts above the flooding, squeezing himself deep into a fork tight enough to support his exhausted being. The root, twenty cubits in diameter, rode the water with remarkable stability and the lad was soon asleep.

As night matured the flood carried the root and its captive into the inner sanctums of the desert where no man had ever penetrated before Wilkulda. Rain stopped somewhat before dawn and at once the flood began to disperse itself in an ever broadening swath over the wastes.

When the boy awoke he saw that he was afloat on an expanse several fathoms deep. Floating alongside the root came any number of drowned lizard and mice, on these he feasted. The flood's momentum carried Wilkulda yet deeper into the Dreamtime lands. Thus rafted on the new sea, his tendril swarm drifted on this day and again a night. On the second dawning, the passenger of the redgum root found that the sea was already leaking away into the flatness.

The root mired and came to a halt as the vanishment of the waters accelerated. Timidly Wilkulda tested the water's depth and found it not above his thighs. And he set out through the miniature ocean as a wader. All this day he plodded westward as the level of the water receeded to his shins. At dusk he came upon a hillock crowned with spinifex in fullest bloom, and here, in comparative dryness, he made his meager camp, even igniting a tender fire of water deposited twigs.

Harshest light awoke Wilkulda at midmorning and as the boy sat up and viewed the world he saw that the now bankrupt flood had delivered unto the desert a rare garden. Flowers regal and obscure, labyrinths of exotic hue, stalks and stems joined to embroider the wastes with an exquisite burgeoning that had vanquished the endemic sterility.

Purple nipples guarded by coves of yellow caressed blue leaves and petals. Ringlets of red bulbs stroked into virility by white-pink fronds, all protected by a green heather, that tangled with the desert sky. Wilkulda stood a moment to reconcile his mind to the harvest of marvels and then left the sand hump to walk bedazzled among the living plants. As far ahead as behind he could see the profusion of flowers. Already a hum of tiny insect legs was emitted by the herds of cicada whose elderly eggs had been fertilized by the warming flood.

Wilkulda continued to track westward. Everywhere the flood had fructified fields and the air was thick with reborn spirits. To the flowers his fingers plucked ceaselessly as he dined on the scentless bounty. The desert blooms seemed all without odor. In his mouth the coolness of the squashed plants liquified to assuage thirst. The flood had impregnated the mummified seeds of an age long trapped by the discarding sands. Excepting the transformed insects, Wilkulda was animal alone in the garden of the flood's aftermath. Nowhere in the endless bogs of flower did there appear a shadow. Treeless, ridgeless, plateauless; the spavined land chewed the living wetness dry. Alone and weaponless, Wilkulda strode the magic flowers of the flood. Sun had filtered the water's mist from the air and was even now recapturing the desert. Wilkulda, the first human searcher in these lands, was happy and even giddy with the juice of the petals as he marched. Night and sleep arrived and he dreamt that he was a blue heron steering out of the sky into a lake's glade, there to copulate with a galah.

False dawn awoke the boy and he observed that the garden was dying. He sought among the dead plants for those living flowers not yet refossilized. As the sun unhinged itself from night and began its circuit, Wilkulda thrust legs energetically westward. And on this particular day, after a meager harvest of shrinking plant stems, when yesterday's posterity had faded, the Sky Father came to visit the lone adolescent who raced the wasteland. Wilkulda noted first only that the flat desert was gradually giving way to a rising ahead.

Moody studs of titanic rock poked upwards from a plateau's decayed ravine. Stilted tall were thousands of phallic boulders gathered close on one another in this vale of mystery. Each penis rock portended efficacious magic. None is less than forty feet high while the tallest project themselves two hundred feet boldly upward like sky trees. This then was the very nucleus of the Eternal Dream, this host of granite penises proclaimed the beginning creation's proximity. In these very studs the Ancestor Spirits had been germinated by the Sky Father. And now in a primal encounter, a man strutted into this universal womb to be transformed.

Beyond the plateau a vermilion hued escapement rose up, mellowed in tincture only by the faint rainbow that was etched on its bulk. The predominant color of this place was an ochred, dulled red. Here in this place of primitive procreation did Wilkulda arrive at mid-day. And as if in a drama's bidding the winds slowed the revolving of earth, and in a world of rivers a few priests became aware that beneath the axis of the cosmos a choosing had taken place.

Now the lad, Wilkulda, became aware of an abounding strangeness. For there, by the Sky's hugest genital, near left of a grove of stubby limestone thrusts, there in the promiscuous center of the universal penises, the Entity could be seen in its enormity. A claw's nail, ripened white, coiled on the earth's loam.

The boy had not yet spied the Eagle perched on the two loftiest rocks, as his soul was gravely excited by the penises themselves. He wished Tjundaga had lived to witness the splendor of the Dream's womb. But then the lad finally was stopped by the hint of a shadow. Looking sunward, Wilkulda saw the Sky Father. At once Wilkulda began to singdance with heaviest emotion.

> *"The Sky Dreamer gave*
> *his Blood Penis a*
> *Circumcision Rare,*
> *"Wonder at the Dreaming Wanderer*
> *who Gifted the First Penis,*
> *"Wonder at the Dreamer Sky*
> *who Favored men with*
> *the Penis and Blood,*
> *"Wonder at the Hugeness*
> *of the Sky Penis,*
> *"Wonder at the Eagle*
> *who is the Sky's*
> *Metamorphosed Penis."*
> *"Wonder at the Universal Penis*
> *that is the Sky."*

And the Eagle was pleased, and he viewed Wilkulda as a noble communicant. And the Eagle was not angry with the boy for he, the Sky Father, had not abandoned Wilkulda, and indeed, he loved the grandson of Tjundaga. The lad stared transfixed as does the mouse who watches in trauma's protective blindness as the hawk's talon breaks the membrane to consummate existence's second marriage of death. The youth wondered if the Eagle would swallow him quickly in one mouthful or spear him into the land with a peck to create a blood soak. Father Sky came to lean out above Wilkulda, and the bird's regality inspired the boy and he wanted to sing again but it seemed inappropriate and he did want to behave with exact correctness for the sake of Tjundaga's training.

The Spirit Bird cocked its head toward Wilkulda and then without sign or shriek of explanation the Eagle wept. The Sky Spirit permitted himself one, inner-rayed, emblazoned tear to roll from lid to beak to pour down in an avalanche of pure wetness. The huge tear sailed downward with an audible sigh, enveloping Wilkulda and drenching him to his original soul, even as the Eagle tilted its extravagant profile upward into its empire. From the Sky Father's beak rushed out a moaning of joyful sorrow. To Wilkulda it seemed as if a newer soul had been infused into every cell of his structure, as if the teardrop had unstained his past shame and washed bitterness away. The air above the two, boy and God, was flamed light as if the sun had settled to rest on one of the infinite penises. The Father thought Wilkulda beautiful in his tear raiment, and every watching Spirit, the Ant and Termite too, also believed that Wilkulda was radiant. For the lad indeed was in a state of creation, he was a newness upon the land.

The tear's magic had unshackled Wilkulda's insight and he entered into canted corners that had been but faint mysteries previously. He was immensely grateful for the miraculous drop of wet as it had created simplicity where fear's dread had settled before. The Eagle was justly proud and in approbation he began to gently step from claw to claw upon the penises, as if performing a dance that applauded the boy.

The Spirit bent low and whispered so that the universe could hear, "Come next to me, child. Closer, for I wish to

inspect tomorrow's embyro. All else had failed but thee,
Wilkulda. You are strangely new, even I did not guess at your
new strangeness. You represent my last arrow and you must
pierce the target that is peculiar man. I have been waiting
ages, ages of frustration, futile ages, long even for a creator,
and I am impatient for an ending. Come my chick, my egg's
fruit, come to me and I shall recite my eternal puzzlement
into thee. We are weary, despondent and weary, and some
spirits, as the Whale, are melancholy. We need some slight
success to renew our hope, for it would be shameful if all our
efforts are seeds that never sprout. You, Wilkulda, shall be
our victory over the cannibals. You are the child of superb
sorcery, of redundant chant and mystic song."

Blackness of stretched skin, of anus, of ear's ornate
intricacies, all that was Wilkulda smiled in rare intimacy. The
boy came to stand joyfully beneath the Spirit's oceanic
breast, near the Eagle's wetted eye. Closer he was to the very
Sky Father, close to him who had birthed the original earth.
This was the very Spirit that had stroked the pregnant shell
with its famed penis until the calcium walls cracked and fell
down to reveal profuse life.

Birthing egg-earth had not enervated the Eagle, nor the
lesser Spirits who had performed as midwives. But
afterwards, when man came, they had wished to loom away,
even as a great iron ship suddenly veers too late to avoid
collision with unchartable iceberg, from their arduous work
and see respite in the sheltered reaches of the dying, birthing
universe. Multitudes of forms and mentalities had been
prodded into dominance before man came onto the land.
Man seemed to have potential but he proved peculiarly
nervous. And in despair the Spirits began to enact miracle
after miracle in attempt to stimulate man if not into
enlightment than into quiescence. Eventually the Spirits,
overwrought as they were, forgot that their dream was
fantasy and took some men past death that these few might
stand in awe of life and crown ordinary man with
thankfulness. Alas, this also failed.

Things did not improve and the Spirits suffered. Yet earth
still desired a fond husband as a procreator, that it might
reproduce itself. The Eagle, though stirred by the beseeching
Spirits, would not release them from their commitment to

earth. The lesser Spirits had surrendered faith in attempting perfection and now they only wished to leave the place in some sort of harmony.

Man was the single animal on earth not created in the image of one of the Spirits. Mighty winged lizards, fabulous mice, fishes improbable, all had Sky progenitors, all but man. Man had no Spirit of his own and it was said in the Sky that man's parents had been an elderly baboon and a young, unworldly, bandicoot. Whatever the disputed parentage, man was cruel. Yet man learned not to mate with his daughters and was the only species to refrain from this. And it was true that in spite of man's innate savagery, he did become aware at last of the Eternal Dream's existence. After an age or three the Spirits viewed man as a beast who thrived on suffering, although a beast with a protean mentality. Man luxuriated in cruelty and the Spirits wondered if the species was incurably defective. Yet there was something of worth that persisted in men, for a few rarest grains of gentleness were observable. And it was with these rare individuals that the Sky had decided to share its burden.

Everywhere the universe hesitated in its respiration and marveled at the wonderment of the Sky Father mated to the boy living in the teardrop. Death paused throughout the universe as the two blended their souls. Patiently the Eagle had waited for this day when the first grain of gentleness was to be sown among the tribes. And the Sky Father was exquisitely moved by the courage of Wilkulda who would be his messenger.

Peering into Wilkulda's tear roofed awareness the Spirit spoke: "I am fatigued. Yes, even those of the Sky, those who created the Dream, may feel impotent and cousined to humiliation. But now I possess you, you shall be my messenger. We of the Sky have worked overlong with man and must have respite. We have devoted our wills and love, that a species of merit might be birthed as gardener to our earth. I for one am still confident that man can be that cultivator, although I admit, he seems to wallow in brutality. We believe that a special person, as you Wilkulda, may be able to cure mankind of cruelty. Through your life we hope to implant a new idea in the souls of men. You will teach man forgiveness. Forgiveness will instruct men that they may forget cruelty. In order that men, who are perpetually distrustful, may listen and perhaps abide your instruction we have decided to invest unique magic into your being. Magic that will be remembered throughout the Dream's time, that creatures trapped in frustration on our egg shall respond ecstatically to the very mention of your name."

The Eagle, still taloned to the red columns, lowered its tremendous bulk directly over the boy and with the swiftest of lancements the Spirit pierced his own massive penis that a fount of blood did come to shield the Sky from the land. Instinctively, Wilkulda standing in the tear drop, fell down and covered his head with cradling arms as the foamed geyser descended onto the tear, washing it away and coating the boy's person with the Eagle's blood.

Wilkulda lay in a widening pond of penis blood and the Sky Father, after some moments, commanded the spouting of his blood to cease. And the Sky Father gaped his beak that the tongue of ochered hues exploded from within to scour the soaked boy. Finished with Wilkulda's absolution the Eagle rose from the Dreamtime land to loft to the universal boundaries. Earth was eclipsed by his lingering shade until the Sky Father redeemed his shadow from earth. Wilkulda was metamorphosed. Mysteries and lesser truths he now understood. He knew what his role of messengerhood implied. Fulfilled in his transformation, he stood up in a caking globe of blood and went to the pillars the Eagle had perched upon. Here in the sand between he washed his skin black.

Alone again on the desert of clotted rock studs, scrubbed and changed, Wilkulda contemplated his response to his new destiny. First, it was obvious, he must return to the lands of the pool, to seek out his father, Lillywur, and begin to instruct his own mankind. Without remorse or deceit he gaited east, southeast down to the world of the Eagle-men, re-creating his path's faint trace across the wilderness. Quickly he repassed the place of Tjundaga's burial, but as the lad was in haste to initiate his new role he momentarily rested to weep a little at the base of the height and then continued on.

## three

Centuries had been shattered and husked and chewed
when Kalod, who had served Wilkulda for many seasons,
spoke to a smallish horde of exceptionally tall and heavily
muscled elders in a northern coastal world where there were
many interesting details. Kalod was now a tiny man after
four hundred and thirty-seven years of defecation, urination,
mastication, and prophethood. Thus and indeed, he had
withered. Yet his skull was firmly implanted with a thicket of
white hair which was complemented by a voluminous hoary
beard. As Kalod orated to the Crocodilemen, secretly he
thought of past things. Of that first day when Wilkulda had
healed men in the sea, when the crippled and diseased had
been healed.

The event Kalod remembered best was when a blind infant
had been raised into the Sky on Wilkulda's hands. A girl born
blind was a frightful omen and normally such malformity
ended in instantaneous suffocation for the infant. However, a
male child without eyes might be considered as marked with
magic as he would be able to enter the places where the dead
spirits congregated without harm coming to his being. A girl
so bred was monstrous and thus dreaded. Memory of that sea
dawning when Wilkulda held the girl babe by her neck and
ankles and lifted the she-thing high, existed in Kalod's mind
even as his tongue spoke to the Crocodiles of responsibility on
that older morning, Wilkulda had moaned as his silent cure
was effected, and as he had uttered this painful croon the
illumination that circled his head had blossomed to flood the
beach with a special radiance. And the clustering of watching
mankinds, and those persons waiting in the tide to be healed,
also moaned in concert. And on the infant's entrance into the
Sky World, in the hands of Wilkulda, her hollow scones had
been filled full with gurgling, lavish eyes. At this creation, the
multitudes on cliff and beach had cast skyward a paean of
triumph. It was a simple matter to view the babe's new eyes

as they were reflected in Wilkulda's light. And the messenger
had taken the child into the Sky a second time that the Sky
might share the joy.

But Kalod had work to do here among the Crocodile-men
and he tore his mind from the beautiful memory to speak a
forceful peroration to a tale of forgiveness. But Kalod was
older now than ancientness, and he was satiated with his own
lectures. The little magician permitted his mind to flow back
again in memories of Wilkulda as his tongue labored among
the Crocodiles. For endless decades, Kalod had associated
himself totally with the sorrow of the Sky Messenger, yet the
Eagle people's rejection of Wilkulda still grieved Kalod and he
mused on the oddness of men.

On his return from the wastelands to the tribal camp, again
cycled back to the pool in those months of his epic run, the
people had welcomed Wilkulda not. They greeted him as a
pariah, a ghoul who still presumes to live as a man when an
honorable ghost would have admitted death. His mankind
realized not that the lad entering their camp had been
transformed into a newness, he then possessed no light about
his head. Wilkulda studied their faces beneath false
expressions of composure. Thus, at once, he learned that he
was a stranger and no longer remotely a favored person.
Though a metamorphosed newness, the boy was unprepared
and depressed by the miasma of hostility.

Wilkulda had expected the tribe to be eager to share his
adventure and to be made aware of his novel magic, and of
the new idea. The lad had not considered the
self-incrimination of appearing alone, without Tjundaga.
Standing mute in their united distrust, their nakedness a
shield to their emotions, the council of elders intently stared
as Wilkulda approached the rise they had assembled on.

The Eagles had known of his returning some days back
when a hunting party had spied him running below his dust
cumulus. The emu hunters, ladened with their weapons and
with nets and dizzy powder for the bird's watering places had
collectively decided not to go to the boy's assistance but to
give up their quest for the delicious fowls and to report the
sighting, and the absence of Tjundaga, to the council.

A clump of whitegums blocked the view of the deep worn
path that rounded slowly up to the rock contained pool. An

invisible, earth imprisoned, spring exhaled its water into the sculptured basin and all about was fat greenness, although the indigenous mankinds remained severely gaunt even when encamped about their precious water source. Wilkulda had paced the spring rebirthed sun up to the camp. The smokings from the fire made Wilkulda admit to himself how much he had missed his home when still ten miles distant. It was quite early in the day when he entered into the camp grounds and happily observed that the entire mankind was awake to greet him, except he noted ominously that the women and children had been sent to the area's fringes as if for safety.

Lillywur, his father, stepped out alone and somewhat in front of the grouping of astonished elders. He spoke as if he might have been practicing his words since the creation of the Dream itself, "Who are you? If you are Mamu the deceiver demon, who eats the souls of sleeping children, then know that we have magic to hurt you."

"Father what do you mean? It is me, Pilala, I mean Wilkulda. I am your eldest son."

"If that is fact then where is Tjundaga my father and father to this people?" Indeed, as a ritualized sorcerer, handsome Lillywur had an obligation to quiz any person or object in a manner he deemed appropriate to the circumstances. However, to use such accusatory language and grimaces to a thing that might still prove itself to be a son was rare and quite prejudicial.

" . . . grandfather is dead," quaked the nervous boy, "and his ghost is content and I think I did the right songdances and bloodied my face and chest with cuts and wailed and groaned a very long time where I buried him."

" . . . dead, he is dead . . . Have you murdered my father, you dirty ghoul. And it was you who caused my valuable daughter to be speared, and you couldn't even lay down like a real man." Then Lillywur turned away from Wilkulda to address the elders, "We have given the Sky our finest rituals, and look at our reward." Lillywur turned again to the boy, "How could you kill the world's greatest man, our best father since the Dream began?"

This last came with a sorrowful wail and runnels of tears even as Lillywur debated no longer the future of the object before him. Although debased by the words of his father,

Wilkulda replied as the new man, as the messenger, "Sir, I am your oldest son and I will never be less than that. Call me never ghoul again, or murderer, for I am the messenger chosen by the Sky Father. It is certain that I am to be the teacher of forgiveness and the one to reveal cruelty's existence. I am the digging stick of tomorrow's fruit, I contain magic in my kidney that can chastise even the winds."

Not intimidated and not reproved, a hysterical Lillywur shrieked out at the chagrined Wilkulda, "My real son is murdered and you are a ghoul, a horrible ghoul who has only assumed the shape of my dead boy. But we Wedgetails know how to deal with such as you. Our magic is twice as powerful as any that a brute like you can have."

And Wilkulda felt fear in his stomach, for he was now aware that the council had judged him as an evilness even before he had returned to the camp. The Eagle-men viewed him as the arch-defiler of circumcision and as the ghoul that had pointed the sorcerer's pointing bone that had slain Tjundaga. However, Wilkulda even in his terror could not divest himself of his new magic and he spoke out authoritatively, "I am Wilkulda and my spirit is answerable only to the Sky Eagle. The Sky World has arranged me into an original intactness. If you will only allow me I shall confer forgiveness unto all of you."

Again Lillywur of the nobly bulged brow and the proud eyes refused the meaning of his child's words. Shoving his own pointing stick into the youth's face, he shouted, "How clever you are, fart-mouth. You lie, you blowing ghoul. Don't speak the name of the Great Penised Eagle for you defile the Sky with your lips of offal and your tongue of urine. Awful ghost, you are a stenched sacrilege to proper males." Raising his spear as if command to the other elders, Lillywur raged, "We must kill this weirdness. Here, step back, make room, all of us together fling our spears into this strange ghoul. Be careful not to hit one another."

As the council reared to cast their spears, Wilkulda appalled by his father's pronouncement, bounded pridefully to where Lillywur stamped the land with angry feet, and in anger seized his parent's spear from stunned hands. Wilkulda balanced the weapon on his fingers and with three leaps hurled the spear into the dinged sky of the wet season.

Watching, the tribe cowered as the shocking, abnormal, flight of the spear cleft the horizon. The mankind understood at last that serious magic lived in the lad. The elders attempted to chase the women and children from the site, but the spear had worked its route beyond the punctured sky and a ponderous velocity of cold, heavy wind flowed down upon the heated depression that was the land. Gigantic booms caused the women and children to huddle miserably, howling abjectly, like puppies thrown into cooking pits. And a dreading Lillywur did believe that an ogre had been summoned by the weird ghoul that inhabited his son's form.

The drumming intensified and the mankind of three hundred elders believed that their world was being squeezed back into its hidden Dream bowels. Even the children recognized that Wilkulda indeed was a potency, a living magician who could bid the Rainbow Snake to come forth from its daytime places of sleep. Snake of misty fantasy appeared rarely and only at the beckoning of master sorcerers. If not propitiated carefully the Snake would eat the world and defecate it out metamorphosed, perhaps without men.

An earthquaking of severe trembles had been released by Wilkulda and mercilessly the quake fell upon the nude trotters of the pool world. Massive slabs of sheared mantle rose from their sockets to slam down and slay any creature of soft blood who might be trapped. Ruptured ground assaulted the eye of man and the bucking land taunted the arrogance of the powerful elders. Bloated sun cast loose from its dragging sky anchor to careen toward insignificant man. The sky's fire crashed to earth and blazed the universe with a harsh furnacing. The land swelled and rolled apart, exposing to man's view the rust stretched layers of blue clay and crusted, green, gravel. The females present profoundly understood their fate, they were to be killed by the murderous magician, Wilkulda. The elders held fast to the faith that Wilkulda was not of man but was ghoul. Even in their terror there were a few elders who believed themselves hunters and dared the fate of the capsized sun by thrusting their spears at the moving shelves of earth, as if they might wound or slay the quaking.

Infants, girls and boys, clawed to female buttocks as the land emitted clenched grievances. Not one person dared to raise his eyes to the single solid, rock island where the sobbing Wilkulda waited. The tribe clung to the shuddering earth, digging fingers and toes into the quivering loam. At last Wilkulda could suffer no more of his people's terror and stretched upward into the infinite void where his father's weapon had stuck into the outer rim of the sky. At his tug the wood lance fell out and drifted down to the Dreamtime earth. And harmony cloistered the land as Wilkulda plucked the sun from its foreign grave and tapped it eagerly back into its sovereign circuit.

Planet's shivering extended several instants before men realized that they had been reprieved. Males re-established their upright postures while their throats startled out stunned gasps and astonished, "huhs." The elders were amazed that Wilkulda had not slain them when the opportunity had been available. Mercy dumbfounded the elders, for each and every one of them would have carried the quake to conclusion., except that they would have undoubtedly spared their own families and the youngest, prettiest females available. The elders viewed kindness as a flaw, they saw Wilkulda as irrevocably imperfect as a man, or even as a ghoul. They had insulted and degraded him to the utmost by denying his person as man, yet he had exhibited pity. He could not kill, he was flawed.

Wilkulda was in despair. Although he was disappointed with the people, he was despondent with himself. He had brandished his anger's punishment and Wilkulda berated himself for straying from forgiveness. He held the once sky-glided spear in hand and now the earth was budgeted with security. Sky was swept clean of dust and the blueness became ambiguous as always. In false obsequiousness the elders laid their weapons to earth and whispered to Lillywur that pacification would do and that killing the ghoul was unnecessary as it was a womanly beasty.

Lillywur was beset with jealousy. Tjundaga was dead. He should be the greatest man of the Eagles, yet his uninitiated, awkward spawn had superseded him with intolerably big magic. Wilkulda's father saw the messenger as an abnormal specimen who by unnatural method had acquired magic beyond contemporary scope.

As the boy watched the cringing subterfuge of the elders he thought, "It has started all wrong." But he fitted a mask of sternness over the truth of his lonely immaturity. And yet, he was old enough to sense in Lillywur's hostility a future scorning by those who he wished to best love him. He commanded the tribe to stop their wailing. Gently then he spoke to his father, softly rebuking him for failing to identify his true son. And shyly Wilkulda returned the spear to distinguished Lillywur even as the people ridiculed both in their secret minds. Namana, his mother, he observed defending his own reality in a cluster of deprecating hags. His mother's defense gave Wilkulda heart and he smiled at the arguing woman, but this strange expression of tenderness only caused suspicious silence among the females, including Namana.

With a self-defensive hotness, Lillywur dismissed the tribe, commanding them to go and concern themselves with normal preoccupations while he discussed serious matters with, "Wilkulda, my son." Gratefully the people fled, although several of the big men did not completely leave but instead walked in pairs some distance from where father and son stood. These elders pretended disregard for the pair as they spied on the weirdness.

"My great parent is dead, you say," said Lillywur, "and you now possess excessive sorcery. Well, I do not charge that there is a connection between his death and your novel powers, but it is fact that these coincidences cry out for explanation. I loved your grandfather well, too well perhaps. I am not like the average son who only wishes to see their fathers dead that they might inherit the old fellow's women, and the power that the female distribution brings. It is none of your concern but I have already divided my parent's wives and daughters as I saw fit. Obviously you are my true son. I was just testing your fitness as a newly circumcised man. After your coming seasons in the bush, for you will continue to be made a man by the initiations, you shall return to my fires and be known as my child. However, in all things I expect respect or you will be exiled. The mirage of the earthquake proves to me that you did reach the Eternal lands as my father planned. You must have stolen big magic from there. Oh, don't deny it, what person could resist such

temptation? Whatever the weirdness of it all, you have
become a great man before your penis is trully prepared and
years before your septum is to be pierced. Well no matter,
you will take your place in the initiate's camp under the
instruction of Uncle Mushabin. Remember to keep away
from the females, including your mother, even I could not
protect you from the council's spears if you did forbidden
acts with any woman.

"Now, let's get some information that makes sense. I
presume that somehow, without my guidance, you satisfied
the frustrations of the ghost of my father or it would be
among us now creating baseness in men. Young man, I had
not intended to exacerbate the situation but I can not
contain myself. Why, when you had the opportunity to
humiliate or even harm the elders during the quake and
afterwards, did you let them off without punishment?
. . . What, what did you say Wilkulda? Forgiveness, what is
forgiveness? What sacrilege do you spit out now? Why do you
throw up this forgiveness? It is like when a dingo crawls
unashamed with the body of his father half-devoured in his
blood stunk jaws . . . Think of the favors you might have
controlled if you had only prolonged the quake, or at least
crushed a few women under those blocks of snapping stone,
if it was at all real. Why you could have been promised
twenty wives if you had handled it in a mature manner. You
should have squeezed them until they begged you to marry
their youngest daughters. I can only conjecture why the Sky
permitted you to possess such magic, a weakling like you.
Why, you hardly shamed me after I condemned you to death
by calling you a ghoul, or rather by suggesting that you
might, might, not be quite, quite, normal. Wilkulda you
certainly must change if you want to be the great man that
your magic entitles you to be."

Wilkulda listened respectfully to Lillywur's lecture but in
his mind he chafed at his father's words. "What does he know
of the Sky Father's torment," thought the boy. And
Lillywur's casual dismissal of forgiveness burned in his
stomach. Then, when finally he raised his eyes to stare up at
his handsome father, Wilkulda realized that the man was
expecting some reply. Deciding not to dare eloquence or
authority, Wilkulda simply said, "Father, the Sky Eagle

decided to invest the future of men to my magic."

But such passivity only exasperated Lillywur, and he snorted, "Well, you are the end. The Sky Spirit invested, huh, well if that isn't heresy I don't know what is. My old father probably began your path to insanity, you can't be blamed for all of it . . . Now, let's get a few things settled. I admit you're my son, I will publicly proclaim this. Now, your grandfather was the archetype Eagle, no doubt about it. However, you must understand that in these last ten or so seasons his dream of a great manhood for you became an obsession. And while we're discussing his peculiarities, as he got older, your grandfather became overly attached to the Sky Eagle to the exclusion of the other Spirits, and he relegated them to minor creatures. This was certainly an absurdity on his part. We of the council believe this attitude might have angered the Sky World and brought on us the disgrace at the Holy Cave as the result of their displeasure."

" . . . the Sky Eagle gave me a message, father," interposed Wilkulda.

"what, what . . . who gave you what?"

"the Eagle, he . . . "

"Shut up you little fool, I heard you, what a profane idea, even taking your magic into account this is all insanity. All right let's hear it all. What is this message, what is the meaning of it all?" queried Lillywur of his son who would be the healer.

"Father, it is my responsibility to teach men that cruelty abounds and that only cruelty can kill cruelty but that forgiveness can make men forget how to create the beginning cruelty; but first I have to teach men what cruelty is and how to know its spoor," did the boy conclude. " . . . ah,ah, how very fascinating, nicely said indeed. You must tell me more about it, at a more convenient time. Now, to important things. How did your grandfather's face look after death strangled him? Was it contorted or afraid as after an episode with murder magic sorcered on the poor old fool by some son-of-a-bitch? Probably it was one of those Mallee Hen-men who killed him. Just because our northern neighbors possess a part of our creation ritual they think that they can get away with anything . . . I sense that you are entirely innocent of his murder. It must have been the Mallees who sorcered your grandfather dead. Now, remember carefully, tell me about it all so that I can discover exactly who did the sorcery. When we raid the Mallees we have to know which one to kill," said Lillywur.

" . . . but father, he seemed to have died very happily. His face was fat and young. There was not hate in any crease, in truth he seemed quite pleased about one thing or another."

"What nonsense you do invent, stupid boy. Now, let's get on with it. Did you find any strange stain or spot in any of his orifices? You did examine him for such, didn't you? It was your duty even though your penis is not full grown. You did spread open his orifices and explore, didn't you?" implored Lillywur.

"Yes father, I did widen his rectum and penis holes to see if the sign of witchery was present. I found no impression of a hair, or a tooth, or a fingernail in any hole. I pried open his dead, sweet smelling, jaws and pulled long his tongue to the roots but there was no disorder there either. Afterwards I filled every orifice with sand, as you showed me, to drown any evil ghost. The corpse made not a noise of disapproval. I did everything I could, the best that I could do alone. I did my best and I loved him," sadly finished Wilkulda.

"Did you not examine his kidney fat," inquired Lillywur.

"Father, I am far too young for such secret rites. It is forbidden to peer in at the kidney fat unless you are a fully degreed elder."

"But of everything that was most important! We know nothing unless we know how much fat was stolen and from which side by the Mallee killer. That would have provided the information we needed to point out the murderer. You broke so many forbidden laws, at least you could have ignored this so I could have peace of mind and not be forced to send sorcery indiscriminately against every Mallee, as I will have to do now. Oh well, you are such a failure already, in such brief years too, it is what I should expect. Where did you bury him, what kind of tree was it? Remember exactly where you left him, for you realize that some day I must go there and collect his bones . . . yes, in a season I will go to father and carry his skeleton home where every elder may have a bit," nobly said Lillywur, true son of Tjundaga.

Solemnly responded Wilkulda, "If there had been any kind

of tree, or even a mulga about, I would have placed the body in it. But there was nothing but the gorge. I carried him high there. It was very high and empty there and he will be safe."

"Well, I suppose that you could not do more than take him high. You say you did dancesing, and I see by the red scars that you visibly mourned him. If it had been too execrable a burial I suppose his ghoul would have been bothering us by now," shuddered the elder.

"Father, I loved him . . . Father, the Sky Father came to me and spilled his essence into my soul, and into me he shouted for help."

"What probably really happened was that you created an imperfect dream during your sleep right after your grandfather died. Well, every important sorcerer must have his magic dream, perfect or not. But please stop making an issue about the Eagle's interest in you or the Rainbow Snake will be angered. Besides, you are much too emotional, it is unseemly. You have been circumcised, show some restraint, remember you will be an Eagle soon."

"The Sky Father came to me! He spoke to me! He touched my being with his being, he gave me a duty I must excel in! He is very sad about men. He made me see cruelty. He gave me forgiveness to transform everyone," implored the lad.

And Wilkulda's words now firmly penetrated Lillywur's pride. The elder, grey with quake's dust; hair, jowls, ears, all feathered with beige-grey curd, skin everywhere greying except where sweat had made dark creases in the body folds, Lillywur became afraid, in his vitals of the boy Wilkulda. For he realized that indeed the lad had voyaged into lands where a visitation by an Ancestor Spirit might have taken place. Lillywur desired to run away, as he had sighted imponderable changes that would be wrought by Wilkulda. Changes that were queer and not of man's way. Yet before this feeling of fear, Lillywur was a warrior and he must stay to speak in dignity, "I will hear no more. It is quite abnormal, all of it."

Lillywur paused to urinate into the earth. He momentarily studied the patterns the liquid created in the dust, murmuring to himself; "It is too bad the old man died. I could use his insight into the meaning of all this queerness. Cruelty, forgiveness, what kind of words are these? Yes, I

need father, even this peculiar lad sees through my bluff,"
then Lillywur stopped to begin again in a louder, firmer,
voice, "tell me again about this . . . message."

With a fog of hope in his throat Wilkulda said, "I am to
make men aware of cruelty and when they know what
cruelty is they will run to possess forgiveness. I am to
metamorphose cruelty into forgiveness."

Lillywur coughed and spit a phlegm of sheer white down
to the place of the urine's lingering dampness, as if to purge
his throat even as he had emptied his bladder. "There's no
sense to this thing, 'forgiveness,' I can't understand, 'cruelty,'
at all . . . My son, a strange spirit has entered your soul and I
am not competent to judge its merit. We must forget your
message for a season or two, and, yes, come back to it
another time when we are both deeper in wisdom. Don't ever
mention your message to anyone else. They might take fright
and spear you too quickly for you to work countering magic.
You shall go to the camp and join the other initiates. Uncle
Mushabin is there even now. Yes, it will be good. You will
live by your own little fire and eat only the food of the
newly circumcised. The old men will prepare you for an
elder's responsibility. Yes, it will be good. It will be good."

As father and son were leaving to go to Mushabin Namana
ran up to her son and in obdurate silence handed him the
magic phallic fringe she had pleated for him. Her son must
have such a fringe about his waist while living in the young
men's place of solitude. It would protect his kidney fat from
theft until as a young adult his first wife would pleat him a
new belt from her hair.

Wilkulda gazed compassionately at his hag mother as he
tied the guarding shield on. Namana was in her thirty-sixth
dry season. He noted how diffidently and obsequiously she
behaved before Lillywur. He had never been aware of her
cowed nature before this insight. Namana had smeared
herself with the silver mud from the far end of the pool. This
was her badge of mourning for Tjundaga. The lad observed in
silence the fresh cuts bleeding from Namana's bagged breasts
where she had welted them to honor her father-in-law's
death. Wilkulda knew that every Eagle woman would do the
same and that Tjundaga's wives, even though they were now
possessed by other, living men, would cut their hair off to the

scalp. It was unfortunate that Tjundaga's corpse was unattainable for there could be no sharing of grief by the entire mankind beneath a burial tree. Yet even without palpable evidence of their loss, the Eagles would deeply mourn the death of their father.

As Wilkulda watched his magnesium painted mother woefully retire from the presence of his father he recognized cruelty. Namana had borne him as her first child after being twice a barren widow with other mankinds. She had been bred as a Mallee Hen and although married twice as a Flying Squirrel, their ways had permitted Namana to remain a Mallee Hen. Tjundaga had bartered for her with a promise of an as yet unborn daughter. The Flying Squirrels had let her go even though she was comparatively young, twenty seasons. But as she had not been able to bear children in six seasons among the Squirrels the trade was made and Lillywur received a first wife much younger and more desirable for laying down than was usually available. Tjundaga had bartered wisely, for Namana soon conceived with Pilala and then she was fruitful wife with five additional children, including the executed Kitata.

The hag had come to love her father-in-law better than Lillywur. She looked forward to those rare ceremonies when a father-in-law could lay down with a suitable daughter-in-law, for Tjundaga was the kindest man she had ever known. Never in anyone's memory had he been observed spearing or kicking a female although such gentleness was considered queer. And besides, as Tjundaga had loved Wilkulda beyond any other object or person, thus Namana trusted Tjundaga as she too loved Wilkulda above all things.

Lillywur and Wilkulda entered the dense mallee patch by a magic bluegum that was the discarded skin of a lightning bolt. They found Mushabin by a smouldering fire. He was sitting in the sand, staring morosely into the tentative flame. Mushabin, who had purified Wilkulda in the cave of shame, turned to gaze at the approaching pair with a brooding despair. The boy saw fear in his uncle's eyes and wished to speak out to say that he would be obedient and cause the old man little concern. However, Lillywur had·immediately at the old man's rising begun the transfering chant that would place Wilkulda in Mushabin's power for the term of the initiation. Lillywur and Wilkulda would now be forbidden to speak to one another until the traditional nine years had passed in separation. There were many other complicated ideas and magic that Wilkulda must revere and practice as a growing Eagle.

Yet as he heard Mushabin join in the transfering song, Wilkulda was beyond sadness. In his thoughts the boy berated his failure, "No one understands anything. The earthquake was a silly thing to do. What a coward I am. I did not dare to tell father that I oathed myself never to lay down with females. I should have died in the wastes with Tjundaga. I should not have taken father's spear away from him, that was cruel of me. I will be with Mushabin a very long time. Maybe I can think of new ways to tell people about forgiveness by teaching them to see cruelty. I am still only a boy. I will have time. I will try again."

# BOOK III
# THE BONE DRILLER'S ODE

## one

I am Kalod, first friend to Wilkulda who stood in the sea of the Turtles. He had been in the tide nine days and nine darks when on the tenth dawn I was summoned from the beach to participate in a judgment with the Wombat-men who lived in an eastern bush world. A young female of this rather unimportant mankind had been accused by a notoriously jealous hag of laying down with a wolf.

Since the matter appeared slight, for it dealt with women, I decided to travel without my family, and the Wombats were only a half day's journey away. I wanted to refuse going altogether but as the paramount Wombat elder was one of my fathers-in-law I did not wish to offend him. Actually the girl should have been speared immediately at the pronouncement of the accusation, innocence notwithstanding. However, as her father was a terribly potent sorcerer among the Echidnas, the troublesome trial had been arranged so as not to cause lasting feuds between the two mankinds.

Before noon I had gained the site of the proceedings, a spung hole left behind by a withered river. My manner was distracted, as in spirit I was still with Wilkulda in the shallows. I had sexual intercourse with several of the younger Wombat wives in too great a rush to present the behavior regarded as affable to a good guest. With this traditional hospitality concluded I could gratefully sit down and eat my brain of emu which had been mutually agreed on in hand words as my gift for attending an insignificant judgment. I adore emu brain.

As I finished licking each ridge and crevice of the bird's skull clean I gestured for the trial to begin. Since it was but a woman who had been accused I permitted the females and children to sit quietly behind the assembly of males. The initial spiritual preliminaries were conducted by my father-in-law, Midjaumidjau, and as he mumbled on I studied the Wombats most sacred thing, a giant bulb-tree that had dried out generations past but had remained without rot.

This tree was unusually big even as these hollow bulbs go and I would think that a fellow could walk ten or twelve paces before he crossed the enclosed space. As a Turtle I, of course, could not enter the sanctuary, but I have a strong feeling that the Wombats stored their holy boards in the bulbtree.

My information as to the Wombat Dreamtime was limited and all I could gather was that the bulbtree was the metamorphosed turd of the Wombat Ancester Hero. I have always thought, I hope without prejudice, that the Wombats lacked distinguished magicians. However, it could be said in their favor that they were always good natured, and even charming in certain circumstances. Wombats were a small-statured people whose tallest warrior barely reached my armpit.

A young woman was brought to stand in the shadow of the bulbtree. One might sense the general character of the Wombats in that they allowed females in the vicinity of their Holy without restraint. The girl was impressive in appearance, with such open and clear eyes that for several moments I did not realize that she was the accused.

My father-in-law was the only Wombat who could be said to possess any remarkable talent. He had ten wives, but his talent was shown rather in the fact that he had slain five men in separate spear duels. I must add that I was quite fond of the rather dwarfish Midjaumidjau, for the old fellow was father to my second wife and had always been fair with me as regards father-in-law food-gifts and such. Midjaumidjau's consideration toward me grew out of his deep regard for my dead father, who had been a true and staunch friend to the Wombats. Over the seasons I had come to respect the old chap in spite of his ready spear and his quick temper. I had arranged seven or eight marriages for the Wombats that had gained them some repute.

This particular trial appeared to be a boresome dither about very little, for the accusation was utterly implausible. Unfortunately, in my immature nonchalance I allowed myself to lapse into inattention and to arrive at my final verdict rather too impulsively. As Kamal, the accused, was a most choice girl with considerable ability at laying down my decision would be acceptable to the Wombat males, and they were all that mattered. Kamal's pleasing nature undoubtedly had caused pettiness and jealousy among the hags. There seemed to be more hags among the Wombat women than anything else.

Besides, her boor of a father, the wicked Echidna sorcerer, the Echidnas are dirty offal eaters anyway with their filthy fur spikes, was seated directly in front of me with three brothers, five sons, and assorted sons-in-law. These Echidna representatives were all fully degreed, with the bone of a bandicoot snout through each man's nostrils. This bone decoration among these loathsome Echidna cannibals supposedly symbolizes fierce warriorhood.

Midjaumidjau's most ancient wife, an ugly bitch if I had ever seen one, had dreamed up the absurd tale of wolf-wiving while dreaming of lost lovers during a defecation. Kamal's fool of a husband, my own brother-in-law on Midjaumidjau's sister's side, was an object of ridicule among us males for allowing the incident to come this far. If he was not such an old, fat, fart he would have killed the hag before the other hags had backed her up in the foul accusation. And now sweet Kamal must be judged in her very existence.

The Echidna faction began pounding their spear butts into the ground while exaggerating the size of their eyes by not blinking. The Wombats were exceedingly nervous, as they knew that Midjaumidjau would accept such bad manners for only so long and then he would start spearing the obtuse Echidnas right and left. I had lain my own spear across my squatted thighs and was ready to spring at Kamal's dour father in self-defense, to kill him if necessary. However, I was surprised and relieved to see that the Echidnas had responded to my raised pointing stick and had become still. I then set into action my ill-thought-out plan.

To Kamal I turned my sorcery stick and touched her with it on both kidneys. At once the girl was in my command. With the pointing stick severely pressed into her side I drew Kamal to stand on the single exposed root of the bulbtree. Hurriedly I professed a formal singing of transference and took responsibility for Kamal's safety during the judgment. Soon now I could conclude this fractious lunacy and lay down with the appealing Kamal. Then, I savored the idea, I could rush back to join Wilkulda in the sea and continue our stimulating exchanges.

I began to quiz the bespelled girl. "Kamal," I sounded as
she sank deeper into my entrancement, "Kamal, did you or
did you not dance into the scrub and there seduce a young
wolf into caressing your organ?"

As I quizzed her I could imagine her portly ass of a
husband being speared dead; but my lazy spirit sprang to
attention as the quiescent little slut astounded all of us with
her response. In the insipid tone of the entranced she
exclaimed, "Oh yes, the grey wolf with the brown muzzle is
my dear love. He has the finest and broadest black stripes
down his flanks of anyone in the pack."

What a bewilderment is man. Humbled to my soul I now
regretted my eagerness to place Kamal under the pointing
stick where she could not lie. If I had any idea that she was a
criminal I would have preferred a base falsehood rather than
a public admission that had been witnessed by the women
and children. Inwardly I castigated myself for my
carelessness. Beyond my disgust at my own stupidity I was
desperately concerned that the Wombats would be
universally degraded by Kamal's perversion.

My pointing stick still controlled Kamal even as her
people, the Echidnas, groaned in shame and rage. The filthy
Wombat hags clicked their teeth stumps and petted their
stomachs, gloating in fetid joy. Though I had made an ass of
myself, and had deeply endangered the Wombats' will to live,
I affected a smile as the turbulence rose. I hopefully glanced
down to where Midjaumidjau sat, thinking that he might have
a way out of the doleful affair, but he assiduously avoided
my beseeching eyes.

How I wanted to banish the putrid wolfess to a long life
with her wolf husband. The wolves are such ugly beasts, with
striped pelts and jaws that hinge under their eye sockets.
Thanks to the Rainbow Snake we have killed most of the
packs off, even ripping puppies out of their dead mother's
pouch to ensure that the species would diminish and die out.
The remaining wolves are slowly being driven further south
each season and one day we will hear no more of them. Why
a woman like Kamal would lust for such brutes I will never
be able to answer. Yet throughout the seasons great men such
as myself have been called to judge sexual crimes. This was,
thankfully, only the second sexual crime I had judged. The

first had been among my own Turtles when a father had begun to lay down with his young son. We had to spear both dead. I earnestly hoped that Kamal's perversion would be my last experience of such horrors.

To exile her would only accede to the disgusting habit, I believed, yet the spearing of a young woman is abhorred by the Wombats as they have much difficulty in arranging marriages due to their bad looks and meager sizes. Idiotic girl, standing there with her goodly breasts as tempting as a gourd of water to a parched man, how indeed should I rid the Wombat soul of such a hideous dishonor? Kamal was quite pretty, with a charming face whose nose curved liltingly upwards. Such a pleasant eyed girl, whoever the ghoul was that had sorcered her into committing the ugliness must have been misanthropic indeed.

There seemed but one punishment equal to her crime. Yet, even as I uttered the words I regretted their harshness. I commanded the hags to seize Kamal and cut away her outer vagina in a mock circumcision. Such an act would be a true severing from the Wombats. At Kamal's age of sixteen such slicing would not kill her, but the conclusion to my verdict certainly would. For after the flints had finished their mutilation Kamal would be set out where spoor marked the wolf trail to a high watering place. No doubt her lover would find her first and attempt to protect Kamal the wolfess, but the pack would pull him down and then devour her quick enough.

That afternoon, many generations past, when the hags dragged Kamal away from my pointing stick, she awoke screaming. Even her sadistic father wailed piteously in response to her appeals, but he was powerless before such confirming magic. The Echidnas, with her shrieks searing their sensibilities, bolted away from the bulbtree's magic and out of the land of the Wombat.

Kamal with a heroic effort freed herself from the hags and ran to me where she struggled to take hold of my pointing stick and thus be protected from the hags' intent. Kamal was even then sliced as I leapt out of range of her imploring hands. She rent her nipples with fingernails as in despair, and she wept out to me that I must reduce her punishment. In

Kamal's paroxysm of terrified whimpers I watched the hags have done with the thing.

It was nighting now and Kamal's butchering was hours past. I could no longer stay in that place and I have never since returned. Midjaumidjau saw me off without protest. Normally he would have feasted me on goanna tail, which is a special favorite of mine since childhood. After a repast we would have lain down with many women. My favorite father-in-law allowed me to go into the dreadness of night without a chant. He nodded his slumped, disheartened head as his only bestowal of safety.

Fortunately there was a breasted moon and the eyes of the Salmon Flock that sleeps in the Sky lustered the land with reflections. I ran speedily with the night glow clearly detailing each tree and boulder in my path. Leaving the marches of the Wombat world I entered my own land, which began at a redgum perched on a big island in a river. The stream, alas, possesses water but every fifth or sixth season of rain. From here to the sea was a lengthy run but it would be upon flatlands and thus not difficult. About me was an ineffable stillness. I sensed that ghosts were all around, preparing to pounce whenever their appetites demanded me.

Somewhere in the hollow distance, before my pounding legs, there appeared a ghost. And it was my father's ghost. I knew at once that it was his. Ahead, thrusting up from the darkly copulated earth to console me on this alone run, my parent's spirit materialized. Swiftly his wispy being was by my side, measuring his slightly longer stride to mine, he had been somewhat over seven feet tall when alive. Undefined was his face, as if the flames of death had ashed his strong features. Here indeed was the shade of a greater man than I, even his ten seasons' old ghost was proud and forbidding as suited the father of the Turtles.

I was most grateful for father's ghost and as we ran together the route to the coastal camp my unrepentant soul was calmed by his presence. Too many men do not take the time and mental effort to distinguish what may well be a beneficent ghost from a killer ghoul. Prejudice dictates that every spectre must be evil, this viewpoint is quite fallacious for many good shades trot the night's vacancies. To me the ghost of my father represented no trauma but an ideal of severe justice that I must try to emulate.

As we lapped the spongy flatness of clay, I began to sing songs of filial devotion. Without my father's prodigious instruction during my boyhood, never could I have risen from mediocrity to arrogant magicianship. I had been considered a sickly lad with a rather retarded personality, but father had not given up on me and had sustained me through my initiation phobia. It was from his strength of character that I acquired the will to enter the shallows and be befriended by Wilkulda.

I do not mention my father's name aloud, not out of fear of the forbidden, as Wilkulda has illuminated the spurious nature of the childish prohibition, but out of respect for my father's heritage. Before we had gone a league I began to feel that father's ghost was angered, and at me. The spirit's hostility made my stomach and kidneys tired. In an effort to appease the ghost, I began to talk incessantly. However, the shade did not respond to my chatterings, and at last I begged it to reveal what defect of my nature had provoked its disapproval.

As we ran on, the ghost remained silent even though I pleaded for an admonition or criticism. The bush trees became shorter and bent over to foretell the approaching sea and its endless wind. As I anticipated the good smell of our fires with the sea odors, pleasuring from my memory, suddenly the ghost zoomed up into the blackness to ascend even as a falling torch plunges from the cliff into the storm-driven seas. As he burned in the void, the head of the ghost broke off from its body and soared upward, even as the body evaporated in a shower of sparks onto the beach ahead. High up, among the stars, the head began to dissolve, but as it dwindled my father's voice came from the contracting glimmer to command my mind even as I tried to hide myself in an empty, aged, termite hive, "Kalod, thou are a barbarian. Go to the sea. Go to Wilkulda and search out his forgiveness. We ghosts have been advised by the Sky that Wilkulda is the new mankind."

Dawn was slanting out from the marrow of night's skeleton as I gained the stone spine overlooking Wilkulda, who still stood in our sea. Famished and fatigued, I still decided to visit Wilkulda before refreshing myself. From the spike of rock that projected from the beach below up to the cliff's height, which hid the cave of paintings where our metamorphosed Turtle souls were stored as stones, I studied his figure in the hazed sea. There he was, erect and proud, facing outward away from land as was his wont. Thick cords of seaweed, brownish with protruding black and purple carbuncles, were wrapped about his stance and spear. I could hold myself no longer and after jumping back to the cliff, a distance of twelve feet, I bounded down the steep path to the beach. The white-black sand was strewn with mud bandings off the sand bar's base that the night ocean at times spews out.

I splashed into the altered sea, and as the water surmounted the scar of my first duel at my knee I did not hesitate, as I had before, but pressed outward. In spite of this show of confidence I was disturbed and dreading, but I could not disgrace my father's spectre. A sudden puff of wind blew a surge of the outbound tide at my testicles but I struggled through to attain Wilkulda, shouting to attract his attention. He ignored my presence. Closer I went until, in salutation, I placed my hand on his hand that circled the decaying spear. I tensely vibrated his arm and even the weapon, but Wilkulda remained imprisoned in his concentration.

As the fog filtered from the sky, in the glare of the rose flame that was the sun being flinted into fire, I, muttering a well known security chant, pushed ahead and turned so that I stood directly in Wilkulda's vision. And just at that moment, my foot slipped, and the bottom went out from under me. In absolute terror I felt myself sinking into far reaching depths. Flailing my arms frantically did not stay my plummeting, for here, just a few feet from where Wilkulda stood, the ocean's floor sheered off into an abyss. Wilkulda, standing in the apparent shallows created by the blockage of returning silt by the sand bar and reef, actually stood on the last ledge before the depths.

Slipping under the surface my body was hurled deeper by the falling tide's undertow. Quickly I was dragged to such a depth that I could no longer hear the thunder of the flowing surf. I was propelled outside both the sand bar and reef into the outer sea. Here fortunately I smashed up against a rock. I was now in such a state that I welcomed death, for I ached with the ocean sitting on me. Even in the distress of being crushed by the sea I wondered if Kamal's father had sung death into my soul.

Yet just in that instant of suspecting the Echidna of evil I remembered poor Kamal and at once the tide seemed to relax its grip. Prone on the drowned corpse of a large animal, I realized that now or never I must attempt to rise. Shoving hard with my knees and elbows I began to float upward to the hidden sky. Sluicing through the surface I gratefully sucked air into my chest despite the painful rawness of throat and lungs. I floated on my back until I had recovered breath. Then I tilted my head and discovered that I was not too far from the sombre Wilkulda. With a child's stroke I paddled over to him. Hauling myself upright by benefit of his spear I found that the tide had played itself out.

"Did you see that, did you see me almost drown? The tidal flow had me choked but I escaped at the last moment. Was it you, Eagle-man, who tried to sing death into me? Was it you? I thought you were my brother."

Having said these foolish words I immediately regretted them, and told Wilkulda I realized it had not been his doing, at least that there were others with better reason to sorcer my end. However, he noticed neither my insult nor the silly apology. His absorption was clearly with matters far beyond my worry that some person might intend to murder me. Staying with him seemed meaningless. I was tired and hungry. I began to think of sneaking away and letting him dwell on whatever it was. But before I could make a move, Wilkulda boomed out at me in an extraordinary tone. "Kalod, why did you judge Kamal as less than a gnawed reptile's tail? Kamal was but a pathetic stranger to wisdom, for was not her soul infirm and crippled? Why did you, Kalod, the bone-driller, act as a wolf?"

In a frenzy of hurt I shouted, "How, ignorant fellow, is it of concern to you what judgment I choose to give on any subject? That you should know about Kamal is of least importance to me. Undoubtedly it was you who disturbed my father's ghost with some barbaric chant. I am Kalod, elder of the great Turtles, not an outcast savage of a paltry desert clan as your stupid Eagle-people must be. Your mankind acted brilliantly when they exiled you. Dirty Kamal fucked with the wolves. She disrupted the entire well-being of the Wombats! Dirty bitch daughter of the evil Echidna filth. Really, Wilkulda, I would expect a magician such as you pretend to be to commend me for the severity of the

judgment. It required courage to send Kamal as a bleeding
stump to the wolves. It was I who heard her scream as the
beasts ate her! Yes, it was I who heard the wolves in their
feasting frenzy! You didn't hear it; I heard it. I took it. I
faced it that the Wombats would not be destroyed by her
degradation. Where were you? Why didn't you send a
judgment into my stomach if you possessed a better one?

"You, Wilkulda, are a miserable sorcerer, not a wise
magician. It was you who sang me down into the sea's belly.
You shrunken-penised fraud. You half-man who declines to
enter the hole of a woman out of fear. I offered you my
friendship, me, Kalod the bone-driller, and you shit all over
me. You get out of my sea, get out or I will spear you with
your own weapon. My council wanted to kill you and place
your body into a termite nest so no spirit of man would
know we slayed you. But I said no. I said you seemed a likely
chap. Go elsewhere and see if others treat you with the
consideration I gave you."

Even to this day far in the future I remember exactly my
words and their inflections. Yet Wilkulda ignored my tirade,
and with a compassionate tone that cleft my heart, said,
"Kalod, when you stood there close to your best
father-in-law, as Kamal began to scream, did you not suffer
for Kamal?"

" . . . It was my duty," I answered unabashed, "I had a
responsibility surpassing pity. Kamal had to die. She had to
die in a manner that would prevent any Wombat from
becoming a pervert for a thousand summers. If she did not
die cruelly and so avenge the Wombats' honor with her
screaming, they might have died out in the next generation.
There would have been no end to it unless I acted
forcefully."

Wilkulda did not reply. Instead he pulled his weathered
spear from the sea bed with a mighty tug as if uprooting a
tree. And as he cast the spear, it fell far out to sea at the
horizon and vanished forever. The messenger, with his freed
hand, soundlessly beckoned, as if his fingers were the gently
flapping wings of a dove, beckoned something from the
narrow puncture that the spear had left in the ocean.

A wind vented from this space and formed a water spout.
The water and wind were mated and reached out to the Sky.

And the water spout became a huge column looming over the sea, so high that it seem'ed to hang from the moon. Then a sound came from the water spout that I could not identify. I though perhaps it came from the camp, where a dingo pup might have been thrown on a fire for an early breakfast for some elder.

Now the pillar of water began to twirl violently even as the strange sound increased in volume. This incredible noise rebounded from the spout to sky, and then to sky again, amplifying its voice with each circuit. Finally, the water spout was near enough and I saw and I heard what it was. It was a giantess Kamal, the sound was her screaming as the wolves bit into her firmness. Screams that fractured her throat even as she was at last masticated by that very wolf who had been her lover.

I became weak as the groans shook my soul. In a tiny voice I begged Wilkulda to send Kamal and her screams back into the Dreamtime rent that his spear had created. But she came closer and her screams sent the flocks of seabirds, and the turtles that abound on our shore, scrambling into the air and water. Kamal was a hugeness and I could view, only too vividly, what the knives of the hags and the fangs of the beasts had wrought. And I saw my own fate in Kamal's plight, she would eat me even as I had given her to the beasts. My bowels loosened to drip down my thighs and I whimpered, "For pity's sake, forgive me, Kamal."

Her ghoul was directly over my head. She was a silhouette of scarlet-blackness except at the edges where the morning sky glared through her. Kamal opened her jaws magnificently wide even as if they were hinged to her ears. The growing incisors were monstrous. From the essence of her dead spirit Kamal cried out to me as if she were a great wolf-bitch in heat. And as I watched in horrified fascination she lurched upon my life's hotness and her awful mandibles closed on my neck to bite it through.

Some unaccountable moments after she had devoured me I found myself floating out on the sea where the foam signifies the reef that rears up at slack tide. From my prone position I could see Wilkulda where he waited, contemplating and proud. The sea abruptly tilted itself toward the land that I was glided to my instructor. The ghost of Kamal had

vanished. However, as I thankfully crept on hands and knees
in the liquid sand to where he waited, Wilkulda began to
admonish me in resounding tones: "Kalod, your beginning
crime has been your refusal to admit that cruelty exists. I
came into the sea that every mankind shall become aware
that cruelty proliferates and that forgiveness is the ultimate
magic. I am the Sky's only messenger and forgiveness is my
only gift to men. It is true, Kamal was guilty of degradation
to her own person, but only that, only to her own self."

Before he could continue, still in the jagged crosses of my
mind I denied his meaning and said sophistically, "Yet you
do see her crime. It is only the degree of her punishment that
we debate. Someone had to be punished. Who was I supposed
to judge, the wolf-lover?"

"Yes, finally you begin to see truth behind your own
cleverness," answered Wilkulda. "For Kamal was a wolf. You
should have judged Kamal the wolf not Kamal the woman.
Kamal had become a wolf yet you slaughtered her as if she
was still of men. Kamal was born beautiful, as are all
children. And she did birth beautiful children. Was she
pervert when she was child and when she bore children? If
Kamal was a woman and not a wolf when she took the beast
into her person, then are we not all wolves, even you and I
and Kamal's fine two babies? I say that when Kamal laid
down with the wolf she was no longer of men but had
metamorphosed into a wolf. Why she prefered to become a
wolf and renounce men is not her crime, it is our crime. The
crime was of men. We are all Kamals in that we secretly
harbor or nourish bestial thoughts. None except the Kamals
dare to act as man thinks. Why, Kalod, did you not pity
Kamal and send her into the wilds as a wolf instead of as a
butchered woman? Why did you betray yourself and create
every man as a wolf? Did you truly shield the Wombat
mankind from disgrace? No, never, for it was Kalod and not
Kamal who disgraced the Wombats and all the mankinds.
Thus, Kalod, it is you who must be forgiven for your cruelty.
Only Kalod can forgive Kalod."

Now I did understand that Wilkulda was the rarest of
magicians. It is because of Wilkulda the messenger that I pass
among the mankinds as the seed of forgiveness. That far day
past when Kamal's ghoul came upon the ocean she ate not

my soul, nor my being, she only chewed away my cruelty. Since that day I was no longer Kalod the bone-driller, but became Kalod, brother to Wilkulda the messenger. Wilkulda continued to speak that far lost morning, "Be cleansed by your crime. Be renewed by your shedding of cruelty. You shall be made anew if you but forgive yourself."

I had sagged down on my side into the wet of the tidal flat. My body compressed the sand and a miniature ocean was raised about my form. I lay in this on one side with knees tucked up into my chest, even as an infant sleeps. My being knew a weakness as does the mucous sprayed, featherless swanlet that has finally pried apart its shell. My being was in rebirth. I saw my Dreamtime spirit as it truly was, a wondrous oyster that had become tainted with disease. I shouted to Wilkulda, "I confess, I confess." Hushed sobs came from me lying in the sand as I cried, "Kamal was innocent of crime. I, Kalod, was guilty!"

He answered, but first he moved, he moved. He came over to me and lifted me from the flats and then together, holding hands, we went to stand facing the sea. Wilkulda said unto me, "I long to be a light. A triumphant light that every child can plainly distinguish. If a man but seeks out forgiveness then at his soul's new beginning, cruelty is banished."

"Teach me Wilkulda the magic, no matter how difficult, that will purge Kamal's screaming from my soul. Show me a dancesong that will mask the wolf's blood from my own vision. Teach me to forgive myself that I will be as you are, as the light that grows from your head. The light, the light, your light, Wilkulda, is getting bigger!"

Said Wilkulda, "Kalod, you shall be my brother."

"I am your brother, why that is very good, I am your brother. Brother to Wilkulda whose head grows a mighty light and who summons ghosts and ghouls into existence from the Dreamtime."

"Kalod shall carry the Sky's gift of forgiveness to the peoples of the worlds. Kalod the Turtle shall speak of forgiveness even when I am dead ten and twenty generations. Men shall become aware that cruelty proliferates and is evil and that only forgiveness can redeem cruelty."

The sun was now highest and I noticed that my mankind

had crept up to the edge of the cliff to observe us. Our hands
were still clasped even as young girls go into the bush with
their wooden bowls held on hips to gather in plums and
apples. A happier Wilkulda now said, "Kalod, can you love?"

I replied without fore-thought, "Love is itself of no
consequence." But Wilkulda did not answer, and I felt I
should embellish this statement. "Oh yes, love is an
insignificant whimsy. It is an emotion of females and of hot
testicled young men who have had little, or no, experience
with girls. Love is a phase in life that everyone must
encounter and survive. It is a minor spirit and not comparable
to the spirit of forgiveness which you have revealed to me."

I thought I had spoken rather well, and was surprised
when Wilkulda, took his head and said thoughtfully, "That
is what I once believed, but recently I have explored the idea
that perhaps love and forgiveness are one implication. I had a
friend, Mayawara, it was she, Mayawara, who wakened
intimations in me that the love spirit may be child, or even
parent, to forgiveness. Even after the Sky Father
metamorphosed me it was not simple to understand
forgiveness. I am glad you have consented to be my brother,
Kalod, for I am lonely since Mayawara."

Wilkulda now let go of my hand and placed his
concentration out into the sea. The candent about his head
had increased mightily in size and brightness. His need of me
was a bewilderment and my spirit expanded. Never had I
known such a welling in my soul. It was as if I had been dead,
then he had come into our sea to awaken me to life. As if I
had been born with a bough shadowing my spirit. Now
Wilkulda had revealed me to myself. Intuitively, without
logic or rationality, I accepted my right as bearer of
Wilkulda's forgiveness when he was dead. My world had been
transformed by my inward nakedness. Wilkulda had seen me
truly as a wolf and it was not until then that I became a man.
And he chose me to be the carrier of his magic.

Day and night flooded down onto the sea even as a
whale's sperm reaches every wave until it is flecked apart and

abandoned. Newest dawn stretched to the far quadrant of the ocean and the swells brimmed with the reflected sky spirit. And the sea became the sky in rebirthed light. Malediction of night withdrew into the mortuary pit and the air was pure. Two magic persons, restored from the catharsis of Kamal's innocence, rested in the awe of the rescued morning sky. Tide had concluded and the shallows billowed with its accomplishment. The multi-white beach was festooned with lazy crabs, dying shrimp, and all manner of animal life. Above, in air supported weavings, the flocks swooped low to harvest the ocean's wastage. Marveling gulls circle highest over the magicians, they were first of any species to discover the drama of night gone and now of the future to be.

And the two men waited for this day to be unrolled. Wilkulda, wet now only to the arch of his beginning self, stretched tall into the sky but with his eyes fastened to the sea. Kalod stood staring into the eyes of the messenger throughout the unfolding day, as he had stood all night. Nothing is actually known of what passed between the two, but Kalod became the truest bearer of Wilkulda's message.

Turtles, men and the herds of reptiles warming in the sun, watched the two on the tidal flats. Women who should have been foraging, males who should have been hunting, fishermen who should have been in the shallows with their nets and spears, watched Wilkulda and the bone-driller stand as one transfiguration in the sea.

Day again failed its recurring hopes. Dimness yawned under the heroic sky. Night blankly guarded the cliffhead where the Turtle elders performed a simple ceremony in commemoration of the Rainbow Snake eating one of its countless daughters, the day's light, who was also a Kangaroo.

Night hung low on the campfires of the dancing elders. Kalod escaped neither the stranger nor the sea although the elders chanted that he might flee. Tide plunged onto earth and the moon bulged from its cloistering blackness, but unsurely as if disbelieving in the ode to come.

Kalod fled not the sea that night and his mankind stayed to witness the monthly rip currents destroy the two magicians. Water rumbled yet higher on the coast's complacency. The ocean progressed up to Wilkulda's neck and in order that the shorter Kalod, who was three fingers beneath a full seven feet tall, might not drown he held him on his shoulders even as if the elder was a small boy needing to be carried on a far walk through the desert.

Night climaxed and vapor hid the sea's prostration. Newest dawn could be anticipated and the cliffside Turtles awoke. They were gratified to find the night ebbing for it was chilled sleeping there close to the ocean. They had long since extinguished their fires as they cared not to attract dangerous magic.

Light crept back. Wilkulda and Kalod could be sighted in the timid daybreak. As if the effort entailed pain, Wilkulda began to speak and the ocean quieted. In this perfect silence those on the cliff could hear, "Kalod, go to the mankinds of the world and inform them that I wait here in the sea for their arrival. Tell man to bring me the sick and the dying, for I shall heal every affliction. With gentleness I shall cure their festering sores and renew their flaking skins. Tell the mankinds to meet here in the sea and I shall heal deformities and create flesh ripe firm where it had been cankerous."

At once Kalod came out of the shallows and made to his people, who stood numbed by the immense words of Wilkulda. Kalod assembled the males of the Turtles, old and young, to inform them of Wilkulda's kinship with the Sky World. Thus, this was Kalod's initial voicing as Wilkulda's brother. Kalod did commission the young men as runners to the mankinds of the worlds. Kalod rehearsed these young men in exact repetition of his words, "Wilkulda shall heal the ill, the fatigued, and the dying. All peoples will be cured by his magic. Bring to the Turtle's sea the circumcised and the not. Bring females and their young. Bring every person to Wilkulda in the sea."

The runners swept up from the tiny clustering that was the Turtle-mankind to race out in every direction. The young men ran with purpose and with pride, for they recognized that theirs was a great mission. They went among enemies and friends, and to each whether sick or strong, they ended with Kalod's final injunction, "Come to the stranger Wilkulda who is the child of the Sky. He shall heal even those who trust not the Sky Spirits, for he excludes none and is the Sky's single messenger."

And a host began to gather there on the cliffhead to view the sea surrounded healer. Wilkulda stirred not from his station as the mankinds arrived to gawk. Lo and behold, Kalod went among the diverse peoples and taught them the songs of the Sky. Quickly even the staunchest cynic was caught up in the fervor and all committed many holy dances.

Then, while the mankinds arrived, as the host grew large, Wilkulda began to heal the sick and dying. And the people came into the sea to be in his presence.

# BOOK IV
# JOSEPH OF BRITAIN

## one

Thus my greatness of an uncle, Joseph Atkins, had been captivated by Frecht the Lowly, and thus he, Joseph the Proper, had become wedded to an aboriginal Christ. It was the dainty Kukika the Whore who did flare the mature seaknight into a novel chivalry. For he, Britain's commonest Noble, was truly metamorphosed. Without salute to Jackson Harbor, that Cook knew not was there, he did chart the Harvester to the west coast of Australia to search the littoral for proof of Wilkulda's verity.

If any sensible and knowledgable boat-person compares the Hartlepool Harvester to the Rainbow of 1855, then he be maddest. For the heavy keeled Harvester, with her barrel bows and casket stern, could do 3½ knots at best as average while the clipper, even prototype Lightning which was built by the Yankees to compete in the China opium trade, could slice the seas at 6 knots while beating to Foochow. And this Lightning was but the testing of the concave hulls of a ratio of six to one, length to width.

Yet the Harvester would toil and earn profit for her varied owners a century full while the gay clipper would be hogged or sprung in ten years. Cook had sailed a coal collier to New Holland and abandoned the aborigines to extinction by dying too quick in the Sandwiches, for it was reported that Captain Cook did think well of the Australoids, and that was surely a lonely love. His Endeavour was a fine craft, however, the Harvester was even sturdier as she had iron ribs built into her during a refit in the 1830's. Hartlepool Harvester was a full rigged ship: three masts square sheeted except for the lateen boomed to the mizzen. Joseph Atkins was a Prince of Gold and a sweet rigger of a ship of sails. His vessel was an 800 tonner and could haul out 550 tons of clip in the hollows.

When on the outbound voyage from Sutherland she stowed
650 ton of general cargo. Bruce and Whoor, owners of the
Harvester, were ship builders and traders who worked their
ships from the channel port of Sutherland. Their ships
free-traded the globe's waters wherever profit might be made.
Atkins, by mid-century, was a full partner in the Harvester
and several other Bruce and Whoor square-riggers. This
accomplishment was not a small deed when many a captain
would strain a lifetime to possess a sixty-fourth share in his
own command.

The Honorable East India Company had ceased to be
involved in cargo and passenger haulage by the 1830's, the
very years that Atkins began to accumulate his riches. Bruce
and Whoor, and hundreds of other concerns, with men like
Atkins available for hire in the tens of thousands, carried
large volumes of the world's wealth in their copper sheathed
wood bottoms. Until 1869, when Suez opened, the sailing
vessel was incomparable; after Suez the engined iron steamers
took into their own hulls the profitable cargos. The cubic
space of a ship's haulage was not identical with her tonnage
capacity, for that would vary considerably by density from
cargo to cargo. Tea from the China ports would pack light,
but the tea-brokers in England would pay a high premium for
fast ships that could reach home before the market opened.
By 1849 the English Navigation Acts had been reformed and
the sailing ship entered a twenty year period of enormous
trade growth. By 1853, when Atkins sailed from Sydney, the
haulage of tea leaves surpassed even the profits in opium.
Every sailing ship laid down in the world's yards was a
clipper, yet the Harvester worked on.

It was January, the wool market in London was at its
most frantic, ships arriving now in England with clip would
receive the highest price. The Harvester was overdue, several
months behind her average sailing as she cleared Jackson
Harbor. The trades had shifted, the prevailing monsoons in
the Arafura and Timor Seas were against him, yet in these
waters Atkins must fight through to reach Australia's western
shores. The Harvester would have to sail in contrary winds
and in waters proliferated with uncharted reefs and isles. If
Atkins could have waited until the rotation of the seasons the
winds would have been with him, but as the very idea of the

side voyage would be anathema to Bruce and Whoor, and as
he was already badly behind schedule, he set the Harvester to
seas as soon as the new rigging had been tarred.

Normally, he would have tacked south out of Sydney to
pick up the winds in the constant flow known as the Roaring
Forties. There blows would have sped him east through the
Southern Seas and down under Horn Island into the Atlantic
trades which would have dispatched him to England except
for the delay of sailing the doldrums in the equatorial zone.
In expectation of fighting windward around northern
Australia, Atkins had rerigged the ship by setting fore and aft
sails on both mizzen and main masts, leaving only the
foremast square rigged. This arrangement would permit the
Harvester to sail somewhat closer to the wind than the
squared masts would. Frecht and Atkins and planned the
change and spent several weeks supervising the installation.
Without the new rig, abnormal to the decade, the ship might
have been demasted in the Torres or blown back onto the
Great Barrier Reef that she must round to make the
westward passage. A day would come when sailing ships
would dare reach West Australia from Sydney by use of the
southern route through the millrace of the Bass Straits. This
would be accomplished by prudent utilization of the
off-shore currents, but many years would pass before such
passages would be attempted.

Atkins had lied to his undermanned crew that he might
keep the thirty hands on board as the gold strikes continued.
He had told the men that gold had been traded from the
blacks by sealers working the west coast. The men did not
believe all that Atkins said, for they expected a captain to lie
that he might raise a crew. But they trusted that a rich man
like Atkins would scent out a profit before raising sail on a
journey to a vacant coast, and the hands and mates expected
to share somewhat in the rewards.

Yet even as Atkins stood out from Port Jackson, to gain
sailing room to clear the Great Barrier in an enormous
seacurve, he could not control his feelings of remorse at
deceiving the poor sailors. Thus, three days out from Sydney,
Atkins assembled his thirty men and his two officers and
without prettiness of word informed them that there was no

gold strike in the west, but that all hands would receive double wages for the extra sailing days above the average return passages.

The sail maker, who was carpenter too, quiered his master at this news, "Ye mean, sir, the cannibals got treasures other than gold?"

"No," with thrusting pride did Atkins reply, "if there are rewards they shall be of honorific ribbons and not of wealth. For we shall return with treasure suitable only for the Lord God, if indeed we have success. I trust that we shall sail back to England after a mighty exploration with tangible vindication of a most unique blackfella."

It was an absurd statement and the crew did not believe him. They were convinced that there had been a gold strike along the dismal shore they beat for, but that the captain, like all captains, was acting in profound greediness. The men were used to that. They would wait and see for themselves. However, by his admission, Atkins had irrevocably jeopardized that which formerly he had held in the highest esteem. His reputation for sobriety could now be openly cursed by honest men as false.

This fundamental passage of the Harvester risked both the ship and the men in an adventure without sober cause. Little was known as to the tides, currents, reefs, and winds off Australia's western shore. A rogue by the name of William Dampiers had made several voyages to this littoral centuries past yet his books on the subject were still regarded by English-reading seamasters as the definitive guide to the waters. Flinders had charted somewhat on his courageous circumference of the continent in the early 1800's, but this was meager. Dampier, like every European observer, including the Dutch discoverers, had reported that no trade of consequence could be expected from the subhuman species that inhabited the awful place.

Atkins' wealth had sprouted from his right to haul freely, 'captain's cargo.' For a free trader's master could expect but £10 a month, if that. However, he was given the privilege of hauling in his cabin, and in a specified space in the hold, his private goods. These he could sell or trade to his personal advantage. Owners of ships valued a captain's acumen as a businessman as much as his abilities in handling a vessel for it was the captain's responsibility to sell the ship's cargo at a profit, as well as his own.

At mid-century the length of a ship's season between ports was becoming more important in the light of competition from steamed vessels, but time was still not urgent to a sailing ship's value except in the Flying Fish trade, the tea haulage. A three masted keg like the Harvester needed a full year to complete the round voyage betwixt home and New South Wales and home again. A ship from England would invariably call at a port on the Brazilian coast, perhaps at the River Plate. Then across to Table Land for trade and revictualing in the Cape Colony. Finally the long sail with fulfilling winds in the sheets for the entire six thousand miles to the east coast of Australia. After cargoing the vessel might double back along the coast of Africa clearing India. If the wool clip at Sydney did not fill her holds she might sail to the Chinese ports, or to Malay for tea, or rice, or spice, or hemp, or a little of each. However, the wiser captains steered south from Sydney and let the Forties take the vessel speedily into the Atlantic. By either route it took a year to complete the round trip passage.

By 1853 Atkins was a man of wealth based on his thirty-six voyages to and from the Australian colonies. His success could not be compared to that of the East Indian Company captains of the previous century, whose personal profit from one journey at times reached £20,000, but then Atkins could never have been employed as an officer on an Indiaman as his birth's station was altogether too humble for such prestigious employment. To be signed on in a midshipman's berth in the Honorable Company a lad had to supply a £50 fee and be of good family, even if a bastard his father had to have social standing.

Factually, the Harvester's general cargo to New South Wales was mainly of illegal spirits; rum from the Brazils, gin and whiskey from Britain. Spirits were the demand, some iron manufacturies and sundries, but it was alcoholic potables that were barreled in an endless gout to Sydney. Rum was the call. What else could be expected from convict societies artificially created by the Acts of Transportation except uninterrupted corruption. The decades of degradation were closing as Atkins fashioned his last voyage. Transportation to

New South Wales had ended ten years previously, but penal
servitude in the form of agricultural and construction labor,
continued until the older convicts slowly died out or were
given freedom to settle in Australia. In Tasmania,
Queensland, Victoria, and West Australia the demand never
ceased for convicts to work the metamorphosed Dream into a
new form. Only Royal Navy ships or those chartered directly
by the admiralty could now haul convicts, and the earlier
abuses lessened.

Joseph Atkins never spoke of his shame at accumulating
wealth for himself and his family by rum. The guilt, however,
existed and had nubbed his inner serenity, thus when
salvation through the act of authenticating Wilkulda
presented itself, Joseph lunged at this opportunity of
self-redemption.

## two

Joseph Atkins sailed the Hartlepool Harvester from
Sydney on January 7, 1853. Aged ship, loose in her new
rigging as a barquentine. She screeched in her hull timbers
from the novel task of sailing degrees off the beam leeward
because of the lateens on the two rear masts. Mis-matched
masts made tight gyrations and emitted preposterous groans
as the rounding wood bases chafed in the imprisoning iron
rings. Yet in spite of a certain spinsterish rigidity she was a
well founded ship and a fine sailor. She had been laid down
at Hartlepool in 1810 during a brief hiatus in the hostilities.
The shipbuilder had been able to give her seasoned wood and
not German fir, or Canadian oak which would decay in a few
years from dry rot. Ferguson Brothers built her with oak
from the Forest of Dean in Gloucestershire, timber saved and
hidden under canvas and roof for a decade and more. She
wasn't a Blackwall Indianman laid down in Brunswick Basin
where the Company's floating towers were normally
carpentered. The Fergusons were partners in the ship with
Bruce and Whoor and that is why she earned the rare
Gloucestershire oak. They put elm in her hull planking where
the twisted, tenacious fibers would not melt away in the sea's

kettle. She possessed Maine pine masts; light, supple wood all the way to the highest pennant pole.

The knackers, or the sea, would eventually wreck every wooden ship, but the Harvester would float ninety-five years before she saw the light obscured by the fathoms deep. The Fergusons had built her under cover in the dry months of July and August, this alone was sufficient reason to give a ship a chance for longevity. If a ship was made in the open where the rain would cancer into the wood such a vessel might last a few years at best. During the Napoleonic wars too many ships were thrown down by wormy wood. Her first seven years she worked the Baltic among the Finn islands and north of Petersburg, where English firms held fish and lumber charters from the Tzars. Then in '17 she was given a new copper bottom and Atkins was made her master. She was placed in the Australian trade hauling rum, wool, and immigrants. A man could pay £15's for a second class berth, or £5's for stowage and start a new life in New South Wales as a settler.

Atkins was a sober man and that is why in 1817 he had been chosen by old man Bruce to command such a prize as was the Harvester. His reputation had been enhanced in Bruce's eyes in that Atkins was believed to be utterly honest in an age when neither sobriety nor honesty was a common characteristic among sea officers. They were not considered louts as in Portugal's halcyon days when she forged her primal empire, but too many chaps did gild their purses by signing for more saltbeef, or biscuit, than was actually stowed below. Even among the prideful East India captains such traditional thievery was not unknown. A captain was required to be an entrepreneur, and this attitude perhaps prompted him to succumb to the available temptations.

Atkins was twenty years old when made captain of the Harvester. His first command had been on his previous voyage as master to the packet Orion. This was a three-masted ship built of Huron pine on the Derwent in Hobarton basin. She was a small two hundred and fifty ton square-rigger. Atkins had served aboard the Orion for one voyage, 1815-1816. The vessel had been chartered in the Thames to transport convicts back to Hobarton, where the prisoners would be reshipped to the cruelest of all penal colonies on Sarah Island. This isle was located on Tasmania's brutal west coast in Macquarie Harbor, actually an inlet carved in the land by the furious storms that blew continuously on the shore. The Orion's captain had hanged himself by his cabin's lantern chain off the Crozet Islands in the Great Southern Ocean, some thousands of miles west of destination. Atkins had been the ship's first officer and he assumed command of the captainless Orion. The Orion carried eighty-seven convicts of which fifteen were females. A ship even as small as the Orion was worked by a large crew in those years when seamen were lucky to have a ship to call home. Young Joseph had upwards of forty men to contend with, and prostitution and drunkeness became rife three days after he had dropped his predecessor's corpse over the gunnels. Such low behavior was habitual in convict ships that carried female prisoners.

The majority of such women had at one time or another practiced whoring, even though they might have been sentenced to transportation for other crimes. These women actively encouraged the officers and crew to use their bodies. Even desperately they plied their loins, for by sexual favor they might hope to raise gold, or rum shares, or even, if they were truly fortunate, to charm a captain to supply a citation releasing them from penal servitude. Such documents did not include return to England, but they did permit the lucky woman to participate in the thriving debauchery for which the Australian colonies were justly renowned. In the Pacific during these decades only the blackbird slavers, who bought men, women, and children from the islands with ship's bread, were held in less esteem than the transportation ships.

As a captain Atkins was that rare-individual of self-discipline, no matter the carnival taking place all about. Remarkable young Atkins, recently married as virgin to virgin, halted the Orion's dissolution by the simple and not uncommon expedient of locking the crew's rum in the powder magazine and convincing sailors and convicts that he would not hesitate to blow the ship to kingdom come with his flintlock unless decorum replaced sloth. And they looked upon Joseph's youthful countenance, and they saw death therein, and they ceased sloth. He sailed the sober, solemn, clean Orion smartly onto the Derwent in the winter of 1816, July it was. When the Island's governor came on board to inspect the ship, as was his duty to each Hobarton arrival, the unaccustomed order and seaworthiness of the Orion, crew, and convicts inspired a letter of commendation into Joseph's steady, dry, hands. This encomium directly aided Atkins in securing the command of the Harvester on return to England.

His initial passage in the Harvester confirmed Bruce's verdict: Atkins was sober, industrious, and foremost he was a shrewd businessman. In November of 1817 the Harvester had sailed into Port Jackson with a general cargo enhanced by a highly profitable purchase of cheap rum and tobacco made at Rio. Bruce and Whoor had encouraged the water stop on the Plate. They had hoped, rightly, that their young captain would not be able to withstand the perfume of huge profits that the rum purveyors waved under his nose.

The trade monopolies held by army officers and clerks in New South Wales had been weakened by 1817, and Atkins had little difficulty in tripling the cargo's profit by engaging in the illegal convict commerce, and also by trading with the short-lived whaling men who were then thick with their ships in the animal teemed waters. The owners allowed Atkins a £100 bonus for the rich voyage. This, when added to the £550 he had earned for fifteen month's work, (he had not a shilling to invest in captain's cargo on his first voyage in the Harvester), permitted Joseph to enter the lists as an investing capitalist. Joseph allowed his youngest sibling, George, £50's and with this minuscule sum the tiny Brighton Iron Works was inaugurated. Joseph, even from his limited funds, was encouraged by the elder Bruce to buy into the Harvester.

By 1853 the ship had been resheathed in copper eight times, and had been given a costly iron ribbing in 1838 after a dockside fire in Sutherland burned her insides out but left the rigging, outer hull and keel intact and afloat. It was a measure of the owners' confidence in her seaworthiness that they spent good money to rebuild the Harvester when she was in her twenty-eighth season at sea. Ribs of iron replaced the huge oak timbers and beams, and thus the ship became stronger, though lighter in displacement and more capacious in the holds.

On January 7, 1853, when the Harvester cleared North

Point, the last refit of '49 had rudely worn and the ship had a pooping tendency in the stern. As long as Atkins commanded her the Harvester was a trim vessel, for under his surveillance she was superior to many a new ship. Her bulging hull, though a throttle to rapid voyaging, was superb at weathering ocean blasts. With old-fashioned copper astrolabe did Joseph Atkins navigate the Western Ocean and the others too. Sextant was also used skillfully in his stout, calm hands, but he rather enjoyed the operation of the clumsy astrolabe, which required three men including himself to handle its sighting. Perhaps Joseph's contentment with the bulky astrolabe was based on his erroneous belief that Prince Henry of Portugal had invented the instrument, and Henry was half-English. How disappointed would Joseph of Britain have been had he known that Jews and Moors developed the star sighting tool.

Despite, or because of his meticulous perfection as a navigator, Atkins was also skilled in commanding his crews. Not once in his career had he resorted to paying a crimp to shanghai a hand for the Harvester. His mathematical mentality seemed to aid him, instead of hindering, in his relationships with the men. To Joseph it was apparent that a fairly treated man was a loyal, productive sailor. With this irrefutable theorem of Christianity as his guide, Atkins had become respected and well thought of by his crews in an age when to treat a sailing man with kindness was considered a weirdness. Joseph ran the Harvester even as the excellent executives of the East Indiamen had managed their fine ships, cautiously and prudently. It was damn the speedy passages if it meant sailing at night with tall canvas spread. It was damn a fortnight gained if a valuable mast or spar was lost in payment for the damn, clever, quickness. Damn the speed and in darkness take in the royals, damn ye. Before bad weather take in the damn t'gallant and the damn fore-mainsail, damn ye, and put a damn reef in the damn t'sails, damn it hurry there men, take the damn sheets in.

Quickness in serving the ship, yes, but damn the clippers and the damn wood burners, damn them all. That was the way of Cook and that was the way of Joseph. And yet because both men were sea-wise, their passages were better than average by far. Joseph begrudged the loss of a line or of a wet bale of clip. He would run from a storm or fight through if need be, but whatever the decision, it would be based on what action was safest for the ship. And he masturbated but once a month, Joseph carefully disciplined himself in that.

A beautiful ship of sail, even with her ribs of iron settling her somewhat too deep at mid-section. The men sing as they round the capstan block aft to take up anchor. No man on board, including the renowned Atkins, could conjure that only the vessel herself would be left untainted by this queer voyage to be. The ship would continue to wend her way for some fifty more honorable years while those who worked her on this voyage would be forever stained afterwards. The ship would last into the era of the oiled dragons and the coaled tramps. The last twenty years of her service the Harvester would serve as a coal barge between Wales and Dublin. Bruce and Whoor had been forced to sell all their sailing ships to satisfy the creditors after the bankruptcy. The haulage rates had diminished far beneath the golden years of mid-century, and the Clyde concern who purchased the Harvester castrated her masts and chopped away her rigging. They gave her an iron prow, where Atkins had always carried the old fashioned spirit sail, that the tow rope might not break off her bow.

In 1898 the Clyde coalers sold her to ship breakers as scrap. There could be no salvage for reselling, as her appointments were antiques. They towed her north past Hartlepool, where the Fergusons had built her almost a century past, up to the Firth of Forth at Buckhaven. Here hulks were burnt out. After firing a ship the knackers would recover whatever metallics were in the ash; copper, brass, and iron. Some of the iron would be loaded on the lingering clipperships, who scrambled as starving children for freight and would sail the scrap to Shangai and Bombay. At Buckhaven the Scots tethered the Harvester close to the shore so that her bottom dropped into the mud at low tide. This was very bad, as it ruined whatever water security remained to the old ship. But the knackers had no other berth open and she waited for her turn on the pyres. There were hundreds of dead wood and iron composite sailing vessels that had to be fired before the Harvester could be blazed. As it was, five years passed before she could be loosened from the shore moorings and hauled by a small, steamed, whaleboat to the winch hook that would fish her out onto the land. The seasons of tidal corruption had filled her bottom with silt and had seriously weakened the wood timbers. A cable length from the railed trundle wheels that the winch would tug her up onto, the Harvester's keel fell out. The copper sheathing, though worn thin, still was quite heavy and it tore away most of her lower hull. Without pause the ship fell rather magically under the waters.

The Firth was quite deep here and as she formed no navigational hazard where she had gone down, the Harvester was not raised. To this day she rests there many fathoms deep in the firth. No man remembered the Harvester until I, Avery Morrison, began this work. No person but I knows that down in waters off prosaic Buckhaven are timbers that once participated in a momentous adventure. For indeed, in the southern summer of 1853, the Harvester had carried Atkins to the ancient lands of the Turtles, there on the western slopes of Australia. Joseph did land where Wilkulda had stood in the sea some thirty-five centuries earlier.

### three

*Ship's Log, January 25, 1853*

Eighteen days out of Sydney. Winds light and contrary. Reached latitude of Cape York forenoon and sailed new course W.N.W. Waters shallowed and treacherous as turned. Much shoal. Ran aground 2:00 P.M. Lost topmast on the foremast. Recovered some rigging. Pulled off reef with boats towing. Was four hours aground. Tops'l hand Thomas Evans was lost when ship struck. Evans was reefing the top gallant, foremast, when we struck and he was thrown from yard onto the reef.

*Personal Diary of Captain Atkins, January 25, 1853*

Ship ran aground while I was below studying Frecht's charts of the western coast. This coral reef was not indicated on any maps, including an old copy of Flinders' work that I had secured in Sydney that I might seek his passage. Was standing four leagues off land when struck with blue water on larboard and starboard. Lost quite a bit of the rigging, both standing and running, besides top mast.

I blame my chief officer, Ryerson McKough, as he had watch when we grounded. He blames a sudden absolute calm in the winds, so that the Harvester would not respond to the rudder but kept drifting after the lookout shouted down warning. If I had smelled rum on his beard I would have left McKough on the reef with a tumbler of water and a wormy biscuit. Christ knows I don't mean that kind of talk, Jane. God knows these be terrible waters for any ship of sail.

Jane, have I and Frecht truly plotted the correct place where he stood, south a little of Cape Leveque. I don't know. Frecht was there twenty-five years past but he did not know the legend then and did not explore.

I have not yet dared to reveal to the men the exact nature of the Harvester's quest, of Wilkulda. I attempted to put aside my lie of gold but the men falsely cling to my cruel yarn. One day I suppose I will have to pay the piper for the conniving.

Tom Evans was catapulted onto the coral when the vessel ran aground. Eight men I have lost in thirty-six voyages in the Harvester. Many a captain would crow about such small losses but I am ashamed even for eight dead souls.

Terrible sight when we got poor Evans's corpse together. The men are cruel sometimes just to hide their own fears. They laughed only because the pumice type of coral Evans squashed onto made thousands of little holes in his skin. The men joked that poor Evans was tatooed to death, not crushed by his falling heft.

Said a full service for Tom Evans. He was with me eleven passages. My best topsail hand. He would be difficult to replace at any time and especially now with the Harvester so underhanded.

Leastaways it was better to lose only one man and not like my crossing of the Horn in '41, when the sea came up over her stern at mid-day when all was clear and quiet and stole half my watch from me. Four men, remember their names, Jane, I cannot, I have forgotten. I will make a place for Tom

Evans's oldest boy next voyage and give his poor widow, his second wife, a suitable purse.

*Personal Diary of Captain Atkins, February 2, 1853*

Accidents and delays plague this sailing, Jane. Thank Lord we rigged her as a fore and aft on the two back masts or we would have lost the ship and all hands perished half a dozen times. She sails well into the wind with this splended rig but this crossing of the Torres in summer is quite arduous. Going downhill in an easy eastward passage under the Horn in the gales of winter is pleasant against the stupidity of the contrary winds here'abouts.

Jane, I am sleeping badly. First time cannot sleep since apprentice days so long ago. My conscience is bothering me as to my duties to Bruce and Whoor Company. Even with old Bruce dead so many years I feel deeply obligated to him, and it bothers me to take the ship away from profitable work to try to search out relics of some supposed nigger magician.

Forgive me. God forgive me. I believe. Oh Jane I believe something grand and awful in import has finally come to your old Joe.

The owners will understand. They will be proud to bask in the reflected glory of the Harvester's exploits.

But Jane if I fail to find proof of Wilkulda's existence surely the owners will look askance on my fitness to master this vessel. Young Jack Whoor will be good about it but the son-in-law of Bruce will be rude even as is his nature unless I bring back profit. He will say blast the relics. They will not dare discharge me after all I have done for them these many years. Indeed, am I not a major partner in the concern? Charles Tawn will have a battle on his hands if he thinks he can sink me so easily.

Alas, my dear wife, I must admit that I am besieged by doubtings as I cannot justify this excursion as a proper venture for either the ship or the company. Where's the profit they'll say and I can't argue it. She's packed with clip, late, too late for the high prices but good wool by any standards no matter the lateness. I am going to risk the cargo by extending the sailing by some ten weeks, or more. If we do burst apart on one of these reefs the bales might keep her up long enough to beach her on one of these channel islands, or even hold her up until I steer her to the mainland.

Damn that Frecht. Rum crazed madman has infested my mind with his delusion.

Kukika, Kukika, Jane, she was a pretty thing for a nigger whore. She worked in the house of Frecht. I've told you about his house before, about the apricot groves and the people there. Kukika told me the tale of Wilkulda. It was little Kukika who spliced this legend of an elder brother of Jesus into my brain.

Frecht has entrusted me with a copy of his will and testament. Jane, although his early life was that of a profligate, in his approaching dotage he has become a changed man. He says he began to become a different man some years back when Kukika first told him Wilkulda's history. He is diseased, horribly, and besides he is too old to attempt a return voyage to the western shore. But whatever comes of this passage, Frecht shared half the cost of the Harvester's rerigging. In his will he has left his considerable fortune to the blacks of New South Wales whereby a retreat will be set up for them on his farms off the Paramatta road in perpetuity. The house and the apricot orchard will belong to the blacks also.

God knows Jane those few coloreds left in New South Wales are needful of succour. Why even in '17 when I first came out to these parts there were hundreds of specimens walking the poorer streets. The niggers that remain in Sydney be a wretched lot today. Crippled and scrofulous, and worse beyond telling but they must have been a strong folk once to have survived in such a hard land. When we English came here the blacks faded into the ground just like a dead butterfly who in a few days is eaten by other insects and worms.

So carefully did I plot the reefs of life until this burdensome venture. It was Frecht that did it. Before meeting him I would have stayed with good cuz R. Marsden on his farm in Manly while riding into Sydney on the white gelding I purchased in '49 to conduct the ship's business. I saw cuz Ralph and Nan but a few hours this passage. My mate tells me that Ralph came down to Darling harbor where we loaded the clip to see what had become of me. I left a

note for him and Nan with Frecht trying to explain my
enthusiasm for this peregrination on the sea.

My darling Jane I wish you were here to guide me.
Without this diary in which to speak to you soon I would be
mad as poor Frecht. This will pass, this journey will end and I
will be sitting with you at Sunday table. Jane I ne'er touched
Kukika, I never did. If Ralph Marsden writ you saying I been
unwell or that I touched Kukika, both lies. Jane, what
damage this must do to my reputation. This lunacy. I am an
Englishman and an Anglican and I cannot fathom my present
decline. This heathen's tale of a Wilkulda has stirred me so
very deeply. Wilkulda is like a fiddle string in my mind that
won't stop humming.

Since a boy at sea I have been sober and industrious. I
have striven to improve both my character and the station
that I was born to. Jane I ne'er touched the lubra no matter
what Ralph Marsden inked in his dirty letter. Sweetheart you
may never fear I have lain against but one woman's belly and
that be yours. Untainted we came together and I vowed then
ne'er to seek out another, and I have kept my promise.

Most of the lads I went to sea with as apprentices are
dead. Too many were killed by rum and corruption and most
were claimed as the sea's forfeit. Do you remember George
Feekles, Jane? He was a goodly lad. My only true friend cept
for you dear Jane. In some strange way Frecht reminds me of
George. Yet two moralities were never further apart. George
kept himself pure same as I did. A sound lad he was and
surely would have made a master if he had not the bad
fortune to go down with the Liverpool Corinthia off Sandy
Hook in '22. Damn the Yankees and their damnable clippers.
Damn them with their six knots average. They'll kill off all
the Indiamen, all of them. During the winter when George
Feekles was lost the Western Ocean is terrible hard.

I have rested an hour or two and as I could not find sleep I
have risen and turned to the diary again dear Jane. As I write
to you I hear your voice consoling my anguish. I hear you
even as the sea sounds outside on the boards. Dear wife it
makes my bosom glow with pride and affection to be sitting
on the very pillow you sewed me in '51. Tis a sad little thing
to think of all the dainty cushions I have worn out with my
spiney bottom. I should not complain but only thank the
Lord for the good years we've had.

We're off the north head of this lonesome continent and it still be apoor even here in latitudes where the rains are heavy. The boat crews that I land for victualing and fresh water return only with the water and though I am grateful for that it is unhappy to see the land lie uncultivated. There's no moon tonight and thick fog hides the foremast from the steer's man. My chained lantern seems a poor dim spark. I know you have not forgotten I love you and when you read this at home in a few months, April or May I hope, Jane you will see how precious is the cargo I carry in my heart for you.

Sad I am now cause I know I'm an old man. The lantern hangs from the cross beam so steady I can be sure a quiet sea runs. I wonder Jane if my heart and liver, or the spleen, inside me swings so evenly side to side as does my cabin's light.

I cannot seem to end tonight's entry. I am too excited by thinking of this exploration. I cannot calm myself even with an hour of reading from the Testament.

The Harvester's wheezing a bit since she went on the reef and is even wetter in the stern. I fear a gale under the stern will spring her boards apart.

Is this not a strangely long entry from your tight lipped Joseph, as if I were afraid to snap shut the lid of my inkwell. Evans is dead. You remember him, he came to our house in '47 to beg a quid to bury his eldest daughter and her unborn child.

I could feel the reef chewing into the Harvester as if it was me being bit into. Her pain was mine, poor ship. First officer McKough said there was no sign of race water and after we rowed her off I had the lead heaved and it was true, more than fifty fathoms under just a scant cable off the coral. Still I don't trust the mate as he is a drunkard. It seems every time the vessel has troubles he's held the watch. But I don't want to make a scapegoat out of a man under me, there's too many captains that practice such deceits.

Jane, Frecht as boy-man purchased a China girl had child with her but he lost both badly which may have deranged him for some years. I think he's a good man now and I trust him.

It is my burden to trace this tale of an earlier Christ to truth or to falsehood. A profound bewilderment has uncaulked my soul's seams. Frecht is convinced that Wilkulda

was practicing a Christian life ten or more centuries before
Jesus's stationing. And Lord forgive me, I am believing in
Wilkulda also.

There is supposed to be a cave near where Wilkulda stood
in the sea. Kukika had told Frecht that the cave has a
painting that shows him healing the tribes. This rude, native
painting is the proof that I am to search for. I have tracing
paper to copy it or if the stone appears suitable for such a
task I will attempt to pry the painting out and carry it
directly to Britain. This is my fond hope, to carve the
painting from its rock mother and return it on the Harvester
to home for all to see.

God forgive me for wailing of a newly made heretic Christ.
Jane what am I to do. I must seek the proof, I must. I will try
and sleep again.

I could not sleep.

Before meeting Frecht I have attended to only matters of
commerce. No doubt commerce is crucial in the aggregate
but still it is but commerce. Now I must dare to be a
discoverer. The very idea of a Wilkulda has unbalanced my
compass and disturbed my wake.

Thank God for the westerly current along this shore or we
could never manage to beat westward even with the new rig
as the prevailing wind as both contrary and altogether too
listless.

## four

Ship of general cargo, ship of wool clip and rum, a
passerby of Australia's currency boys and of a seemingly
vacant continent: Harvester storms the bulge and the land's
current carries her against air movements down the ugly west
coast. A prosaic vessel mastered by a pragmatic man of his
season. She never failed Atkins, the men yes, but never the
ship. The Harvester would lumber from out the eternal clasp
of terrible waves sending spumed and aroused foam from her
bows to stain high on the royal studs. A thousand
summations of a boastful ocean forever thwarted by the
ship's will to float in the lowest sky.

To three generations of seamen she made a secure home.
She did not have the speed or the grace to outrun a gale but

she failed not once to box her way out to calm waters from cruel danger. Hartlepool Harvester, perhaps too alliterative a name for some tastes, but the title fits the ship in perfection. A sturdy, stubby, carrier of produce, a commercial success, a reaper of fair winds and heavy gold; a vessel fitted to her essential requirements as a tool of man on the seas, and as a mother to men alone.

No cannon snouts penis arrogantly over the hull to falsely intimidate the waters. Four brass hand pieces did swivel, actually they were perpetually lashed, on the after deck railings. Today as yesterday, she carried bales of clip back to the looms of Britain and Flanders. By 1853 the days of exorbitant profit were drained in the Australian trade but goodly fortunes were too be made on the land in beasts and minerals.

Thus, in the middle of a fair century, a century of sunny confidence, when previously the Harvester and Atkins had been as dray wagon and driver, Joseph steered a course far removed from his own self-interest. His two mates, McKough and the junior, Donaldson, after six weeks of forcing the ship in and out of the Torres Straits had come to believe that Atkins was mad. At first the officers had disbelieved Joseph's recantation of the lie for they viewed him as a golden man of luck, a fellow who would rather sell his mother cheaply than not sell her at all. The mates thought the westward sail would lead to a virgin gold field and they would finally share in a pot of gold that the two had almost consigned to the grave.

When McKough and Donaldson at last accepted the newest disillusionment their minds burned hotter than rage's cauldron, and the men dreamt only of retribution. They accepted the truth, that Atkins was pursuing a nigger Christ, and the officers thus viewed their captain as a debased object fit for overt ridicule. Before they thought him mad the two had aped Atkins fulsomely, but now the angry mates betrayed every acquired gesture and habit. Instinctively the two men realized that the shipowners would condemn Atkins' extraordinary passion as unfitness for continued command of the Harvester. Joseph once returned to England would be discarded, and perhaps one of them might have the opportunity to become master of one of the luckiest ships then working.

Silently they gloated at their vision of Atkins felled. They saw their own phoenix rising from his charred reputation. Without style or pity his two mates facilitated Atkins in his desire to reach his mad destination. The sooner finished with the lunacy , the closer the great moment of his removal from command and their own promotion. They ordered the short-handed crew to ignore exertion and blamed the onerous schedule on the derangements of the captain. As the Harvester rounded Cape Van Diemen to make southward, the mates had convinced the crew that indeed there was no gold strike and that Atkins was seriously flawed.

The two officers manipulated the men's hate with fantasy's delight. In devout pleasure the two contemplated the rupture of Atkins with the owners once back at Sutherland. They waltzed in their working sleep at the eventual denouncement, when the sailing brotherhood would be made aware of their captain's strange obsession for a stone age Christ.

*Personal Diary Of Captain Atkins March 5, 1853*

Jane, the difficulties of this sailing have eased on passing southward along this barren land. We are forced to hug the shore to take advantage of the coastal current but thank God the reefs and shoals are less abundant here than on the eastern shores.

I imagine during the typhoon season these waters are very dangerous as west there is only empty sea until the tit of India and then Africa. Below, to the south, the ice blocks the water only after thousands of leagues of open sea where the storms can build up without hinderance. The typhoons must be great enough to sway even the earth. Storms shall ne'er whip my vessel's soft bottom onto nearby lee shore of rock. Monster storms must visit this coast spearing their wrath as undigested sea bowels against my disheveled ship, even as an immortal storm sky fades like a woman's red soaked bandage.

Ancient mold that was I, that was Atkins, is demasted. This beard that I methodically play among its whorls with my hand was once the beard of a Joseph who used to be I but in this latest hour when I rub the damp hairiness I touch the face of a stranger than I was behind the spiral coils.

Jane, my heart beating is agitated, my crew is ill-content, my mates treacherous, my ship spouting in water from sprung joints, yet I do believe an immense reward is to be spooned into my empty porridge bowl.

Jane, help me. My penis has not raised off my belly even with the aid of my clenched fingers since we crashed the reef and lost poor Evans. It as if my gonads were jolted and set awry even as the ship's compass shifts when nearing a land's mass. But the metal arrow I could reset while my own member seems not repairable. Jane I think I am finished as a man and am dying from sickly innards which make my movements bright red with blood. Save me Jane for my soul has been wrested from my discipline since I began to believe in an aboriginee Christ.

My crew is wild with fear of me. They and I mutually pretend that nothing has changed and that my rule of the ship is unassailable while the truth be that with each league deeper into the voyage their loyalties and respect further erodes. Without good Cecil Smith on board I would fear the crew's dread of me could lead them to violence to my person. They shrink back even as I pass among them, but Cecil is my friend and is the crew's true leader though he is but carpenter and sailmaker. The crew will stand faithful to me by his good example.

Ten passages have Cecil Smith and I made as shipmates. What a nimble boy he was when he first came aboard. Away into the rigging he flew when ordered without that cowed faint start that bespeaks an apprentice's will to flee. Cecil showed even then that he was born to be at sea. If he had not broke his legs in that fall in '50 as we closed into home harbor and the wind suddenly blew us back on her keel, I would have promoted him to mate then. As carpenter and sailmaker he is the cleverest I've seen and is too valuable in this station to change, but I will think on it. He is the finest man on any ship, to return to the Harvester knitted and strong boned after but three months laid up, even with his limping he is my best man. Cecil is as full of devotion to me as he was when he came unlettered from the orphanage and I do believe he looks upon me as his father. Next journey I shall make him chief officer not withstanding his skill with the needle and saw. I will ask Charles Tawn to find other berths for McKough and Donaldson. They both are opposed to me and wish me only evil.

This is a life of hardness, this sea life. But then the sailor is part of something bigger, grander, than a poor dolt trapped on the land. Wind is the primitive force of my being. My only hate, abhorrence is a better word Jane, at sea are the doldrums. Windless seas are the devil's work. I shall never trust the steam engines. No good can come of it Jane, mark my words. The piston and the steam as motive power is wicked and harm shall come to those usurpers who trick the owners into forfeiting sails. Why every English child knows that tea hauled in steam powered ships has a stink to the leaves from the coal smoke that will destroy a person's sense of taste.

Free winds, God's winds, how does anyone but fools think that an open sail could ever be surpassed as a ship's engine. As little as I think of those scrawny clippers at least there's speed enough for any owner without trafficking with coal and pistons. Personally Jane I observe that the steam driven craft has already seen its best day and that the sail has won hands down.

*Personal Diary of Captain Atkins March 6, 1853*

Sea proves in every way the Lord's omnipotence. We puny fellows fight the gales but no matter our victories we see in every encounter our own meagerness even as we think we have steered the ship into clear sailing. Hell itself must be the womb of typhoons. I have been at sea too many a year yet I have ne'er forgotten my first typhoon. Today I have studied out the signs of approaching typhoons and yet a storm as big as that can be staring you in the eye before you can blink. Quick they can come without a warning, without a drop in the glass. There's been the times I seen the glass drop so low you'd think the mercury had leaked out in some kind of breakage. You shout yourself hoarse battening the ship down yet the day stays bonny without the smallest scent of a storm. How they do smell bad, a typhoon does.

I firmly believe that the truest weather gauge is the sky's own color. This is useless at night except for the color of the moon through the sky. Whatever, it is a lengthy labor needed to learn even the rudimentary shadings of the sea and sky. Winds are secret and betray not their ways even to virgins. The sky is the wind's womb, yet it all seems foolish wisdom to acquire as the coal burns away at the inner veins of the earth. Pristine white skies are the most dangerous, beware the world itself when the color of the sky is as an old egg shell.

Yet it is true, there have been days off the great tail of Horn when there is nothing except a zenith of calm blue overhead while on the ocean incredible winds are shredding the sheets and the ship threatens to throw her masts from out the holes. I've noticed that the blues in the sky are ne'er the same when nearing landfall. The sky shades change so fleet it is as sometimes when I pass my hand over a misted mirror to wipe on a new reflection.

Wilkulda's people are said to be poor sailors. With these Southern Seas you'd think any race would take to the ocean but it isn't so. They've dugouts and rafts of course but these are poorly fashioned. Most curious aborigine craft I ever viewed was in Hobarton my first visit there in '16. T'was a reed affair, tied at each end with string and shaped like a broad beamed canoe. Only difference between that reed boat and the Pharaoh's ships that are illustrated in my books is that the Egyptian craft was big enough for a single mast and had a line taunted betwixt stempost and bow-sprit so that the ship would not hog.

The Hobarton canoe was too small for any rigging. In its bow space was a little place all smouldered where coals were kept alive that when landfall was made a fire could be started right away. There's those in Hobarton who believe that in these canoes the niggers crossed Bass to reach Tasmania. The aboriginees might be bad seamen but they be a brave race if they faced the awful rip currents and seas that blow in those straits and especially bad they are on a crossing passage.

Without Frecht and Kukika I'd ne'er seen beneath these niggers' filth to find secrets undreamt. To me, before I met Frecht, they appeared only as monkeys trapped in the perpetual heat of their loins. True the nigger is scummish to look at and they give off a stench that is remarkable in its puissance, I saw them as dogs except their pricks are not bright red, but now I've learned about Wilkulda.

Most of the settlers consider the niggers vermin, not

human they say and that the blacks must be killed off even as a shepherd shoots wolves, Jane, these aborigines are a most religious people and there are some among the colonial clergy who hint that the abos are descended from the lost tribes of Israel. There is a tale told late at night around fireplaces with pots of rum in hand, even in the best houses, that the abos are a mixture of Hebrews and an invading negroid people who destroyed the civilization that was based on the Old Testament.

To sail thousands upon thousands of leagues as a stern shipmaster and then when ranked high and the possessor of not inconsiderable wealth and a honorable name to become involved with a negress and a scoundrel in this mad attempt to verify the past reality of a aborigine messiah. I have become infected with Frecht's madness.

Jane my soul is flooded and awash. I am not equal to this quest. What matter can it be to any Englishman if a Wilkulda could heal? Then what is it that I have become, who am I? I thought I knew my character's chart. I was an Englishman who worked the seas as if they be his Monarch's patrimony. But before I was sailor, before England hoisted sail o'er the globe, I and The Queen God Bless Her, were yeomen. I am a believer and I am a man of goodest will, always victor am I o'er whores and rum's seduction.

Jane tell me, am I mad? Who have I become Jane?

I am Atkins, father to tall sons and virtuous daughters. Am I not Atkins? I am Atkins who has bested Drake's passage in winter. Wilkulda was at best a magician to a race of low curs, naked and filthy smelling, of perpetual and loathsome abominations before the Lord of Hosts.

Lord help me. My mind has become as a sunken, rotted, mainsail thready and hung on a weeviled spar on one of those devil's convict hulks anchored in the Thames when I was a lad. Poorest of all men were those chained in those prison ships. What a poor wretched lot they were who be made captive in such wicked wrecks that did float on the Queen's river. Jane it twisted my heart mournful when as a lad I sailed past men so ill treated.

Perhaps it is true, perhaps Wilkulda was what Frecht thinks he may have been.

# five

*Ship's Log March 20, 1853*

Captain Atkins still be sick and I, Chief Officer Ryerson McKough, commands this vessel in his stead. Captain Atkins is feeling somewhat better today after his dreadful incapacitations of late. Captain Atkins continues to write queer scribbles in his diary that is not of the Queen's language at leasts as far as me and Mr. Donaldson can make out. Captain Atkins was up and down the ship this dawn in his night shirt scouting out every nook like a red indian would for God knows what purpose.

Still holding due south as Captain Atkins demands.

*Personal Diary of Captain Atkins March 20, 1853*

Lord let me sleep. My soul is outraged by my failure. I wander my ship even as if spying out foreign kings secreted between decks.

Wilkulda has won me over. I struggled but his magic has bested my Christian severity. For I am now convinced that there was a true healer on these raw, desperate, shores and that he was named Wilkulda.

I loathe myself for my quaking of faith. If this nigger was a Christ then what are we and what was Jesus? Forgive me for my heretical quizzing. I believe, I believe he was the anointed one. Which one, both were one.

But if the black one was of holy pity, who am I?

I must discover the chart to my mind's new channel before I can decipher the riddle of His two Sons. Perhaps this voyage is but a stroke of my body's dying despair. It is incredible that such a limitless unease has invaded my vitals. As a boy I was not irregular and created a goodly quantity of defecations in the hut without mother's help. In truth I was a cheery lad even though forced to be the eldest in a fatherless brood.

It is an ever lengthening scroll since I was in mother's arms. It was a happy home even if poor and scanty of bread and fire wood. But mother's faith and readings in the bible made us children feel very rich. Mother was a fineness of manner. Oh Jane how the consumption suctioned out her lungs. It was a hard time especially that night when she died.

I was twelve years old, no, what am I thinking of, I was sixteen and home after my voyage as junior officer in the Thrush under Captain McGonigle.

What a long time it has been since McGonigle called little Joe Atkins to his cabin and signed me as second after the old second had died. What was his name Jane, that poor man who died when his neck boil sulphurated and poisoned him. McGonigle was a kindly man. Where would I have ended without his interest? He was a widower without sons and because I was a good, polite, lad who shirked not at the ship's labor he showed me kindness.

I shall never forget how McGonigle's Thrush took the sea over her bowsprit with that wicked figurehead of a naked nymph piping on her reed flute diving below the water line. Deeper and deeper the Thrush would slip into the sea when the sea rose. Even with the sheets bunted during a gale the water would run a foot deep back to the stern castle. Then when she must broach, the Thrush would toss the water off as if she were a fashionable lady opening her parasol to a spring drizzle.

Once off the Orkneys, when we was blown out of the Sleeve by a great winter gale, she wallowed badly in a fierce quartering wind. She threw her sails backwards hard against the rigging and masts. I felt sure she was going to lose everything aloft and then be dragged under by the drowning sails. The masts loosened and shook as if they was already out of her when McGonigle took the rudder and brought her around to slide her beam ways over the huge sea and take the wind abaft to pull Thrush safely through.

Thrush, at last she so bit into a storm with that nymph of hers that even McGonigle could not burst her free. Down she went in '21 off the Skag with all hands, with good McGonigle and the nymph too.

## six

After this entry a most unfortunate gap appears in my uncle's diary, a period of ten days eludes him, thus all of us. We only have the ship's log to relate of the period from March 20 to March 30, but as this journal was then under the authority of the disreptuable mates it offers small enlightenment into Joseph's feelings. From the transcript of the naval inquiry it can be assumed that Joseph was able to keep the Harvester sailing south along Australia's western coast by promising his two mates that they would sail to the inconsequential penal settlements of Albany and Perth for re-stocking. After her water barrels were refilled the Harvester would run east through the Bass and then, caught up in the Forties, she would burst around Horn and make to England.

Atkins' original plan had been, after chiseling free the cavern's sacred mural, to sail the Indian Ocean to Singapore and run in the trades to Africa where he would pick up the Agulhas current down at Hope and then sail north. This would be a longer passage but safer, as going down hill around the Horn in winter time would be too risky for a man who stored in his cabin locker a fragile historical relic. Joseph had accepted the mates' demand to use the southern route only as an expedient to keep Harvester prowed to that seafront where Frecht had indicated the correct location.

The mates did slander at the inquiry that Atkins had offered, "One hundred soverigns for the man who sights a black man standing in the sea." That this tale, even though verified by each crew member's affidavit was allowed to stand by the court, bespeaks the low tenor of the inquiry. What may be verified is that when the vicinity of the Turtle land was reached Joseph was able to invoke his captain's prerogatives, if only momentarily, and to send several shore parties out in search of topographical and anthropological data to compare with notes supplied by Frecht. We may safely presume that Joseph did offer a substantial reward to the sailor who discovered the holy cave.

Joseph's entries in his diary begin again on April 2nd. The ship's log shows that on the night of April 1st, McKough and Donaldson had decided to take the Harvester off the shore and stand out to catch the prevailing winds of the season north to Timor. Why the two schemers had decided to run to that pesthole of what empire remained to Portugal, is an enigma. Actually, their earlier plan to catch the Forties off Perth was logical and even superior to Joseph's dawdling plot to cross into the Atlantic from the east. Perhaps the crew was becoming difficult and had pressured the two mates into sailing for Timor. Sailors seemed to relish dying in such corrupt hell ports.

There is no doubt of Joseph's serious debilitation throughout this period, but there is sufficient proof in both journals that Atkins was able to put aside his emotional suffering long enough to convince the mates of the authenticity of the Harvester's strange quest. Somehow Atkins was able to induce McKough and Donaldson to peruse the information supplied to him by Frecht. When the Board of Naval Inquiry exonerated the officers and crew for the marooning of Captain Joseph Atkins, the august gentlemen had overlooked the causes for the ship's abrupt changes of course on the 1st and 2nd of April, 1853. When the Harvester was headed north to Timor, Joseph, in spite of his infinite despair, had enticed the two officers below to his cabin to read the spreadout maps and notes of Frecht. These lost papers convinced McKough and Donaldson that there was some possibility of finding proof of Wilkulda's life. It was then that the two brought the vessel about and sailed back to the littoral. They had decided to rid themselves of Atkins by marooning him there. Thus, it was their conversion to believe in the quest that forced their hand. They dared not have Joseph return with palpable vindication of the voyage's value, even if an esoteric value.

Acclaim would be Joseph's if he returned with proof of a past demi-god, even if a nigger. The 19th Century was a season when novelties of exploration were the rage. Fame was not yet debased by over-abundance and falsity. As a hero, Atkins could never be replaced as the Harvester's captain, and a shadow of mistrust would inevitably threaten the careers of McKough and Donaldson, no matter their legal right to command a vessel when its captain has become melancholic and incapacitated.

## seven

*Personal Diary of Captain Atkins April 1, 1853*

The port ahead tis always nearest and the one left behind the blinded stern is death. The thing is to reach out for the harbor that is forever unattainable as is the final port closed by the coal's smoke in the dark of day. Never the answer is contentment as loneliness dogs even the cheery stranger. Sooner on morrow's breech we shall slip anchor of rambled free iron throating down into the harbor's pocket.

Harbors are the brats of tearing seas that languidly crack the earth's vertebrae. Harbors create men who slay dainty eyes and whiskered snouts sleeping beneath the sea's surface. To sight after arduous watches of clay waves to squat for men to peer between a fairy woman then ever before. A place of green squares and white stairs holding tall doorways rectangled by pavement's arched chimney brick. A place of courageous men who died in servitude beneath their convict masters. I loathe-adore Sydneytown.

We should have settled there with Ralph and your cuz Anne in '35 even as they, I would have pricked my roots in that charming farm on Cook's river near Canterbury hamlet and becomed a landed gentry instead of this awful revealment.

No. Men still refuse to trust in harbors. They pretend not to ken such designs.

Jane my men have turned against me. Cecil, faithful Cecil Smith, came to me on deck in view of every Jack Tar and said I was ill and that the Harvester must be steered directly to Timor without further spurious investigations on my insistence. Jane, t'was I who taught him his letters that he now fouls my heart with refined words. Cecil scorns me, all of the crew see me as dishonored by this holy search for Wilkulda.

Soon, tomorrow, the ship shall stand by the shore where he did heal the tribes. Here at the faded anus of a tiny, lost, stream I shall be a newest man, a glorious vase of redblack clays. The mates are convinced of his verity, I am sure they believe though they admit it not. The Harvester stands in for the final, just, exploration and I am exculpated.

Now I feel I am fully appraised of this effort's meaning, this thrust from east to west, from where whored roof Sydney to this uncivilized, better, cleansed land. I am reminted in gold plate. I am a chalice to the Lord's chart. The poor men of the Harvester, unhappy lads, are blinded still by my brightness. They think me mad. Do you read closely Jane, the foolish men believe I have sunk down into the drippings of insane delusions. Cannot they see that I have been uplifted. Tomorrow, on the morrow, we find the place I promised. Then to Perth for succour and then to fly to England in the great dashing winds. Thank God I was able to convince McKough and Donaldson to back the sails and come about from heathen Timor. Wilkulda will be safe, soon safe.

England will greet my treasure with a stirring, the priests of God will ponder forever the mystery of Wilkulda. Jewel's rubies shall gleamcrowd my chest and boxes. No, I shall illuminate the world with this treasure. For that there was an earlier Christ is a mighty glory. This must ignite the hollowness of men into a dazzling intensity. Without this richness of Wilkulda soon all men shall wrinkle and be inert.

Indeed as the historied Navigator of yesterday cargoed rarest gifts to monarchs royal, so I Joseph shall burden to Victoria a crown of marveled strangeness. I am convinced that the Queen will reward me graciously, perhaps the sword's tender tap is not a pipe dream, Jane. As the deeds of the Navigator progenitored both the Indies west and the Americas, thus my recital of Wilkulda's identity will proclaim a new age for men and women and boys and girls everywhere on this goodly earth. On bended knees before Victoria I shall give utterance to the best tale ever told, that Christs are multiple.

But Oh Lord of Lords why could I not have remained Atkins, captain to Harvester instead of Atkins, Apostle to Wilkulda. Too old am I Jane, with a weathered cock that has gone bad. Kept myself pure for what, hundreds of young, soft warmings beckoned me to their scented places. I, the biggest fool to ship the seas, took pride in the staunching of my manhood. Too many months without cuddly women beneath my young cock that's now aged beyond repair. Jane, what comes over a man to make him write such as this. I think your Joe Atkins is near death's estuary. This is how I end the coil of my life's line, to an anchor sinking rapidly.

Ships are living bird-dragons. There is unsureness in my mentality that I believe that when the petrels and dolphins come upon a sailing ship they believe them to brother swans. Fowls that seek not the sky's refreshment but as clipped cormorants of yellow fishermen, sip the sea but dare not swallow. My gullet too is strictured.

I dream of a monster wave that will come off the Horn's sweep to burst the hatch heads with a massive sob that will snort the Harvester bottomward. Lord let me be not mad. Let Wilkulda have been reality and not my own insanity. I am convinced that this creaking cabin of the Harvester is not the universe, no not even its replica.

## eight

Winds skirt the belching sea billows and the Harvester's bow, beneath figurehead of woodengirlchild grasping wreath of rose ivoried daisy in white cracked paint hands, cleaves the bruising storm. Wind has lashed the castled wave as if into a froth of beaten egg whites. Flecks of crisp water heave over the railings followed by huge cubes of water meters thick. The crew furls the final sail except the jibs on the foremast. Even the spanker is tightly clenched to the boom. She keeps her head up. The men are bent small as they muscle in the wind and water to secure the whipping lines of tattered sails. At the foremast Donaldson, the second officer, has worked with deeper labor than any other in battening her down. That is a second's role, to work and lead the men by example and fists. Cecil Smith, the best man of the Harvester's crew, stands strong by the mizzenmast, which is his responsibility. He has done well as always and his station is first secured.

First officer Ryerson McKough alone at the wheel, alone
on the afterdeck, all hands in the rigging or at the winches to
battle her sheets in. McKough is a good seaman but weak in
character. He has succeeded in turning the Harvester about
on her track and is beating through a storm for the coast he
left the day before to sail to Timor.

Atkins half sprawls in his bunk. He is awake but has not
noticed the off-shore gale. He remains below while the
Harvester fights for her life. His shoulders are propped against
the bulwark. He is writing in his journal although the cabin is
dark and he has forgotten to kindle the lantern above.
However, in the lightning reflected from the sea, the space of
his self-made confinement alternately brightens and fades.
The room is never completely dark.

*Personal Diary of Captain Atkins April 2, 1853*

Tomorrow is my anticipated landing, tomorrow I claim
Wilkulda as prize. I will soon claw up the spirit from the rock
hidden behind heaven's garment. Tomorrow tomorrow he be
mine, what a prize.

Cherished Victoria shall come down to Thames dockside
to greet Harvester even as the Virgin Monarch came to caress
Drake. Very first after ashore I must seek out the cave where
Wilkulda resides in paint. Cecil will follow me as second. The
two of us alone will gently strike out the holy rock from its
cup. Good Cecil and I will transport the painting, we shall
first construct a wee wagon to sled it over the grains, no, of
course, we must build tracks of beam and a wheeled trolley
to be safer. And wrong, there must be more than two in the
cave as it will be a painting beyond ponderous. Winch, slings,
ropes, spikes, hammer, what else? I shall carry it securely
hulled to England where the whores will curtsey as it wagons
by, the truest passion.

The crew was captivated by my sermon this morning. I
awoke all slumbering watches with the bell of this fine ship
and congregated them below my deck's pride. Surely now the
men regard me as a man transfixed with a goal so pure that it
sweeps the skies clear. Now they too are apprentice converts
to Wilkulda.

I Joseph Atkins was set on earth to bring men the fact of

Wilkulda. Mad I ne'er be fore I am fulfilled with God's trust. Among the English race I will be elevated to the rank of seer. Wilkulda will be made fast to everyman's soul by my travail.


## nine

At dawn the winds fell and McKough tacked the Harvester into an enormous basin. The water was shallow but there was no need for a chain to be thrown, as visible beneath the keel was the white sanded bottom. And as the Harvester settled deep into the hollows between waves, a series of small sand bars, garlanded with streaming plants that flooded in the tide's rhythm, would rise up abruptly as if to strike the ship's bottom. A sailor lounged on a plank fitted from the bowsprit that angled slightly out over the sea until it met the hull's bulge some yards rearward. This plank served as the crew's lavatory. They would sit with their legs dangling betwixt plank and ship while they performed their evacuations. Normally on approaching an uncharted shore the sailor would be casting a leaded line for measurement, but with the pristine shallows he could call back from sight," 'af a dozen,' in relative leisure.

"Five an' we're clear thanks Christ," blessed the bottom's observer as the ship flew over the range of bars. Harvester glided through a patch of bulb and weed-surfaced sea garden. The hull burst apart hundreds of the miniature gourds and a livid tint drifted from the crushed black bulbs to dye the clear waters. It was the 3rd of April and but a day since they had sighted land again after returning to the coast. Atkins had thought that yesterday would have presented the moment of cherished arrival, but the storm had blown them too far north and the ship had to be worked south to the bay noted on Frecht's chart.

During the forenoon of the 2nd Atkins had come on deck. Bobbing about the decks he had encouraged and cajoled the crew to herd together by the primal mainmast that he might sermonize beneath the banging sheets. He had lectured a dawn previously and the mates permitted the crew to congregate again in the hope that Atkins would further

degrade himself before them. By this juncture every man
aboard appraised Atkins as possessed by lecturing but Atkins
noticed not their scorn, for even as the wool laden Harvester
floated below the pure sky his mind had risen from his
corporeal self to mate with the sun.

His very appearance bespoke derangement, for he had put
aside even a brisk toilet and was filthy. A noxious stench
clung to the air he moved through. And the sailors, who
prided themselves on cleanliness, saw his dissolution of dress
and person as proof of his insanity. Uneasily they watched
his frantic hand jabbings and his short bursts of pacing about
the mast butt. He was attempting to force his thoughts into
logical procession, however, before he uttered a word at the
mast's base, with a beatific smile in his ashen face, and
swarming his arms above his head even as if his twisting hands
could sing without words, he led the men from mid-decks to
the main capstan block that fronted the mizzen mast. This
was that very block on which the master anchor chains were
chanted in and out of the sea.

Sullenly, muttering of disaster, prophesying ill-luck, the
crew with hunched necks, bare-footed, came to the block
with their euphoric captain. Panting, his fringed skull wet
with rising sweat. Atkins struggled to attain the top of the
wooden buttress. As if to prove his debility he slipped and
crashed to the deck, but prodded his nervous bulk again onto
the large wheeled peg as the crew, mutely, surrounded him.

"I am free," he began, as the sea and sky bleached sailors
of the Harvester elbowed each other and muttered curses,
"always I have lusted for a wind not of earth that I could
neither compass, nor map, no, not even identify. I have
found my breeze and it has offered me liberation. So long
was I without the wind that I have been concerned it was
non-existent. But my wind is true and it shall leave me alone
never more. Too many men of ships eat the passion of their
freedom but although my balls have shuddered for the want
of a brown girl beneath my cock, yet, I have found my wind.
All about on each tack, girls were profuse, but I resisted and
instead have found my wind."

At this mention of brown women unlaid the crew
interrupted Atkins with obscene cackles. The two mates
guffawed even as they seized Joseph's trouser belt and rushed

him off the truncated cylinder of oak. The mates were good natured as their huge fists flailed his person. Thus, Atkins in the midst of his sermon of love was dragged from the ray blackened stump that wombed the ship to earth by its iron links.

The crew observed with astonishment the enfeeblement of once mighty Atkins. And most of the men were amused although a few felt the tradgedy of his fall and were degraded by his humilation. These few who felt a caustic hurt of betrayal were most dangerous to Atkins. Sailors all crowded onto one another's shoulders to peer down at the foundered captain as he lay stiffly booted to the deck by the mates. Yet, as the score and ten of sailing men joked and winked at his fate, Joseph with welling spirit pried himself free of the mates and with his ectasy as goad he regained the ascendancy of the capstan block.

Standing high on the spool, even as mutiny burned in the crew's desire, he attempted to speak but the laughter bested even the sea. The few old sailors, men in their forties and ancient with life's logic, banged their solid palms to the gunnels so that a thumping drum sounded throughout the ship's beam.

"Let 'im speak," quoted an old one, "he's ouren cap'ain, he's Atkins the proud un' an' the owner's fatted calf." Thus said Cecil Smith the crew's best man and Joseph's friend. It was Smith's finest moment, as if he were both a sword's edge and a gouged shield boldly defending his fallen prince.

Smith held the anger of the men back as Joseph swayed and began to speak, "I am free." He said this thrice more from the blood speckled block.

Staggering yet still standing, redness majestically pouring from torn ear and raptured nose. Rubbing green silk shirt sleeve across his blood designed mouth, Atkins became motionless as if wafted into some remote dreaming. Then he smiled, even as if he were some highborn, charming, noble's boy, and said, "Fear me not for I mean no harm. I ask nothing except that we be delivered. Forgive me as I have somehow bred violence into this discourse of forgiveness."

The majority of the Harvester's crew remained grim and brooding at this statement, but a few frankly expelled farts, or picked nostrils, or squeezed yellow creamed pus from

boils. The two mates reveled in the morning's entertainment
as Joseph continued. "My task is not opaque though my
mind is timid before my discovery. Let me tell you what has
been resolved in my heart's soul. I demand nothing from thee
neither approbation nor love, only that thee listen. That I
once panted as everyman to fondle and suck at the soft secret
places is not urgent. What is important is that I have been
chosen by fortune to announce the second, no, the first
Christ."

The men thronged about in the afterwake of the weird
heresy. Those closest heartily swung fists until Joseph's being
was crumpled on the block. A rib was snapped by a left
handed blow and a sailor lad swept a knotted line to slice his
forehead, leaving flesh spread wide even as if Atkins was a
bitten into, ripe plum. And still he clung to the block and
rose again in an attempt to speak. Impressed by his resolution
the crew's fury was lanced.

With the pain of the rope's burn as his north star, Atkins
directed his soul to be composed. And went on with his
confession, "Somewhere near our voyage's final plot, on
those squares of precise degree, a black fellow was anointed
by this same sea to be brother of Jesus and this lonesome
black did heal the dying-diseased."

With abhorrence the men stepped away from the figure on
the block, away, as if Joseph were a rotted corpse of
odoriforous chemicals. Silent to their very skeleton structures
the sailors dared not speak and the joisting squeals of the
rigging were suddenly awesome in the men's inner ears.
Slowly the crew measured the vileness of the devil that was
Joseph Atkins. A whispered threat did escape from jealous
Donaldson, the second officer, who a decade previously had
forfeited the privilege of penis erection when a London bred
whore, queer with gin, had bitten somewhat too deeply
during oral delights, and now the stunted Horace D. heard his
fury screech, "Kill 'im, kill the bloody shitface," thus
bespoke the severed Donaldson.

Atkins acknowledged the threat only in one corner of his
metamorphosed brain. For though he was now doomed, to
himself he was a refreshed Joseph, a true worshipper of
Wilkulda's myth. The crew's confidence in violence rose
when they saw him not respond to Donaldson's fuming; and

thus each man nursed the forbidden dream that he alone would become the single captain on the primordial oceans. The crew became boastful, as if the demented plan to kill a captain was a daily sport. A shrill giggle was emitted by the eleven year old, flaxen haired galley-boy who was the cook's arsehole whore. Gladly had the lad prostituted himself, for extra rations of raisin biscuit were a most desirable reward.

"Let's take 'im an' 'ang 'im, the doity shit's cockhead," stamped out a handsome ablebodied who owed Atkins a gold sovereign for payment of a proper burial for brother and brood dead of smoke inhalation suffered in the firing of their slum dwelling.

" 'e's a 'eathen, a cannibal's brat from Africa Atkins be," exclaimed a newer young, top's hand, a chap born in Liverpool to a washerwoman whore. The whore part of his mother had contracted syphilis from his unknown father, by which disease the sailor lad was being eaten up.

Laughing and jesting, with some playful arse goosing, the men of the Harvester gathered in their brains a hot wind of intended slaughter. "Well, should we 'ang Joseph Atkins for his blasphemy?" queried Cecil Smith, carpenter, sail mender, astrolabe assistant; the best one of all was Cecil Smith. This man Atkins had tutored and trusted, he alone of the Harvester's signed crew would not suffer materially in the future for the marooning of Joseph Atkins. Cecil Smith as an aged captain would die six decades hence when his cattleboat would be sunk off Caracas by a submersible's iron tooth.

As no answer was given to his question, Smith cheerily responded to himself, "Well, 'e's a queer brute no doubt at all. Let's 'ang 'im high so 'is lousy prick juts out red blood from 'is jerkin' legs." Thus spake the orphan who Atkins had purchased free from a convict's ship surgeon at Adelaide, the man Joseph viewed as dear. At this ultimate treason Atkins made a slight shivering of arms and spine. But Cecil Smith, the best one, lurched his hefty shoulder as pivot and slammed his heaviest fist into his captain's throat. Atkins dropped as a deadness to the holystoned plankings.

Crew came around to make a hedge of scorn about the unconscious man. A few kicked at him as if he was a skull-ball, and his chubby form rolled from deckside to deckside. Yet after the first circuit Joseph roused himself.

Again he rose to make to the warm-wet-red capstan block. Crew watched with greedy fascination as if Atkins was a forbidden puppet performance. With spasmodic belchings of blood Joseph stood erect once more on the chain's wrist. Crew howled in delight at the marvelous spectacle of their grand captain sacrificed on the block of blocks. The men garbled among themselves even as barnyard roosters who by some cabal of sorcery have gained ascendancy over the axe wielding farmer. Anticipating butchery's merriment the crew jabbed each other with eager elbows and fingers. Behind the backs of the ringed crew the cook's passion overwhelmed the elderly, arthritic, fellow and he kissed his boy helper fully on the lips while wetly fondling the lad's parts. But the youngster with a teasing leer ran away to dodge into the first row of sailors ganged about the unsteady but upright Joseph.

"Let's drop 'im offen the yardarm all naked with the rope tied to his cock," screamed the overly excited cook who from his rearward security masturbated with hand clenched in pocket.

A taciturn Irishman from Derry, who kept beads and a tin cross carefully hidden in his box so that his mates would not abuse him as a popish dog, spoke out in a tone of pity, though he instantly regretted, and retracted, his sympathy: "No, we should not lay hands on the captain. We should force the heretic over the side wit' boat hooks. That way he'll drown without a sin on us for cohabiting a criminal deed." The Irish sailor knew the word, 'cohabiting,' for as a lad he had borne witness with his mother against his father for 'cohabiting,' with three daughters.

Shrewdly McKough now spoke from his canker infested throat, the souvenir of scurvy first contacted when as a child he had served under a miserly Yankee captain who sold his crew's anti-scorbatics to a slave trader who had run short at sea. Ryerson growled in a not unpleasant voice, "There be but one way to deal with this. Captain Atkins will be safely left ashore in this bay that he has navigated us to. We are low on supplies due to the extra sailing and he will have to live off the land like the niggers do. Many a white man has lorded among these Australian niggers for years and years, enjoyin' all that is offered, ha, ha. This is what Atkins wants it to be and so be it. His brains be plagued but I understands his speech makin' to be his commands to be left behind so's he can explore and teach the niggers Christianity. We must do his bidding even if we sees that he be disordered, for he is ouren captain."

Sonorously did McKough, master to be of the proud ship Harvester, continue his ploy, "When we drop anchor in the Thames an' unload the clip we'es gonna tell the authorities the absolute truth that Atkins was left behind on this terrible shore as consummation of his own command. His diary is full of madness and will show his unfitness to command. It will show that Atkins is mad enough to order his own marooning. We'll work the story out on the inboard passage so's we won't cross ourselves. Tomorrow we will maroon the devil, the rest of today we'll turn out the rum and Atkins' brandy and celebrate the voyage home."

Joseph, as if he had not heard his crew's merciless ranting, began to speak, "Men, the Lord has," but Donaldson kicked him off the capstan block. The crew carried and and pushed the unresisting Atkins to the ship's lowest deck that covered the bilge. Here, aft of the wheel, with the rudder's massive pinion revolving nakedly, Joseph was flung into the wet cupboard that served as the Harvester's brig and chained to the iron rings that were skewered into the hull.

On leaving the cell the cook's helper, the biscuit prostituted boy, suffered remorse at the pitiful appearance of his captain and hastily tore a sleeve from Atkin's shirt and wetted it in a puddle of leaked-in seawater to wash Joseph's face and neck and welted torso. The liquid was astringent to the man's mentality and Atkins strove to his feet. And he did succeed in standing, but feeling the weight of the wrist chains in his soul, Joseph collapsed despairingly.

An unlit lantern swung on wearied hemp line outside the solid panel that was the cell's portal. And though Joseph could not see the lamp twisting and straining ceaselessly, by the vibrating sound of the bracing hemp fibers he felt the sea's pulse and was comforted in his solitude. Atkins called out to where the dry oil lantern swung in the empty deckway, "Men, I am your benefactor, I am your captain. I am master to the Harvester."

The lack of response forced reality upon Atkins, but he could not yet surrender, and with misbegotten energy began

to batter his chilled iron manacles on the hull. It was but a
meager drumming he produced and dispirited he soon
abandoned it. He wished for light but there was none, only a
patch of grey on the cell's far bulkhead from a tiny square of
bars set high in the oak door.

A droning boom quivered his cell. He knew the source but
was astonished that the sound was so tangible, as if he could
be bruised by the noise alone. It was the rudder of the
Harvester held over hard as the ship was run out of the bay to
stand safely off shore at night. The vessel was brought about
in a quartering wind and the sheets with their running rigging
briskly rumbled as the keel fell across the waves.

Awake, Atkins peered up from the brig floor to seek out
the unoiled wick snuggled in its empty copper bowl floating
to and fro outside the door, but he could only visualize it
deep in his memory. Crawling along the deck he groped upon
the bucket that should have contained drinking water, but it
was empty. Angered at the disobeyed regulation, Joseph
banged the wood container at the door slab. His hands were
jaggedly cut by the iron nails protruding from the pail's
frame, but he did not desist.

From decks above running bare feet sounded down to the
bilge deck. A hatchway was lifted and instantly a liberated
square of twilight entered the space of Atkin's confinement.
A ladder was let down to this the lowest level. Five
ablebodies came jumbled down as if they were one clotting
of men and cloth. Cursing with vigor they shouted out that
Atkins must cease his thumping. He did cease and the men
happily rushed to climb back to the main deck where the
rum was uncovered with none to act as overseer. Before they
made up the ladder, Atkins in a voice of trembling clarity
provoked the men's collective guilt, " . . . is this how an
English crew treats the ship's captain. I have ne'er been a
Bligh to any man. Did you men know that I knew Bligh when
he was governor of New South Wales. He caused himself the
same type of troubles as a governor that he had at sea. Men, I
am not a Bligh. I am disheartened that thee men would
forbid me a keg of drinking water. I would ne'er do the like
to any of thee. And the lamp boys, please strike the lamp
that I may have a bit of light as comfort during this night."

No answer came from the now solemn five, and Atkins

sensing their conflicts, rapidly continued, "Men, why am I in these chains? Do I deserve such a plight? There is still opportunity for reflection men. Tomorrow, after I am marooned, thee will be doomed, if not by England then by God. Release me and I shall make the morrow's exploration and when we return to England with the rock painting I shall ask the law to be lenient with you poor men."

Although the thick door separated the five from Atkins, the sailors huddled by the ladder's base as if seeking protection from doomed captain. After a short exchange of whispers the five, without a word for Joseph, speedily went up to the next deck. Atkins shouted for them to stay and heed his instruction for light and water. From the encirclement of the brig the timbre of his voice was as a child shrieking. The five ablebodies secretly waited above and thus realized Atkins' true emotional state from the plea squeals. Because they were five, which is not a magical number, nor even a mysterious sum, the sailors felt deeply the captain's cringing. The men hated him hotly for his pain and fear, as this made Joseph their brother.

A fattish chap, fated not to finish the voyage due to a dropsical death from a strictured kidney, was incensed that Atkins would hurl his own fear at their souls and he shouted down the hatchway, "Ye damn heretic, we'z gonna leave ye wit youse nigger prick kisser. Ye damnable old fool shut yur hole." The defrocked captain heard the confirmation of his judgment to be and lay down wearily on the brig deck, disappointed and yet relieved. After staring at the idea of marooning Joseph convinced himself that he would be grateful to die in the world of Wilkulda.

## ten

Atkins' wife Jane had been a doe of a girl when they wedded. Fifteen years she was when shaken and yet willingly, she had become wife to the strong cocked youth. She was flagrantly ignorant of how to make a man feel safe in her concavity and in his own innocence Joseph knew not how to teach Jane to be unafraid of his passion. In a few years,

during Joseph's short stays at home, a pattern of infrequent
sexual indulgence was established.

The trouble had begun during their first fortnight of
marriage when Joseph, dismissing Jane's wretched sense of
self-degradation as a passing phase, did not ease his lust until
her fears had been magnified beyond recompense. For after
this initiation into the storming of a man's cock, Jane
withdrew her being from Joe, convinced of her mother's old
tale's truth, that men became insane with an excess of
sexuality. Her mother had informed her of this fact in
childhood, and the young couple lived in her mother's home
for the first year of their marriage.

Joseph had driven the Harvester hard that they might
purchase their own home. Yet even with his haste's success
he was disappointed to find that Jane, even distant from her
mother's will, was intolerant of his bulging manhood. After
thirty years of marriage Joseph still had not viewed his wife
completely ungarmented. In the beginning seasons of their
copulations Jane would raise her nightgown no further than
her thighs. However, after several pregnacies she relented
somewhat to her husband's suggestions and allowed a drained
Joseph to rest his head upon her naked breast, with her gown
pulled down over his head.

These habits of Jane he dreamt not of as he lay shackled in
the brig. He dreamt instead of Kukika, of her charms and of
her availability that he had denied himself. Safely at sea,
Joseph could allow absent Kukika to be his inspiration. He
attempted to think of the lubra's odor, of how she smelled.
For her distinctive scent had both repelled him and drawn
him to her. Yet he could not remember the odor's
composition there in his cell. And Joseph did not hear his
own moan of relieved tension as he drifted into a depth of
slumber.

And thus, Joseph knew not of the fabulous dreamings he
did create there on the brig floor. Behind his closed scalp he
at once envisioned the embroidery of a vividly hued coverlet.
A cotton blanket that had once warmed his boyhood straw
mat. It had been a stained, poor cloth. Ragged blanket with
bands of brown upon brown, but with a wide, boldly bright,
red knitting betwixt the two duns. In his dream Atkins was a

young child garbed in a tiny nightshirt that exhibited his genitals fully before his mother, who was washing his face, especially rubbing at eyes and nose, with a patch of damp cloth. Truly he knew he must be very young there in the dream, yet his bulk before his mother was of an adult.

It was summer and the two persons stood alone now in a small, meagerly furnished bedroom that was his mother's sparse space. It was the room he had been conceived in and born into. It was the last room his father had left before he drowned in the South Brighton creek when the rotted bridge collapsed under a spring hail storm. It was the room where his father as a corpse had been redressed in a rented suit, to be returned before interment.

The dreaming flew from this sacred room and no longer boy but instead, in the huge canvas cloak that he wore on winter crossings on the Western Ocean, Joseph stood on the bowsprit of the Harvester as it floated in a doldrum. Dreaming Atkins was astounded at the cloak's weight. Wondering if the garment carried ponderous cargo he felt into vast pockets. From within these cloth containers Joseph scooped out tiny anchors cast in gold. The cloak was overburdened with these gold miniatures and he could sense that the garment was being torn apart by the weight. Desperately he began emptying the pockets of their treasure and as he did this, dreaming Joseph, discovered that his boots were aslosh with blue cold water that drained down to drench the bow nymph.

In his dream Atkins bent down to tug off flooded boots and as he did this the dreamscape filtered once again and the fantasy's backdrop became an orchard of orange, coconut, date trees, and pomegranate vines netted above. An English sky united with a soft, wet, meadow from which tall trees towered among the vines of fruit and bloomed chestnut buds. There, behind a pear tree, he spied the town of his being, Old Brighton.

He looked upon the town from an unkempt corner of the orchard. It was a sea village with manure, sheep, cows, apple groves, and finally, ultimately the harbor and its ships of sail, royal swans of tree and linen. Atkins, a boy still of dreamings, but also huge as man, cloak now cracked with

drying salt careening down creek road to Sunday church. A
stone fence bordered both sides of the pleasant dirt lane. The
fence was prettily grown with green and white flowers
sheltering the smooth stones below. He came to sit with
mother in church, in the second to last row at the rear, under
the choir balcony. He could sense the strain and tension in
his mother. She was quite alone and provocative in her
widow's blackness.

Yet the dream's shutter lensed wide and Joseph was in
poor cottage of home staring over the edge of the coffin that
vised his father's corpse. Joseph kneeled on knees and the
cheap, pressed-woodchip, coffin reared high above the
lad-man. He saw how his father was minutely and exactly
dead, just as he had seen it decades previously. Except that
his parent's brown, softly waved hair and beard were
seemingly blueblack against the ivory deadness, the very hue
of his ship's figurehead. He saw again the pauper's coffin with
its woodknots plugged with unbaked clay.

In dream's reality Atkins sensed that he had returned from
a justly renowned adventure. And yet elation floundered and
Joseph turned in despair to trudge morosely from the empty
parlor.

Again a shifting and he in exhilarating race went to seek
mother. He found her at once which was the dream's single
lie. Joseph bent to mother but noticed now at last that she
wore no widow's black but was nakedly black in skin.
Agonizing dream suddenly revealed to Atkins that nude,
black, mother lay quite still in the coffin of finest walnut he
had purchased for her corpse on his returning from the sea as
a young man of prospects.

And dead mother spoke to her son, "Sweet child how wan
and chalky you look. Are you constipated? How many times
have I told you not to oversweat when you move your
bowels. Your pallor tells me that you and Jane have been
fighting again. Not Jane, not Jane, stop fighting with your
little brother or I shall never kiss thee again. Come, it's an
early bed for bad Joey."

Dream stimulated inert Joe and in his imprisonment he
attempted to reply to his mother. Alas, as he began to speak
the woman rose from her coffin and drifted slowly out of the
church into kitchen of the cottage he had been raised in until
shipped out to sea at age eight. Joseph of the dream ran after

mother's bobbing form into the hearth space. His enormous boots sloshed out pristine founts of sea water onto the earthen floor.

Then he observed, standing still and silent at the food table, his four brothers and two sisters neatly ranked by height. At the onset he noted that the room smelled not of cooking vapors but of church candles, melting smoking wax. In his dream, Captain Atkins understood that he was seeing his sibling-fellows as they had been when he took leave to journey on the seas.

"How sad and alone they were to see me go," thought Joseph in his dream, "and Unice and Hobart and James and Prudence all gone now."

Glancing toward the fireplace, with its soot blackened iron rods and prongs, he became aware that the oven was abnormally dusty, as if it had not known a blaze for a very long time. Turning his eye from the cold hearth Joseph saw that his six brothers and sisters had taken their places on planks upheld by milk stools around the table. As the eldest he made his way to the right of his mother's place, which was nearest the oven. At the end opposite from mother should be an emptiness reserved for the memory of dead father and husband. Then in trauma's dream Joe realized that he had inadvertently sat on the stool of his father. He attempted to cry out but instead of a wail a spout of seawater sprang from Joseph's throat.

In the dream his mother rose in terror from the boards to rush past the chopping block through an inner door. Running after her, with arms throttling up and down as if he were a little boy, massive Atkins ran after mother while in an adult voice he cried plaintively, "Mama, mama."

Following mother through the doorway, all the Josephs of every world screamed. For instead of entering the sleeping area he fell a long way down into the Thames' estuary. Floundering in panic, wildly did Atkins of both dream and brig twist frantically, as if striving up toward the safety of the kitchen exit from which he had fallen. Alas, he was captive of the outbound tide as it streamed back into the ocean. And just then, and only for the briefest of instants, Joseph in both dream and brig became aware that this dreaming was a final testing and that death was warped near his dreaming soul.

In the dream he was beneath the river's placid, refuse
tonsiled surface. Here the true vigor of the stream ruled
without restraint. Above in the sky's white space, although
somewhat disturbed by the prismatic green weaving, he could
distinguish the vast swollen sun. The tide took him yet
deeper into the river's intestine. And in his maturing dream
Atkins in the Thames passed under a brace of anchored
sailing ships. He could hear the sea gurgling in his stomach
and tasted its astringent foulness on gums and teeth.
Intermittently his hands would strike on black logs,
half-devoured by sea beings, still buoyant enough to float
laboriously at mid-depth. Several fathoms of slate water
separated his drowning state from the green mossed hulls.

The vessels were tethered by bow anchors alone and thus
the ships streamed backwards in obedience to the Thames'
flow. Joseph was too deep to read the stern plates; however,
as this was a true dream, he could see clearly the distance
reduced titles even in the shifting light of the river. And the
anchor chains of wrought iron seemed not to be of heavy
hammered metal, but rather, bright cords of glass balloons
that held the sea imprisoned castles afloat.

These chains swept mightily up from the shadowed
bottom in parallel gratings that clenched the ships to earth,
for without the metal cord the vessels might leap high into
the universe. Hulls heavy in hirsute green velvet, yet dreaming
Atkins judged that this fact of plant growth on keels must be
mistaken as ships of commerce anchored in the Thames had
not the leisure to beard so richly.

*May's Misstress. Hamburg Hanna. Nancy Bosse. Honor
Jenkins. Maurice Fendem. Cox and Turner Mercury. Bourge
Virgin. Jonathan Thomas Millhouse Esq. Mighty Baltimore
Red. Norse Princess. Sea Stallion. Apollo's Head.*

These were the vessels he dreamed as he drifted in the
Thames. Ships that he had never set foot on, nor transacted
business with. These were trim and doughty craft that at one
time or another the Harvester, with Joseph on deck, had
passed on the open sea. Gently he rolled down the dimming
Thames. He floated twenty fathoms down from surface glare
and when a convulsion unsteadied the tide's pattern he was
softly weaved into the river's bed. Joseph experienced neither
pain nor fear, passing unhurried in a natural voyage of return
to the ocean's depths.

A pause in the current dropped him into the deepest pit of the river bottom. And here, at last, he became confused and thus afraid of dying. Violently he kicked into the muck and a cumulus of decayed mud was ejected upwards by his energy. For a moment Atkins successfully rose toward the atmosphere, yet even as he neared the surface some power possessively reeled him back down.

In this dream of optimum genus, Joseph observed that the constricted river had dramatically widened into an enormous, candleless place. In a moment of calm terror he noted that the gentle but omnipotent tide had carried him out of the estuary into the channel between severed island and continent matrix, that the sea was now sucking him down into its nether regions.

Oldest of the brain's sections began to race at the approaching numbness of death. Atkins exiting from life burst on a word into the ocean depths, "Mother!" And as the magic term mingled with the water, finally at end now, the sea pressed past his lips and broke into the last reservoir of air he had been holding safe in his rectum. Victorious was the dream and Atkins began to whimper in sleeping as death triumphed.

Yet he was succoured, saved by a dreaming transportation from the channel depths to the kitchen threshold. His mother was climbing the sawed board stairs, and he followed her on narrowing steps, seeing himself as clumsy, too big even as a dream truth. Musing at the silence of the stairs that should be creaking, cracking, he said aloud, "How well have I proceeded in the world of gold."

Joseph watched mother's immaculate, severely held rump ascend in proper, humorless dignity. Then, in a staggering hush of awareness, he realized that his mother had never lived in such a commodious house as this. Indeed, this structure was the very one possessed by Jane and himself, rich Joe.

Dream swiftly beheld another scene, it was the place where the cresting South Brighton creek had destroyed the bridge and his father had drowned. Yet, in fact as in dream, when Joey had raced here he found the bridge quite intact though worn, as he had always known it. He remembered in the dream as he looked down at the bridge from a knoll how his mother had to struggle daily in the golden world to keep firewood and gruel and cottage. Mother had succeed in this.

They were never evicted although there were times she had to
work the nights through some other place, washing clothing,
or something, to get the gold to exist.

Dreaming Joseph was at the uppermost stair landing where
she had turned off to enter a brightly lit room from the
dimness. He saw himself, soaked with the ocean's substance,
enter behind the woman's shadow. Inside he discovered that
the room was the cottage's loft where he and his four
brothers had slept. "There, here, what a good place this was,
the very best place of my life."

A small window emitted a hazed moonlight, the tiny pane
of glass was in the shape of an inverted triangle. There were
no beds, only mats of straw. The one underneath the window
was Joe's. "How little everything is," spoke Atkins quite
distinctly in the brig and dream dimension too. Suddenly
without effort he found himself sprawled over his mat,
overwhelming it with his grossness. Water sluiced from his
cloak but instead of sopping the floor the liquid dropped
through space into invisibility.

Mother drifted to bend over him, seemingly unaffected by
the floorlessness. She hand combed back his damp sidelocks
and rubbed her yellowed fingers back and forth on his sparse
haired scalp as if he still might be fully maned. She spoke
aloud but Atkins could not or would not comprehend the
words. She repeated the simple phrase again and again, even
spelling it out with her lips forming each syllable. Atkins
could not identify the meaning of her silent message.

Closing his dream eyes Joseph hoped that on reopening
them he would be able to understand his mother's warning
but instead when he did look onto the dreamscape again it
had passed elsewhere. When he blinked dreaming lids he was
horrified to discover three nude ladies swaying in Oriental
dance about his mat in a stoop of larking sadness.

Sweet naked females, hands and braids entwined in highest
harmony. To himself the dreaming Joey felt as an ungainly
whale smothering the loft space with queer lusts. Sombre,
and like a fat spectre, he lay upon the rectangled straw. Three
women gracefully smiled and their costume of nakedness
wore no masks of deceit for the boy Joseph to misconstrue
the smiling.

The dream hesitated as if afraid, and then moved rapidly

even as if it scorned its own timidity. Joseph dreaming lay
still on his straw mat but now truly as a boy of seven years.
The age was but one season before he went to sea. It was his
seventh birthday and he was ill with croup. Mother had not
allowed him to come to the kitchen to eat his holiday gift of
pudding. Mother, fully clothed and English white, briskly
appeared by his side with the rare, sugared, delicacy held in
long fingered hands. Withered yet energetic, Mary Atkins
settled herself on the milking stool that served as the loft's
single chair, and relentlessly spooned the pudding into Joey's
oval mouth as if the treat might possess an unknown magic
quality.

Finished with the feeding of her dreaming son, she did not
leave but patiently stayed a longish spell on the milking stool
keeping her eldest child company on this, his last birthday at
home. Finally, after a deep sigh of resignation, Mary spoke,
"Joey must go to sleep. Birthday is over and you must wait
till some other time before I can play with thee again."

His mother arose and at once diminished in size as if she
had been punctured balloon. Mary reached to the base of her
son's pallet and unfolded an insignificant, tawdry, blanket
and tucked it about him. But as Mary's body had shrunk,
Joey's had again become corpulent and she had difficulty in
covering his bloating chest with the thin coverlet. Satisfied
with her efforts, Mary Atkins straightened up and in total
calmness took from out her pocket a carved wood toy horse
with wondrous rider. Magnificent white stallion with fore
hoofs determinedly upraised, astride on a red saddle is a
prince all blue except for his pale face and hands, his jacket is
emblemed with gold paint. What a delicious, noble toy, it is,
a gift for a king to be.

In his desperate actuality, Atkins, behind the dream,
realized that he had never possessed such a handsome toy,
but once, somewhere, he had indeed seen such a wooden
horse and its finest rider. Then in his dream Joey, and
Captain Atkins, remembered where he had seen it on the day
of his father's funeral. His cousin, son of his father's brother,
a wealthy man who owned his own tools as a cabinet maker,
had come to the funeral. Edward Atkins, a lad his own age,
five years, owned the toy and had carried it into church
under his shirt. The cousin had shown it to Joey as they

together had watched his weeping mother sprawled over one end of his father's coffin. And for the remainder of the day Joey could think of nothing but the handsome toy.

And in his dreaming Joey took the horse and its splended rider from his mother's hand and cradled the toy under his bearded chin. And this simple dreamt act brought a mirage of contentedness to the dying seamaster. As he rested in his sleep the relentless intensity of the dream eased and his contracted muscles, formidably taut, released in an abrupt spasm. Then Atkins slept relieved of strain.

## eleven

Time of a small glass's volume drained and Joseph was awakened by a block of light that torched down the opening hatchway above. Many men squirmed down, clamoring as they came. First sailor to reach the brig door shouted in mock outrage, "What's ye lordship annoys us for?"

"I called for no man," cautiously answered sleep exhausted Atkins.

"Why ye old fart we 'eard yese screechin' already a bell's sand or more. We've 'nough of yer witch's blather." authoritively spoke the paunchy cook.

"I called for no man, surely not for you," replied Joseph through the thick wood base of the door as he lay propped on one elbow on the deck. This disclaiming only infuriated the sailors and they discharged gobs of spittle toward the small crisscross bars of the door's grate. Shouting and shaking the portal's panel did not intimidate Atkins but instead provoked the dreamless captain, "You men act like brutes, where is your Christian charity?"

Heartily they laughed and one, the bastard of a prominent royal wet nurse, roared back, "We'se brutes but still better Christians than you could ever be with your freak's lust to fuck the backside of a nigger witchdoctor."

Atkins attempted to reply to this specific calumny but the men created too great an uproar with coarse suggestions. Then a sailor advised him not to disturb their fun again, "if ye knows what's good for ye."

As the men made up the ladder several sailors continued to

jeer loud obscenities out, Joseph softly spoke, "Kindly bring to me my diary for I need to write an entry. My soul commands me to prick ink into a manifestation of my suffering for Wilkulda my Christ."

The last sailor, tipsy, caught the meaning of the request if not all the words. This fellow quieted his carousing compatriots as leaned back down the ladder to ask with head canted, "Wa' ja say, ye old turd?" A squall of laughter punctuated the question.

"Bring First Officer McKough to me at once," issued Atkins.

This initiated raucous hilarity that continued several moments until one venomous sot spoke out, "Ryerson McKough the Harvester's captain now, whiles yer only the pig's arsehole."

"Bring him to me this instant," enjoined Atkins with a resolve that tamed the mindless circus. Habits of discipline reasserted themselves as Atkins' tone invoked stern, punishing power.

"Maybe we'ed better," said a gaunt chap who was the ship's nimblest topside hand. A clustering of men followed this with many a "Pipe down, ye bastards," and "Shut yer whore's hole." Thus the crew discussed the request to bring down Ryerson McKough. An agreement was finally distinguished from the hubbub and the cook's young lover ascended earnestly the Harvester's multi-decks to fetch both mates down to Atkins. The remaining group now conversed behind cupped hands in excited asides as they awaited the officers' arrival. Joseph rested, lying supine with his arms as pilow.

The ship's officers rumbled down the ladder, "What is it, ah, Mr. Atkins, what do you want with your blasted journal?" asked McKough the parvenu captain.

"I am aware that you mean to maroon me tomorrow, allow me a final entry for my family," was Atkin's lament.

"Listen here man, don't make me out to be a fool. You are a pretty queer monkey, and monkeys don't need quill and ink," responded the first mate.

And the cook could not resist belching out, "Ye snot, ye 'ad us goin' all about the seas an' now ye made a mistake, ye fancy bastard. We's correcten' ye's mistake so's ye could be wit yer nigger boy."

A rather meager round of laughter accompanied the cook's remarks, but Atkins ignored them and implored, "You have my ship and my crew, Ryerson McKough, give me my diary that I might say goodby to my dear ones."

"What do you really want with the blasted thing, to trap us an' make us look like we've committed a criminal mutiny when all we've done in God's name, is saved your family and the owners from a terrible mortification. Why, man, you're finished. Your mind has gone feeble. The diary will be evidence that you're mad, and a warlock besides. I seen the years tally up one on another and sees you thought me a drunken failure but men like you could never grow so mighty without men like me. We're the manure, the shit, that made you grow so big. We's does the real work, makes the ship work in winds and doldrum. We's fight the sea alone whiles ye yells outa that damn trumpet. I have that fuckin' horn now, ye damnable bastard. I ain't gonna give ye the damn book, ye thinks me stupid . . . Certainly at the very least you would attempt to trick me with yer writin', ye bastard anti-Christ," spoke Ryerson McKough.

The men were silent. One, his face bloated with fear, filled the sole lantern with oil and tindered its wick so that a feeble glow created only deeper shadows, not of more light.

"So this is how it ends," said Atkins behind his door of imprisonment. The timbre of despair in his voice shivered the men. "My discovery of Wilkulda Christ is to be lost. Wilkulda should have been of great benefit to the nations of this listing world, but to such sloths as thee of the Harvester, I appear only as a line of unraveling strands. If you be a man, Ryerson, you would drop me into the sea. For if you dare leave me marooned there is always the outside chance that I could be rescued and brought back to testify against all of you. Drop me in the sea, for by this marooning you will cast profound doubt on my reputation and my very sanity."

No man was at the helm or in the rigging, the crew was compacted in the bowels of the old ship. They understood Atkins not. Yet his words terrified each man for they had thought of the thing too. "If 'es rescued by 'nother ship wes will all 'ang."

A great argument ensued but Atkins spoke and the men listened most carefully. "If you men but give me the diary

for one final entry I shall include a paragraph exonerating
those of the Harvester from the crimes of mutiny and
marooning. Then you will not be murderers and no
Englishman can blame you if I am eaten by cannibals. If I am
rescued the diary will stand on your side against me.
Earnestly I will write of your complete innocence. That all
that has taken place was a result of my own will. I will tell
the world how my spirit yearned for contentment on the
shores of my discovered Christ. Give to me my book of
self-taught songs and I will forgive all of you in such a
manner that even Jane Atkins will believe in the rightousness
of my abandonment."

   "You give us your word on it, Captain?" questioned the
glum, emasculated second officer.

   "Aye, Donaldson, I give you my word on it."


## twelve


Thus Joseph Atkins was gifted his personal journal for an
hour, more or less, of impassioned composition. And it was
this very same journal that has become the primal document
of the book you now hold.

   From this diary came my volume's revelations pertaining
to the Australoid messiah. From my great uncle's script, I,
Avery Morrison, have undone the past bitterness into a future
redemption. Joseph Atkins' search was not fruitless for this
very book is created in testimony to a Christ's lost existence.

   That the writings in my relative's journal were almost
unintelligible even to me, who as a boy with working eyes
surveyed the pages freshly, yet even to a veteran of the Great
War they boast an ecstasy that precludes cynicism. Firstly, as
a youth before my sight was stolen, I translated the diary
into rational coherence. A thing the naval inquiry might have
done a half century previously if the bench had not been

made up entirely of bigots. As a boy of eleven I began the transcription of Atkins' passion into logic's clarity. The hidden truths remained sealed to me until I forfeited at Ypres. No, not at Ypres, lost them at Loos. True it has been difficult for me, Avery, myself to be logical since the voracious gas feasted on me. However, I proclaim myself as the second truest believer.

Joseph's family had paid for a copy of the court's minutes after the crew's exoneration. Even as a child of eleven I was cautious enough to reject the court's verdict that Joseph Atkins, master of the Harvester, had by unknown cause become demented. And soon after this reading I came to love our family blacksheep and his bush Christ.

"Hosanna, hosanna He did live twice and perhaps a third waits to be found." This was Joseph Atkins' last extant sentence that I discovered in his private written parts. How could I not love him after reading those words. How could any man deny Joseph of Britain as a spirit of great vision.

Joseph's lack of coherence was overcome by the purity of his passion. To me as a boy before puberty, the diary was climactic, as if a birthing could come to a virgin, eleven year old bachelor. An utter transparency and lack of sophistication pervades the journal. Simply then, I was a romantic lad. As if I was a sexless, quite extenuated, poet. A seedy and lonely poet, who recognizes that his best meter must be inherently clumsy due to his honesty. A poet too old with experience who comes upon revelations before he himself may breed life.

His vision had flared Joseph's common sense to abstractions peculiar. He, quite alone, had discovered a unique and original universe stranded in that falsity of time and space known as the industrial revolution. The language of his diary, as I decoded it, seemed the patois of unexplored Atlantis. The song of a sunken city, a fragment of disappointed but portending lyricism. As if Joseph's journal were a Rosetta Stone that led me into an awareness of his second universe.

I have judged that you should see a section of the diary exactly as Joseph entered it. It is part of the concluding orchestration done in his cell aboard the Harvester. A segment that has mystified me since boyhood, since reaching maturity I understand it far less.

*Personal Diary of Captain Atkins, undated*

Wailing small the Christians devour the lion's tail and reincarnate sometime in their intestines. For as the ship's manifestation illuminates the Hebrew's revenge. As Bloodleaks outbecoming cruelty and anti-brother to Prince Wilkulda. Spatters mankind does Bloodleaks as moaning for forsaken christus as did the saintly virgins lust to create foolishness. Lazarus and Moses too were comical christs and danced beneath death's masks even as if I were a ballroom of larks fluted by a cagekeeper. Moses also with pealing screams did endlessly repeat that there was more to life than an universal fornication. That there were better things to do than scream in pleasure. That in a heathen's unhygienic heaving founded a kingdom of Christs all. Love becomes a bound trusting that forces Prince Wilkulda and his follower into a quiet madness. Pounce nakedly on deserts bloomed with forgiveness. And exactly does New South Wales belong to. Wilkulda when convicts do eat one another at highest teatime.

Why did not God have the confidence to speak to say to dare that he had sired more than a virgin Jewess. Was not God ashamed. Ashamed that we might applaud the grandeur of his dreamtime.

Ah, to breathe from out one's personal cock the seas that sweep the land's wound healed and freshed and gaily signature death. Dreaming was Wilkulda when he laid on his virgin sister to create forgiveness from her screaming menstrual rents.

I too would have liked to jam my smallish cockiness softly into divine rear and hear the guests laugh gratefully for it. And to possess an infinite realm of orgasms while betwixt the grunts I would testify that I was an elegant lover compared to pharaoh and his sibling's vagina. Risked all and yet have been lonely since died as deads utmost power and yet now squirm with new life in my spine's foliage. My feathers are luxuriant but the penised downey's finer softness than all the wooden ship's white plumage. My wondrous wood thrush ships.

Abel was a diamond merchant while Cain was a despised leper. Cain slew Wilkulda that I might love Jesus. Hail Cain Thy are Thee Omnipotent Murdered. See my lucious flesh harden and then swiftly mandibled by effusive maggots and glamorous beetles. My putridness shall fog the sun.

Frecht is my better father than Atkins who suicided in South Brighton sewage stream shall die and Wilkulda is died yet Napoleon lives to lust even for my baby grandsons. I too now die proudly as commissioned. I am a patricide who loves the christs of humanity. Why could not one be birthed today now. Let there be simultaneous resurrections now, I love Wilkulda who is my christus. I love my dead christus who is my Wilkulda. Man is never forgiven for Abel's appointment with golden glass.

I will not give in, not in giver. For from each narrowness of closeted greatness despised earth shall circumvent the powerful admonitions of the powerful and a requiem of man shall be understood by the children, And men everywhere will be undebased and un-degraded and upthrown by the Captains of God. Naked and washed, shaved and crowned, the anointed processional shall purge into the brine of existence. Shall purge, and all shall enter into the sea's brooding for instruction.

As is plainly seen, the metamorphosis of Joseph was now complete. A newer human had wiggled free from the rejected navigator's skin. Magic's ultimate hope had refreshed a man with an original soul.

## thirteen

Joseph sat huddled with his soul in the sternboard of the Harvester's whale boat as six rowers pulled toward the comber hidden shore. Atkins no longer questioned reality, for by his juncture he had lost all interest in the ship and its betraying crew. Askew in appearance but dignified in contemplation of prospects, Joseph casually noted the enormous reef glide omnipotently below the boat's shadowing. It was afternoon and the tide was running in but its very propulsion caused the rowers awkwardness. Exchanging curses they thrust the open craft toward the place marked on Atkin's private charts.

Oar-planes invariably slithered too deeply into the waves

that gravely rose over the iron locks. Sullenly, as if eager for day's conclusion, the vermilion disk of hungry light sought the ocean's shelter. Against enroaching night the eroded ocean basin was indistinguishable from the stumbled cliffs that lurched behind the shallows in receding procession.

Suddenly Joseph remembered. He emitted an audible sob and recklessly sprang to stand erect on the stern seat. His mind had recognized the boat's destination as Kukika's description of her homeland, and the place of Wilkulda's healdom. Sailor closest to Joseph dropped his oar and with expression of boredom, with a broken, rust eaten oarlock, gnawed and pitted from seasons forgotten of rest in the bottom of the whaleboat, savagely struck at Atkins' left shin while shouting, "Sit down ye arsewipe 'fore I beat yer dirty face to mush."

And pain's intensity did drop Atkins back to the seat, but in the excitement of the approaching shoreline, he disregarded the exposed white shin bone and its trembling pain. Blood softly unraveled from the swelling wound, and Joseph raised his voice in prophetic intonation, "See, lads, where that particular spur of white stone juts above the cliff line, here on this very lee shore, where sea and wind have raped the rock to its bare roots, here Wilkulda healed men."

Whaleboat's crew rested from the monotonous rowing to listen to Atkins with baleful interest. He, sensing their curiosity, again stood up on the tilting seat. The men, observing that he was not nervous, permitted him to speak upright as blood from the sheared leg clotted trouser cloth to exploded flesh.

"Here," Joseph spoke as if lecturing from pulpit, "or quite near here, a Messiah true did perform his holy miracles. No cross he had as marker to end his journey into Sacred Spirit but my Wilkulda was consanguineous to Jesus the Jew."

These varied blasphemies carried no threat to the rowers as they knew that quite soon the Harvester would be rid of its odd albatross. They now bent earnestly to their work as Atkins continued his speech, but the men heard only the sounds and not the meaning of the language. "True, he was not an Israelite circumcised in the Temple of the manger, but he was similarly ritualized and thus cannot be cast among the camps of the gentile. For though he was bred of savagery, was he not a rare sacredness? Blackness was his eye and hair and skin for he was a defeater of light with his perpetual shadow. Yet never was he a fornicator nor liar, as he forsook the urgency of his mighty prickhood to become lifted high. Tall and morose he was, yet his gracefulness made his gentle features radiant. And it was said that his very skull shone with the sky's bright vigor."

Careened with tremoring and vibrato, the whaleboat struck earth at its bow. Uncoordinated did Atkins sprawl to twist limply among the limbs of the oar pullers. Without discourse, without ceremony, the sailors hoisted the exiled disciple over the thin, curved gunnels to drop him, as a trifle, hastily into the shallows. Chest and knees broke through the sea's placidity and Joseph sank into the dense sea-vegetation that had been nourished long ago by the silt of the desert devoured river. Where the oarlock had gashed his flesh the sea's salt purified and healed the tear with caustic swiftness.

Flowing weed of tide's garden came in waltzing tempo to shackle him even as adroitly as had the iron hoops of the brig's confinement. Stinging eyes opened full and he watched his own beard flow in unison with the undulating yellow sea vines that laced him to a drowning death. Sea itself, without conscious intent, came to rescue Atkins from the plant mesh. A rolling wave reached down to pluck him from the sea forest and tumble him even as an emptied shell onto the tide wrinkled beach. Cloth torn and seamed apart fell off his washed hulk that he became an exposure of whiteness.

Lying on the beach Atkins thought himself saved, but the wave returned to drag him back down into the sloping shallows. Again the ocean vomited him out as unharmonious and spewed him mightily onto the land's cruel shock. Feeling the tide rising behind, swaying in its greenness to shatter his being's source, hearing the sea fulfilling itself and preparing its strength to seize him once and for all, as if he were a single clawed crustacean scurrying sideways to confound a diving gull's beak, Joseph scrambled up the beach to a safe place.

From this place he now turned to search at sea for the whaleboat. Perhaps hoping to signal it with begging gestures and have it return, and he would then renounce Wilkulda to gain a seat. But the waves were too tall and masked the retreating boat. Exhausted, naked, his clothes lost in the tide, Atkins succumbed to a weakened sleep.

## fourteen

Moon was unconcerned by night's throttling of Dusk. Blackness came brazenly and without pity to the seaside. Atkins slept like a drowned badger, except for meager pulsations. And as darkness was filtered by sun's broach, still he slept. Minerals of the ocean had destroyed the germs in his lacerated flesh, however a drenching chill had surreptitiously invaded his respiration apparatus.

Droves of flies hovered over his being and feasted on the salt of his body. At mid-morning, without cause, Atkins finally startled himself from a dreaming's dread and awoke alertly to greet the fly convocation with tense shivers that forced the insects from his skin. As he tried to rise, the new man Atkins, the movement unbalanced his soul and created nausea. The dying sailor man retched vacantly with dryness into the beach.

Chancing to gaze up from his sterile puking, Atkins now saw, a quarter mile up the beach, camouflaged by the cliff shadow, five black spearmen stalking his proneness. A very old man, with a wallaby skull perched tightly on his clipped hair, realized that the prey had become aware of their presence. He abandoned all stealth and with spear taunting the air with aggressive jabs, the old one raced forward in a concert of nimble to and fro retreatings that he might confuse the prey. The old man moved as if he were a choreographed spider probing its secreted catch.

Joseph intuitively understood that some sort of ritualistic killing dance was being enacted as the four other men joined the oldest in the strange back and forward dance-charge. He glanced northward along the beach behind him. Here from his rear came three additional warriors racing with spear throwers at ready. These were younger men and had huge chignons of hair mud-plastered high on their heads.

Joseph remained quite still as the eight spearmen coverged

on him. Now he could see that the five elders were decorated with red and yellow chest bands painted between series of raised scar rows. A stench did envelop these fellows—this tribe habitually applied fish-fat as emollient to their persons. Silent was he as the eight stood over him and utilized their spear points to examine his nature. A particularly aggressive younger man dashed his spear into Atkins' thigh. As the queer albino screamed the warrior laughed and his seven companions also chortled in relief. They had feared that the Rainbow Snake had sent a terrifying big, white, grub to eat them all up.

Casually the hunters came to examine the prostrate man. They discussed Atkins as if he were a sea turtle flipped on its shell to helplessly stare into the hollow of the sky. While Joseph observed the savages in their quiet conversation he was amused to notice that their penises were no larger than his own. For he had falsely conjured their private parts huge even as the African fishermen he had observed urinating from their dhow when he had taken the Harvester into Madagascar port years past.

Looking with greater concentration, Joseph noted that the blacks were different in appearance from those he had seen in New South Wales, even in the apricot orchard. These follows were as muscular and as lean as ebony egrets. The men carried themselves with confidence and pride. All eight were circumcised. The young chap who had speared him took out of his waist pouch a quite large seashell in the design of a spread fan. Delicate fossil, rim thinned to sharpness, served as knife and magic device. As Joseph was absorbed with the seven others, smelling and hearing them, the young spearman reached down complacently to seize the captain's uncircumcised genitals. Joseph groaned with the abuse and at the dreadful consequence the pearl shell implied. Cheerfully the athletic warrior lowered the white-blue artifact toward the fleshy pale externalities of Atkins' malehood. Joseph, watching in fascination, momentarily glimpsed the shell's interior of crenelated ribs.

Alarmed to defense, Atkins urgently lifted an arm to guard his parts. But the savage ignored his protest and with zest bent to curve the shell's task complete. Then Atkins in ultimate terror shouted, "Wilkulda, I am a believer in Wilkulda." And then he fainted.

Some few hours later Atkins swam back to consciousness. However, as the shock of the episode lingered in his esophagus, he screamed even as if the shell edge had torn and still was tearing his being. As his screaming diminished he eagerly searched his arch for his genitals. Joseph was gratified to poke and flap them still whole. With further perusal of self he discovered that a kind aborigine had placed corrupting seaweed over his leg wounds.

Now he realized that he had been moved several hundred feet from the sea and was under the protection of the cliff. A small driftwood fire smouldered by his chest and Joseph was overly warm in spite of his nakedness. Covertly Atkins spied out his companions there on the beach of Wilkulda. There were some forty individuals, including women and children, huddled about similar driftwood fires. They nonchalantly watched every move for portents of evil sorcerey.

There were no structures of any type, but the camp was laid below a line of weed-caped hummocks that slanted northward from the base of the sandstone walls. By the seaside there were several dozen tall and massive mounds of some extraneous material. These heaps were some fifty feet in diameter and perhaps twenty in height. Until Joseph was able to investigate he believed the mounds to be platforms erected for religious purpose. Eventually he would discover that the mounds were refuse and nothing more. Shells of oysters, mussels, and clams tossed one on top of another until miniature peaks were formed. There were neither trees on the beach nor could any be sighted leaning away from the wind on the cliffhead.

In the sky, squealing flocks of seabirds paraded in clever swoopings, and solitary herons made solemn glides. On ledges of exposed shelf rock were thick accumulations of guano. The five elders Joseph had first seen were engaged in vehement argumentation. Atkins, hoping that the people had known contact with British ships, cordially cried out, "Do any of you boys talky whitefellas talky?"

Politely the assemblage pretended to have a complete lack of curiosity. But one or two older boys could not help smiling at the interesting albino's twittering. He was so different, so unusual and abnormal, they were enchanted with his baldness as they knew not that hairlessness was an affliction but thought the exposed pate to be magical. And

what little hair he did have was putrid hued in flaxen fringes.
To the savages his grey eyes were of fishes and not of men, as
were their own brown candles. His pouched stomach of white
folds cringing one into another was fascinating compared to
their rigid leanness. Joseph's stubby fingers on massive paws,
so awkward compared to the boys' narrow, sensitive hands.
Fleshy, massive, thighs, albino calves, gross as set to their
bird-trimmed limbs. Indeed, Joseph was revealed as the most
abnormal specimen the sea had ever burped up into their
world. At this primal meeting the elders had decided that
Atkins was an undeveloped embryo of the chummy Dugong
and the elegant Tunafish, true residents of the Dreamtime
World.

Seeing his attempt at language communication fail, Joseph
regressed into his essential humanity and by gestures of hand
and mouth was able to signal thirst and hunger. Immediately
a middle-aged woman, perhaps in her late thirties, a rather
rotund female especially about the buttocks, came
obediently from her place among the women's huddle to run
to Joseph with a gourd of water and a strip of fish on a wood
platter. These items she had secretly prepared for the stranger
as he slept after his fainting. She shyly placed the offerings at
his side while timidly, in a lowered voice tinged with fear, she
said, "Wilkulda."

"Yes, we are all brothers and sisters in our devotion to
Wilkulda Christ. I am pleased to be among the children of
forgiveness," spoke the Englishman as he swallowed the food
and drink in a trice. Unfortunately the odor and slipperiness
of the raw fish nauseated the foreigner and he vomited out
the delicacy. The woman, who kneeled by his squatted
thighs, watched his spasmodic rejection of the fish. Without
discourse she took out a handful of black seeds from a woven
bag tied to her waist. These she flowed down into Atkins'
cupped hands. She had previously roasted the seeds on a flat,
thin rock placed in a fire's embers. The seeds' aroma was
pleasant and the albino hurriedly ate them all.

His fish vomiting was licked up by a host of large pawed
dogs who tongued even the scented sand as they snapped and
nibbled at one another. Later Atkins would see the uses of
the dogs in the hunt when a wounded kangaroo, attempting

to leap to safety, would be brought down by the pack. Weakened by the events of the past weeks Joseph lay back, resting as best he could among the dogs and flies. The heat was dreadful even here in the cliff's shade. He was thankful as dusk presaged day's end. Additional driftwood fires were ignited and he saw that each adult, or clutching couple, had two fires to sleep between. Children curled about parents and survived in this constant warmth. People were sleeping already, it was not a ceremonial night. They seemed undisturbed by the hot cinders that sparked out to die on their nakedness.

The same closely cropped, robust buttocked woman who had fed him came to light a second blaze in back of Joseph's neck. Her shortened hair indicated that she had recently shaved her skull as obsequy for a husband dead. Immediately this second fire exploded bits of burning wood that ate on his moist skin. The sparks caused his body to reflex grotesquely. Soon he would become complacent to the burns and to the hundreds of tiny scars.

This first night among the savages he did watch this same female who had tended him stoop a few paces from where he lay and urinate in the sand. Her release caused Joseph to stand and free his water, even as had the men and boys about them. Later this same night, when another need became urgent, he was informed by the female's gesture that defecation was a most personal matter and especially to a woman. A cultivated person was expected to walk to a hidden place along the cliff to evacuate bowels, except for the children who were not restrained in these movements. Yet disease and endemic diarrhea were absent even though no regard was paid to hygienic laws. When Joseph had completed several migratory walkabouts with the horde he theorized that the very frequency of camp changes reduced the risk of sickness.

In Kalod's day, three millenia past, the Turtles foraged the cliff head and hunted well in the interior bush. But in the age between them and the people Atkins had come upon, the drying up of the small cliff river had changed drastically the survival habits of men. The tidal flats were the horde's major foraging resource, and the underground springs that gushed

to surface at lowest tides were the only dependable sources
now. Wallabies, emu, and some kangaroo could still be
hunted on the plateau that began at the cliff and extended
many miles inland, but since the total drying up of the
stream the bush lands were strikingly barren.

Among the mankind Joseph had come upon the females
provided the larger share of the mankind's daily sustenance
by digging for shellfish in the tidal flats. However, the
dexterity of the men at hunting and fishing was marvelous
and their spears seemed as flesh extensions rather than
inanimate tools. The ten foot spears ended with a barbed
point hacked from a kangaroo shinbone, while the kinky
mulga shafts were straightened by a tempering fire and the
heads attached with treegum and animal sinew bindings. The
males also controlled reality by their magic.

On that first night ashore, after the woman had completed
her urination, she went to the tiny fires flanking Joseph and
poked the three burning sticks closer together. With a
contemplative pause the female then lay down by Atkins'
side and curled herself into his white warmth. Startled, her
stench abhorrent, the European jerked away, but Joseph had
forgotten the fire at his neck and his instant reaction to the
hotness was to bring him back in closest contact with the
savage. She, without concern, cradled him into her being and
stroked his genitals.

Aghast at her effrontery, he was bitterly ashamed to sense
his formerly exhausted member's immediate response to her
ministrations. As excitement rose Joseph forgot the purpose
of his quest. Now he understood the why of his survival that
morning of threat. "They've taken me in to be husband to
this bald bitch," he thought as the woman continued to
manipulate his manhood. And softly she spoke as her own
passion was increased by her efforts, "Wilkulda, Wilkulda."
Joseph Atkins now became aware of his placement in this
original world. He was Wilkulda, they had taken the word
symbol of his idealized brotherhood as an introduction of
self.

Yukari, that was her name, had interceded with the elders
as they were measuring the magic needed to deprive the
albino of life. She had been a widow but a fortnight when the
sea had deposited Joseph in her arms. This particular
mankind forbade themselves a widow's flesh as every wife

was sister-in-law to each male who was not husband. Thus
Yukari must be bartered for another woman from some
neighboring tribe. But Yukari was happy with her present
mankind and desired not to be uprooted again. Her children
were young adults and she wished to stay with them now
when they could provide her with a little extra in the way of
food and magical protection. The sea's renunciation of Atkins
had given her the opportunity to remain with the
Oyster-men. Previously she had lived with a poorly fed inland
mankind. On coming to the seaside with a new husband
seasons past Yukari had learned to relish the meat of the
Oyster Ancestor.

That first night Atkins attempted to refuse his manhood's
heat. Yet the persistence of Yukari had encouraged his
self-esteem and his vision of saintly behavior was soon
faulted. A part of Joseph yearned to escape his own passion
and the woman's ugliness, but Yukari was far too
experienced a lover and she held him captive in spite of her
stink and her general uncleanliness. After some moments her
dirt no longer seemed a barrier to his prick's extension and as
Yukari stretched her flesh along his person, Atkins came to
mount her. In his heat he bent to kiss the woman but she
turned her face away, not understanding such a caress and
thinking it unwholesome. This did not stay his confidence
and Joseph swelled with sureness and did a mighty
fornication with Yukari. And she was happy. And he was
proud to have achieved a fine success with his woman.


## fifteen

As the remainder of his life was subtracted day by day,
Joseph became convinced that without Yukari's enormous
skills as a forager and as an aborigine wife he would have
been dead in the first week of his experience among the
Oyster-people. Even with the spear gifted to him Atkins
could neither hunt nor fish, which mystified the tribe. Under
Yukari's patient guidance he did acquire the method of
digging for shellfish. The Oysters neither ridiculed nor
complained when he gave up attempts to hunt after a few
failures to keep up with the others and did a woman's work.

Each morning before the sun's heat became impossible Joseph would strenuously walk the shallows prodding the sea's land for the contact of a shell discovered.

He could make only the smallest contribution to his own daily consumption. Joseph was not well and could assimilate but the briefest blast of the Australian day. Every object in this world was a marvel to Atkins, from the mankind itself to the alternating black and white sanded beaches. Above, diminishing the cliff and the shore to petty rubble, the gigantic sun ignited this world to a prehistoric scale. The mankind, now but a tiny segment of the original Oyster tribe who had inhabited the southern shore of the bay in Kalod's time, persisted in calling the albino Wilkulda.

Never in his season among the Oysters did Joseph acclimate himself to the harsh environment of this furnaced littoral. At the beginning he would go about under the sky of day without concern, but the flamings roasted his delicate whiteness to a purpleish hue. Patches of his scorched skin would crumble and flake while ubiquitous covens of flies came to glutton on the wet pus erupted. Thus, from these initial torments Joseph hastily acquired the necessary skill to construct a weed and stick windbreak. He struggled to curve the structure's frame that it might resemble the low cocoon huts the savages made in a few minutes whenever the idea of protection became interesting. In these abodes he would sit the daylight hours through wondering at the Harvester's progress home and her welfare.

Worms with wings flew into his soft beef and tunneled therein to bowels and muscles. Joseph then suffered blood in all his orifices. He gratefully accepted the protective applications of fish tallow that Yukari pressed into his being with her compassionate hands. Periodically she was able to acquire a handful of emu fat from her eldest son, and Atkins would be luxuriated in that balm. At darkness, as the rainy season approached, no matter how many fires Yukari lit about him he would shiver with chill. It was only the compressing warmth of the woman that kept him alive. At dawn Yukari and the other women would go up onto the cliffhead where the bush began several hundred feet inland. There they would forage with digging sticks and platters gathering fruit, tubers, and varied insects. Honey ants were eagerly sought as their crushed bodies in a bowl of water was a most delicious beverage to the Oysters. In the afternoon, as the tide ebbed, the women would wander the tidal flats reaping the sea's tailings.

At the end of his first month with the mankind Atkins sadly admitted to his soul that the Oysters seemed to be untransformed savages, as if a link to a past healer was so unlikely as to be ludicrous. The Englishman pondered their state of savagery and his belief in a past Wilkulda withered.

Although Joseph could not acquit himself in the labor due existence as well as a girl-child, the Oyster-Males humilated him not. And in spite of his penis malformation with its hideous foreskin, the albino was a male and that was sufficient proof of Dreamtime origin. The elders led him reverently to the sacred places and then encouraged Joseph in fondling holy boards. If he could have only guessed that one particularly aged and time stressed, rubbed-thin stick was the metamorphosed soul of the bone-driller Kalod, Joseph would have been elated.

As Joseph was accepted as a male elder he was included in the laying down privileges of malehood. Thus, at appropriate myth ceremonies he could lay down with other females besides Yukari. And one night after a religious dance with a neighboring horde Joseph could not restrain himself and did lay down with an appealing fifteen-year-old girl. This fornication did not bother his conscience in the least and Atkins was even tempted to steal away with the visitors that he might remain with the girl. However, the glances of the elders from both mankinds persuaded him to forget his lustfulness.

After his horde returned to the campsite Joseph laid down only with Yukari. Indeed, Yukari was his salvation. When she would return from the flats, Yukari would go to the windbreak where her albino husband sprawled comatose. Quickly Yukari would awaken him to drink and food. And as he ate she would rub magic fat into his person. Yukari kept Joseph safe from an angry father's spear when he unintentionally placed his hand onto the shoulder of a youth who was to undergo circumcision the next moon. And when Joseph was in severest agony from a night chill and its resultant fever, it was Yukari who gifted the Oyster's sorcerer her human hair armlets that the magician would dancesing a cure for her husband's relief. The sorcerer succeeded in this by drawing a large wood spur from Joseph's head, at which the albino felt immediate relief.

Why Yukari cared so deeply for Joseph is beyond knowledge. Though he made love to her each night, and though he became a stronger cocked fellow with each successive copulation, Yukari's needs were but partially satisfied by his efforts, she thus took several daytime lovers during the moments of respite while foraging. Joseph guessed about Yukari's paramours but it jealousied him not for he realized that it was not done to belittle his agedness. Atkins cared for his mate, Yukari, and he knew not the cause for the mutual affection. Yukari had no interest in the logic of their love but Joseph had hours in which to dwell on the seeming absurdity of the relationship. He came to think that Yukari pitied him as a mother suffers for a weakling child. He did not understand his own tenderness for the scarified Yukari, but he learned to accept that he did respond to her, that he was happy with the woman. Joseph desired that he might one day be able to return the care and protection that she effortlessly offered.

Days shriveled as time itself was fired to ash by the sun of West Australia. Joseph accepted his predicament as final. And he thought he had processed Wilkulda out of his soul. Yet one day, alone in the camp except for a playful group of ten and eleven-year-olds, Joseph began to weep in the sparse shade of his windbreak. The youngsters, an independent and snippy lot, rushed over to witness the albino's strange sobbing.

Two boys and a girl came closest to stare in at the watering man. The girl was ten years old, her name was Nantjinjin. The boys' names were Naniwayya and Inakinya. The girl was quite short and squat but her face was radiant with a fantastic smile of joviality and charm. The old hags were already warning Nantjinjin that if she continued in her manner of boldness and fearlessness, surely one day as a young wife she would elope with a young lover. And that the elders would as surely hunt them down and slay the man and make her life miserable for many seasons. And as the bitches spoke, thus destiny years hence would confirm their urine's portent.

Fascinated, Nantjinjin observed the lamentations of the albino, Wilkulda, as he sat there in the ephemeral protection of the twisted sticks. She felt instinctive pity for the wretched man. Poking him rather too heartily in the biceps, she said in her own language, "Ah Wilkulda, poor albino, why does a man cry? You can lay down with me if you want, all my friends do and you too can be my friend."

Tiny black girl with nipples slight, tiny black girl with a woman's foliage slight, offered herself to Joseph. He, as was normal, understood the words not. Yet Atkins was sincerely moved at discovering a person besides Yukari who seemed to express Christian kindness. Joseph attempted to reply, and with a smile of sadness and a flutter of hands he signified a wordless communion with the child. Alas, he remained despondent and lay back into the slanting curvature of the hovel to weep fitfully on.

When Yukari returned that afternoon from her work she found her husband very sick and in an irregular coma. She ignited a large blaze at the open side of the windbreak and forced the protesting man to swallow water. Yukari begged a bit of wallaby tongue from the Oysters' paramount elder. She cut the meat into smaller parts and poked them onto Atkins' tongue but he had not the energy to grunt the food down. The woman took back the wallaby meat and masticated it and then mixed the mash with water. Using her fingers Yukari fed the albino.

Two days did she spend by his side that he might live; but on the third dawn Yukari had to resume foraging, as the elders could not provide them with more food. Joseph had recovered somewhat, in that he could now keep his eyes open for some moments and stare out to sea as if in expectation.

That night, by sign language, Yukari made Wilkulda the albino understand that the Oysters must migrate to the next site on the second dawn after this primal night of coolness ended. Unless he could keep the pace he would be left to die alone without even a ritual burial as he was a stranger. Wilkulda, Joey Joe Joseph, Atkins was aware that he was succumbing to an infection of the lungs, for he could plainly hear the mucous oceans drowning his brain. He knew that soon, when the brain could absorb no more, he would suffocate in the blindness of his mind.

Dawn but one rotated and Yukari lowered on pleasant

thighs of limpid blackness into the beach's whiteness to pick
up digging sticks and platters. Atkins, the true albino, from
his drowning mind clawed at her wrist. Bone delicate in its
imperial structure of thinness, yet he reached up on her tiny
arm toward her sunken tits as if he were a baby in reflex of
life's feeding. Yukari was impatient in her sadness at the
dying of her charming, gentle, albino husband, and in
frustration at her inability to keep him as living flesh she
abruptly freed her wrist from his terrified grip.

She relented and sank to knee by his sand encrusted head.
With a forefinger stiffened by resolve, the marooned sailing
master began to draw a picture in the sand, a thing he had
tried several times previously, but at each instance had been
stopped by either his wife or a nearby elder. Anxiously
Yukari surveyed the deserted camp, for if a stray elder
happened to see the albino creating forbidden magic, and in
the presence of a female, both would be slain. Picturing by
finger either in ocher or dirt was forbidden to all but the
mankind's magic artist. However, as an elder was not about,
Yukari cautiously glanced sideward at the drawing's
formation.

The dying Englishman depressed two circles, two fingers
wide, into the sand. Then he drew inner straight lines
between points on each circle's border. Now there did exist
in the sand a volume of perspective in the shape of a large
rod. Wavering lines below he marked as the fictitious sea.
Quickly sand indentations became a mankind reaching out
from the sea to the rod. In the sea of sands he drew simply as
he could, a child held in a man's upheld hands. A man who
stood alone in the pretense sea.

Joseph gazed in sincere admiration at his own finger's
work. It was a goodly depiction and accurate in detail to his
mystical imagination. Confidently, Joseph returned to the
canvas of tiny, mobile, grains and with emotion he fingered
in cliffs and sky above his sand mapped ocean. Yukari had
been following the sand mural, for its scene interested her,
and she was about to question the albino when the calls of
the females on the cliffhead distracted her. She luted back an
answer to their cries that she join them in the day's effort.
Without asking her husband about the drawing, Yukari
hurried away up the cliff path. At her disappearance the rare

albino began to weep and his being to founder in his chest's leakage.

"Ah, what an utter fraud I am," did the sorrowing fellow wail to the sheer rock wall," a failure, a minus sum is my life's record." He curled in the sand, below his creation, wheezing. And now the melancholic Joseph was rapidly failing. The girl Nantjinjin and the boys Inakinya and Naniwayya had been secretly observing Yukari and the albino from behind a hummock. Now in perfect composure and with bold intent, Nantjinjin came alone to examine the drawing while giving an impudent smile to the dying Atkins.

Gaily she called her chums to view the drawing. The boys dashed to Nantjinjin in a race of spraying sand. The three youngsters, hands on knees, bent to absorb the picture with pleasure. They were not afraid of magic, for the children knew that Yukari would not have stayed if anything serious was intended by it. Nantjinjin suddenly became sombre as she studied the narrow lines in the sand. She spoke a word to the albino which invoked no answer. The girl smiled, and taking up his hand and placing it first onto the drawing, she then pointed Joseph's hand to a place at the cliff base.

Frantically, Joseph cried out, "What is it child, what is it you see?"

Nantjinjin stretched her young arm toward a point beyond their position on the beach.

"Where is it, girl, where is the cave," Atkins cried with fierce energy.

Intelligent Nantjinjin perceived his desperation and went to stand by Joseph. Raising his hand again in hers she curved their entwined limbs exactly at a knobby column of sandstone that stood some yards away from the cliff itself. It was perhaps a half mile north from the camp. The column rose from a shallow breakage in the cliff even as if exiled into eternal solitude by an ancient anathema of the Dreamtime.

Naked in the heat of midmorning, the three children and Atkins together ran toward the cave's guardian pillar. Joseph led the three youngsters as if he were a sprightly lad racing to be first to reach the t'gallant of the mainmast on McGonigle's Thrush. Merrily the three juvenile savages chased after the foolish albino, Wilkulda. In the excitement of the adventure the three emitted hunting shrills. The Englishman had not

felt so young, so manly, in a score of autumns, and his
congested lungs were momentarily, magically relieved.

Deep sand softly clotted about the stubby pedestal of the
bleached rock tree. Atkins tenderly fingered the wind creased
column, ignoring the intense heat radiated by the sun
captured stone. The children were around his legs, playing in
the beach's oven. Nantjinjin giggled at some prank Inakinya,
the youngest lad, performed with an urination directed at the
rock jutting. Without hesitation, after his yellow wash had
steamed on the pillar, blond haired Inakinya, as if in
confirmation of his prank, fearlessly skipped behind the
stone's bulge into the shadow of space behind.

All followed Inakinya into the cave. Atkins, the aged
albino, entered last. It was a very old hole, older than
humankind. It was a magic forgotten even by the Oysters.
For when the cave was already ancient, many springtimes
past, the Turtles had celebrated the cavern as the Rainbow
Snake's penis hole. Smoothness of the cave's surfaces
suggested that at one time the sea had dwelt in this
stone-blocked temple tunnel. There was a goodly volume to
the place. At one age or another men had lived in the cave.
On a certain forgotten day a man alone had gone into the
space to slay the monster that occupied the cavern. And
when the man slew the occupant the cave became possessed
by men.

At the beginning, the cave's nude walls shone in
unadorned splendor. After one age or another, a peculiar
fellow could no longer resist the virginal rock. He was a
young man as magicians are considered. He lived in a season
before man had been gifted circumcision. He created magic
on the cavern's black skin even as he had learned to grow
magic on the scars of his own personal tissue. From the
charcoal of a dead fire, with white clay from a dewed pan,
with yellow ocher found in an outcropping and red from a
hidden high place, blue from a certain rare clay: the young
magician drew fertility itself, and surcease itself, where
before only emptiness had clung. Today, the day of Joseph,
it was miraculous to behold. Ages of hardened and harvested
drawings that represented universal ideas in the shapes of
kangaroo, lizards, wombats, fishes, birds, dingos, and ghouls.
Today, as yesterday, they resided in an immortality of magic

truth. Symbols portending beyond death and rebirth urgently fulfilled the walls: the Dreamtime bred and launched there again and again in mighty peals of repetition. The cave's being was of holy magic. Warriors as hunters and magicians thronged the rock in dancing action. Here and there in strange proportion pregnant women did exist.

Joseph swept the walls of the decorated cavern with bewildered gaze. The vividness of the hues bespoke the painter's boldness. Sunlight unfiltered and harsh in direct reflection from the sea was diffused by the portal's guardian pillar to illuminate the inner space with translucent wonder. Joseph became aware of the ceiling. Fantasy of symbol portrayed as incredible, swarming vitality bathed the albino in sacred awe. He sank to his bared knees in the sands. Joseph was credulous in the beauty of his discovery. Yes, oh yes, his head flung itself backwards as if independent of his wholeness, swiveling eyes explored the ceiling's tableau.

His emotion could not be constrained and Joseph cried out, "Thanks be God for thy witnessing. My spirit has been victualed and my hope vindicated. Thank God for this parade of majesty that looms infinitely above my head. My faith is confirmed by this bright tapestry of stone. Forgive me for my doubting. I know now who Wilkulda was, I know truly. But Lord, who and what is man?"

His emotion of transcending reverie was not imitated by the three laughing children who caroused in a far nook of the cave. The Oysters did not hold this cave holy and women were permitted to enter an insignificant space. The three children, engrossed with a detailed scene on one wall, bothered not to glance up to the ceiling where the healer Wilkulda lived. The particular drawing that had captured the three youngsters' imaginations was of a faded man of red ocher whose yellow penis extended through four outlines of females. Finally this drawing ended with the penis's enormous tip being devoured by a small turtle. This was the original depiction of Kalod's mankind's sacred myth. But as the Turtles were long felled by time's defeat, the three children could safely look on the Dreamtime symbol as a hoax. Mischievous girl reached up to the ancient painting and as a prank she patted the ochered member. At this her two companions shrieked in glee and then in raucous disorder pulled the giggling, enchanted Nantjinjin outside where in the coolness between cliff and column the lads laid down with her.

Joseph was alone in confrontation with the ceiling. From his kneeling self he studied the treasure above. The painting covered the entire roof, which ran thirty-seven cubits to the rear. The painting approximated fifteen cubits in breadth. As the cavern's roof was vaulted, there was a deepening sense of volume enclosed and yet unstable. The painting's background was a sea of fading yellow streaks. Joseph could not have guessed at the incredible sacrifices the Turtles had given in women and magic to obtain the necessary ocher to complete the painting.

Kalod, brother to the healer, had returned to his people in the seventh century of his life. Before he died he had recreated the vast episode of Wilkulda healing on the roof. All the emotions he had experienced in his career he transposed to the rock. The Turtles contributed to their very demise by the bartering away of too many women in order to supply Kalod with sufficient ocher.

Sky was white clay, the humans were blackred with blue mouths and private parts; Wilkulda was also a figure of blackred but the huge proportion of his figure overwhelmed the raw stone ceiling. From Wilkulda's red head a circle of white light banded by yellow-blue was etched onto the rock.

Joseph began to speak in reverential tones to the painting, "Help me die as redeemed. I am perpetually alone and a failure except that it is I, Joey, who found thee. Too soon I must swallow dust. Give me a sign Wilkulda Christ that you still live. Tell me that I and every man shall be saved by your recoming. You shall come to this world once again, oh please. Tell me that thou and brother Jesus and perhaps others to come shall stride earth that the children of man might be redeemed. Tell me at least that the children are to be delivered . . . I love thee Wilkulda!"

Joseph stretched out to lie on his spine that his view of the painting might be of its entirety. And in this strange prostration he did find voice and spirit to enter into joyous song. He sang to the painting of the cavern roof. Previously to this instant his voice was not appropriate to song, but now he sang with a pure gusto. Never had the seamaster possessed such a voice as this. It was as if his voice had been purged of dying.

As he continued to sing, Joseph rose to his feet in his
nakedness. A joy surged into his being, silencing his dròwning
cells. Rising on his toes Joseph was able to press his finger
tips into the mural's volume of space. Touching the ancient
ocher viewed a contenting balm into his beleaguered spirit.
Ecstasy forced Joseph to break his song off and cry out in
rapture. He tilted his head backward, like an infant searching
out newness, to keep the rushing tears from inhibiting his
renewed singing. Indeed he refreshed his song with an
exultation due Wilkulda of the sea. For as he fell into the
accumulated sands of the ages, Joseph believed that the hand
of Wilkulda had caught him safely.

Following down came the entire rock canopy of Kalod's
creation. It had been dislodged by the straining fingers of the
albino. The tableau of Wilkulda in the sea had slipped from
its rock socket to crush the dead believer.

## sixteen

Some hours later the youngest boy, Inakinya, returned to
the cave to seek a special pebble that he had dropped in
chasing Nantjinjin. The two other children followed and
together they found the nakedly soft albino sticky cold with
blood weeping from cracked frontal lobes. The three were
much intrigued by the smile flowered on the impacted white
face of dead Wilkulda.

At once the two boys importantly set off to bring the
Oyster mankind to the cavern. Nantjinjin hunched down by
the corpse to wail as was the custom of her people, even
though it was but a strange albino corpse. Quickly the people
attended a brief autopsy of the albino. Only the shrieks of
Yukari reached the peal's note essential to intensive
mourning, but hers alone was sufficient. Yukari borrowed a
spear thrower and reversing the implement struck the
flint-adze deeply into her scalp that blood might accompany
her grief. This blow caused a sensation of sadness among the
women attending Yukari. And the combined screams of the
Oyster females now competed with the squalling petrels for
the sky's attention. Even tiny Nantjinjin was affected by
Yukari's reddened head and redoubled her weeping.

After a perfunctory exploration of the albino's kidney fat the elders decided on the sparest of funerals. Wilkulda the albino, alias Joseph the metamorphosed, was carried up the cliffside and buried in a paltry grave under a dying mulga root. No Oyster inquired of the magicians as to the cause of the albino's death, for such information would be needed for revenge and this was not deemed important to any person. The funeral was accomplished with extraordinary haste, and with alacrity the Oysters moved that very day to a new campsite.

Several years had passed in peace when the Oysters, in one season of dryness, did return to the very place where the albino had originally been cast landside. The Oysters, except for one person, had forgotten the albino's name. That person was not Yukari; indeed, she had misplaced even the memory of her season with Joseph and was far inland with a new husband from the Grasshopper-men. It was the girl Nantjinjin who remembered Wilkulda the albino. And she knew that it was time for the dead man's spirit to be absorbed into a living being's soul. The elders dismissed the idea Nantjinjin offered, that she would become the dead man's spirit repository. It was established fact that a thirteen-year-old girl was too young to hold the large spirit of an adult male. At the very least such an act would leave her own soul diminished.

But Nantjinjin insisted, and as she was quite the prettiest young female along the bay shores, the council relented and a ceremony was performed. Thus Nantjinjin did store the albino's spirit in her stomach. And as she lived ninety-six years of adventure, Nantjinjin always considered the albino's spirit to have been most lucky.

# BOOK V  MAYAWARA

## one

Kalod had forgotten how to die . . . He, who had been a bone-driller until metamorphosed by Wilkulda, was now as bent and twisted as a dusty crow's skeleton from the intense friction that bears on a perpetual prophet. He had traveled in many worlds and slept by the fires of diverse mankinds. Kalod meditated much of the day now that he began to remember the preparatory signals of death. Kalod had investigated hundreds of tribes in search of the one that would weld itself to forgiveness. Along valleys of shrub and on red crusted plains he plodded on in search of a faithful people, yet it was all for naught and Kalod ceaselessly crossed over the wilds in pursuit of human habitation. By the south side of the Kanajong tree, by a fine river beach; by a desolate fire in an empty circle of hotness with a mankind of fifteen souls; Kalod would challenge men to accept forgiveness.

To whomever he met in his journeys he revealed his own being in hope of a response. A decade past he had decided to return to his Turtle-people that he might be buried in the land of his Dreamtime Ancestor. Now home on the cliff of his people, staring out to sea as he had six centuries before, in the era of Wilkulda's actuality, Kalod began to draw the story of the healer in his mind that it might be transposed to the sacred hoard cave.

He began painting in the spring of his six hundred forty-seventh year. The story in ocher would be completed in five years and then Kalod would die and be buried in the deep sand of the cavern beneath the holy mural. And thus, as we study the fragments of rock for remnant artifacts of the Wilkuldian legend, we are indebted to the bone-driller.

It was but a few months after Wilkulda had returned from the Eternal Dreamtime lands to his instruction with Uncle Mushabin in the initiates' camp, when Lillywur, son of Tjundaga, vanished. At first nothing extraordinary was assumed, as it was thought that Lillywur had turned to the habits of his dead father, that he had sought solitude in order to better concentrate on magic. After a season had passed

211

without Lillywur's return a hunting party was directed to
search for him or his corpse.

Never was Lillywur found. When the reports of the elder's
vanishment reached into the secluded mallee where the
young initiates lived apart, Wilkulda, taller and wiser,
remained silent. To his own soul he acknowledged the ending
courage of his father for he knew that Lillywur had
attempted to return alone to the burial height of Tjundaga at
the entrance of the Dreaming lands.

It came to pass, as the seasons mounted and tottered, that
the women of the Eagles discovered that Wilkulda was
confirmed to chastity. Mushabin, who had come to love the
young man during the years of training, pacified the elders
when they wished to punish Wilkulda for his effrontery in
refusing the wives pledged to him since childhood. Mushabin
could not silence the women and they publicly ridiculed the
perpetual softness of Wilkulda's manhood. By this time he
had finished his circumcisional ritual and was free to marry
and raise a family. He chose to sleep by the fire of his
mother. Namana was an ugly hag and an unimportant figure
since the scandal associated with Lillywur's absence. But even
as a powerless hag she defended her son Wilkulda from
ostracism.

She, and Lillywur's other wives, had been divided by
Mushabin among the men. Namana had been given to a
young fellow as his first wife after he promised Mushabin his
first daughter as a future mate to Mushabin's fourth son.
Namana's vigorous husband soon arranged for a second wife
and as this was a young, pretty girl, Namana's duties were
confined to food and firewood gathering. She regretted
deeply, and felt humiliated, that laying down was now a rare
act and Namana looked forward to the ceremonial dances
when the men entered an excited state of passion and then
the hags could enjoy a man again. Namana, toothless, breasts
folded down flat to the navel's crease, scalp bald from endless
funeral obsequies was mother to the messenger and rejected
him not.

On the day his scrotum piercement was healed, Wilkulda,
with Mushabin at his side, left the mallee camp to re-enter his
mankind's society. Namana sang of her joy as he came to her
fire. Only Mushabin had remained an ally to Tjundaga's

grandson and he was dying from a tumor in his bowels. At Mushabin's autopsy the malignant growth was discovered and this led to a feud between the Eagles and the Wallabies.

Wilkulda had asked Namana's husband if he might stay by his wife's fire, and as Mushabin had already interceded with a promise of food gifts, the fellow granted him permission. At night's issue Namana would timidly approach her son with a platter of seed cakes and perhaps a few wild plums or apples, seldom would the messenger eat flesh. He did not hunt with the men nor forage with the women and children. Wikulda's contribution to the food supply were the eggs he cradled against his chest as he brought them to Namana. Endless searching for bird's eggs soon made Wilkulda an expert at scouting the mallee-hen and plover nests.

In spite of Namana's attentions, and her love, Wilkulda was aware that he was detested and believed to be the essence of queerness by the tribe. When mother and son would squat around a night fire Namana's conversation seemed to be one rhythmic sigh composed only of the repetition of her son's name. Namana was burdened with the tribe's hostility and felt it more keenly than Wilkulda.

He would try to distract his mother by engaging her in trivial comforting gossip; "Mother, how is Juuh's third son, who opened his thigh while sharpening his spear? Is it true that Moog's baby cried out last night in a strange tongue? Mother, I hear that your sister's youngest daughter, the Moth-man's wife, has run away with a Kangaroo. Mother, it is said that Badinjau's lumbago was healed today by Uncle Mushabin, who does not look well himself, by use of the magic sea shell he traded for three seasons past with a handful of ocher."

Namana's answers would be brief and apathetic although gossip was normally a vital stimulant to her. But Wilkulda did not worry over much about himself until his own soul was profoundly scalded by a cruel act of the elders. In his wanderings in search of eggs Wilkulda frequently came among groups of children who found the mallee bush entanglements ideal for game-playing. Here they would pretend to be on hunts or in battle forays and in the ravines that were bare of foliage they would play at kick and ball throwing. Whenever Wilkulda came into their midst, trying not to notice their covert staring as if he was a queer beast to be slyly studied, he would join in their games and talk to them of his strange ideas. And soon the children looked forward to Wilkulda's coming among them.

However, as the seasons passed he stumbled on such groups of youngsters less and less often, and if he did happen to find them, they became still as if afraid. Seasons fell into vacant wombs and time became wind funnels of dust and if Wilkulda did find company with the children it was a rare occurrence. Yet at intervals Wilkulda, in the vigils of his solitude, would come upon a child alone. Perhaps a small boy or girl would leave the camp grounds to gather up a few dried twigs for the fire. At these discoveries the messenger would smile tenderly as he approached the child. Wilkulda would instinctively sink to his knees that he might hold the youngster about the waist. At Wilkulda's touch the children were never afraid and they eagerly snuggled into his being.

Undoubtedly he played with them, poking their bellies and tickling their cheeks and patting buttocks firm. The child might croon as it moved closer beneath Wilkulda's head. And notwithstanding the age of the child Wilkulda would attempt to teach of forgiveness; that children should not be cruel to baby birds or snakes or lizards, that tearing off feet, or heads, from small animals to observe the funny jerkings was a cruelty to the Sky. He taught that children should not drop a live dingo pup onto a fire, and not to disembowel a frog to see how far it could hop with its intestiness held as anchor. And not to mock at a playmate's odd sized ear or laugh at a playmate's failure in games and life. These things did Wilkulda say to the children of the Wedgetail Eagles. Thus he taught of cruelty's existence and that the scream of a silent lizard could be heard in the Sky.

Wilkulda's reward as a teacher of forgiveness was his contact with the children. He would hold the child to his chest as long as he could without boring the youngster and without alarming a waiting mother in camp. Unfortunately, as Wilkulda entered his late twenties he rarely came upon individual children anymore. The elders long before had found out his pleasures and put a stop to the youngsters playing in the nesting areas. And now each child was instructed never to leave the encampment alone, but to remain, or else go in the company of an older comrade. Again and again the children of the Eagles were taught to distrust Wilkulda as the strangest man in the world. As the youngsters were quite intelligent they soon acquired skills of hate and thus scowled at Wilkulda even in the security of the camp.

Wilkulda's quiet but firm questions forced Namana to inform him the reasons for the children grimacing at his appearance. Her answers disturbed the messenger to the denseness of his magic soul. In this retching pain he left the Eagle people for several days. Distracted and dismayed he wandered in the bush until finally he decided that he must not abandon the tribe to cruelty. On returning to his mankind further indignity awaited Wilkulda: he discovered that the people had hastily moved to another site, hiding their tracks carefully. After fruitless searching along the traditional foraging route Wilkulda came to realize that the entire tribe had sought cover in the sacred hills where the despoiled cave of circumcision lay. That the elders would lead the women and children to such a magic place bespoke their dread of Wilkulda.

Fires had been left unlit that smoke might not lead the weird person to their hiding place. When on the second dawn of his searching Wilkulda came upon them clustered in a secret ravine of the Dreamtime, the people were in miserable condition from lack of fire's warmth. It was a hideous moment both for the mankind and for Wilkulda when he spied them tightly packed and hunched together in the grey pre-morning. Despondency was the language of the Eagles that bitter dawn.

Yet they were his humankind, his people. It was the world of the Sky Father. He could not yet admit the depth of his failure, of the people's refusal to accept the presence of cruelty. Wilkulda tenaciously re-established his identity. The elders dared not refuse him the ceremonial rights due his age, but Wilkulda would eventually learn that the men were secretly re-performing those rites that he had participated in. His spirit was low and yet he could not relent. And Wilkulda began to publicly rebuke instances of cruelty. This lecturing created tension in the tribe and private debates were held by the council on how best to rid themselves of the monster.

Frustration upon frustration brought Wilkulda almost to

despair. Yet it was his recognition of defeat and his admission
of failure that gave him the courage to seek in his soul for the
way that forgiveness might be taught. It was during these
seasons of deprivation that Wilkulda began to dare think of
healing the ailments and the deformities of men's bodies and
spirits. His first experience as the healer happened one day
when three infant males became deathly ill with vomiting and
diarrhea.

The Eagle sorcerers labored on the infants from night to
dawn without result, and by morning the babes were nearer
death than life. Namana was mother-in-law to two of the
boys' fathers by the flesh of her sister-in-law. The elders,
convinced of the futility of the act, permitted Namana to
creep from camp to find Wilkulda. At this juncture he had
chosen to make his night fires in a secluded place. He had
slept alone since the tribe had attempted to hide from him in
the sacred ravine. When his hag mother explained her
purpose, Wilkulda was eager to try and heal the dying boys.
With excited leaps Wilkulda came into the camp, overjoyed at
the summoning. The three babies lay sunken and inert, close
to the fires. He came unto the infants and unwrapped the
kangaroo pelts from their forms. The magicians had used the
pelts to liquefy the ghouls in the boys' beings. To Wilkulda's
touch the three were as hot as embers yet they sweated not.
He took up a gourd of water from a mother's listless hands
and attempted to leak water into the babes' mouths. The
liquid splashed away on the cracked lips.

As the elders clicked their teeth and tugged frantically at
their testicles, Wilkulda unsquatted and leaned over the three.
Although infanticide was a matter of the season's order, to
lose three males, with the youngest already a year old and
past the time of smothering, would be a tragic event to the
mankind. The messenger pondered the challenge. In order to
exorcise the ghouls every curing chant had been used and
then tried again by the elders. The sorcerers had sucked
dozens of wood and bone splinters from the flesh of the
three yet the babes were nearing death. All the magic objects
possessed by the Eagle-people had been manipulated to no
avail. The very rare curved crystal belonging to the
neighboring Fly-man had also failed.

Wilkulda saw the life essences of the infant boys draining

from toes and fingers to sink lost into the sands. In his
profound fear for the fleeting lives Wilkulda must create
extraordinary magic. He concluded that to repeat the chants
and dances would be foolish. And he would not use the
sorcered pointing stick that the dying Mushabin had
bestowed on or bequeathed to him. Wilkulda knew
spontaneously that he would perform a dance unique to this
situation. Swiftly, as if contorted by a giant spasm, he flung
Mushabin's sacred pointing stick into the Sky. And this
object of magic floated away into eternal flight. Wilkulda
without regret began the chanted ceremony of childhood
betrothal: the sacred song of promise between fathers of son
and daughter who one day would be mated. The tribe
recognized the song at once and thought its inappropriateness
a scandal.

Lean jowled, sunken titted, flabbed hags covered their
eyes at the horror of the sacrilege. And Wilkulda was
surprised himself to hear this particular chant issuing from his
own tongue. Incredibly, as the words of symbolic copulation
were expelled from his constrained throat, Wilkulda felt a
satisfied warmth enter his loins. A sense of sureness now
radiated from his singing. His deep but lilting voice seemed to
turn into a mist directly above the babes. Though the words
were alien to the infants' needs, a quiet came to the scornful
tribe, for every person suddenly realized that immortal magic
breathed again.

It could be seen that the eyes of the dying babes had
focused with clarity on the singing healer. A silent sharing
was felt among the mankind as in spite of their cynicism they
began to respond to the ecstasy of Wilkulda's giving. He was
radiant with forgiveness. Intense pain was Wilkulda's face and
the people understood not, as this type of masculine agony at
childbirth was novel to their experience. Indeed, the agony of
forgiveness was original to Wilkulda. And yet in a strange
manner the people were fulfilled by Wilkulda's sorrow.

Wilkulda danced on as the father of sons betrothed to the
Sky. And in his dancing Wilkulda was metamorphosed into
the healer. Gently Wilkulda lay his hands on the foreheads of
the three and the babes were healed of death. Though no
person could yet see it, a slight glow was kindled deep in the
ear canals of the healer.

The wrenching gasps ended and the boys slept in a normal way. A surging love escaped Wilkulda and he wondered at the hope of liberated forgiveness. Gratefully he lifted his face to the Sky and heard the three frustrated ghouls burn in the substance that was the fog of his healing. Behold, the sleeping resurrected did seek nourishment from tender nipples. Mothers moaned in joyous disbelief as they fondled the living infants: Hastily the three females squeezed milk into their waiting, dried, tissues.

Wilkulda, in the afterbirth of his success, continued to dancesing poetry. Alone, he had destroyed death and secured suckling life for the infants. Never had he felt such pride. It had ended, the years of hope in a coming destiny yet doubt that his life would be lengthy enough to gain it. He had found his role and was fully aware of its enactment. From this fulcrum of creation he would be essentially a harmonious messenger, happy to himself. He could now respect his appointment by the Sky Father. For he, the queer despised fellow, had healed three. Wilkulda believed the magic of healing would pierce cruelty and give forgiveness freedom.

## two

As Wilkulda lofted the blind female infant, that the Sky might judge his fitness as messenger, he was unsure. Never before this day in the Turtles' sea had he been asked to create eyes whole. Even as the blind child was desperately placed in his hands by a beseeching mother, old and sterile until this birth of last opportunity, Wilkulda had wondered at the child's survival. A blind male birthed might signify sorcerhood to various mankinds but such crippledom in a female occasioned only infanticide. Wilkulda was aware of the mother's courage in that her baby still lived. He felt her will to create in the infant's intactness. And thus, with pride for the old woman, he raised the blindness into the Sky. As Wilkulda did this uplifting he was momentarily startled for he had caught the unsophisticated sun staring greedily at the child.

Landward the viewing moved Wilkulda's spirit deeply, for sprawling lines of supplicants from every world bridged the

spilling surf to beach and along the cliff trail to surmount the
heights. In the ages of the planet-island never had so great an
assembly of the mankinds gathered. Four thousands and
eight souls, young and aged, had ventured to the Turtles'
shore that they might be healed. To Wilkulda, this particular
day overawed all previous moments except for the moment
when the Sky Father had named him messenger. Serenity was
Wilkulda's as he took the blind child atop his fingertips to tap
her being into the Sky. As he did this, at the extreme top of
the shoreline's single spiked projection, Kalod with solemn
joy studied the miracle.

The tiny girl's shadow became huge on the sea and she hid
the sun's bounty for a brevity. The baby shuddered on
Wilkulda's quiet palms. This peculiar vibration passed into his
wrists and now his own being became a trembling, and the
infant was cured and eyes had been created for her. A
crescendo of excitement mounted from those nearest to him
in the shallows and was taken back by those who thronged
the earth's ridges and spaces of flatness. The babe's new eyes
clearly reflected the excited sun.

They came from the furthest parts. From lands sacred to
the Eternal Dream the mankinds approached the sea to be
healed by Wilkulda. Gently he would lay his hands on the
adult brows while the young he upheld into the Sky, and
thus the curing was effected. With each healing the glow
about his head intensified. At night the beach would be
brilliant bright from the campfires of diverse mankinds and
the gleam of Wilkulda's glow.

At night Kalod would sleep on his shoulders safe above
the tide's hunger. Then Wilkulda too would dream. Above all
things and events past and future, Wilkulda's mind dwelt on
Mayawara. It had been her fault that the Eagle-men had
exorcised both of them from their homeland.


### three

Why Mayawara was interested in Wilkulda is a riddle. It
had been five seasons since he had cured the three male babes
of death to be. Among his people he was considered a

gigantic weirdness, for he still kept the ancient promise and
did not lay down with females. Mayawara was the cherished,
absorbingly lovely prize of the pool world. At fifteen, the
season of her mindless involvement with Wilkulda, she was
formally wifed to her childhood bethrothal, Yokunua of the
Cockroach people. Jabiaba, Mayawara's father, was an
important elder of the Eagles and he considered Yokunua his
best friend among the foreigners. Seasons past when the two
comrades had arranged the future of Mayawara, Yokunua
had presented his widowed mother to Jabiaba as gift
bestowed for gift, favor for favor.

The two men had become dear comrades from an incident
twenty years past. During a mutual myth enactment shared
equality by the Roaches and the Eagles, there had been a
serious disputation. A Roach, Tjupuna, had offered a
calculated insult by eating Jabiaba's alloted portion of a
kangaroo killed by Tungulla. Tungulla was Jabiaba's
father-in-law in his sister's nephew lineage. Yokunua had
taken Jabiaba's part although Tjupuna was son-in-law to his
flesh father and thus his brother-in-law. Moanya, who was
Yokuna's father and Tjupuna's father-in-law, some seasons
previous to his regrettable demise, had married Jabiaba's
daughter, Punipuni. Punipuni was then Yokunua's
mother-in-law and Jabiaba became Yokunua's father-in-law.
Thus, the two elders were deeply obligated to one another
although Jabiaba was somewhat more important due to
having twelve wives while Yokunua had but eight. Yokunua,
on marrying his ninth wife, Mayawara, had moved his entire
family of thirty-nine souls to the Eagle lands for an extended
visit with Jabiaba. As the world of the pool was one of
plenitude, Yokunua's presence did not overstrain the
available food resources.

At the beginning of her marriage, sultry Mayawara was
happy to be sleeping by the fires of Yokunua. He spent much
time with her and laid down exclusively with her, his ninth
wife, for one season. However, the excluded elder wives
remonstrated and as their power to cause fractious discord
was limitless, Yokunua put aside Mayawara and indulged his
eight senior women. Without his constant attentions
Mayawara became bored and sought diversion.

That this highly desirable and esteemed female should be

attracted to the patient and gentle Wilkulda was a mystery. It was not that Mayawara was deprived of paramours, for several younger men in their infatuation had dared to risk censure by laying down with the pretty girl. Perhaps her taste for Wilkulda had been nurtured by his constant denial of available women. And he had rejected the four young wives that Tjundaga and Lillywur had arranged for him during his childhood. These four females were Mayawara's age and thus deemed especially desirable.

Mayawara was beautiful even to the oathed discipline of Wilkulda's awareness. She was small in structure, yet wide of hips, and her buttocks were as plentiful as the fruit of the plum trees that groved near the pool's sanctuary. In her sixteenth year, Mayawara's passion for Wilkulda outbalanced her caution. She began to seek him out in his lonely apart places. Mayawara, in her lust, attempted to persuade Wilkulda to become her lover. With a child's charming guile, she daily contrived to seek him out as he walked along his accustomed paths seeking eggs.

Mayawara plotted to seduce Wilkulda and to force him by the pressure of his aroused needs to elope. For she knew that if Wilkulda would lay down often with her Yokunua must discover the adultery and then Wilkulda would prefer to flee rather than risk killing the old man in a spear fight. Among the Eagles elopement was somewhat traditionalized and rarely ended in death as was the rule with other mankinds. Lovers would sneak to neighboring tribes for protection and normally these mankinds would welcome the pair as persons of interest and excitement. If the cuckold husband, usually an aged man, was adroitly handled by his fellow elders he would be secretly pleased to be rid of the mischievous young wife who ate more than she brought in. The old man would be mollified by sympathy, gifts and favors, and by the certainty that his brother elders respected his wise prudence at avoiding an ugly spearing incident where countless feuds would breed.

Mayawara's plan was of simple manipulation; to excite Wilkulda to coitus, to escape the dullard Yokunua and begin life anew among an interesting people elsewhere. Things would be good in the world with such a handsome young magician for a husband, so plotted comely Mayawara. The girl intuitively understood that her father, Jabiaba, would be hugely delighted if she could become wife to Wilkulda. It was generally thought that Wilkulda could still become the greatest man in the pool world if he would accept the merest modes of a traditional life.

Daily Mayawara slipped away from foraging duties to ferret out Wilkulda in his vigilant solitude. During the five seasons since the cure of the three baby boys his favorite place of meditation was in a cluster of sacred boulders hued dull ebony. Twelve rocks full of blackness, even as twelve moons would be without lustrous reflection. These twelve relics were the remains of a giant massif frictioned by remote interludes of time into spherical boulders a child's size. In the Dreamtime a Wildcat Ancestor had come among twelve pregnant women rooting among tuber growths. The Wildcat was famished and devoured the women, but that he might not offend the Sky he ate not the twelve embryos. The Sky metamorphosed the embryos into boulders that men might be aware of the Wildcat's wisdom.

Nearby a cache of sacred boards was masked in a redgum's petrified trunk. The boards had originally resided in the cave where Wilkulda first spoke to the Sky Spirit, but the holies had been transferred to the tree's vault after the incident of shame. On the day of Mayawara's profanation, brooding Wilkulda sat in the shade of a thirteenth boulder. This potent monolith was greater in volume than the combined cubits of the twelve metamorphosed embryos. This was the twice hued stone of superior magic. Its upper level was red while the base was chalky. An oval structure, it balanced out of the earth like a spear head spiked into the land. It is not permissible to inform strangers of the exact symbolization of this shaft of marbled shades as its holy memory is still ineffably linked to the existence of the remaining mankinds.

Wilkulda was gloomy in his solitude this day as he despaired at ever accomplishing his messengerhood. Since the three infants' cure he had healed but a paltry few. The Eagle people were profoundly healthy and Wilkulda did not think it just to rescue aged men and women from the spirit of death. Egg gathering was not enough satisfaction measured against Wilkulda's need to help his mankind by instilling in them a hope of forgiveness.

The messenger was in a state of depression and self-loathing at the moment Mayawara, emboldened by her lust, chose to enter into the limits of the petrified twelve's sanctuary. This was a criminal intrusion and demanded an axiomatic death penalty if discovered. In her passion for Wilkulda, Mayawara entered the dead lake bed where the relics reposed. She came to stand by the red-white rock and merged her shadow with the bigger shade that cooled morose Wilkulda. Astonished by her presence he peered at her uncomprehending as the sun stenciled her body against the boulder with a white flame. Afraid for her and aware of the severity of her transgression, Wilkulda bolted to his feet and spoke her name aloud for the very first time, "Mayawara," the potency of her name's sound gave him pause until he exclaimed hurriedly, "Mayawara, you will die if the elders see you here. Run away Mayawara, run at once!"

Softly and without terror she asked Wilkulda if he did not wish to lay down with her there in the coolness of the rock's shadow. Startled both by her absence of fright and by her appeal of intimacy, Wilkulda in stutters informed Mayawara that although she was beautiful he had invoked the Sky's aid as a boy by sacrificing laying down. And besides, she was wife to Yokunua. "Young woman, you must leave this sanctuary of the Dreamtime at once," he ended his admonition.

Comely Mayawara did love and lust for Wilkulda beyond safe guarding's inhibitions. She was a loving girl, and without tremors she pleaded with Wilkulda to renounce his childish oath of dependency that he had taken while under the influence of ghouls. "Be my husband, it would be easy for us to leave this place and go to the Ant people who have a big stream and eat emu every day," Mayawara insisted.

In joyous confidence she came close to Wilkulda as she spoke. Before he could comprehend her intent, Mayawara took his hands and placed them over her breasts. And it is reported that Wilkulda, stunned by the tissue's delicacy, did not immediately remove his hands from their encirclement. Ever shyly he began to drift into Mayawara's being. However, he held himself intact and though hesitant, gently took his fingers from her teats. Then, with apparent sadness, Wilkulda turned from Mayawara and ran toward the encampment some three miles distant.

Gracefully, yet somewhat unbalanced in her rapid motion, the young woman leapt after her love. In her eagerness, Mayawara slipped on a too smooth pebble and fell askew against the red-white rock at a peculiar angle to its fulcrumed base. Disturbed by the blow, the sacred boulder vibrated in its socket, but it settled back without damage. Perhaps the holy had moved a fractional distance, however, it was enough for a large tailed lizard to scamper frantically from its lair beneath the monolith.

Fallen and fearful, Mayawara shrieked while with palsied hands she sought to comfort her stomach which she had bruised and scraped against the relic. Halting at the sound of her accident Wilkulda turned and ran back to help. In her trauma at touching the actual Dream in the boulder's substance, Mayawara had forgotten her boldness of the moment past. Quivering, she hid her face against Wilkulda's chest as he pulled the girl upright. Standing her erect, Wilkulda tried to calm her terror: "It will be all right, Mayawara, I will tell no one. It will be our secret. The rock has returned to its original posture. No man could possibly know that it had been shaken. You will not be harmed, but you must be very careful never to mention that you have trespassed in a Dreamtime sanctuary."

Mayawara was calming down, and Wilkulda made to lead her from the place of thirteen stones, when a shrill yelping slandered over the plain. Horror was intense and Mayawara swooned as she became aware of the warriors closing with spears prepared. First Wilkulda attempted to lift the fainted girl but even as he bent to her the weapons were loosened by the arching throwers and he stood up to protect her. Ten Eagle elders, paramount in the tribal hierarchy, now reached for bird boomerangs as the first release of spears erupted short into the earth. Holding the thin planes tightly the warriors sped the land towards the transgressor who had despoiled the rock of their origin. One boomerang was freed some hundreds of feet from where the messenger defended Mayawara. Decorated wand of contoured wood lofted in threatening gyrations. Such flimsy winged weapons were normally hurled only at roosting birds. It was a long cast and the boomerang pathed in elongated vector to Wilkulda's skull. Near it came and he could see the freshly ochered yellow bandings atwirl on revolving axis. Wilkulda recognized the thrower by the color's design. As Mayawara awoke sobbing, death's swaying instrument wafted down at the girl's slim head, but Wilkulda uttered a magical grunting and the boomerang swerved from its trajectory to dash perpendicularly into the sky.

Ten warriors neared. A lithe chap, full of his good looks and the plumpness of his hopping penis, tautened his sinewed spinal column to unleash a spear in mighty pride. Warrior left earth in his hurling ejaculation and the loosed weapon devoured sky in a vast curve. Mayawara, in the wisdom of transfixed prey, judged that the spear when spent of energy would cleave her navel. Panicked, she bounded away in the stiff legged run of the hunted attempting escape. But spear's victory could not be overcome by such a soft sprint as this, for the throw was perfection. As Mayawara cringed from the downing weapon she thought, "Oh, it is not bad to die under the spear of Tjalerina. He is our best hunter and is the biggest penised and he has beautiful magic in the wood spear."

And quite suddenly the spear was on her, puncturing Mayawara's wondrous neck. It projected from the rear through strong tendons that now twined about the shaft as the point burst artery and frontal throat. Vermilion bloomings stormed the land's dryness. Awkward, clumsy, slow, the girl fell askew onto the spear, and as its point skidded in the dust, Mayawara bit through her tongue and died.

Wilkulda heard the life essence flow from Mayawara and he sorrowed. Sibilant swishings of airborn spears awoke his senses from mourning to his own danger. Yet he knelt by the dead female even as the warriors closed in furious heat. The men feared Wilkulda and thus wished desperately to kill him. As the males raced over a spur of clay, cracked in myriad webbings by the unrelenting sun, rage fountained in Wilkulda. He recognized that indeed he had been attracted to the girl Mayawara. That she had been responding to his own unspoken, unacted, lust for her.

In his self-hate, Wilkulda reared to his feet, severely jarring the red-white boulder. The relic, as if inspired by Wilkulda's anger, sprang from earth into sky. Tormented rock screamed as it crashed back to the land, and fell into shatterings.

Precious, twihued monolith was extinct. The ten warriors moaned in disbelief to witness this ultimate desecration. Surrounding Wilkulda and the woman's corpse the men snatched up previously spent spears and jabbed frantically at Wilkulda from a distance of fifteen paces. The messenger stood passively as if in reverie. The spearmen focused their lances and flighted them in terrible concert. The spears came at Wilkulda, intent to skewer him. But a wind lifted from the moon and bent the spears to earth far from their target.

Not to be so easily defeated, the elders next gathered up the shards of the red-white relic. Fisting the missiles, they loosed the stones at the weird healer. As the first rocks assaulted his skin Wilkulda awoke. Disregarding the barrage he took dead Mayawara up in his arms. Seeing this the spearless men ceased their skillful stoning. Prideful and aloof was Wilkulda as he uplifted Mayawara's deadness over his head. Her blood sogged hair matted down to paint his face with gore. The weapon protruded from her neck wound but Wilkulda made no effort to remove it. He tilted the stilled body toward the inspecting zenith.

Loudly, with eyes wide in anguish, Wilkulda spoke to the Sky. "Here is the proof of my deceit, of my futility as the messenger. Each day I trusted that soon I would pronounce forgiveness, but I am hopeless. All those whom I love, Kitata, Tjundaga, Lillywur, Namana, and now poor Mayawara suffer because of my perversity. Because of a false promise made when I was a child she is dead. Mayawara longed for my member stiff in her sensual self. She yeared to lay down with me and comfort my strangeness and ease my loneliness. She died while trying to be my friend and lover. Forgive me for her death. Give Mayawara warm flesh again and renewed spirit. Restore passion to her eyes and wind to her mouth. Let Mayawara live once more!"

Warriors, with fragments prepared to batter him, heard Wilkulda's plea and they hesitated to let the curious scene transpire. Wilkulda lowered Mayawara's body to the planet's dust. He crouched by her and drew from her shrinking neck Tjalerina's exceptional spear. Wound's leakage twirled the mulga shaft spiral crimson. Cautiously he revolved the weapon clear of its entrance and as there were no barbs, and as the girth of the spearhead was no greater than the whole, it was accomplished.

Again Wilkulda raised her into the Sky. A pale mist coagulated about the two in a denseness. Wilkulda in the stricturing fog felt someone groan. Swiftly he became aware that it was the gasping of Mayawara. The haze evaporated and she lived. Wounds healed, mouth sweetly wetted air into lungs, and Mayawara lived.

Ten elders forgot stones and dropped their hands to each other's stomachs in soothing rotation that the tension caused by the exhibited magic might be relieved. Though jealous of Wilkulda's potency, the males were pleased that Mayawara lived. She was quite beautiful and temptingly young. Cleverly the elders surmised that erotic Mayawara could be spared any future punishment, as had she not already paid the penalty of death? Wilkulda placed the uncomprehending, exhausted, girl to ground. In his ecstasy at her life returned he forgot the presence of the warriors and their intention to slay him. He had not dared to believe that such magic truly existed. Now the enactment had been done in the simplicity of a murmuring light. This new gift from the Sky exalted Wilkulda and inspired him to trust that with such aid he might lead men into an abhorrence of cruelty.

Assured of Mayawara's continued availability for laying down, the elders made a congress of nakedness. Though the situation was novel, the correct course soon became obvious and was agreed upon without argumentation. Wilkulda would be taken before a sanctified judgement performed by his peers. Such a judgement could legally slay him and the trial's innate justice would, must, annul Wilkulda's magic. That Mayawara had participated in the defilement of the Dreamtime navel was either an innocent mistake or more probably, the doing of Wilkulda the ghoul. She would not come before the judgment, for Mayawara was an innocent. A big trial would be arranged. Guests from neighboring mankinds would be invited, many big men would visit with their retinues. The inquest would bring fame to the Eagles and would establish the utter exactitude of their laws.

## four

Runners were sent to the various worlds in search of important elders who would wish to participate in judging a

ghoul. Such an event was delicious and soon entire peoples
began to assemble by the pool's luxury. As the full moon
approached, which would inaugurate the trial's opening, the
encampment became merry with great men and their
families. Forty-eight elders were joined by ceremonial law to
adjudicate the proceedings for Wilkulda's conviction.

Among the visitors were desert folk who had never viewed
such an expanse of water as. the Eagles' pool. These men of
the wastes believed themselves fortunate to peer at the
mighty pool without the immense spirit residing in the water
eating their essences. The strangers from the wilds of stone
and sand would sit placidly about the pond staring down into
the water in metaphysical admiration for the Dreamtime
abstraction. Wilkulda and Mayawara were forbidden access to
the pool's proximity and were held under strict surveillance
near a solitary whitegum a mile from the camp. As the elders
urged the moon on to fruition they, in sequences of quartets,
nervously guarded Wilkulda in a squatting position across a
fire's limit.

To one side of the whitegum Mayawara was occupied by
ceaseless laying downs with the Eagles and their guests.
Yokunua, her fat mate, that he might win favor and be
absolved of associated guilt, implored every male to partake
of his wife's beauty. Thus, in the nineteen days preceding the
judgment, scores of hearty fellows had sexual intercourse
with Mayawara close by the whitegum in Wilkulda's
awareness.

At night, when every person slept including his guardian
elders, Wilkulda became free of humiliation and
imprisonment. In the darkness he would wander seeking that
meditation that would guide him from mistakes and the
futility of the past. Among the black ravines the messenger
traced his plans for a coming tomorrow, after the judgment
found him not guilty of sacrilege.

The moon did become full and hatched the world reborn.
And on the following morning the judgment began. The
forty-eight great men in dignity arranged themselves about
the living whitegum that was the claw of the Sky Eagle.
Wilkulda was directed to sit on the tree's exposed primary
root. The elders were painted and oiled and many had designs
of heavy blood and feathers sealed to their beings. Women

and children crept within hearing distance of the proceedings,
but they seated themselves backwards to the tree that they
might not view the Spirit's metamorphosed claw. Mayawara,
who had been ritually cleansed by the laying downs, sat
safely beneath the last shadow of the whitegum.

Wirultjurkur, who was the biggest man of the Eagles, began
the accusatory peroration. This elder was father-in-law to
Wilkulda as his daughter had married Lillywur's second son
by Lillywur's fourth wife. Thus, Wirultjurkur's language,
though arrogant, was not petty out of regard for the deceased
Tjundaga, who had been his own father-in-law. "You,
man-person-ghoul, you are a thief of kidney-fat, a murderer
of the spirit, and a profaner of Holy Dreamtime. It has been
corroborated that you are a cannibal and devoured your
father as he lived for we have found not even a bone's finger.
Indeed, this was a heinous crime. More, it has been
substantiated that you gifted your meager penis to the
ghoul-domain in trade for loathsome sorcery. You are proven
to be an obnoxious heretic and a rebel against the sacred
Dreamtime. You are an abomination beneath the Sky. You
are a ghoul who does not recognize your own ghoul status,
indeed you are the queerest ghoul even investigated by men.
But you will be expelled from our rectums. We shall be
finished with the wickedest ghoul ever inflicted on a
mankind. You are obscene and less than dingo filth."

Eleven brothers to Wilkulda, sons of Lillywur's many
wives, came to stand on the root-artery of the whitegum to
bear witness to the foulness of the accused, of the healer's
perversion, of his criminal murder, of his queerness surpassing
abnormal ghoulhood. Thus, did the brothers of Wilkulda
testify to his wickedness. Uncles, nephews, and
brothers-in-law continued to denounce the ghoulish
weirdness of the messenger. At mid-day the denunciations
paused for refreshments.

Afternoon came and the elders did boast fatuously of the
judgment's auspicious beginning. To open the postmorn's
testimonies they chose to lead a despondent Namana to the
vicinity of the sacred claw. Her eyes were sealed with arm
blood and pink cockatoo feathers. Seldom were females
permitted to speak on matters pertaining to judgments, and
even more rarely were they permitted to step into the space
of a consecrated Dreamtime relic. Namana was under the

restraint of severe magic that she might not commit even
unintentional sacrilege.

Wirultjurkur nervously prodded the hag with his spear that
she might stand to the rear of the Tree. Indeed, Namana was
placed exceedingly close to the protruding knob of the
master root. With calmness and stately composure
Wirultjurkur did sing magic into Namana's soul. And to
secure the magic's grip he did dance on the metamorphosed
root-claw. Carefully Wirultjurkur, with a sliver of flint,
opened a tiny penis vein. With his fingers he caught a sprinkle
of blood. Using his thumb as swab he smeared the blood
upon Namana's lips. The elder was still for a profound
moment as he held the sanctifying fingers to the hag's mouth.
He used the last droplet of blood to draw a careful zigzag line
on the woman's stomach. Then Wirultjurkur propped one
end of his pointing stick in Namana's navel and the opposite
end in his own.

Wirultjurkur and Namana were now entranced into a
mighty single nature. Their beings clung to each other
through the mutuality of the pointing stick. From a squatting
gaggle of visiting elders a small man arose. He was aglow with
yellow ocher from scalp to toe nail. His oval face was cradled
in an immense bush of white cockatoo feathers. This fellow's
pointing stick was thick with the caked, combined penis
blood of the forty-eight elders. Swiftly the guest sorcerer
strode to the merged two and placed both his hands around
the connecting pointing stick while holding his own ritualized
stick alongside of Wirultjurkur's. The elder spoke with the
combined vigor of three sutured souls: "Womb of the ghoul
Wilkulda, reveal to the Sky the essence of your ghoulson's
perversity."

Namana spoke. Her silent utterance was transferred
through the two pointing sticks into Wirultjurkur. The
pronouncement of Namana was uttered in the cultivated but
booming voice of Wirultjurkur, "He is my son who healed the
three babes and who pleases the Sky and is child of the Sky.
Wilkulda is a warrior defending the Sky's kidney fat.
Tjundaga dug a path from the Eternal Dream to today so that
my baby Pilala could become Wilkulda the good."

The assemblage was horrified and exclaimed in bursting
voices that were soundings of fear rather than meaningful
words. A predictable verdict had been transformed by the

authentic spirit of Namana issuing an unknown and
forbidden dimension of truth. She spoke again without
prodding in the awesome voice of Wirultjurkur, "What is
wrong with the Eagle people? Why do you hate Wilkulda who
has helped us in sickness and is nice and quiet. You hate him
because he doesn't expect big favors for his magic and that
makes you all so little. What wrong is it that Wilkulda doesn't
lay down with women? Yes I agree it is strange and more
than once I have told him to lay down with one wife at least
to get you big fellows nicer. But what is wrong if he
doesn't . . . ahee, ahee, I am tired."

And Wirultjurkur and Namana both slumped their heads to
chests in sleep. However, the guest elder holding the two
pointing sticks securely in their navels, chanted a command
and her soliloquy continued, "Why don't you big fellows
spear me and my son dead. . . . This is a bad joke. Wilkulda is
the best wizard among you turds. Didn't he make Mayawara,
the little bitch, live after Tjalerina's spear had split apart her
neck. Now you big turds can lay down with pretty Mayawara
as much as you want. Her fat husband will even help you get
your pricks in . . . You'll see, one day Mayawara will be as
ugly as I am, it all passes . . . Wilkulda is the best magician.
All that he wants is for us to be better than we was. Why is it
bad to be better? His message is very nice and it doesn't scare
anyone like the Rainbow Snake's voice does. At last he treats
us women kindly which is better than all you turds put
together. Nobody understands Wilkulda's message anyhow so
what harm can it do. My son is just what Tjundaga said he
would be when he was a little boy and we people were going
hungry and Pilala threw a stone playing and it rolled down a
hill and when he chased it he saw five kangaroo and the
hunters caught three of them. Tjundaga said then, 'He is boy
of goodness and strange potentialities.'

"Just because the Sky likes him better than you, you hate
him. Did you turds think that just because I talk through a
man's balls that I would betray my gentle Wilkulda. As I
stand here with Wirultjurkur's and the Honey Ant-man's
pointing sticks in my belly and hear my soul in Wirultjurkur's
mouth, how could you think I could betray my son? I am
only a dumb woman who don't know what cruelty and
forgiveness is, but my Wilkulda knows and that is good."

Namana had completed her statement and fell from the

pointing sticks in exhaustion. The Honey Ant-man then
sprawled into the dirt besmirching his lovely yellow ocher,
but as he fell he still held fast to the sticks. Wirultjurkur
awoke and remembering the words he had spoken for
Namana, he screamed. Forty-eight elders were in an uproar.
The trial came to a halt as they disintegrated into acrimony
and accusation. Namana had fooled them in the lengthy
quizzing that had preceded her testimony. She had pretended
to be against Wilkulda so that the elders would allow her to
testify while protected by the holy relic root.

Forty-eight elders debated the best method to deceive
themselves over Namana's testimony. They arrived at a
unanimous conclusion: disregard the hag's words completely
and overwhelm her regrettable impression with a galaxy of
incriminating witnesses. And man followed man onto the
root to libel the messenger. Dusk pursued the daylight's
lingering outposts. A few females separated from the huddle
at the back and in abnormal quiet they ignited blazes from
fire sticks and prepared food for the one large meal of the
day. Soon all the women and children had drifted away to
join their compatriots in the evening labors.

Wilkulda, hunched listlessly by the gigantic root, had
listened to his mother and had been inspired by her staunch
defense. However, the day's summing of lies from the
subverted witnesses had emptied his being's courage.
Forty-eight elders were hungry and irritable. The hours of
spurious testimony had sounded absurd even to their eager
ears. Forty-eight elders were lethargic and bored as new fires
shed dimness into the obscured dusk. Wilkulda became aware
that the trial had reached its conclusion. It was the verdict
first agreed upon some centuries past by rainbow termites in
the concavity of a decimated coral starfish.

Wilkulda was to be killed. Children gleefully raced in the
ever spreading circles of fire light. Delicious smokings of
sandfurnaced kangaroo created juices in mankind's mouth.
Wilkulda was to be killed. Mayawara, who loved and desired
Wilkulda, was allowed to be among the giggling, unrestrained,
women but she was mute. They could hear Wirultjurkur's
injunction for all uncircumcised males to leave the environs
of the sanctuary as consecrated weapons were to be
unleashed. Namana wept as she knelt to blow her own fires

to flame. Man was hungry and except for Mayawara and Namana, all looked forward to the celebration that would follow the act of punishment.

Forty-eight elders urinated on the metamorphosed root in concert. Yellow ochered Honey Antman came upon the root itself as the urine soaked the earth about the relic. He took Wilkulda by the arm and took him off and away from the protection of the sacred whitegum. Honey Ant-man left the messenger standing alone many paces from the root. The elders now came to encircle Wilkulda as the spaces of earth were fulfilled with darkness.

Wirultjurkur sweetly, and willed with pity, intoned, "We your brother Eagles, and our honored guests, have studied your crime. We have made ourselves knowledgeable as to the essence of the dispute. The punishment is based on our defense of the Sky World of the Eternal Dream, and of men everywhere. Mercy is not our way as you are well aware. I loved your grandfather who was my own father-in-law. Your hag-mother's evidence has been dismissed as it was polluted by some esoteric song of evil that you chanted into her belly. Do not refute me, for I am your friend and doubt your ghoul nature even now. Personally I believe that you are not a monster. I believe you are demented, which perhaps is far worse because of the danger of insane sorcery. I, Wirultjurkur, your fleshed kin, ask that you die as a good person and not harm the Dreamtime with distorted magic. Die in a normal manner and do not vent your rage on those who have been forced by your own actions to judge your aberrations."

Softly the elder walked from the weeping Wilkulda. Wirultjurkur called the elders into rows of ordered warriors fronting the sobbing messiah. Wirultjurkur in a bold voice said, "The name Wilkulda is forever banished from mens' lips. By the highest ethical codes I now command that together we spear this crazy man dead ... All at once now, throw your spears!"

Precious quartz points, flint heads, simple wood points, pierced the messenger. With eyes closed, cheeks dampened by glistening tears, Wilkulda felt the two score and eight spears slide into his inner hollows. From far off he could hear the wailing peals of horrified Namana intermingled with the screamings of a younger woman. Inwardly Wilkulda wept in dismay at his own failure. Even as he died he wept at the defeat of the Sky's newest Dream.

Now Wilkulda was dead. He was sprawled backwards, grotesquely propped up on the maze of puncturing weapons. Wilkulda was dead by forty-eight sockets burst into his exploding flesh. His corpse was slowly forced by gravity's will to topple the spear entanglement and he lay face to the dust. The elders found another argument to debate: what, if any, obsequies should be granted the dead man. Finally it was agreed that the corpse should at least be buried and not left to the birds and dingos, this out of respect for Tjundaga. But it must be a petty burial without honor or ceremonial grandeur.

The younger elders picked up the corpse and carried the deadness on their spears that had been roughly pulled out of the chilling tissue. He was taken some miles to a gravel pit hard by a large, brilliantly white clay pan. Namana wept and clawed her breasts blood red. With sharpened stick she poked holes in her face and skull until she was but a wailing contusion. The foreign, visiting, elders dealt with Namana. The stunned hag was pushed out of camp by strong kicks to her sagging rump. A young, weak bachelor of the Flying Squirrels was sent away with Namana as her husband. He would take her as his first wife. Wilkulda's brothers and brothers-in-law were instructed not to mourn the spirit of the corpse as there was some question whether it was a human ghost or not.

In a brief star hazed journey the impatient and rude funeral procession reached the gravel deposit. Here a river, several ages beyond the Dreamtime's past, had left its skeleton. Quickly a shallow grave was shoved apart in the friction-bred stone. There were no green leafed branches to grace the meager grave. Wilkulda's spear, gifted by dead Uncle Mushabin, was thrown brusquely into the hole and then his corpse was dropped alongside the weapon. Wirultjurkur farted as he bent to perform a cursory autopsy, expertly slicing apart the lower abdomen to expose the kidneys. Beneath the flaring torches of the elders the exhibited fat was luxurious beyond previous experience. But the rare fullness of the kidney fat was misconstrued by the males as tangible proof of the ghoul's weirdness. The burial was completed by Wirultjurkur as with kangaroo sinew he tied one thigh of the corpse to its chest. There was no further interest. Stones were scooped over the body even as canines hind-leg their feces covered. Then a mound several feet high was heaped upon the corpse.

## five

The elders returned to the fires and in sequence of authority did lay down with prettiest Mayawara. Thus the night's celebration was inaugurated. Gaiety became intense as the people reveled in the death of Wilkulda. Inhibitions, guilt, grief, all were shed and pleasure exceeded expectation. Men had a marvelous evening and relaxed in the triumph of their true science over wicked sorcery. Sexual intercourse was ignited even as a bush blazing in the advancing dimness. Elders permitted ancient feuds to be dissolved by the sharing of antagonists' wives. Wirultjurkur felt that this was the finest moment of his long, successful, life in that he had destroyed a powerful weirdness. In his gratification he gave his youngest three daughters, eight seasons of age, nine seasons of age, and again from another wife, nine seasons of age, to unhurried copulation with several of the greater elders.

Mayawara was grateful that she had not been punished and that she had survived death. In her delight at being spared she smiled eagerly throughout the eighty-four copulations she performed this day and night, although during the last six of them she was unconscious. At the night's beginning the hags were desperately jealous that Mayawara seemed to have monopolized the stiffened penises. However, in the elation of the night, each female present was favored with a minimum of three copulations. This then was a night of festival and joy at the release of tension accomplished by the execution of Wilkulda. Indeed, it appeared that woe itself had vanished. Disregard for traditional sexual proscriptions was actively encouraged by the elders in order to dissipate the lingering dread engendered by Namana's soliloquy, especially in the women. A grand celebration was performed and sons-in-law

and mothers-in-law were jocularly mismatched even as fathers
lay down with daughters and daughters-in-law. Even the
dying hags, Namana's cronies, had delicious spurts of ecstasy
to ease their dreams of death. The frivolities entered a second
night after a day of refreshments. Nine kangaroo were
speared and roasted with seventy-two dingo pups in an
unheard-of expenditure of meat. Man's capacity for
copulation had not been diminished by repletion. And the
forty-eight elders sat contentedly about fires waiting for
gonads to be refilled.

At the clay pan, near the gravel burial mound of Wilkulda,
something was stirring on this the second night of
exaggerated celebrations. The pan's night hue was blue and it
sparkled with tiny beads discovered by the moon's reflection.
On three sides of the gravel soak mulga bush protected the
stones. This night a wild pack of dingos had come to explore
the gravel deposit. With their large paws they scattered out a
conical shape into the stones. The wind had borne the odor
of corrupting meat to the pack and they had traveled one
hundred miles to investigate the bounty.

As they neared the corpse the dogs were set into a frenzy
of hunger and nipped and bit each other. Their snouts went
deep and it seemed that they must be at their reward.
However, even as the form of the deadness bulged in the
gravel, the dingos, for no discernible reason, fell back and
became silent. The omnipresent noises of the land, the birds
and wombats and kangaroo-mice and worms and moths and
termites, grew still. Only a single owl emitted demented
screams as it flew off into the sky.

The dingos assumed stances of timeless wariness. A
whoosh of air from the cooling desert stirred the fur of the
dogs and instantly they leaped out of the gravel into the
protection of the bountiful bush. Wilkulda had come to life.
Tiny stones had compacted under their own weight to
oppress his flesh. As he spread wide his eyelids in the
blackness, Wilkulda's lashes forced the gravel to fractionally
give way. A slight hollow appeared above each eye. Wilkulda
became aware that life had returned and that he had not been
the creator of his renewal. By the minute sounds of the
rolling gravel Wilkulda perceived that his wounds were
moving together in healing resurgence. Hundreds of grubs and
worms were fleeing his breathing body.

The messenger lay heavily settled. He was conscious of
death yet he stirred with hope of existence. Intuitively he
believed that the Sky had responded to his suffering and had
restored him to reality. Wilkulda was unaware that in the
instant when life had been returned to him as solace from
death, procreation briefly teemed throughout the universe.
And in the seas and on the land everything that was meant
for death was redeemed and allotted a future time in which
to die.

As he lay still and swallowed bits of shattered rock,
Wilkulda debated whether he should return to the world as a
man. He mused that perhaps as a metamorphosed snake he
could burrow into the inner limits of earth to sleep an age or
two until the mankinds had changed. Yet even as he
considered withdrawal the boldness of Wilkulda's soul raised
one arm to force its way upwards through the slippery gravel.
A hand freely projected from the burial mound into a false
dawn of alabaster paleness. With ease Wilkulda severed the
thigh strap and, parting the heavy gravel, stood upright in the
deposit of the extinct river. He thought it curious that he
should gain new life as do the locusts who are born from sand
grains and then fly as a mighty roaring in the Sky.

The grandson of Tjundaga left that place of safe ignominy
to return to the camp's certain humilation. Normally sentries
would be alert and hunters preparing for the day's necessity
but in this dawn the mankinds still slumbered, emptied of
energy by the redundant fornications. Yowlings from the
running pack of wild dingos could be heard as Wilkulda came
among the naked people. They slept in heaps among a
labyrinth of dying down fires. Chilled dawn extended itself
over the earth. Wilkulda saw revealed, in the light's pallor, the
low excess that had shrunk the mankinds into lesser beings.
The grounds about the pond were strewn with the evidence
of unnatural copulations. Crude matings were enacted even as
the participants slept.

Stealthily Wilkulda picked his way among the piles of
humans. By the pool itself the messenger pulled together a
giant heaping of logs and broken branches. Without
premeditation Wilkulda labored as if composing a finer,
better Dream from the firewood. Forming a circle of logs
Wilkulda gathered embers and fired the wood. The abundant
fire flashed skyward in determined self-consumption. Yet

there was neither smoke nor warmth to its searing flames. With unnatural rapidity the fire ate wood until there was a hill of white ash surmounting the red glow of furnacing combustion.

Not plotting his goal the messenger stepped into the high mound of fire's grave even as the remaining log ends at the outer circumference were ignited. Standing in the glowing coals that reached to his knees, Wilkulda reflected on the reason for his rebirth. He suffered not from the fired wheel of wood and he patiently waited for man to awake and wonder at his placement. He believed still that men must absorb his message and be metamorphosed from cruel beings into forgiving humanity. He knew that he would not have been rescued from death if men were not essentially worthy of the message. Calmly Wilkulda decided to call the folk awake to view his recreation.

Without affectation Wilkulda sang the song of marriage to summon the mankinds awake. It was the song he had sung when curing the three infant males. A stifled, haunted moan was the multitudes' response. Women and children at first cringed and wept at the sight of the strange fire and its burden. Males were silent in dreading contemplation. Humankind rose to its feet and in a spontaneous reaction fled from the pond's oasis, leaving Wilkulda comforted only by his fire. In haste the mankinds, hags and infants thrust aside by strident men, raging warriors streaked below this palest of all dawns to the clay pan and its orphaned gravel pit. Tribes of earth made their varied ways through the mulga growth to the stone road where the ghoul Wilkulda had been interred. One idea possessed the elders' minds, that the corpse had not been properly honored by the sparse funeral. This odious mistake must be rectified by homage to the deathness that the fire's apparition might dissipate.

Forty-eight big men, with forty-eight circumcised appendages, in rightous desperation clawed at the gravel clogged grave. A mantle of smaller pebbles was scattered over the clay forefront. The mass of the mankinds collected silently about the frantic hole making. Wirultjurkur, his emotions ever obedient to his stern will, fashioned order from the mad antics by insisting that a few younger, steadier, men dig alone so that an excess of hands might not impede the excavation. A council of the world's biggest elders grouped to one side in a forlorn squatting as the few labored to search out the corpse. Females and their young watched listlessly, drained by the trauma. Wirultjurkur, watching the work fruitlessly mine deeper, offered up to the Rainbow Snake a marvelous gift if only the corpse was found. In loud, sombre tones Wirultjurkur announced that he was ready to give the ghoul's message a fair hearing, if only the deadness was found here in the pit where it must be.

The breach in the gravel became a crater and yet the corpse of Wilkulda was not revealed. Ten cubits of stone were removed and then the clay stratum was fondled. No trace of kidney-fat decomposition was found. Men groped in the floodlike gravel until a poking hand came upon the broken kangaroo sinew that Wilkulda had burst in his self-liberation. At this palpable proof of miracle the humans were perturbed and chastised. Recriminations flew as each blamed the resurrection's success on another. A few tentative spearings were in the offing when the turmoil was quieted by the sound of a sobbing song drifting over the meager tops of the eucalyptuses. A song of weeping, as if a mother was entreating a child to return from death, became lucid in each person's senses. Wilkulda was again singing his bridal chant sadly in the lonely morning by the pool.

Resentful, nervous, balking, the arrogant people came slowly back to the encampment. As the mankinds walked on the white clay beneath a green-yellow morning sky, triangles of dissolving shadows moved and faded below their tall, thin legs. Fingering their accumulations of sacred feathers and sticks, the forty-eight elders preceded the people. Haughty was their mien as they neared the glowing mound of ash. They hid the fears that puckered their hearts and twitched their throats.

Stiffly men came to the fire of Wilkulda. Stillness abounded except for the smacking and squeaking noises of babes suckling at breasts. The hundreds of night fires had died out. Camp dingos, normally ubiquitous in their chattering roughness, were absent. Timorous, expectant of punishment, man approached the soundless fire.

Tenderly Wilkulda smiled at the people who were ranked by sexual precedence around the fire. "Forget suspicion and jealousy, trust in the Sky and its infinite water," he spoke, "trust in my release from death, by your renewed trust confirm your children's destiny. Refute cruelty as base and not of man. Cling to forgiveness as a babe clings to his mother's breast. Be metamorphosed by forgiveness. Follow my words and be forgetful of murder plottings. Deny me not for I am your deliverer."

The people remained unmoved. Inwardly they chose to leave Wilkulda alone in his sadness. The task he had offered was alien to their comprehension. Sensing their rejection of himself and his message, Wilkulda spoke again: "I am not false. I am the Sky's raindrop. Never have I been ghoul or deceiver. I am the rainbow of tomorrow. I am the end of cruelty and the beginning of the New Dream. Is not there one who will stand with me as a defender of forgiveness?"

Humankind failed Wilkulda. They listened as the stone of the Nightmare Age hears the last storm, insentient and unaware, yet arrogantly. Elders pretended attentiveness to the messenger even as they conjured magic to defeat him. Wilkulda smiled encouragingly as the bloomed sky faded the fire's inner conflict. No person, no man spoke out in Wilkulda's favor. Instead resentment swelled in the people for they felt belittled by the ghoul's treachery. It was as it had been before, Wilkulda was rejected by men.

Then, as ridicule began to mount toward open display, a murmuring of shocked reproaches could be heard from the hunched mass of rearward females. It was Mayawara approaching the front. Beautiful Mayawara, mystified by her own impetuosity, dashed through the ranks of sullen men to stand in the outer ashes of Wilkulda's fire. He glowed with pride as Mayawara, her petite breasts abob from the run, did say with her lovely face shyly turned earthward, "I am Wilkulda's friend. He is a very good person and a very good magician too. He never hurt anyone and he tries to help people, I was dead, I was dead. Tjalerina killed me. Wilkulda made me live again. I think we should try his forgiveness. I think we should let Wilkulda be our messenger if he wants so much to be a messenger."

Wilkulda was a truster of men and hoped that the host would be swayed by Mayawara's example. He could no longer look upon Mayawara as only another female among many. By her act she had recalled the courage of Tjundaga. He cared for her. He again believed that all men were redeemable. He felt that a new age had begun when Mayawara had assumed his message as her burden. Thus reassured, Wilkulda did step from the fire with Mushabin's unsinged spear in hand. At once the volatile embers became cold chars.

Wilkulda was at Mayawara's side and was quietly tall above her ringlets. He took her slender, tiny hand in his, and as he looked upon her face it seemed as if Mayawara was a gourd of water gifted to a parched man. 'Why, she is a girl of exquisite sensitivity,' Wilkulda thought as he looked down at her. Keenly sure of man's destiny the messenger turned and stood erect before the scorning assemblage. Alas, he did not see their baleful paranoia or their rage at his renewed exultation. Wilkulda saw them prepared to accept the gift of forgiveness as Mayawara had done. Awaiting their joyous acceptance he stilled his soul and readied his message.

Handsome, regal, Wirultjurkur replied adroitly to the silent passion of the messenger. The skilled sorcerer spoke well, with the potency of a man who realizes he faces the extreme challenge to his faith. Dawn was well past and the flatness of rock and sand was blonded by the early sun's cast. Calmly, with persuasive authority, Wirultjurkur said, "My dear fellow, with respect and hospitality I must tell you that you be altogether too queer, too strange for our simple love of the Sky World. We do not need to recreate the order of existence, for we are wise and are content with the perfection of the Dream. We sleep and awaken in harmony with the relentless re-creation of the Ancestors' voyages. We need neither cruelty nor forgiveness, as these ideas are alien and beyond our sophistication. Go among peoples better educated than we, braver than we, people who will appreciate your outstanding potential because of their own superiority."

Wirultjurkur had said this with a charming tilt of his head and with a most friendly tone to his voice. But now more forcefully, he continued, "We speared you with every legal right, and yet you fail to accept our will. We have rejected you and your unnaturalness ever since you returned alone as a boy from the sacred lands. Without provocation I tell you that you must go elsewhere. Go to a more distinguished people and be their messenger."

Bemused by his own courage before the ghoul, for now Wirultjurkur knew that Wilkulda must be a ghoul, he paused deferentially before saying, "Life is extraordinary, is it not? Stop me if I say something that is offensive. Now, we do request, dear fellow, that you go. Take Mayawara with you. She has chosen to oppose her elders, let the girl be your property now . . . Mayawara, if I might digress, what a disappointment you are. Because of your insane impulse you must leave forever with Wilkulda. We Eagles, and your husband's people, obviously do not appeal to your taste . . .

"And obviously," continued the haughty sorcerer, "you, young sir, possess powers beyond our imaginations. So I do hope that you will practice your magic with a people deserving such greatness. Forgive, aha, my audacity when I ask you to go, please go. Don't let it upset you, old fellow, we respect your magic but it surpasses that contentedness of life we strive for. Go and take your weird kindness with you. We find you distasteful and not as a man should be. Most probably it is impossible for any human to slay you, only another ghoul could do it. You have caused only tribulation to those you say you wish to aid. For your own peace of spirit I wish a human could kill you."

Wilkulda clung to the hand of Mayawara as he commented in an even voice, "I was dead among the grey stones, but I have returned to the living world, that my message forecasting a better age is given to man."

"Now, now," interrupted Wirultjurkur, "we are all male adults here in the front rows. There is no need for exaggeration. We respect your magic, we do. Let's get down to the facts, to what's real and to what we know. We're reasonable and willing to compromise on everything but principle. I admit that it is useless to try and kill you. How can we slay what is already dead? To be quite candid, your message is anarchy and unsettling to our traditions. It is with a serene conscience that I ask you to go. Go without enmity and wander in the nightlands with your kindred ghosts."

With excited curiosity the assembled people waited for Wilkulda's rejoinder. What a terrific display of arrogance by arrogant Wirultjurkur thought his forty-seven comrades in

degreed malehood. They were entranced with Wirultjurkur's
audacity and knew that whatever the ghoul sorcered, it could
never surpass the brilliant oratory of their leader.

Yet simply did Wilkulda reply to the elder's splendidness,
"Yes, certainly, we shall leave."

And he and Mayawara without haste walked away from
the sinking castle of ash. The astonished throng watched the
two depart with consternation. Where was the blow, the
crash and thunder of conflicting magic? The people had been
denied the competition of two great magicians and man felt
cheated.

## six

Mayawara and Wilkulda made to the south. That first day
they loped through uninhabited wastes. By late afternoon the
magic boundaries of the Eagle-land were passed and they
came into a plain of undulating clay pans. To the east was a
ridge roughly projecting upward with a glade of bluegums at
its crest. They climbed the ridge in search of water, which
they found dripping from a rock outcropping. Mayawara was
delighted to be with Wilkulda and trusted that life had again
become agreeable. To be free of her strict father and weary
husband was reason enough for joy. This first day Wilkulda
made camp among the bluegums. They gathered several types
of berries from the thickets and Wilkulda created fire by
friction. Sitting between the fires the two feasted on ripe
fruit. After the meal Wilkulda lay down to sleep on one side
of the middle blaze. Mayawara, instead of placing herself on
the opposite side of the fire, lay down next to Wilkulda. She
wiggled into his arms, saying in a compelling voice that she
was fearful and sad from the morning's ordeal. Wilkulda felt
the need to comfort Mayawara and thus cradled her in his
arms. With her head in the sand, beneath his shoulder, they
slept.

For several days they tramped south through
spinifex-clumped plains. On the eighth day since leaving the
pool world they entered a region of blue bubbled stone. The
illimitable scatterings of rock were spread evenly over miles
of flats. In this place of blue, once molten stone, the two first
ate meat that Wilkulda had killed. He had followed the

exceedingly faint tracks of a wombat to its burrow. The
animal had left a trail from its nocturnal food searching.
Wilkulda blazed smoke bursts into each of the lair's exits,
leaving only the entrance smokeless. Here the wombat rushed
out from its safety and Wilkulda slew the mawkish creature
with his worn spear that had not tasted blood since Mushabin
had thrust it seasons past. Wilkulda did this killing thing for
Mayawara, as the woman craved flesh.

That night they greedily devoured the roasted wombat,
cracking apart each bone for the cavity's sweet morsel.
Wilkulda ate the prey's brain as was his due. Afterwards they
sat with legs extended to expand their stomachs that the
food might be digested. The world of green-blue rock did not
end and they walked deeper into the bareness. No food of
consequence was found to replace the wombat's strength,
and by the seventeenth day of the trek Mayawara had
weakened and could not continue past mid-day. Wilkulda
made camp in the shadow of a plum-tinted boulder, massive
compared to the blue stones that were no bigger than a
clenched fist. Yet the plum boulder reached but a single cubit
into the sky. However, the vaulting above was so vast that the
land's very harshness was overwhelmed and without
definition.

Wilkulda, who had not entered Mayawara with his penis,
now desired to capture meat for her even as any hunter
would wish to feed his woman. That afternoon he lay prone
near a snake's crevice in the earth some hundreds of leaps
from where Mayawara rested in the plum stone's shade. At
dusk the dirt snake awoke. This particular reptile was seven
feet in length and fat with many mice. Wilkulda lay intent
and still; the harmless snake was about to slither safely away
from the warning heat of the man when he awakened from
his motionlessness. Wilkulda's hand shot out to grip the snake
and with heavy jaws he gnawed off its head. With the dead
snake held high as trophy Wilkulda ran exuberantly to
Mayawara. In the shadow of the pumice boulder the two
swallowed the reflexing snake without bothering to sear the
meat. Mayawara ate from one end while Wilkulda chewed at
the other. They ate the squirming deadness with much
hilarity.

Later he made a meager fire of dried weed to defend them

from the cold night. They lay down to sleep by the pumice
rock and the fires. Mayawara slid along his being, settling in
to share his warmth and protection. She now considered this
normal sleep behavior. The young woman had not urged
Wilkulda into lovemaking, she had been patient. However,
this night Mayawara lusted heartily for the snake-killing
Wilkulda and she whispered with her mouth softly pressed
into the sand under his ear, "No one is here. No person is
here who would care what we do. Let us be husband and wife
tonight."

Lureful was Mayawara's being with chin proud between
diamond faceted cheeks. Thick loopings of never brushed
tresses gave her the appearance of an innocent girl-child. Her
nose was less squat than Wilkulda's and somewhat aquiline.
His forehead was heavily shielded with bone projecting over
deep placed eyes, while Mayawara's delicately tapered head
swept to a perfect crown of ovalness. Her eyes were of a
tender brown, while his were as bark. The young woman's
glistening mouth was small even as Wilkulda's although
narrow, was large with protruding lips.

Breasts full and floating with her energy's heat she now
stunned her nipples strongly into Wilkulda's flesh.
Mayawara's eyes were large and lustrous with sexual hotness.
Her entire body was intent and alert to response even as if
her being was sculpted from the moving leg of a mating red
kangaroo. Speaking with the honesty of her passion,
Mayawara enjoined, "The place inside me is warmly wet and
will not hurt your penis. Lay down with me and I will be
happy and you will be happy. Everyone says I am beautiful
like the black swans swimming in the pool at home. I know
that you are a different kind of man but I am not afraid of
you. You are very handsome, Wilkulda, with your pretty eyes
and your fine tallness. I will not tell anyone if you put your
hardness into me. We will be lovers and I will take care of
you and you will take care of me."

Wilkulda could not think of a distraction and his hands
came to rest in the crevice of Mayawara's plump buttocks.
She was a warming in the chill of the dying day. She smelled
of life as he had always known it: of seed cake burning in the
coals, of singed kangaroo pelts, of impenetrable mulga wood
burning, of perspiration mixed with emu fat, of blood and

clay, of urine and breast milk, of offal and death, and of menstruation and creation. Mayawara's odor was of home, of peace and of things in order.

The young woman did not truly sense who Wilkulda was and indeed, he was aware of her ignorance of his nature. She loved him as a man and that washed away all the bitterness and frustration of his role as messenger. A fierce desire shattered Wilkulda's resolve and he dared to please Mayawara. The oath of eternal chastity was an age past and seemed meaningless with Mayawara there close. And Wilkulda said to his soul that he had died and had been reborn, that the promise belonged to the dead fellow he had been. He, the second Wilkulda, was free of the obligation. He loved her. Wilkulda realized that the warmness in his chest was his love for Mayawara. The old sacrifice was the faded prattling of a child compared to being cruel to soft Mayawara who loved him.

"Do you not hurt inside," asked Wilkulda, "so many men have laid down with you so recently? I don't want to hurt you."

"No," confided Mayawara in a low, sweet rustling of a voice as she felt Wilkulda's heat expand. "Women are used to such matters. Those stupid men could not hurt me. Darling Wilkulda, it is our way to lay down often with many men. The law requires it and we are glad to help protect the Dreamtime. Besides, laying down is fun."

Even as she spoke Mayawara guided Wilkulda with sure familiarity. And as his throat made new, strange sounds, Wilkulda did enter her with his penis. She crossed her legs over his back while he lifted her up by the buttocks into his strength. He was not ashamed to thrust with Mayawara. Wilkulda was pleased with himself. He was delighted with the excited Mayawara and he contented her. She now dozed small and damp in his sheltering self as he mused at his sense of accomplishment. And as he too fell into slumber Wilkulda wished that his message could be as ecstatically greeted as was his love by Mayawara.

Awakening before dawn they made love with much lust. During the day's walk they stopped several times in shaded places to love and love again. As they trudged the gibber plains and slept beneath a new moon, Mayawara and Wilkulda were indeed man and wife.

Late in the afternoon of the third day since the moon's rebirth they entered a land of mallee growth. Travel became increasingly difficult. However, as the two strove to create a passage through the dense, snapping entanglements they came upon a clearing, which was the base of an enormous hill set deep in the mallee plants. The mighty slope rose above and out of the mallee, and the pair crawled up the incline. It took them the rest of that day and the morning of the next to surmount the height's crest.

On the summit they came upon a grove of thriving whitegums, and grass and reeds clustered thickly about a small marsh. Following the marsh on the top of the hill they discovered an oasis, watered by a stream that issued from a fracture in the thin stone of the hill's crown. The brook was but three feet in width and less than a foot deep, and ran fifty feet from the rock cap before it was dissipated in the marsh somewhat lower down the summit. The water was cold and pristine. By the plenitude of tracks along the stream's banks it appeared that much game existed on the hill. Before Wilkulda and Mayawara men had not penetrated the mallee to the high but invaluable water source.

The hill stretched two miles in length from north to south and was perhaps one half mile wide. A cap of sheer slate protected the eastern and western slopes, while the north and south sides were thick with mallee. Flocks of cockatoos nested in a copse of ironwood trees that clung to the inner fringe of the slate on the eastern edge of the oasis. In the marsh itself, lilies proliferated but shared the wetness with turtles, frogs, snakes, and herons and cranes basking under the gigantic sun. At the western part of the marsh hugely tall trees grew. Trees without branches except for a meager tuft at the apex of the extended trunks. These trees, which sprouted several hundreds of feet into the sky, served as nesting places for a covey of wedgetail eagles. These lords of the sky were proud and heavy birds, for food abounded. The tracks of a score of species identified the watering place as a matrix of life, except for man.

The tribes to the east and west of the hill had not yet made their way through the miles of mallee that blocked off the hill. To the south a world of sand inhibited life for ten leagues. Wilkulda and Mayawara were the primordial pair of their animalkind to exist on this high table rock. In five

centuries a mankind from the eastern dunes would explore
the mallee and discover the hill and its precious water.
Wilkulda and his love Mayawara made their camp on the
verdant eastern bank of the brook. Here plum and apple trees
had rooted luxuriously in the dust accumulations of the
aeons.

That first day while bathing downstream Mayawara found
the fresh water crayfish that spawned profusely in the brook.
Shellfish and fruit and the eggs from the roosting flocks
supplied the two fully and they waxed fat on the stone
capital. As they were the first of men to live at the spring, the
birds and the wallabies and the platypuses and the wombats
and the bears feared them not. The animals came
unhesitantly to drink at the stream in daylight although the
humans were camped nearby. Mayawara sought eggs in nests
and the birds in their great multitudes shrilled not at the
thefts. Wilkulda did not kill and the animals established
personal relationships with the couple.

Wilkulda restrained himself not and pleasured with his
woman. Mayawara was happier than she had ever
remembered. She believed that they would settle
permanently by the brook on the burgeoning rock meadow
and birth a new mankind. Even she, a stupid woman, realized
that the oasis could support a large mankind. The girl no
longer feared Wilkulda's refusal of love, for now he was a
spontaneous and inexhaustible lover. In the first week by the
stream Mayawara had pleated mats and a sun screen from the
water reeds. Each day she would work at the making of the
many thing necessary to a civilized life. She diligently scraped
wood platters from the cut lumber that Wilkulda had
chopped with the adze he had fashioned. With her delicate
fingers Mayawara wove a seine from human and wallaby hair
she found on trees and bushes where the plodders had lost
tufts of fur. With this hand net she chased the crayfish and
minnows in the stream.

It was Mayawara who foraged in the new world for
wonderfully rotund berries and tubers. Wilkulda filled his
days in constant dialogue with the comrades he had found on
the spur of the slate height. Here a large family of kangaroo
lived among the fine meadows cracked apart in the stone
shield. These grand leapers liked Wilkulda and thought him

quite an interesting chap. Without initiation they accepted
him as a kangaroo who had no tail. And in their language that
is how Wilkulda was named, Tailless Leaper. The weeks of
jovial contentment and mutual meditation among his friends
the kangaroo gave a sense of purpose to Wilkulda.

This particular hive of kangaroo had come to the rockhill
before man had lived in the planet. They found Wilkulda
charming and insisted on permitting him precedence in their
rituals which deeply flattered the messenger. Several younger
female kangaroo were tendered him that he might satisfy his
sexual needs, but Wilkulda cheerfully explained that he was
provided for in this by his mate at the spring. Eventually
Wilkulda invited his comrades to visit Mayawara. One
afternoon, as she was standing in the brook with the seine,
Wilkulda, in two footed leaps, followed by fifteen large male
kangaroos, came bounding over the slate cap. It pleased
Mayawara that Wilkulda jumped further and higher than any
of his peers. With civility Mayawara greeted the marsupials as
Wilkulda introduced each by name with due respect for
appropriate seniority. Smiling in hospitality the woman
offered platters of berries and plums to her guests. Graciously
the kangaroos refused, except for the youngest who forgot
the visitor's law and munched down a heap of strawberries.

Mayawara quietly sat and listened to the discussion of the
amazingly fine weather that had persisted into the rain
season, which was winter to this planet. That Mayawara
could comprehend the language of the marsupials did not
surprise her and she enjoyed their company at ease.

After this meeting the entire tribe of kanagroo felt no
shyness in visiting Mayawara and Wilkulda at their campsite.
The young woman became fast friends with several of the
marsupial females. And the kangaroos were happy to have
man on the table rock, as it added a dimension to their
knowledge of the world. The wedgetail eagles, who kept the
stupendous flocks of roosting birds in balance with the food
supply, were also delighted to share the brook with man. The
blacked eagles would glide down from their surmounting
nests to swoop gently above the listening kangaroo and the
speaking Wilkulda. One day in a discussion Wilkulda
discovered that both the eagles and the kangaroo believed
that today was tomorrow and also yesterday. That the days

were identical and in fact were but one repetition. That seasons were of food and that death did not exist; their symbol for death and season was food. Man, Wilkulda, was saddened by his friends' lack of cosmic imagination. Wilkulda suffered now for he realized that his message was meant for men alone. That the other animals had no need of forgiveness as they were innately without cruelty.

The marsupials were much taken with Mayawara and were astonished at the volume of her visible breasts, and indeed, her extraordinary lack of a pouch. They would come early to the morning campfires, as at their first visit with Mayawara she had presented each female kangaroo with a small seed cake hot from the embers and they had become enamoured of the baked food. Each morning they would patiently sit on their great tails waiting turns for a mouthful of the delicious cake. The kangaroo were not greedy and a mouthful sufficed; besides, they did not wish to tire their hostess. Although it was laborious to prepare the seed dough and cook it for so many guests, Mayawara loved her sisters and minded not the task.

At noontime the kangaroo and the wedgetails would depart as they were aware that Mayawara and Wilkulda would lay down then. Mayawara now believed Wilkulda would remain her husband until death. Darkness or day he was her constant lover, tender and gentle but always a racing of excited potency. For it was as if Wilkulda had become a cloud bursting with warm rain. A spurting of wetness that surged the clay and dust of wasted seasons clean from a rubbled river bed. He loved as if his very living continuation was dependent on his gonads' abundancy. As if uniting with Mayawara he might forestall the future. She guessed not his dread of the morrow's fulfillment.

Mayawara had put behind her the memory of Wilkulda's duality, his appointment as a precursor to the new Dream. What she did know was that she was the most fortunate of women and that soon many fine children would be born. That she and Wilkulda would live peaceably on the grass and tree shattered slate in harmony with the kangaroo and the wedgetail eagles. However, as a wise wife Mayawara did sense that Wilkulda needed challenges and stimulations that she and his comrades could not provide. She was planning to suggest that he might search the mallee country for a small mankind and invite a few younger couples to share the oasis. Then the intellectual company of similarly ritualized men would certainly add zest to Wilkulda's daily life.

And how she inwardly berated the old Mayawara, the little girl who was forever preoccupied with vanity and seduction. Mayawara sorrowed that her parents could not view her circumstance and her transformation. Interestingly her love for Wilkulda was based on those very characteristics that had made him an outcast among his people. For a copulating Wilkulda had remained as kind as the Wilkulda of chastity. Never in her experience had she known a man to hold a woman's hand during menstrual pain. It was a revelation when on her first bleeding as a wanderer he had carried handfuls of water from a tree stump's hollow to her as she huddled by the night fires. Later that same night, when she slept under his shoulder for warmth, Mayawara had awakened and thought about the sweet taste of the brackish water Wilkulda had given her. And he never insisted on intercourse during menstruation as did the Eagle-men, who believed high magic could be performed at the moment of intermixture of liquids. Wilkulda would even say thank you for a leaf of fruit, and this was indeed novel to Mayawara's experience.

Wilkulda was happy. The groves of thriving eucalyptuses, and their nesting flocks, inspired his soul with hope. Existence had never seemed so bountiful and lovely. He hoped too that his message could be redeemed. He would watch the scores of full grown wedgetails circling high on erect wings hour on hour without seeking rest's perch. Their shadows would glide gracefully over the slate garden and his upturned face. The very rhythm of life at the oasis persuaded Wilkulda that one day cruelty among men must be abolished. He sang inwardly of forgiveness as never before and he could sense the growing of forgiveness in his soul. The day would come when Wilkulda must meditate on his myth's enactment, its next testing, but not now, he pleaded with his spurring conscience. Wilkulda said to his soul to be content and not to be impatient, and it was done. All around the tablerock was heavy with the saturation of underground water. To the north the rains had flooded plain and gorge, but here in the

mallee country there was only a scent of mist in the air. The
floods flowed beneath great deserts and only a small portion
of the waters reached the slate oasis by unseen tunnels of
passage, but what did trickle through was sufficient to cycle
life with birth.


## seven

Weeks leached slow, one day burned itself past the last and
Wilkulda was a new man. The lovers had been on the rock
oasis seven moons and Mayawara had not menstruated the
final two. Thus, they knew that the baby spirit lived in
Mayawara and that they would be parents to a child. On
Mayawara's urging he had even fabricated a new spear and
left Mushabin's gift by the reed hut when he visited his
comrades. However a day came when he returned from
dialogue with the kangaroo without the younger, cleverer,
weapon. A kangaroo youth had evidenced interest in the
pretty object, the spear Wilkulda had made, and the man had
taught the marsupial to cast the object properly, using his tail
as a spearthrower. The kangaroo thought the throwing a
game that had to do with the longest toss. But one of the
young marsupial's casts had pierced a toad with the fire
hardened point. Wilkulda and the young kangaroo wept over
the toad's corpse and together they broke asunder the new
spear.

It was soon after the death of the toad that the difficult
morning arrived. While Mayawara knelt by the night fire to
stoke it into a bursting of tiny flames, arranging it for the
traditional platter of seed to bake, Wilkulda said, "Eat well,
little bird, for today we must walk away from this place."

To the east dawn made black the slate's greyness while
hazed columns of light searched the desolate landscape.
Mayawara, as she munched the seed, asked in that tone of
voice that a wife uses only with her husband, "Where do we
go? Why so early? What is so important? Who do you want to
visit?"

It was too sad for Wilkulda, and he did not answer, but
rose from the ground. He took up Mushabin's fraying spear

and leaned on it in contemplation for a briefness. Mayawara ate another handful of seeds. Wilkulda began to walk away from the soaring sun, south, due south over the hump of the table rock. At once Mayawara jumped to her feet and pushed her precious utensils into the largest fishnet that she had woven only recently. Dutifully Mayawara followed as a wife must. Wilkulda did not say goodby to his kangaroo friends but instead fled as if afraid to look back. He walked in shorter steps that he might not tire the burdened woman. This man loved her profoundly and he took up her net sack of possessions that she would only have to carry her embryo. He wondered at her trust and doubted that he would be able to put aside her flesh.

They traveled quickly as young people should, stopping only to gather a few dozen mallee hen eggs to suck at as they walked. With regret the lovers left the world of the brook that had been their good home. Mayawara was apprehensive but not sad, for she felt that they surely would shortly return. Undoubtedly, she thought, it would be a short excursion that was necessary for Wilkulda's magical requirements.

By high sun they were in brazen sand that piled to their ankles and in some driftings, over knees. There was not a dead tree to be sighted nor a single clump of spinifex. This land had been destroyed and burnt to the bare extremities. Faintly, in the western horizon, a slanting, crimson hued escarpment could be seen rising from the desert flats. Wilkulda turned to reach this rising that they might follow its shaded line. As they neared the scarlet ridge that grew arrogantly up from the decayed desert, Wilkulda spied far away a thin line splitting the sky perpendicularly: smoke of a campfire. This smoke was but vaguely distinguishable in the immense vacancy and Mayawara did not notice it. Without a word to her, Wilkulda took note of the wafting beacon as his answer.

By afternoon the ridge rose several hundred feet above the blight, and the pair ran alongside its baseline. Sighting a scoriated relic of a mulga tree buried in a crevice Wilkulda went to sniff the plant's skeleton. Prodding with his spear in the sand about the mulga he touched a rock shelf projecting out from the ridge. Here he began to dig out a deep water

soak. Three yards beneath the surface Wilkulda found a slim
layer of wetness. He stamped on the bottom of the soak to
force the water upwards. Mayawara stretched down into the
soak and Wilkulda lifted handfuls of the liquid to her mouth.

After her thirst was appeased Wilkulda licked the moisture
from his hands and crawled out of the hole. At once they
again pursued the ridge line and were grateful for its shade.
The hot bombast of late afternoon boasted its extreme
temperature a degree beyond human reason. They noticed
that the spur of red rock was receeding rapidly now below
the muffling dun sands. And suddenly the ridge ended in a
vale of iron oxide boulders the size of elderly hills. Wilkulda
recognized the traces of a path leading into the metallic vale
from the opposite direction. This was a place frequented by
men, probably a sanctuary sacred to the people creating the
wood smoke. Even the female Mayawara had now identified
the hanging plumes of ash. Five feathers of heated residue
rose· in the lower sky south, southeast. Taking her man's
hand, Mayawara said, "This is such a horrid place. The color
of these rocks is awful. I think they must be magic. If we
hurry we can be with those people and their fires before
dark. Are they the ones coming back to our brook with us? Is
that why we've come here, to find people to live with us
besides the kangaroo?"

No life but the two lovers existed in the hostile vale of
oxide sterility. Lizards, grubs, locust, even the omnipresent
flies were absent. Wilkulda turned to the anticipating
Mayawara but before he could speak she said, "Why do we
stop? It is no good here, my sweetheart. Let's hurry and we
can be with people tonight. It's so wonderful to find people
only a day's walk from our hill. They'll be nice and give us
roast meat. We will eat and talk among people again and
there will be many fires."

Wilkulda, who loved this one girl, looked into her proud
face and after a moment of regret, he spoke in a low and
unsteady voice, "My little sparrow, we must go separate
trails." Softly and longingly he wavered on, "I have to
complete a thing. It must be done. The Sky is my Father and
I must move on. Only you, little bird, have given me
happiness. You are a very pretty and a very good girl. You
will live a long life with plentiful food and will bear many
beautiful children and have many fine husbands . . ."

"What is wrong with you? Is it you, Wilkulda who teaches of cruelty? Why can't I help you with your duty to the Sky? You are a very stupid man, I see that now. What about our land high up by the stream, and your friends the kangaroos? Oh, don't leave me. I'll do what ever you want. I'll do what ever you say. Don't leave me, don't go," finished comely Mayawara with many swallowed tears.

Wilkulda wanted to stay with Mayawara. He knew that he would be the dominant elder among the desert folk they now approached. He might be able to do great things with this unsophisticated mankind. The idea of training forgiveness into his own children was also a piercing temptation. In truth, he did not wish to leave Mayawara whom he loved and who carried a male child in her stomach that would be his son. Wilkulda did not wish to live alone and apart any more. He did not desire to be cold at night and he pleasured much in laying down with Mayawara.

As he held her close Mayawara's hands caught onto his wrists in silent plea even as if she were a wordless infant. Her tear wet hair was suctioned in by her weeping mouth and eyes. Wilkulda spoke, "My little sparrow, you are so beautiful and so full of love. I would never leave you if the choice was mine but I was chosen to be unique. I did not choose to be me. I am not what you think I am. I am not like other men, not at all like them. I want to stay with you always, close and warm. I want to be your husband forever and grow old with you. I'd be happy with you until I died and you could help me be the messenger. But don't you see, I'm not really a man anymore. I am the white swan alone in the sky at night. I am as strange as the teeth of babies that grow out of nothing. When I was a boy, perhaps seeking death after too much sadness, the message was given to me. I was so proud. It has been harder to be the messenger than I could have ever imagined. But I can no more turn away from forgiveness than can a stick not burn in the fire. It is cruel that I leave but crueler to myself than to you. I must seek those who will carry on the message after me. These people ahead are remote and too uncrowded. They are decent as most people are and will be good to you. They are the Lizards. They have no pool but several springs live on their land. When you go to them you must not speak of our oasis as they believe the Mallee world to be forbidden to men.

"Among these Lizards is a fine fellow called Mjanya. He is
quite young but already a big man with several wives. But all
Mjanya's wives are old. You will go alone to the Lizards and
Mjanya will take you as wife this very night. After a life of
many seasons among the Lizards you will say to your young
granddaughters that in your long life Mjanya was the best
man you ever knew."

A staggered Mayawara said, "But I belong to you. I am
your woman. I am content to stay with you always. Take me
with you. I will be no trouble, I promise."

Wilkulda, with pain's shadow in his eyes, answered in
stutters, "I can take no woman among the strange peoples I
must visit. I love you, Mayawara, and I am grateful that you
loved me. It was wonderful to lay down with you and have
someone to talk to without being afraid of being thought a
fool. I was chosen to make a commotion in the Dream's
projection and to heal men. You will see, little sparrow,
Mjanya will make you very happy."

Mayawara stopped crying and looked searchingly into her
man's face. The Wilkulda she saw was slender framed, with
thin, small hands and feet attached to lengthy, twined arms
and legs. A man whose ridged incisions covered his chest even
as the veins of a leaf remain intact when all else is clay. His
appearance bespoke no exception from her world's
configuration. Mayawara examined a tall want of a fellow
with vines of stretched muscle fastened to the bone even as a
clippership's rigging supports the tall masts. She saw a face
sorrowed and distorted with things apart from her
understanding. And Mayawara said to her lover lost, "All
right. I will go. You are a man with no feelings for those who
want to please you."

"Yes," purposelessly in agreement, "Yes, that is fact. I am
a bad man, but from this time on I will try and be better and
never again shall I hurt such as Mayawara. I am sorry, I
should not . . . but I have learned so much . . . I so needed to
have your love."

Ended, Wilkulda still wished to lean and press his head to
where Mayawara's neck gracefully joined at her shoulder. But
he was afraid to touch her as it might lead to laying down
there by the boulders and that would mean never again

thinking of leaving her. Silent and apart they moved toward the smoke trails. They did not stop to view a wide ravine where hundreds of goanna lizards were clustered. The reptiles lazily baked with their folds of skin loose in relaxation. These lizards were the brothers of the people of the smoke and they trusted men. The goannas heard the two pass by their fissured domain without concern.

A sagging rind of the sun shadowed the land harshly as they advanced to a single bluegum that marked the encampment's boundary. Wilkulda stopped to turn and bid goodby, but Mayawara listlessly trudged on toward the fire without comment. She was gone. He knew it now, she was gone and soon he would be irrevocably dead. He did not want Mayawara to be gone. He wanted to stay with the young woman and grow old and ugly together.

The Lizards were a tribe of thirty persons inclusive of children. Actually it was a family band under the fatherhood of Mjanya's parent. The Lizards would gratefully take Mayawara into their mankind. It was difficult to find suitable wives in the desert. They would not be afraid and think her a ghoul. It was too apparent that she was human with her cheeks glistened with tears. Mayawara's sobbing clearly bewailed the fact that her useless lover had deserted her.

Wilkulda lingered in the circumference of the bluegum's surface roots. Light was vanquished and night was paramount. He stood there with his pain as the noises of the Lizards' evening meal were calmed by sleep. He stood there when he knew Mayawara had lain down with Mjanya and was nestled in his powerful hunting arms. Before he began his running, as if his throat spasmed beyond command, Wilkulda spoke aloud in the darkness, "Mayawara don't go. I don't want you to go."

She was not sleeping. She was thinking of Wilkulda when the sound drifted down from the bluegum to the nightfires. Mayawara lifted her head from Mjanya even as an otter becomes still as it raises its head from a pond to listen to the wind's secret. She listened intently but the sound did not come again and she thought it to have been a dingo yelping. With a woman's sigh of enduring acceptance, Mayawara went to sleep. Wilkulda, even before she had been startled by his plea, began his lonely running to the east.


## eight

In the year of Wilkulda's sojourn, reportings of an impossibly powerful magician were heard around fires in the deserts, in the bush, and in the river valleys of the continent. Sixty decades would have to pass before the rumor of the newest Dreamtime Hero reached from sea strait to sea strait, but it had begun that first season after he left Mayawara. At high ceremonies, where several mankinds would merge their varied myths into one dramatic Dreamtime re-creation, the news of the Hero Wilkulda would be discussed. Hunting parties straying across boundaries would meet and transfer the tale of an exceptionally tall and thin magician who would but touch a sickness and a cure would be invoked. Thus the world was hoed for Kalod to come and seed forgiveness among the peoples of the land.

It was all quite true. Wilkulda would come to a community of men and ask neither for water nor food. Women he refused. He did ask that those who were ill be brought to him. Then the wanderer would lift his hands to his arm's fullest extension, with palms to the Sky. Without incantation or dance, mutely he would place his fingers to the sickness. Thus he healed men. Children exhausted by dry fever, warriors with bellies rent from spear's implosion, females with ulcerated parts: to each person the messenger gave end to pain and a cure. Tribes became beholden to Wilkulda. They listened with polite attentiveness as he pleaded for their recognition of cruelty. However, no matter the greatness of the mankind, after a few days the throbbing light that glowed from his head would force him to travel on. Perhaps it was wise to move on quickly as even the most sophisticated elder would begin to take affront at a man who relentlessly rejected daughters, sisters, wives, mothers, and forbidden foods.

Thus many alien mankinds became brothers to Wilkulda. But with only one people did he stay more than a few days. This was a dense mankind located in the river world at the southeast tit of the continent. These men were an intelligent race who speared other males only at the severest provocation and who did not practice abuse of women. They were skilled in hut construction and their large weedland wood structures overlooked a narrow ocean bay from fat green hills. The men called themselves Whales and Joobaitch was the great elder of the mankind.

Joobaitch was exceedingly proficient at calling the black whales, who lived beyond the channel in the great sea, into the bay close to shore. Sacred ceremonies would be conducted on the beach by the Whale-men as their brother whales in the waters looked on. The magicians of the Whales were keen artists and they had inscribed the Sky's pantheon on the mammoth bluffs of granite that fronted the littoral.

Joobaitch, a man of high humor, enjoyed the dialogue of the messenger and responded with an analysis of the dangers inherent in a too rigorous faith based on forgiveness. Joobaitch's insights into the nature of cruelty and the idealism of forgiveness appealed deeply to Wilkulda. He realized that he had come upon a man whose soul was as curious as had been Tjundaga's. Wilkulda lingered seven weeks with the Whales and Joobaitch became an adherent of the tenets of forgiveness. The messenger desired to stay for a lengthy stay with the prolific and alert Whales but the light about his head urged him on to further healings elsewhere. Joobaitch was eager for Wilkulda to remain and invest every Whale with forgiveness, and indeed, there were thousands of Whales to inspire.

But Wilkulda became a spore of germination before the copious winds. Diagonally he leapt over the lands of the central blights making toward his single, plausible destination. He came among diverse mankinds and spoke to them in their own languages. As he cured men he earnestly portrayed forgiveness as the final magic. Wilkulda raced the substance of the Sky's reality and as he did this voyaging he strained to create a New Dream. Nights were as day to the running magician and in his nakedness he came upon the naked mankinds of earth. In the duality of his light's emission, in its revelation and its blindness, Wilkulda chose to trust, and thus deceived himself. For Wilkulda believed the tribes he healed were entered into forgiveness, and this was not true.

In the acrid wastes he found man. In the swamps of the ·
southwest nipple he found man. With energy he explored the
continent's southern coast from fragrant mammary to the
opposite fertile, wetted gland, between was uninterrupted
blight. This coast was an oblivion of both water and
nurturing land. Yet even here in a funnel of hostility he
found mankinds content with circumcision and the Eternal
Dream. Mankinds who considered themselves rich with the
seacoast pods of seals and dugongs.

He came back on his tracks along the southern coast
through the swamp world on the western peninsula.
Northward now along the western shore, beneath shadows
sweltered by the harsh heat and the blood warm seas did
Wilkulda run. Here on the beaches parallel to Australia's
Western Ocean did Wilkulda confer reality with his trust of
men. And he had finally achieved the discipline of
remembering Mayawara without weeping.

The seacoast peoples seemed immune to deformities and
disease. But his days of healing were fulfilled as there were
numerous stomach disorders to be cured due to the shellfish
diet. This western shore was well populated compared to the
inner wastes and the southern devastation. However, it was
empty of men compared to the eastern lands where the
Whales lived. Northward continued Wilkulda along the west
coast. Huge tides undermining cliffs to perpetually friction
gigantic and exotic creatures out of the pliant stone reduced
Wilkulda's running form to innocence. Outward reefs and
rocks thrashed tidal waves into booming founts as Wilkulda
entered a coastal bay gouged out from north to south in the
shape of a flanged hook. Seaward, beyond the reefs, three
islands break apart the ocean's force and create calmer,
warmer, water in the bay itself. The islands are sparse of
foliage and hideous on their outer faces where the sea has
distorted the rock shield and bitten out ragged slits of
pointed stone. Thus, rock rib-cages of monstrous appearance
sluiced the ocean over the raw isles.

The bay's floor had been secreted with mineral deposits by
now vanished rivers. When Wilkulda walked by the protected
waters had become a hatchery of opulent life. Several
mankinds shared the bay and its plenty, and warmaking was
seldom practiced here. On the sheltered waters of the bay

scores of reed and dugout canoes chased and caught the sharks that proliferated. Delectable sharks in many thousands knew the bay as a nursery and the four tribes inhabiting the shoreline were also Sharks of differing classes. These fat mankinds were virile and healthy, and except for a few bowel obstructions and lower tract adhesions Wilkulda found the Sharks barren and devoid of spiritual curiosity.

Leaving this area after three days he came upon a long and vacant beach. White sandflats veered sullenly northward without distinguishing features. Except for mist and seasonal sprinkles there were no sources of fresh water and man did not exist along this sterility. Wilkulda gained the end of this beach without remorse and gratefully entered a greener land. Here a coiling riverlet led him to a cliff waterfall that fell into a secluded bay. A reef, and then closer to shore a large sand bar, barricaded the bay from the tormenting rip tides of the ocean. In this land Wilkulda was to meet his friend Kalod the bone driller.

Night time was upon earth as he left the splendor of the plummeting waterfall to follow the cliff head above the sea. Ahead he identified campfires of men, beacons most compelling. Moon's iridescent fog drifted on the calm of the satiated tide as Wilkulda came near to a single big campfire. A dancesong was being performed as he stealthily approached. Sorcerers leapt and crooned in simulation of the world's creation by the Rainbow Snake. Wilkulda circled the myth enactment cautiously as he desired not to disturb the elders who were enticing the moon into its fullest birth. Then as he silently, softly passed between two kapok trees he noticed with amazement that one of the participants in the ceremony was a woman. An actual female was fingering an exceptionally heroic ancestor-board. She was caressing the sacred relic with fingers heavy with magic ocher of yellow.

Never in his imagination had Wilkulda dared to hope that he might find a mankind that permitted a female to be involved with a Dreamtime ritual. The woman was absurdly old, and with her two front teeth removed decades past for ceremonial requirements her hag face was tiny and crumpled, yet it was a thing surpassing Wilkulda's experience to witness a woman enrolled as a potent caretaker of myth responsibilities. The messenger was pleased and he could not bring himself to take leave of the momentous scene. Soon he could not doubt, the woman indeed was an authentic actress of magic in the ceremonial event. Then and there he chose this tribe of provocative individualists to die with, that his message might live.

The hag noticed his form between the kapok trees. In an instant she fingered out a flake of her vaginal blood and flicked it at the apparition, chanting madly. Wilkulda was taken aback by her grossness and reflexed away in a tremendous bound. However, as he raced from the ceremonial grounds he paused and considered the audacity of the hag's act. He lingered to meditate and wonder at the ancient sorceress; had she been pretty as a young woman with a face like Mayawara's, was she loved by many men when her menstrual ran deep and full? And he thought deeper of Mayawara and how her fluid would stain the sands as she slept in his arms.

Wilkulda heard a sweet sound and momentarily thought it to be Mayawara calling him to fire at the close of day when they had lived on the slate hill. But it was not the girl, it was the sea's humming volume as it rushed upon the gleaming sand below. Wilkulda decided not to go on to the tribe's encampment but instead to visit the sea at the beach's end. He leapt down a zigzag path and ran across the wide strip of sand to the ocean. And before he could reflect on his logic Wilkulda stopped not at the sea's margin but proceeded out into the waters. He stood there in the high tide. He felt as if the pattern of his adventurous life had climaxed. Wilkulda of the pool world had come to stand alone and to die alone in the sea.

## nine

As Wilkulda held the girl infant of new eyes aloft in the sky, he watched Kalod far up on the cliffside path holding people back that there would not be a dreadful rush down the ·slanted decline. As he lowered the child to her mother the woman sang a simple chant honoring the messenger. The heat of day was as if the sun was a flying cooking stone baking seed cake. The mankinds did not notice the searing

environment as they clamored to be with the healer in the
sea. Movement had halted as he lifted the blind infant, but now
humanity swarmed to be with him in the waters. Males
antique with carbuncles sluicing pus whimpered as Wilkulda
forced pain to vanish. Women bleeding from stunted limbs,
with hands and feet ground into stumps, wept as regeneration
surged in their atoms. Young men with horridly obese private
parts, bulging with infections caused by careless subincision,
cried out thankfully as he cured them. One lad, carried
screaming into the sea by father and uncles, with a penis
distended to the size of an arm, shrieked gratefully as
Wilkulda healed the brutalized member. And the refreshment
caused the messenger to weep. Children came down to the
ocean in scores. Shyly, as if ashamed to bother an elder with
trifles, they showed Wilkulda their burns and broken bones.
And as he healed the sick the gleaming from his head
flowered the shallows with a calm light brighter than dawn.

For thirty-five days he healed the host, and then, at dusk
of the thirty-sixth day, it seemed to Wilkulda that the line of
those from the cliff to the sea had become sparse and less
demanding. Seeing his end apparent in the diminishing
patients, Wilkulda sang out in a voice so pure that at first the
mankinds thought it was the cry of an exotic seabird.

"To me bring the corpses of the recently dead and I shall
blow life into them." The host shuddered as the day's salient
curve came to completion and Wilkulda again sang out,
"Carry to me the dead of this season, those whose organs
have been eaten and whose flesh is rotted, for am I not the
resurrector of the recent dead?"

Man did as Wilkulda bidded. Momentarily they mused at
the confusions that death renunciation would cause because
of the wife divisions. However, they realized such hesitation
was petty and rushed to comply with the magician's
command. Man did not understand that Wilkulda sought a
continuation of his own life even as he created resurrection
for others. Sons and fathers, brothers and uncles raced to
forbidden graves. To tree limbs and raised platforms, to holes
in canyon sides, to bone tubes living men came to uncover
the dead and then bring the deadnesses to Wilkulda.

As the days passed while waiting for the dead to arrive,
Wilkulda became aware that the numbers of the sick entering
the sea were again increasing. He had been foolishly

apprehensive that his labor was finishing too quickly. From
the secret spurs and lagoons of reality the mankinds made to
the sea that they might be healed. And the dead of the season
began to arrive. Some of the remains were complete corpses
except for fringe decomposition, while others were but burnt
bones contained in painted hollows of wood. Wilkulda did as
he had promised and man was exultant to the fullest
measure.

Yet even the recent dead were not infinite sums, and late
one morning the final deadness was carried to Wilkulda. This
was a man of the Platypuses. The deadness had been a living
father to a powerful tribe from the northern swamps where
thirty-foot crocodiles slumbered and where three-foot
wing-spanned foxes glided from tree towers to seize flighted
bird. The corpse was escorted by forty sons. As Wilkulda
looked upon the last deadness he saw wisdom hooded in the
decayed visage. This elder alive had been an originator of
dancesongs and was deeply missed by the Platypuses for his
happy disposition.

Wilkulda scooped up the body and lifted it to the Sky.
There came a spasm in the spine of the dead creator of song
as a gaseous film gushed from his orifices. With a fragile
shudder the cadaver metamorphosed and the man's
appearance became infused with alertness and awareness. An
aged tongue licked stiffened lips and the old man, in the
terror of rebirth, screamed. His sons wailed in compassion as
the old man, fully awake, continued to scream. Then the
fellow glimpsed in the sea the queer stranger holding him
above the waters, and he ceased his screaming. The singer
intently studied Wilkulda who hold him safe above the tide.
A ray from Wilkulda's nimbus slipped into the old man's
brain and he became appraised of the redeemer's significance.

The old man's name was Gunningbal, and Gunningbal now
said quite coherently, "I live. I live. I am no longer dead. I
have bested Wandinyilmernang, that low coward thought he
could sorcer me dead . . . This is not our inlet's swamp, this is
the sea-mother. Ooh, look at all the people on the beach and
up on the cliff. Ooh, what is your name, magician, and who is
your Ancestor?"

"I am an Eagle and my brothers call me Wilkulda. I am the
messenger who heals. I am the defeater of cruelty and the
definer of forgiveness."

Wilkulda tenderly gave over Gunningbal to his sons. This singer was a gentle fellow now in his aged seasons but as a younger man he had been ferocious and had killed often. He was aware that the Heron, Wandinyilmernang, had not really murdered him with magic, for Gunningbal understood that when a man becomes quite elderly he may die of things beyond sorcery. Thus Gunningbal, the singer of original songs, was different from other men. He pulled out of the protective arms of his brood to stand in the sea and squint into Wilkulda's face. Gunningbal perused Wilkulda's eyes with his own. And Gunningbal saw truth afire in the messenger's gleam. He rocognized the lucent ring about Wilkulda's head for exactly what it was, the aura of a procreating Ancestor-Spirit. In a crescendo of new energy Gunningbal rushed through the shallows casting a curved sheet of spray upon the tidal flats. He came onto the beach. Holding his arms high over his head, as if entering the Sky with his space widening fingers, Gunningbal began to dance with spiking knees while in peals of tenor notes he sang,

> *"Blood Red Sky is the*
> *Rainbow Snake,*
> *"Wilkulda is the sea's Penis,*
> *"Wilkulda is bright Yellow*
> *clay and is the Venting*
> *Penis that gifts Blood to*
> *the Sky,*
> *"Rainbow Snake is blue Tears,*
> *"Wilkulda is Yellow clay,*
> *Wilkulda is the magician of*
> *the Rainbow Snake,*
> *"Wilkulda bears Rainbow Snake's*
> *Penis fiery around his Skull for*
> *Wilkulda is the forbidden Rainbow,*
> *"Wilkulda is the Rainbow Snake and*
> *is Penis to the Sky."*

And Gunningbal recited his new song again and again. Soon all men present joined in the new ceremony. Gunningbal by his being's creativity encouraged the formation of the sacred myth with gestures and steppings that depicted the scene before him. Aloof Kalod forgot his impatience and came down from his station on the zigzag path to become an excited dancer.

Wilkulda watched the birth of the myth ceremony and believed that his message had been implemented, that forgiveness had become intimate with man. All that remained was the final motioning of his design, for Gunningbal was the last of the recent dead and there were no more sick to be healed.

## ten

At dusk a bridge of campfires linked beach to cliff with ephemeral sparkings. Wilkulda summoned Kalod into the shallows and spoke to his brother, "It is the time in which I must die. I have cured all those that have entered the sea and I have vanquished death in the recently dead. I must forget Mayawara that I may die and complete this mything. Then you, Kalod, shall tell the mankinds of my message."

Kalod desired to interrupt that he might ask of Mayawara, but even as the sea grew upon the land the healer spoke on, "I am convinced that men now accept forgiveness. Not all men, certainly, but enough for a beginning. You will perform much magic as you walk about the worlds informing men that cruelty is to be destroyed. I never reached the northern coasts, nor the great bulk of the northeast and northwest parts of the planet. Your journeys will be momentous, for indeed the center of the world I barely passed by. You will speak of me and my message, in the world's holy caves you will draw my picture with my head bright with the curious light. You shall live an immense sequence of seasons. You will speak plainly in every man's ear . . .

"At dawn, you, Kalod, will bring the guests and your Turtles to gaze on me here in the sea. When the hot of tomorrow is fullest I shall die. You will tell the people that I chose to die that forgiveness is never forgotten."

Kalod haltingly, in a soft tone, as if embarrassed by the melodramatic pronouncement said, "Wilkulda, you must not become dead. Men are not ready, you are wrong. I am as a wind-tossed ash to your magic. Men, especially strangers, will not trust me. Perhaps you could almost die but return in another man's form to lead me . . . "

"No, I shall die and never return. It will not be a pretense death," insisted Wilkulda, as if convincing himself of the idea's necessity.

Kalod argued, "It is not the right way. It is too extreme and will only frighten people away from forgiveness. What if instead of doing good dying only makes your memory evil? You would be dead, not able to speak out against cruelty."

"No, I must die now, and it may already be too late."

"What do you mean?" asked Kalod.

Stubbornly, as if daring to tug from out his own soul an ineffable truth, Wilkulda said, "I do not think it was right that I rescued the recently dead. Why, it might have been, no, it was a cruelty."

"What, Wilkulda, what is it you say?"

"I thought of my grandfather Tjundaga. If he had lived to be an old man like Gunningbal I would have rescued him too . . . But why? The old ones shall die soon again and then it will be harder for those left."

"But think of Gunningbal's song. It is so strong," spoke Kalod.

"Yes, but his sons and sons-in-law will have to mourn and grieve for him again, and soon, too soon. I rescued them that I might live. I found another magic to perform that I might live a moment more. It was wrong. It was cruel. I must seek repentance for my cruelty."

And Kalod persisted, "You saved the children, the dead children . . ."

"No, it was not right. Before the morrow's sun finishes its passage down the Sky's spine I will be dead. This will be death everlasting and never will I view the Sky again. My spirit shall not be of repetition. My spirit will not rush to the Dream for reissuing. Futility and ridicule and exile will end and I will die knowing that men forgive men for cruelty . . . and I will never muse again on Mayawara . . . You Kalod will be the Sky's messenger. Go to the shore and prepare yourself for the beginning of your own myth."

Sternly Kalod the bone driller rejected Wilkulda's dying: "Don't become dead for them. They can never understand it. That you die, even for forgiveness, is waste. Live for the message. My brother, I have not wanted to tell you the truth. I thought in time you would realize how much is to be done.

Wilkulda, these fellows do not accept forgiveness. They still pleasure in cruelty. Do not die for such savages. If you die now it is too soon. Stay and take them by the hand into forgiveness. Live, you and I will go to many lands, we will find mankinds suitable and worthy. We will go south and find the girl Mayawara and she will be your only wife."

Hushed, nodding gently as if in contented repose, Wilkulda replied, "These are the earth's best peoples. These are to be the inheritors of the message. Have you forgotten so soon that you judged a woman to be a beast but instead discovered that you were the perpetrator of cruelty? Trust my judgment. Assemble at dawn these peoples for I know none else to choose as first."

Chastened Kalod, still convinced of the other's error, could not resist longer. Swaying with grief he spoke, "Wilkulda, let me die with you. Please, let me share your death. I am not worthy to sing of forgiveness."

"I must die alone, but it was good of you to say that you would. Come close to me and I shall drop one tear into your soul and you shall truly know that forever you are my replacement."

And Wilkulda wept one tear onto Kalod's shaken, slumped head as the sea, astounded by the act, fell into itself with a weeping moan. "Kalod, can you see now? Go to the shore and await my soul's end. You will be me in all things except for the magic of healing men. Only the Sky Father can create such a gift."

Kalod waited for dawn on the cliffhead. Wilkulda, alone in the darkened shallows, watched the new moon glint dubiously on a placid tide. He had come into the sea on a full moon and he would die as it was re-created. A quarter mile out from Wilkulda lay the humped sand bar that was the dying waterfall's dust sperm. This splendid custodian of the coast steeped eight leagues in length. However, the actual protector of the shoreline and the sandbar was the massive coral reef two miles off landside. The reef, though broken through to sea's bottom in numerous places, extended along the littoral's front for thirty-six leagues. It was this coral skeleton that throttled the enormous seas that boomed in from Africa's hoof.

At low tide both reef and sandbar protruded into the air. About bar and reef a denseness of life sifts the nutrient rich water. Dugong and white-hair seal and walrus visited the slabs of rock that erupt from the sea where the coral cannot root. The sea-slug, brown with teat feet, accumulates in myriad squirmings, fat and twelve inches uncoiled. The slug knows the reef as a castle, as a wet worm world. Trepang, or Bech-De-Mer, the sea-slugs, white or brown, festoon to the reef's turrets even as powdered sugar to a hot tart.

Toothless turtles gather on the sand mountain at low tide in a congeries beyond computation. Turtles assemble in layered committees on the exposed swelling; two inch turtles and nine foot Luth command the sea equally from their reptilian kingdom. Poisonous yellow-bellied sea-snake wreaths its thirty-six sections with aloof condescension, an ejaculating prince among the sterile drones of sea vines.

Herds of yellowfin tuna, shad kingfish, barracuda, salmon, and shark cluster about the reef in unhurried requiem of an existence seldom threatened. Four to six foot sharks roam the reef crest at low tide even as angry crows pick at a huge carcass. Birds everywhere, over the sand and coral promontories: the Giant Petrel, the Fulmar, the Stinkpot, and ever more glide in to kill and gorge on the heroic reef and sandbar. And from the few tall trees that have dared to grow upon the cliff itself, white-chested sea-eagles float freely on the trades over the exposed coral to pick up and then drop shellfish in soggy bursts.

Reef sharks are frenetic in their voracious anxiety to eat reality itself. They swiggle on the drying crown of the reef with jaws prepared for bird or trapped fish. The fins and tails of the reef sharks are sunburned black by the endless cruises on the sea's surface. These are insignificant shark and dare to kill man only when concentrated in a gang. In the very deepest pool along the entire reef maze at the coral wall off the Turtle's shore, there lurks a Great White Shark. Thirty-eight feet in length from snout to tail tip, eight feet from pale belly skin to dorsal fin; a girth expanded and bulged loathsomely from five decades of gluttony. Its elephantine gills are tinged black at the edges where the blood vessels have died. The monster's hue is that of cement that has congealed but not yet dried. Arrow shafts, pilot fish in swarms, dart at the shark's fleshy, tucked jaws for garbage. Aged was the Great White Shark from its fifth decade of overgrowth.

The old fish was still not satiated. The ugly thing was as
ravenous as when it had been birthed as a smallish thing off
the Solomons. The deepest pool at the coral's outermost
limit was the shark's lair and had been for the past twelve
years. The slightest vibration in the heavy water indicated to
the shark the size and food value of any prey passing its pit.

It was to this peculiar ferocity that Wilkulda turned that
death might successfully seek him out. Wilkulda envisioned
the shark correctly in each detail and thus viewed the animal
as a primordial mishap, a mistake surviving from an age
previous to the Dreamtime. Great White Shark's foretorso
lurched downward so that its huge jaws swung lower than the
outbalanced rear section. Wilkulda surveyed the Great White
Shark and knew him well even to the serried ranks of
mandibles. The healer did not yet speak to the shark, for he
was awaiting the dawn before calling up the teeth.

Dawn sheathed night and laid upon the sea. Wilkulda
observed that Kalod had done as he bidded. Twenty-eight
mankinds congregated on the beach close to the strolling
waters. The mankinds were separated each from its neighbor
by a few yards of space. The elders of each people were at
the very front, some with ankles wet from the sea.
Twenty-eight mankinds danced and sang Gunningbal's
creation in repetitious unison. Each male had attired himself
in highest costume of magicdom. As the type of decoration
varied by mankind the shore was resplendent in novel
diversity.

Wilkulda turned to the beach and in slowest moment
surveyed the gathering from end to ending. First he looked to
the mankind furthest south and saw the starkly white
squared patterns of clay that the Bandicoots had fingered to
skin. Their eyes were dabbled yellow with crumbling,
hoarded ocher, they were a poor people. Then came into his
vision the Kangaroo Rats with their penises vivid in red ocher
coats and heads white and huge with precious kapok
beehived to skulls. Blackness ornate contrasted with white
ash swirls that flowed from thigh to stomach to thigh marked
out the Crayfish. Brilliant pink cockatoo feathers and thick
opossum pelts enticed Wilkulda's sight to the courageous
Black Ducks whose arms and legs shimmered in redness
recently sprayed from open veins to enhance magic's

attractiveness. Turtle elders, caped with full skulled kangaroo shrugs, rodent visaged, open mouthed, shadowed over the men's grey caked faces. Six males represented the Flying Fish-men. They had traveled from a distance greater than any others. From their far ocean lagoons in the north the Flying Fish had burdened a gaily painted hollow tree trunk. They beat upon this object with square cut sticks. The voice from the log of the Flying Fish was overwhelming and females hid faces in each other's breasts as it grunted. Only the Flying Fish had been gifted a drum by the Dreamtime Spirits.

Wilkulda paused to watch the Pelicans prance with their carefully carpentered grave-poles. They had manufactured the burial posts during the past nights after Kalod had informed them that Wilkulda was to die soon. The poles were twice a tall man's height and were blooded and ochered geometrics. Three such posts had been prepared and nine more would be completed to stand at the sea's edge after Wilkulda was dead. Normally a great man required but one such pole in death. The Pelicans staked the three poles into the sand a pace from the ocean's appetite. They weaved in slow dance between the objects of mourning.

Northward went his gaze to the Emus who had no instrument to adore him. They were a conservative mankind, immune to modernity and to patronizing infringements based on obscure rituals. The Emus rejected all adaptations that might dim the purity of their myth enactments. As if to compensate for their austerity and lack of decoration, the Emus were a populous mankind with one hundred and seventeen ritualized clans. These proud elders presented not a feather nor a pelt, nor a dab of ocher to their beings, however from scalp to toe the hundred and seventeen were russet hued with the dried liquid of pierced penises.

Wilkulda hesitated his swerving head to suck in the entire vision of the twenty-eight mankinds dancing Gunningbal's recital. He returned his sight to individually inspect the tribes. His awareness came upon the Owls. These were the fiercest of the world's mankinds. The Owls were arrogant and acted without due heed to ritual or conscience. However, they were a great mankind and numbered to the sum of four hundred and eight males. Their spears were of bloodwood and measured eighteen feet in length. The Owls as their ritual

demanded spilt their penises in sub-incision wider than any
other extant mankind. The Owls took no prisoners in their
frequent feudings and they ate the buttocks of those slain in
battle, those of their own flesh besides that of the enemy.
Owls dominated the inner rivers of a land a hundred leagues
to the northeast. The Owls believed themselves to be the
ultimate mankind.

The infant female who had been healed of blindness was
an Owl. And thus this mankind now adored Wilkulda. In awe
of Kalod's pronouncement of Wilkulda's coming death the
Owls during the night had come to the darkened beach. In
the sparse flickerings of the Sky's night fires and the moon
they had structured a titanic sand-mound by the sea where
Wilkulda stood. The mound symbolized the light about the
healer's head. It was a creation one hundred feet in length
and fifty wide, and the mound was humped twelve feet high.

Upon the foot stamped and moulded sand hill the Owls
had poured out their blood that the mound might be sealed
and secure from both sorcery and the offshore winds. The
magic mound was swathed with alternating white flower
blooms from the bush plants and pink and grey plumage
from cockatoos. The blood was the sea, the white flowers the
infant's created eyes, the grey feathers the earth, the pink
feathers the Sky, and the entire mound's composition
represented his nimbus. The Owls danced about the mound
in exaggerated slowness. Each gesture was in reduced tempo
and they sung Gunningbal's epic stanzas with gusto.

From the cliff above came the throbbing bellows of a
dozen Rainbow Snakes. The vibrating roar disturbed the
nesting flocks of seabirds as the Turtle elders violently swung
the holy whistles. Thus the presence of the Snake was intense
and the pipers and gulls and eagles and terns and grebes
exploded out above the sea in a shivering of beating wings
and screeching beaks. The shelled reptiles massed on the
sandbar heard the Snake's injunction and clacking carapaces
against one another they noisily waddled into the sea.

At sea's side the Heron-men, a northeast tribe, sucked
inwards on their majestic flutes, the didgeridu. This tube of
wood, sectioned by magic membranes, when vigorously
inhaled and then abruptly expelled whined a note that
enchanted the anxious watchers. As the Rainbow Snake and
the didgeridu cried out in a harmony of wails Wilkulda

quietly surveyed each and every mankind to note the commemorative decorations. As the elders continued to recite Gunningbal's work, at their rear, along the perpetual shadow of the cliff base, the women and children squatted in compact tiers. They pressed into each other's flesh even as drowning moths merge in the vortex of a whirling eddy. The dancing lines of men blocked the view and the females could not see Wilkulda except through infrequent spacings. But they partook of the ceremony and participated actively by rhythmically slapping cupped hands to inner thighs. And thus these huddled women produced with their thousands of hands a sound that carried far out to sea, where it frightened off several score of bulky albatrosses who had been feasting off a dying, helpless, sperm whale.

Wilkulda wanted the women and children at the shallow's rim but he had forgotten to instruct Kalod in this. The only words that Wilkulda could hear plainly over the enormous acclamation was the phrase, "Wilkulda is the forbidden Rainbow." It was the moment, and he turned his vision seaward even as the demonstration on the beach became frenzied. He began to voyage his mind to that deepest place at the reef's outer extremity. However, as the mind moved past the sandbar, he came upon a tiny blowfish expelling miniature water spouts into the sand to expose tiny vessels of food.

Wilkulda enjoyed the blowfish's persistence and decided to become the blowfish. And Wilkulda became the small fish. Flicking his fins, he as the blowfish darted down the slope of the bar. He dodged a snapping barracuda and entered the coral ramparts. The fish wound its way through the reef's crenelations. Without dismay the blowfish thrust down toward the obscurity of the Great White Shark.

Even as it dove down an ancient stratum of the tiny animal's brain fought the surging in its being. Wilkulda willed the fish deeper. Down past a hundred reef sharks ripping at the corpse of a diseased tuna patriarch. The tuna was now flimsy shreddings of flesh, but brief minutes before it had possessed fifteen hundred pounds of authority. Deeper, to depths beyond its limits the blowfish pushed and Wilkulda created a sterner structure for the animal.

Finally off a limestone shelf some thirty fathoms deeper

than the reef's original skeleton, the hulking shark was spied
out. Great White Shark floated a few feet off the thickly
manured, indistinct bottom. It dozed after a night's sloth
among grazing mackerel. As the blowfish's vibrations were
meager in these depths, it was the pilot fish who were alert
and they burst out at the thing hoping to inspect dead food,
but they flashed back to the shark after confirming the thing
as repugnant life.

At first, seeing the sleeping predator through the optics of
the blowfish, Wilkulda thought the monster to be an
extension of the shelf, or a tumorous swelling on the sea
bottom. After a moment he recognized the boneless beast
that had been fabricated in a shell of armored teeth. The
beast indolently squished out massive lengths of white
excrement as it slept.

"Biggest fish awake," Wilkulda symbolized into the dozing
brain, "I have a challenge for your strength and a meaty thing
to be devoured."

This shark was ill disposed to challenges and was quite
cross to be so rudely awakened. Great White Shark unlidded
its eyes and saw the little fish. With an abrupt
communication of meshed symbols, accompanied by furious
anal expulsions, the shark grunted at the blowfish, "Wha' ya
so deep." Without another expression of social contact the
shark snapped at the tiny fish. Its teeth missed aim but the
compressing water between the jaws pummeled the blowfish
into its gigantic stomach.

Wilkulda was dismayed at the creature's nature and from
its abdomen he spoke, "Shark, do not behave so badly. You
will come willingly or you will be commanded, there is
certainly no reason to terrorize the blowfish. Now, let him
go!"

Great White Shark was taken aback by the impudence of
the swallowed morsel, and indeed the strangeness of the
entire proceedings panicked the beast. The shark bolted out
of its lair down into the plunging trench that began
immediately by the limestone ledge. Wilkulda felt the
increased weight of the descending sea and took measures to
reinforce the integral strength of the blowfish.

Very deep dived the Great White Shark. Down through
hundreds of fathoms it sped. As the volume of the ocean

increased, Wilkulda probed the skull of the silent beast. Wilkulda again and again issued stringent symbols at the shark, but it was not until the animal reached a thousand fathoms that it was compelled to reply; "What want little stomach food. Better be food or else I kill ya."

"Big shark, fear me not for I shall not harm thee," stated Wilkulda feeling responsible and thus guilty for the brute's overt cowardice.

"Me never afraid," spoke cruel shark.

"That is an untruth, for I am the Sky's messenger and know things that no other may," quoted the blowfish.

There was an embarrassed silence on the cold layer of sea water that the shark had found to rest upon one thousand fathoms deep. Suddenly, as if relieved of anxiety, the shark spoke, "Stomach food, I'ms 'friad altimes cept big now that was so small once."

"I shall not harm you, brother fish, but as you say, you are a big fish now and you will do my bidding," informed Wilkulda.

The brute believed himself clever and during the final symbol it began to thrash wildly in every dimension as it bent its form to either side simultaneously. It tried to suck inward its stomach to crush the blowfish. When Wilkulda attempted to calm the Great White Shark it dove down to a second stratum of chilled water that gave additional buoyancy to its huge body. It was at this depth of seventy-five hundred feet that the shark would hunt the giant squid that drifted by in the current. Great White Shark still felt the presence alive in his belly and rushed down to the ocean floor fifteen hundred feet deeper yet.

At the sloping side of the trench that angled through the bottom the shark came upon an extension of the limestone ledge that adjoined his reef lair. The shark excitedly banged his pale pink underside on the rock in hopes of crushing the prolix blowfish. Cyclonic foam bubbled from the muck that clung to the slanted limestone. As the maddened gyrations of the beast somewhat quieted, Wilkulda in pity for its fear spoke tenderly, "Shark, you will come with me and have a fine meal. You will meet no harm."

"Don' wanna go no more . . . wha meal?" queried the grunting, good aroused Great White Shark.

"You remember the taste of men, you have eaten men before. They are sweetest flesh. You shall feast in your belly and be content with what I provide."

"Wha mean?" interjected the shark, becoming involved at last.

Wilkulda sirened on, "Remember the taste of men. Soft and tender, yet large meat to be chewed longishly."

"Mens? . . . things very shiny good. Blood! Little soft straights shaken, blood lots, smells good," said the shark.

"Yes, a man shall be your reward when you come with me. You will only have to bite. A juicy man eaten will make you feel good all over."

The hugeness of teeth became intent as it listened to the blandishments issued by the smallness in its belly. As the monster squirmed in delight at Wilkulda's description, additional symbols entered the shark's brain, "Now come to where the light begins and you will be given wondrous blood to smell."

With the slightest weave of its corpulent but flowing form the shark rose out of the deep, as the blowfish lent encouragement at every fathom higher. Rising incubus came into the milky glaze of the near surface. Even as the shark reconsidered the mission its dropsy dorsal fin broke the sky with blunting disregard.

"Blood where?" asked the shark.

"Where the hardness begins," coaxed Wilkulda.

"No . . . fear the hardness, safe only where here safe in this safe, no go where hard hurts," announced the Great White Shark.

"Did I not promise a full measure of sweet flesh? I do not lie. I am not permitted to lie. I shall not take you to death on the hardness. You will not be punished but instead be rewarded with an immortality of sorts."

The beast understood but one symbol in three, yet the crooning of Wilkulda's voice was compelling. However, it resisted yet." 'Fraid hard. Never go where soft safe gone. Live Live Live Live Live eat eat eat eat eat," the Great White Shark cried out.

Wilkulda persisted to cajole the poor beast and slowly it eased its ponderous self landbound. At last the manipulated monster was at reef side. However, as the tide was low the shark would not pass through a channel that the blowfish aimed it at. Time and time again the shark turned away from the narrowness. Several men on the cliff head now saw the great animal out by the reef. They shouted and the host on the beach lifted its gaze from the motionless healer standing in the shallows to where the snout could be observed approaching and then receding from the entrance through the coral.

Sadly the blowfish forced the shark with binding discipline through the reef. Thrashing stupendous agitation the monster catapulted itself over the reef in a gusting of broken matter. The hundreds of reef sharks, who had been prowling on or near the barrier, bolted away in swiftest terror.

Great White Shark swam nervously in the longitudinal basin between reef and sandbar. Here it would have been content to stay awhile, but the blowfish offered no rest, nor did it relinquish control. Before the beast could study its new surroundings it was racing toward the sandbar. At a low place, where six inches of sea water still drained over the bar, the shark smashed over into the shallows where the man Wilkulda waited even as the blowfish ended its transcendent performance.

This place of thin water was clear and the shark could see perfectly the uniform ridges of tide birthed sand that strolled along the shallow's floor. The thousands on the beach, awed to stillness, forgot ceremonial duties and groaned as if they wished they could flee even as had the reef sharks. The bravest warriors instinctively stepped backward to pause before with hurried lofting of spears they rushed into the seas toward the brute. The weapons fell short by many yards.

The shallows signified danger and death to the beast and Wilkulda fought the shark's trauma. He had the Great White Shark plainly in his sight and he forced the monster to vomit out the living blowfish. The tiny fish dashed away and forgot at once its adventure in the stomach of the Great White Shark. The shark was still some lengths from the healer and it swam but slowly as if in dread. The warriors ran from the ocean as they watched Wilkulda wave the shark onto his aliveness. Only a few exceedingly bold Owls dared to stay close to the water where the mild waves washed their feet. Kalod the bone driller was hunched down behind a boulder on the cliff path and held his head in his hands as he wept. The females along the cliff wailed lamentably.

The whistle roaring, the bobbop of the drums, the voices of the flocks, all quieted as the shark proceeded toward Wilkulda. Then the shark struck bottom and in fearful reflex jolted onto its back in panic. The animal rolled over and over as if attempting to tunnel through the shallow's floor. Sand, rock, and thin sheets of spray shadowed the Sky and the few men near the surf ran away even as minnows sped outward into the forbidden deeper waters.

Shark warped and canted itself to no relief. It slid on its back along the shallows in terrified capitulation. Then too swift even for the awareness of Wilkulda the fear maddened shark was upon him. Half-aground, the Great White Shark shoveled without purpose to where the healer stood. Spinning and spewing the shallow's substance skyward, even as a whale's tumultuous death breath shoots upward without end, the shark in a simple instant noted the waiting man and struck Wilkulda fully in the small of his back with gigantic skull as ram.

The twenty-eight mankinds fled to the cliff's height as Wilkulda was launched many feet into the sky and fell unresistingly into a deeper part of the shallows. The Great White Shark's momentum carried it sideways up onto the forebeach but with cataclysmic energy the giant fish bounded off land back into the sea. It rushed for the sandbar and the sanctuary of the deep ocean. In panic from its brief conflict with the beach the brute momentarily forgot its stricken prey. However, as it sluiced to the depressed passage on the sandbar, the shark happened to see the floating wreckage of its skull's encounter.

Wilkulda lay broken on the sea's tension, the tide leisurely breasting him outward. He was not yet dead although his lower spine and pelvis had been crushed and fragmented. The flesh and skin of his buttocks had been burnt away by the friction of the brute's linked skin. A flow of crimson fluid leaked from his mouth and nostrils. His face was not quite distorted beyond recognition by the agony.

A few brave elders, including Gunningbal softly chanting his poem, came to water's end to search for sign of the messenger. They spotted his floating form and saw at once that the previously growing glow about his head had vanished. Wilkulda was no longer the healer but had become as he was years before, a person in torment. Without his circle of light Wilkulda was in a denseness as he had been in the cave of shame. His suffering was now dreadful, for although the spinal column had been fractured, the compressed cord was alert to sensation. Agony existed for Wilkulda.

The ending came. The shark, as it made for a successful escape, passed close by Wilkulda. The fish smelt the blood and forgot its flight of fear. The Great White Shark curved mightily and in the beginning of a new snout wave drove its ranked teeth into the man's being. Living men on the shoreline screamed. The sea's hue was fresh green. The sky was a rare translucent blue. The red gilded man dying seemed quite insignificant in the enchantment of his surroundings.

The man had felt and even heard the Shark's teeth grind apart his corporeal self. His mind was unfortunately not ransomed by shock and he was aware of this last experience. Wilkulda relished his coming death, for his pain must soon end or the world's balance would be forever distorted.

Shark settled the man squarely in his jaws and swam comfortably on the surface over the sandbar and the reef into the altered sea. The beast held Wilkulda erect from the waist and the poor fellow's head angled out of the water, his face to the receding coast.

Wilkulda from this grotesque position must refill his lungs. Now he began to scream, a limitless scream even as the agony was limitless. It was the scream of a person being eaten by a Great White Shark, the scream of an ordinary man and not of a perfected Hero.

The scream coursed out to defeat the sea's bass shaking. The scream vibrated along the sandstone cliff to transfix those who also had been screaming.

The water was white whirl as spools of flecked droplets spun in circular designs from the swift track of the shark. Wilkulda's scream was at last severed as the animal arched himself in steep incline to dive down to the first cold layer of water at the thousand fathom mark. Here the chilled water held the shark lazily as it ate its catch.

It began to rain in the afternoon and by nightfall a storm

drenched the transfixed mankinds huddled by the cliff and on its path. In their nakedness they clung to the rock that the storm might not sweep them into the sea. This night they forgot to light fires and by morning all were quite miserable with the cold, the wet, and hunger.

At dawn Kalod the bone driller, without demonstration or weepings, began his voyage among the tribes of earth.

The End